Kevin Linville

THE BIG PEOPLE

THE BIG PEOPLE

K. H. LINVILLE

THE BIG PEOPLE

iUniverse books may be ordered through booksellers or by contacting:

iUniverse
1663 Liberty Drive
Bloomington, IN 47403
www.iuniverse.com
1-800-Authors (1-800-288-4677)

ISBN: 978-1-4917-5454-2 (sc)
ISBN: 978-1-4917-5455-9 (e)

Library of Congress Control Number: 2015900978

Printed in the United States of America.

iUniverse rev. date: 01/31/2015

Contents

The Journey

Seattle, Washington July 17, 1897

It was nearing the end of the century and things were bad all over. The entire country had been mired in depression for over seven years, and a seemingly endless stream of hardships had begun driving people to search for a better life. One such man found himself in the Pacific Northwest. Out of money, and fast running out of hope.

The rain finally eased to a drizzle as Elmer worked his way up the street. The all morning downpour had left him a little depressed, and wet enough that he'd begun to splash straight through the shallower puddles. Eventually he reached the building on the next corner, where he stepped up to the door and knocked. When it opened, he could see that the man inside was quite annoyed that he'd come back so soon.

"Anything today?" he asked, while trying to appear both eager and confident.

"No! Same as yesterday! ...And tomorrow!" the man snapped back at him. Then quickly closed the door with a slam.

Turning away from the porch, Elmer dug the pencil and paper from his pocket and scratched off the last name from his soggy list.

It had been hard times ever since he was old enough to work, so he didn't have much experience for a twenty year old, and though he was usually optimistic, he knew he wouldn't be anyone's first pick. He'd hoped that showing real eagerness might make a difference, and he also hoped that being a bigger than average man might help. Well, stronger than average anyway.

After shoving the expired list back into his pocket, he looked around and saw that he'd pretty much been to every business in the area. Except that is, for the ones with 'No Work' signs in their windows. He'd been feeling hungry for some time now, and knew that it was probably early afternoon, so not knowing where to look next he decided to head home for lunch.

Home was a one-room cabin on the outskirts of Seattle that he shared with his uncle Henry. Really it was Henry's place, as he was the one who paid the rent and bought the potatoes that they both lived on. Elmer had come to live with Henry from his mother's ranch in Oregon, where he'd had no luck at all, and had no real chance of finding work. They got along well though. They were more friends than relatives.

A few minutes after he started walking, a small pack of dogs appeared and began loping along with him. They snooped all over the place as they went, checking everything handy. Then Elmer spied a dime at the edge of a large puddle. 'These days that's almost a windfall' he thought as he bent over to pick it up. "This must be my lucky day."

As soon as he bent over, most of the dogs surrounded him and curiously pushed in to see what he was doing. After all, it could be food related. As he stood up again he said, "Wow, you guys are a real little gang. I mean it." he added, "You're all really little." There wasn't a big dog in the bunch. Most of them stood wagging their tails and staring, as if trying to figure out what he was saying. They were a wet and ragged looking lot, but he could tell that at least a couple of them were Terrier types.

A few of them wandered ahead a little, then saw something up a side street that commanded their full attention. They instantly ran off towards it, causing the others to take notice and bolt off after them. The dogs had disappeared as quickly as they'd shown up.

As Elmer kept walking, he realized the rain had finally stopped, and he hoped it would stay that way at least until he got home. Then as he got closer to the street the dogs had run up, he could hear people yelling about something. He couldn't make it out, but it sounded like a lot of people. He was getting pretty curious as he approached the corner, and when he peered up the street he saw that it was indeed a lot of people, about fifty or so. They were still about a block away, but were all happy and excited about something and standing all over the street. Without realizing it, he'd already started towards them to investigate, probably because in these times a large group of happy people was a rare sight indeed.

Suddenly a loud roar went up from the crowd, and they all surged forward towards the building in front of them. This made Elmer even more curious and he began to walk a little faster. By the time he reached the cheerful mob, the noise had died down again, and they were spreading back out over the street like before. Then they began yelling to a second floor window of a hotel.

He could see two well-dressed men leaning out the window, with the heads of at least three or four women crammed around them. Everyone in the window was laughing, and most of them were brandishing champagne glasses. Then the men threw out large handfuls of corn, and when it rained down on the crowd another loud roar went up and they all plowed forward again.

In the confusion, Elmer noticed a boy standing nearby that had stayed put and seemed to be fumbling with something. Tapping the boy on the shoulder he asked "Hey kid, what's going on here? Did somebody get married?"

The boy looked up with a big excited smile, then yelling over the noise of the crowd he said "No! Those guys up there are throwin' gold out the window! Look!" and he opened his hand to reveal seven or eight kernel size nuggets. "They said they're from the Yukon and they struck it rich!" he added.

Never having seen gold before, Elmer stared at the nuggets intently. After a couple of seconds he looked up at the frenzied crowd, then his eyes suddenly widened and he too shot forward, throwing himself into the chaos.

Meanwhile across town, the sun had come out and forced Henry to shed his heavy Mackinaw coat. He'd been hard at work all morning, driving around town scooping up horse droppings. It wasn't very glamorous work, but he felt lucky to even have the job, especially when so many people were in dire straits. It wasn't very pleasant work either, and even worse when it rained. But the part he hated the most was shoveling up dung in front of women.

The wagon he was driving was piled high with the wet manure, and he'd just wound his way through numerous high mounds of it to pull up to the barn. The company he worked for was supposed to haul the manure outside the city limits, but had figured out they could make much bigger profits by simply storing it in huge piles right there in the compound. Henry figured it was only a matter of time until the city took notice and cancelled their contract. So he continuously worried about his job disappearing. He earned not bad wages though, seventy cents a day, just enough to feed himself and Elmer both, and pay the rent.

After getting a drink of water, he climbed back on the wagon again and moved it to the newest nearby mound to unload. He worked with a half dozen other men who also drove wagons throughout town, and thought it odd that none of them had come back from doing their routes yet. But he just figured they probably had to load up full like he did. For some reason the whole town had been real busy for about a week, and there were men and horses everywhere.

He'd nearly finished unloading when he saw Elmer coming. Running down the mud and manure road and winding his way through the piles, almost like he was being chased. It looked like he was carrying something too, and when he finally reached the wagon, Henry could see that it was a newspaper.

Short of breath, Elmer looked up at him on the wagon and gasped out "Henry! You gotta quit your job!"

"Sure Elmer," he replied dryly as he kept shoveling, "I'll just plant a money tree. Don't know why I never thought of it before."

"No, I'm serious Henry," he added, "look at this!" and handed him up the newspaper.

Henry had no intention of quitting his job, but wondered what had Elmer so worked up. So he squatted down on the back of the wagon to have a look.

It was the 'Seattle Post Intelligencer', and the headline read 'GOLD!-GOLD!-GOLD!-GOLD!' in huge letters. And under that a title said '68 Rich Men on The Steamer Portland', with other lines that read 'Stacks of Yellow Metal!' and 'More than a Ton of Solid Gold Aboard!'

Very excited, Elmer began tapping the page saying "Look here, 68 rich guys off just one boat!" Then he pointed lower on the page to another caption that read 'Latest news from the Klondike'. "It says down here that it's the kind of gold you can mine with a pan and shovel."

Henry thought of himself as a smart enough guy, and far from being naive he was actually fairly skeptical. So he handed the paper back to Elmer as he stood up again, saying "That's a newspaper Elmer, it's probably a buncha crap."

He knew how some newspapers would embellish or even fabricate stories to sell more copies. Then he went back to shoveling again, but thought to himself how the paper was one of the most widely circulated in the City.

"I mighta thought so too," agreed Elmer, "but coming home for lunch I saw two guys throwing gold nuggets out a hotel room window. Look!" And he opened up his hand to show Henry about a dozen or so nuggets, some as big as beans.

Upon seeing the gold, Henry immediately quit shoveling again and squatted down for a better look. "Wow! You must have twenty or thirty dollars worth there." he said, appearing a little hypnotized.

"They musta thrown a year's wages out the window!" replied Elmer, as he too studied the nuggets, "We gotta go there."

"To the hotel?" answered Henry matter-of-factly, partly to tease Elmer.

"Noooo!" he complained in frustration, "To the Klondike, where the gold is!"

"What!" exclaimed Henry, "I think the money tree's a better idea." He didn't like spur-of-the-moment decisions much.

"Aw come on Henry! Why not go?" pleaded Elmer.

"Well for one thing I have a job." replied Henry, as he tried to think of another reason.

"You drive a turd wagon!" exclaimed Elmer.

Henry knew Elmer wanted to go pretty bad, as he'd rarely seen him so excited.

"Even if these stories are true," answered Henry, "getting rich is always a real long shot, and that's not a very good reason to go running off to Alaska."

"Hey! I just thought of something!" replied Elmer, "It said in the newspaper that they sent a tug-boat out to meet the ship, so they could get the story before their competitors. The ship isn't supposed to dock until six o'clock. You're just about finished. We could go down there by then, and we'll ask some of those miners what the truth is. Then we'll know."

Henry was getting pretty curious himself and figured it probably was a good idea, but trying not to encourage Elmer any further, he replied, "Well I guess we could have a look."

At about six feet tall, Henry was a couple of inches taller than Elmer, but as the friends walked down towards the docks, Henry could barely keep up. Elmer was practically bouncing. He was also trying to convince Henry of the almost guaranteed benefits of heading north.

"There's no way for ordinary men to get rich anymore," he argued, "or even make a decent living, and even if we don't strike it rich, I bet we could get good paying jobs working for someone who has. At the very least, it'd be a heck of an adventure." he continued.

As they neared the harbor and could see down to the water, they were shocked! Thousands of people covered the long dock, with many more lining the shore. Neither of them had ever seen so many people in one place before. Henry was thirty years old, and had been to San Francisco a couple of times, but he'd never seen anything like this. He had a good head for numbers though, and knew that this was a large part of the city's population that had come down to see.

Making their way towards a spot on the shoreline, they could see a man perched on the roof of a nearby building with a camera box set up. He was either taking pictures of the crowd, or the newly arrived steamship securing its lines. The ship was 'The Portland' just like the newspaper said, and just when they got to the nearest spot they could see from, the gangplank of the vessel came down.

With this, the buzzing noise emanating from the huge crowd became much louder, and when a man began walking down the ramp with his bags, they erupted with cheering and congratulations. Then as more men with bags and beat up suitcases started down the gangplank behind him, some in the crowd began yelling "How rich is the Klondike?"

One of the men de-barking the ship then yelled back "Ten times richer than California! We got millions!"

The crowd cheered wildly. Many men were lugging bags or small suitcases that seemed to be very heavy, and one fellow carrying such a case and working hard to appear as casual as possible, had the handle snap off completely. Another was dragging a large canvas bag that he could only skid a few feet at a time.

As the procession of heavy laden miners continued, Henry noticed how ragged they all looked. Even more evidence that they arrived directly from mining in the north. As each one reached the end of the gangplank

they were mobbed by reporters and citizens alike. Then people began yelling "Show us the gold!" and many of the miners held their burdens as high as they could to oblige.

By the time most of them had worked their way through the crowd to the Wells Fargo safe wagons, much of the mob had the symptoms of full blown 'Gold Fever'. Extra police hired to guard the wagons seemed to confirm the richness of the Klondike, and as Henry watched some of the wagons leave loaded down with miners and gold, he felt a tug on his shirt. It was Elmer. There was a lot of noise, so he was both yelling and motioning that he wanted to leave.

The people behind them had all crammed forward trying to see better, so they really had to push their way through to get out. Once to the edge of the massive crowd, Elmer said "I wanna get to the shipping office before everyone else does." He was assuming that everybody would want to go to the Klondike, and he was right.

The shipping office was nearby so it only took a few minutes to reach it, but when they did, there was another huge crowd mobbing the office for tickets. In fact it was the same crowd, it simply stretched all the way down to the 'Portland'.

"Let's go in and see what it costs to get there!" said Elmer enthusiastically.

To Henry it looked like a frustrating and probably futile thing to try. So he looked around for a moment then said to Elmer "I'll wait for you across the street by that bench over there." and then turned to start walking towards it.

"Okay" replied Elmer, "I'll be back as soon as I can." then he quickly disappeared into the crowd.

Henry reached the bench and sat down to rest his legs, and soon found himself thinking about how exciting all this was, and how without noticing it, he too had caught the fever. Now his life seemed a lot more mundane than it had just a few hours ago.

He had a good view from where he sat, and as he gazed out over the multitude of people, he could see the man on the roof still taking pictures. Then his eye caught some familiar faces. On the street below the photographer were some of the other drivers he worked with. They were too far away to talk to, but he could see now why the other wagons hadn't come back.

Then Henry felt something push into his side and saw that a woman had arrived with many children, and was lining up the smaller ones on the bench beside him. There wasn't enough room for them all so he offered up his place to her, but she refused, saying that the older ones could stand, and that she was much too nervous to sit down. She thanked him anyway though, saying her name was 'Stanley'.

Trying to make polite conversation, Henry asked her if she'd come down to meet the ship? She said she wasn't sure, and went on to explain how her husband had gone to the Yukon two years earlier, mostly as a last resort, and she'd received a letter saying that he'd be coming back on the next boat, and the Portland was it.

She paced back and forth anxiously as she told Henry how important it was that her husband return. He'd left her with $20 when he went, all they had, but after struggling to scrape by with seven children, she was now down to $2, and very concerned about the coming winter.

As she spoke, Henry noticed that the whole family was virtually dressed in rags.

Before long the sun began setting, and Elmer re-emerged from the still persistent crowd. The bounce was gone from his step now, and his face expressed a look of deep concern. "Well I learned lots in there," he said, "and most of it's not good."

Suddenly the Stanley woman yelled "Bill!" then she and the kids ran towards a destitute looking man coming up the street.

Elmer sat down on the now empty bench with Henry, and as they watched the Stanley family re-unite, Henry said "So what did you find out?"

"It's a long way." replied Elmer, "It's in the middle of the Yukon, almost to the Arctic Circle."

It was very distant, but Henry was pretty good with maps and remembered "That's beside Alaska isn't it?"

Elmer nodded in agreement "Right beside and straight east." he said, "There's two ways to get there. One is to sail about 1500 miles north to the south coast of Alaska, then go inland. The other way you travel the same by ship, but then go around to the far west of Alaska, then sail up the Yukon River."

"How far up the river?" asked Henry.

"1800 miles." replied Elmer slowly.

"Boy, that's a long way." answered Henry, while trying to picture it in his mind.

"Doesn't matter anyway." continued Elmer, "We can't afford it....We could go straight north then overland. But the guy in the office said they're booked up solid for the next four months."

Henry felt his heart sink, and was surprised that he too had become eager to go.

They both sat on the bench staring at the ground, trying to figure out if there was anything they could do about it. Then the Stanley family passed by all packed tightly around the father. Elmer had forgotten all about asking a miner questions, the reason they'd come down to the docks in the first place. But even though Henry hadn't forgotten, he saw no reason to bother the Stanleys about something they wouldn't be doing anyway. Then they overheard Mrs. Stanley say "Thank God you're back Bill! We only got $2 left."

"Our worries are over." he told her, "I found gold, I got $90,000."

They heard her squeal, and then watched as all the kids began dancing around as if on hot coals.

Henry and Elmer looked at each other in disbelief at what they'd just heard, then went back to staring at the ground again. After a few minutes Henry said "You know, if a guy had a good job and saved every penny, it'd take 250 years to save that much."

More time passed, and not knowing what else to do, Henry said "Well, we both missed lunch today. Let's go home and eat. Besides, it's getting dark."

"Yea....alright." replied Elmer slowly.

As desperate as he was, he too didn't know what else they could do. Henry had never seen him so depressed.

As they began to leave, they saw that the crowd was much smaller now and rapidly dissipating. They walked along without talking for a while, both deep in thought about what a wild day it'd been. They also wondered what they should do now. It was like their whole world had been shaken up and they couldn't just go back to the way it was yesterday.

By the time they'd walked five or six blocks, it was beginning to get quite dark and they were finally getting away from the mass of people. Then when they turned to cut through an alley towards home, they heard a loud groan come from up ahead. They looked up and saw two shadowy figures at the far end of the alley, and it looked as if a large man was beating up a smaller guy.

Elmer wasn't one to idly witness injustice, nor to overthink his actions, so he instantly shot off down the alley yelling "Hey you! Stop that!"

The smaller man was laying on the ground now with the big man bent over him. When the bigger man saw Elmer coming, he straightened up fast and they saw a flash of silver as he slipped around the corner and disappeared. Running hard, Elmer quickly reached the man on the ground, with Henry only a few yards behind. They looked down the street but could see no sign of the assailant, and when they turned their attention to the guy on the ground they knew why the big man had run off so fast. He was a little old man with stab wounds all over him!

Elmer knelt down beside him to see how bad it was, and saw that it was very grim indeed. "He's all stuck full a holes!" said Elmer urgently.

They knew the old guy was going to need a doctor fast if he was going to have any chance to survive, so Henry raced off to find help.

"Hurry Henry!" yelled Elmer! "He's bleedin' all over the place."

A few minutes went by when suddenly a young man appeared. He was a small thin guy, a few years younger than Elmer, and he quickly threw himself down by the old man, and began both grieving and assuring him that he'd be okay. It was the old fellow's grandson, and he tearfully wept that he'd only been gone a few minutes. "I just went to get more cigars for him." he sobbed.

The grandfather now lay on his back losing conscious, and faintly mumbling "...he stole my cigar..."

Elmer looked to be in control, but on the inside he was panicking for Henry to come back. To him it seemed like the old man might expire any second.

Very quickly Henry returned with a policeman, followed by a wagon driven by a married couple. Then everyone quickly helped load the old man onto the wagon, and they sped off towards the hospital.

After recording what Henry and Elmer had witnessed, the police officer also departed, but they stayed a little longer, explaining to the grandson everything they'd seen. He quickly thanked them for their help, and said that he too had to get to the hospital and began to hurry off.

They turned to start for home again, but had only gone a few steps when the young fellow suddenly yelled back to them "Hey, you guys want to go to the Klondike?"

They froze in their tracks then quickly spun around.

"Me and grandpa were going," he said, "but there's no way it can happen now. Here." he added, and he held out two steamship tickets. "Consider it gratitude for stopping grandpa's attacker."

Elmer slowly extended his hand only to have the young fellow cram the tickets into it, then run off towards the hospital yelling "Thanks again and good luck."

"Wow..." said Henry quietly. "This seems strange. He didn't ask us our names, or tell us his, or even wait to see if we wanted to go."

Elmer was straining to read the tickets but it was too dark. He looked up at Henry with an amazed expression and exclaimed "Its fate! We're supposed to go!"

Henry knew Elmer was going to the Klondike now even if he had to swim there.

"Well," replied Henry, "Like you said, at least it'll be a big adventure."

Such a constant stream of new thoughts flooded their minds now, that they walked home without realizing it. Neither of them noticed that Elmer had talked the whole way either. His mind had rambled from what they would need, to how well they might do, to how their riches could be spent. Mostly though, he talked about how his boring life was finally going to change.

Henry woke the next morning to the sounds of Elmer packing. "I read the tickets." he said, "We sail for Skagway, Alaska in six weeks. Gotta get ready."

It appeared as though he'd already finished getting ready. He was done stuffing his pack and duffle bag, and over them he'd draped his big buffalo coat and a huge Bowie knife he'd inherited from his father. Really he'd had no use for the knife until now.

In the next few days, Henry learned from reading the newspaper that more than five thousand people had made their way down to greet the Portland, and while it was rumored to have a ton of gold on board, it had actually carried more than two tons. A day earlier in San Francisco the same scene had unfolded when 'The Excelcior' arrived, and now the news was being blasted all over the world.

The greatest gold rush in history was beginning, with every port in North America and many more around the world booming with activity. Everything that would float was being sent north. Demand so great, that virtually all ships regardless of size were being used, and most were being loaded far beyond capacity. Some to never be seen again.

Henry packed his own things over the next few weeks, which seemed to drag by very slowly. To Elmer it seemed like months. He packed and re-packed numerous times, and told everyone he knew that he was going to the Klondike to seek his fortune.

Finally the day came, and stumbling toward the docks under their heavy loads, they saw that the whole waterfront was a beehive of activity. All kinds of dry goods and hardware were stacked everywhere, and hundreds of people with horses, dogs, and various other animals, were milling throughout the piles wherever there was space. Many of the dogs were in cages, and there were signs that read 'Top Dollar for Large Dogs'. When Elmer saw the signs, he realized why the pack of dogs he'd seen some weeks earlier were all so small.

It was near chaos all around the ship they were to board, and as they made their way up the crowded gangplank, they could see that many of the caged dogs were also being loaded.

Near the top of the busy ramp Elmer slipped and bumped hard into the man behind him, and when he heard the smash of broken bottles, he turned around to see a large man that looked very rugged and mean. When the man looked up from his leaking bag to Elmer, rage came over his face. He quickly drew a large knife from his jacket, and trying to keep it concealed lunged toward him! Elmer went into shock! Then just as quick, a huge hand seized the man's wrist with enough strength to hold him almost motionless. The man struggled briefly before realizing it was nearly hopeless, then quickly dropped the knife and looked up smiling, as if not to be looking for any trouble. It was the most insincere smile Elmer had ever seen, enhanced by a mouthful of black teeth and one large tooth that seemed to be made out of lead. The huge man holding him appeared to be very calm and confident, and suddenly jerked Elmer's attacker a little closer and said "This is gonna be a long enough trip without locking horns right off the start....Don't ya think?" then pushed him free.

The thug picked up his knife and smashed baggage, then with a sneer shoved his way off through the crowd.

Elmer grabbed one of the man's massive hands and began shaking

it vigorously. "Don't know how to thank you mister!" he said gratefully, "My name's Elmer Baxter. And this is Henry Browning."

Henry nodded politely.

"My name's Sam, Sam Steele." the big man answered while smiling through his moustache.

"You goin' to the Klondike too?" asked Elmer.

"I think we all are." he replied.

The three of them continued to talk as the ship finished loading, and Elmer calmed down from the knife attack. He couldn't believe that he'd gone his whole life without even seeing a vicious assault, and now in just over a month he'd witnessed two, and one of them was aimed at him. Elmer didn't know that it was the same assailant. The thug had recognized him though, and hated him not only for the smashed whiskey, but for thwarting his previous attack on the old man.

Before long the boilers were fired up, and with great excitement the little ship began steaming out of the harbor. Henry and Elmer quickly realized that the entire boat was crammed with men and cargo. They weren't sailors, but they, as well as most the other passengers, agreed that the ship looked dangerously overloaded. None however wanted to turn back. All aboard were consumed with winning the race to the Klondike.

Moving throughout the ship, they soon found that the sleeping bunks were on the lowest level, where it resembled a castle dungeon in every way. It was small, dark, stenchy, and had extra bunks wedged into every possible space. Then they learned that in the dining room the passengers would eat in shifts, while sides of pork and beef swung over their heads and between the tables. After exploring the rest of the ship, they decided that for the sake of breathing, whenever possible they'd spend their time on deck.

Later in the evening the air was calm and warm so they found a place near the bow and made themselves quite comfortable. They sat on canvas bags with some of the other passengers, while some lit pipes, and everyone talked of the journey ahead.

Soon it became apparent that no one really knew anything about where they were going. It was generally agreed that after Skagway they crossed the mountains into the Yukon, but that's all anyone knew. So the conversation quickly turned to what fortunes the coming year would bring. Most were figuring to prosper, while others were very confident and expecting to strike it rich. With everyone's anticipated fortunes being validated by each other, speculation grew, and prosperity seemed even more imminent.

Eventually the sun disappeared and took the warm air with it, forcing Henry and Elmer off to their bunks. As they walked along the railing, Henry said "You know...If we were to turn back now we'd be in a real bind. No jobs, no place to live. We gotta go all the way now no matter what. So if things start going wrong, we're just gonna have to look at it like a big adventure and dig in."

"I agree." vowed Elmer, "I'm not goin' back."

After squeezing into their bunks, Henry lay thinking about how fast things had changed, and how he felt a little out of control. At least they seemed to be off to a good start. A few seconds later he felt his leg getting wet just below the knee. Then a splash bounced off his shoulder. Concentrating hard in the dark, he realized to his horror that the urine and waste from the livestock above them, was leaking through the deck and randomly dripping on their bunks. He immediately became even more frustrated at their jammed conditions, which left him no room to move at all. "Oh yea." he mumbled through gritted teeth, "This is just peachy."

For the next two weeks, a near constant wind pounded big waves at the little ship, regularly threatening to sink it. The steady rolling of the vessel made many of the passengers deathly ill, yet most chose to suffer on deck, as the dungeon had become an almost unbearable hellhole. The choking smell of ammonia and methane completely permeated the lower parts of the ship, so much so, that many of the passengers feared a possible explosion.

Eventually the gale subsided and the people began feeling better. The fact that their voyage would soon end helped a lot too. The boat had wound its way north through the coastal islands for the entire journey, and now it turned up the Lynn Canal. A long narrow inlet with Skagway laying at its head. As they steamed along the now glassy water, the passengers began filling the deck to see. Henry and Elmer stood leaning against the railing with everyone else, keenly watching for their destination. They'd been lucky to not run into the man with the leadtooth again, but Elmer was still regularly looking over his shoulder.

Steep mountains on both sides of the canal sloped right down into the water now, and there didn't appear to be room for a village or town anywhere. Soon they were rounding the last bend of their voyage, and the crowded ship buzzed with excitement. Then Skagway came into view and the deck became as loud as a party. They could see two other ships anchored in front of the town, and everyone's mind raced to assess the situation and form immediate plans.

Henry was wondering how many people were already in front of them bound for the Klondike, when he heard Elmer say "Howdy Mr. Steele, I like your coat."

Sam was standing beside them, and sporting a large buffalo coat similar to Elmer's. He smiled at Elmer's politeness at calling him Mr. Steele. "It'll be good to get off this floatin' cesspool." he replied while staring at Skagway.

Upon reaching the other ships, the anchor dropped and a chaotic struggle began to be first ashore. Sam turned again to Henry and Elmer and said "I know a bit about this town, and I highly recommend that you do your business, and then leave as quickly as possible. It's not a safe place....And don't gamble! Every game in town is rigged."

Then he wished them luck, and seemingly not being in any hurry, went to retrieve his belongings from the dungeon.

It was low tide in the harbor, and the shallow water kept the ship some distance away from shore. The crew wasted no time in beginning to unload, and it apparently involved throwing much of the cargo overboard. The passengers were told that the tide would take it in from there.

Soon the longboats were being lowered into the water, and were quickly surrounded by boxes and crates, and jumbled piles of lumber floating around like giant toothpicks. Then they watched as half a dozen horses were loaded onto a platform with high sides on it, and the ship's crane lift them up and over the side. Just as they were wondered where the crane was going to set them, the bottom suddenly fell away and dropped the terrified animals about sixteen feet into the icy water. This shocked the passengers almost as much as the horses. It was then assumed that the animals would swim the shortest distance to shore, then be rounded up on the beach.

After Henry and Elmer secured a place in a longboat, everyone took oars to poke and prod their way through the floating debris. Then they all rowed steadily towards the beach, which would have been uneventful, had not one of the swimming horses seemed to try and climb in the boat. A brief battle of oars and hooves ensued, before they and the horse continued towards shore.

Upon landing on the beach, Henry and Elmer helped unload the boat, then push it away to return for more passengers. It was then that they realized they had a very pressing problem. The tide was coming in, and the mud flat they were standing on barely had a slope at all to it. This left the water free to rush in very quickly. The ocean was going to rise up about twenty feet, and the high tide line was a few hundred yards away, and to make it worse, the entire distance was a sea of mud.

They quickly grabbed what they could carry and began trying to run. But it didn't work. Every step they took would sink in then have to be pulled free again.

Before long it began to look doubtful that they'd make it back to the rest of their things in time, and a quick glance around told them that everyone else had the same problem. Many worse, because they had much more baggage to move.

By the time they returned to the waterline they expected to see the rest of their things floating, but instead, they saw an old man skidding their stuff along keeping just ahead of the tide.

When he saw them approaching he let go of their bags and stood up. It was an elderly priest, complete with frock, collar and cross, and a fair amount of mud. "Hello, I'm Father Charles Bowers." he said, "I thought you may need a helping hand."

"Yes we did, thank you." replied Elmer, while introducing himself and Henry, "We're lucky you were here."

He was a small gray haired man, and his eyes twinkled when he smiled. "I'm here most the time." he said, "Every day I find many of God's children needing assistance. It's a good place to do his work."

They thanked him again and after hoisting their remaining bags, the three of them plodded up the beach together.

"I'm assuming you men are bound for the Klondike." suggested the reverend, "Have you made your provisions for food yet?"

"What do you mean?" asked Henry.

"The law says that each person must have a year's supply of food, or they won't let you into the Yukon." he replied, "Do you have horses?"

"No." answered Henry, "Do we absolutely need them?"

"You do unless you can carry a ton of food on your back." said the Reverend.

This was getting stressful for Henry. He had a reasonable nest egg saved up, but he really wanted to keep it for emergencies.

Finally off the beach, they placed all their things in a single pile and began to ponder their next move. Then the saintly old priest said "I must return to help others now." and he began shaking their hands. "Be careful my sons. Skagway can be a dangerous place. If you need to purchase horses or supplies, I recommend you go to Jeff's Oyster Parlour and ask for Jeff Smith. I can vouch for his honesty and character. Many of the outfitters here are quite disreputable." With that, they thanked him once more for his help, then watched as he tramped back towards the waterline.

They could still see many men running up and down the beach, and much of their stuff was starting to float. There was a sign posted where everyone could see it that read 'Help off the Beach' 'Tide going out-$20 per Hour' 'Tide coming in-$50 per Hour'. That was insane they thought. Who would pay that much?

Hundreds of piles of goods were stacked along the permanent shoreline here, as much as in Seattle, and Henry and Elmer sat down on theirs to discuss their situation. Their feet hadn't even dried off yet, and they'd already been warned about Skagway twice. They decided that they should indeed get everything done as quickly as possible, and the point was driven home completely when they spied yet another ship steaming in towards Skagway. They had to get moving now.

They figured their stuff would be okay where it was, at least for a while anyway, so they started into Skagway.

As they headed into town, they began noticing for the first time how far north they really were. A slight breeze went wafting by, with a surprisingly cold bite to it.

Skagway was a small community that was absolutely overflowing with people. And besides all the stampeders, there were dogs and drunks everywhere. The whole town was made up of tents and buildings of rough sawn lumber, and new buildings were going up all over the place. Most looked like they were going to be bars and saloons.

By the time they reached the center of town and Jeff Smith's Oyster Parlour, they'd figured out that the whole town was also a giant sea of muck. While crossing the street in mud half way to their knees, Elmer was almost run over by a young girl in a wagon being pulled by a moose. He looked back at Henry smiling and said "There's something you don't see every day. This must be Alaska alright."

Then he saw the telegraph office not far from Jeff's Parlour. "While you're dickerin' for horses, I'm gonna wire my mom and sisters." he said, "Tell 'em what I'm doing so they don't think I'm dead."

"Okay," answered Henry, "and if for some reason we miss each other, I'll meet you back at our pile."

Elmer entered the telegraph office, and saw that a rich looking couple was already waiting at the counter. Patiently waiting his turn, he noticed that in the corner they had a large parrot in a cage, a great big green one just sitting motionless. "Hello Polly." said Elmer, while trying to touch its wing through the bars.

"Hello stinky." replied the parrot. Then it suddenly shot forward and bit a chunk from the end of his finger.

"Damn!" blurted out Elmer grimacing. "That really hurt!" He'd gotten the attention of the other people in the office, and they all watched as the clerk threw him a rag to tend his wound. Upon catching it, he realized that the rag was already covered in blood, and that the parrot must've bit a lot of people.

As he wrapped his bleeding finger in a piece of the cloth, the parrot let fly with a stream of expletives that would've made a sailor blush. Many of the people then looked at the clerk, who simply shrugged his shoulders and said "He was raised on a ship."

Still waiting his turn, Elmer overheard the man at the counter say "We'd like two first class tickets to the Klondike please."

"On what?" responded the telegraph operator.

"Train, stagecoach, whatever's quickest." the man answered back.

The clerk laughed out loud, "There's no train or anything else to the Klondike." he replied.

Partly confused and depressed, the couple left and Elmer moved up to the counter. Then he saw the sign. $5 for ten words! That was more than ten times what it cost in Seattle! He had to do it though. If anything happened, his family would probably never find out what became of him. So after laying out nearly all his money, the clerk asked him if he wanted to wire any currency. "No!" he snapped back angrily, "You already have all my currency!"

Meanwhile, Henry had entered Jeff Smith's Parlour. It was a straight drinking establishment with a desk in one corner. He walked over to it, and asked the man sitting there if he could speak to Jeff Smith.

"He's with someone at the moment," the clerk replied, "but I'll tell him you're here."

Henry had no way of knowing it, but the person Jeff Smith was with at the time, was Leadtooth from the ship, and he was delivering things he'd acquired in Seattle to his boss. One such item was a very valuable silver cigar case that he'd stolen from an old man he'd stabbed in an alley.

Soon a dapper dressed man appeared, and announced "Captain Jefferson Randolph Smith, at your service sir. How may I assist you?"

He was an affable gentleman, with a soft spoken drawl.

Henry introduced himself, and said "I need information. I'm unfamiliar with how everyone's getting to the Klondike."

"Do you have horses?" asked Smith.

"No." replied Henry, "I want to fully understand my options first."

"That's a wise decision Mister Browning," he said, "but really there are no options. If you have horses, you can take one of two trails, the White Pass or the Chilkoot Pass. The Chilkoot's a little shorter, but the White Pass is lower through the mountains and much easier."

He then led Henry to a large map on the wall that featured the trails and most of the surrounding area. As they talked, the bar began filling with boisterous men, and it soon became very loud and confusing to do business, but Henry and Smith pressed on anyway.

Elmer had just reached the front of Jeff's Oyster Parlour, when Henry came out. He wasn't smiling, but said to Elmer "Well, I bought the food and horses we need."

"How much did they cost?" he asked.

"Why, a testicle of course." replied Henry, greatly perturbed that he'd spent nearly all his money. "I only have $6 left."

Elmer had spent all his money too. He hadn't spent nearly as much as Henry though, so was still optimistic as always. "Look!

I bought a map." he said holding out a rolled up paper, "A store by the telegraph office was selling them. It's of the Klondike."

"That's good." replied Henry, not really hearing him. He was still thinking of his lost savings. But he figured with luck they shouldn't need to buy much more from now on anyway.

So he explained to Elmer what he'd learned about the trails to the Klondike, and how the White Pass seemed to be the best way to go. It was too late for them to leave town today, so Henry had arranged to pick up everything in the morning. They just had to get one of the horses, and take it down to collect their belongings from the beach.

Arriving at the livery stable, they found that the horses they'd bought were a sorry looking lot indeed. Henry swore that at least a couple of them were part mule. They took the best looking one, and struck off toward the waterfront to retrieve their belongings before it got too dark. Then all they had to do was find a place to sleep.

Plodding down the muddy main street towards the beach, they noticed that the saloons and dancehalls had begun to come to life. Many of them dubious joints at best, judging by their own names. Places like, 'The Bucket of Blood', 'The Mangy Dog', and 'The Blaze of Glory'. Hundreds of men were milling about now, and a great many of them were already drunk.

With the start of the gold rush, Skagway's population had exploded like a bomb. Thousands were transients bound for the Klondike, while others had come from the goldfields with money to spend. Any kind of census was impossible, but about seven hundred to a thousand people were permanent residents, and a huge number of them were criminals. With no mayor and a benign sheriff, Skagway ran wild to the point of anarchy. The sale of alcohol was illegal in Alaska, but an estimated eighty saloons, dancehalls, and gambling houses sold liquor around the clock. Gunfire was frequent, murders were common, and someone was killed almost every night. It was absolutely lawless.

When Henry and Elmer reached their belongings, they were pleased to find them undisturbed. There were men around their pile though. Men who'd bought the longboats from the ships, and were now taking them apart for building materials. There were also a couple of men with wives who'd just finished moving their luggage ashore. "We should be there in a fortnight ladies." they overheard one of them say. These people had no idea what they were in for.

Henry and Elmer loaded their things onto the horse, except for their packs which they themselves carried, then made their way back to the livery stable. After putting their horse and belongings away they wandered back outside again. They had to find a place to sleep now, but they really didn't want to venture back into the streets again. It was beginning to look quite dangerous. Everyone seemed much drunker now and fights were breaking out. Even more stressing, was they could hear occasional gunfire.

As people walked by, a man and woman came to a stop in front of them. They were charity workers, but were dressed more like singing carolers. When they asked for a donation for Skagway's widows and orphans, Henry became a little anxious as he had almost nothing left. He and Elmer were both generous fellows though, so he dug deep and gave them 50¢ anyway. Elmer too searched his recently drained pockets, and was surprised to discover the lucky dime he'd found in Seattle. He gladly gave it up though, figuring it might bring him more luck this way.

After the workers thanked them and left, they heard a booming voice behind them. "I thought you guys were gonna play it smart and get outta town!"

It was getting pretty dark now, but they knew by the voice that it was Sam Steele.

"Hi Sam." replied Elmer, "We're leaving first thing in the morning. We were just looking for a place to sleep."

He smiled at them like they were a couple of kids. "Intelligent people shouldn't be on the streets now." he said, "There's men in Skagway that'd cut your stomach out if they thought you'd swallowed a nickel."

"We were thinking the same thing." said Henry.

"I'm waiting for some men to meet me here." answered Sam, "I leased a bunkhouse, and I think you fellas better stay with me tonight for safekeepin'."

"That'd be great Sam!" they both answered thankfully, "We're a bit stuck."

So they strode off with him towards the bunkhouse, and quickly found themselves marveling at his bold and powerful demeanor. Confident in every way.

When they entered Sam's room in the building, they saw about a half dozen empty bunks lined against the wall, and after they'd each crawled into one, Henry mentioned how good it felt to be in a clean, dry bed again.

"I've gotten used to the ship." kidded Elmer, "I don't know if I can sleep without my eyes burning."

Both Sam and Henry burst out laughing, which made Elmer begin to giggle too.

Then suddenly they heard a loud bash from the wall behind their heads. It was quickly followed by three more loud smashes, and then another.

"What the blazes?" growled Sam while raising his head up to look at the wall.

Then a final wall shaking bash brought a huge spike spearing through, exactly to where his head had been. He sprung up angrily from his bed, and out the door wearing only his giant red long johns. Henry and Elmer were amazed at how fast he could move for such a big guy. They then listened quietly, but all they could hear was parts of a conversation that seemed normal in tone and volume. Of course it was mixed with the street noise, which was becoming louder and sounding more chaotic all the time, and the occasional gunshots had now become frequent gunfire.

After a few minutes, Sam returned to the room shaking his head. And after settling back into bed again, he said "The guy was nailing a soap dish to the wall....with a foot long spike."

They all laid quiet again, trying to block out the sounds of the town going wild, when suddenly bullets began ripping through the wall narrowly missing them. It scared Elmer half to death, and he curled up small waiting for more. Henry too was shaken, but didn't know what they could do about it. Sam never moved at all, but they heard him mumble "Bloody idiots." and within a minute was snoring loudly. Henry thought about how all the warnings about Skagway had been true, and how glad he was going to be to leave in the morning.

It had taken Henry some time to fall asleep, so when he woke in the morning Elmer was already dressed and ready to go. While Sam had gotten up and left even before Elmer woke up.

They felt great while walking to get the horses and supplies. The sun was warm and bright, the sky all blue, and they hadn't been robbed or attacked either, but mostly because they were finally on their way.

They were awhile organizing their newly purchased dry goods to be carried. There were many hundreds of pounds of flour, cornmeal, sugar, beans, raisins, lard, dried potatoes, and more, as well as candles, blankets, coffee, tea, ropes, shovels, saws and files. A stove, stovepipes, soap, salt, lamps, coal oil, etc, etc, etc.

After loading up the horses with all their food and property, they helped load their own packs onto each other's backs, and when they were finally ready to go, it felt to both of them like it was the real beginning of their journey.

"Well Elmer. Let's go get rich." declared Henry.

Elmer didn't need any encouragement. He was already wearing a great big grin and feeling like he could out pack the horses. So they started their adventure by pulling their new pack train through town to where the trails began.

Where the trails forked in front of them, a man had set up a fancy portable bar, and as they passed by he spoke up, "Gentlemen. A drink to toast your impending fortune?"

"That's a good idea!" said Elmer looking at Henry, forgetting that he'd already parted with his last dime.

Henry thought it was a good idea too, but he really didn't want to part with what little money he had left, that he didn't absolutely have to.

The man's sign read '25¢ a glass', and that was very expensive. In Seattle a forty ounce bottle was only 40¢.

"It's a capital idea," Henry said to the man, "but we're already short of funds. I only got a quarter left."

It wasn't true, but Henry was trying to get out of spending anything.

"I feel like talking." replied the man, "Tell you what. You buy one, and I'll give you one. And consider yourselves fortunate, it's a rare occurrence in Alaska when a bartender buys a customer a drink. As rare as…. well, as a quiet night in Skagway." he added chuckling.

He appeared to be out of the old west, with curly black hair and a buckskin coat with fringes on it. "I'm Charlie Meadows." he said, "But people call me Arizona Charlie.

They introduced themselves as he poured the whiskey into glasses, and Elmer asked him "Do you live here?"

"No." he replied, laughing at the very idea, "I'm heading for the Klondike just like everybody else. But I had a rather unfortunate gambling experience, so I too am short of funds. But with my mobile establishment here, I hope to remedy the situation shortly."

Then he shot back a drink he'd poured for himself.

They talked with Charlie for a while, but before long their feet were getting itchy, so they splashed down their drinks as they wished themselves good luck, then after thanking Charlie for the rare occurrence, the friends took their first few steps up the White Pass trail.

"Whoa there boys!" Charlie yelled at them, "Where you off to?"

"We're taking the White Pass trail." Henry shouted back.

"No! No! No! Not under any circumstances!" he declared.

"Why not?" asked Elmer confused.

"There is no trail." Charlie replied, "Oh it starts out like a wagon road, but a couple a miles down it turns into a trail, and then a bad trail, and after that, barely a trail at all. There's so many dead animals on the White Pass, they call it 'the Dead Horse Trail'."

"Are you sure?" asked Elmer, not knowing whether to believe him or not.

"Positive." replied Charlie, "I've seen people come back off that trail wanting to kill somebody."

After pausing in thought for a bit, Henry looked at Elmer and said "I guess we'll have to go over the Chilkoot." Then he asked Charlie "Do you know how long that trail is?"

"About forty miles." he answered, "But it's a very formidable forty miles."

Then Henry asked him "How long do you think it'll take us with the horses?"

"You can't use horses." replied Charlie, "It's too steep. ...You didn't buy these animals did you?"

"Yes...why?" asked Henry, as he started to panic inside.

"Let me guess," answered Charlie, "Jefferson Randolph 'Soapy' Smith?"

"Oh damn." groaned Henry, as he realized how much they'd stolen from him.

They both sat down on Charlie's bar stumps and stared at the ground in disbelief.

"How come they call him Soapy?" Elmer finally asked.

"They've called him that for as long as I can remember." said Charlie, "I heard cause he's so slippery when he separates men from their money."

"Do you know him?" asked Henry, still hoping there'd be some way to get his money back.

"Not really." answered Charlie, "I know of him. Back when I was in Colorado his gang ran the city of Denver. I heard when he learned of the gold rush, he moved his whole gang up here. Now he's the dictator of Skagway and his gang robs everything that moves. Usually repeatedly. You guys didn't wire anybody money did you?"

"No," replied Elmer, "why?"

"It's one of his scams." added Charlie, "He gets people who want to telegraph someone, and if they wire any money, his gang just keeps it. No one ever finds out cause they leave town, and no telegraph is ever sent."

"I didn't wire any money," said Elmer, "but I did send a telegram. It cost me everything. But I watched the operator send the message."

"Yea," said Charlie slowly, "but if you follow the telegraph line, you'll find it goes along a few poles into the bush where it ends tied to a tree. There is no telegraph line to Alaska yet."

Elmer dropped his head into his hands and said "Aw damn, I been fleeced. I feel so stupid!

"Don't feel too bad." said Charlie, "They get everybody, and I mean everybody! They even got people dressed as charity workers going around collecting donations."

Henry was sitting calm and quiet, but Elmer knew he was as angry as he'd ever seen him. His head just kept getting redder. Finally he stood up and tied the horses to a tree.

"I think I'll try and reason with Mr. Soapy Smith." he said, and started walking back towards town.

Elmer quickly fell in behind him, with Charlie yelling "I think it'd be wise to just swallow it up and go!"

He saw they weren't listening so he poured himself another drink and yelled again "Best be careful boys, Soapy's gang is ruthless!"

Henry marched through the mud with a vengeance as Elmer hurried to keep up. "Maybe he's right Henry, maybe we should just hit the trail." he suggested, hoping to persuade him from confronting Soapy.

"Damn Elmer, he stole everything I saved for three years!"

Elmer was almost as mad as Henry, but he was angrier about being made a fool of, than losing his money.

When they found Soapy, he was standing on the wooden sidewalk in front of the livery stable they'd gotten the horses from. He had three men with him, and was talking to an old woman. She was small and rough looking, and had a large six shooter stuck through her belt. She finished talking with them and left before they reached Soapy, as did one of the men. They recognized the departing man as the Reverend Bowers. They'd forgotten how he'd steered them to Soapy's Parlour.

The mud became deeper as they approached, forcing them to stumble over and use the wooden walkway. Soapy was flanked by two large men, and a cold shiver ran through Elmer as he realized one of them was Leadtooth. When Soapy saw them coming and they got near enough, he said "I thought you boys would be long gone by now."

Blinded by rage, Henry almost ran the last few yards to Soapy and piled headlong into him, sending them both careening down into the mud.

As they fought to both get up and keep the other down, Henry saw Soapy's cigar case slip out of his pocket and into the mud. He'd never stolen anything before, but in this fight he wanted to hurt Smith anyway he could. So with his pocket only a few inches away, and a momentary free hand, he quickly slipped it into his own pocket, and resumed trying to smash Soapy's face in.

Soapy had men hired so this sort of thing didn't happen and quickly yelled "Mace! Do your job!"

As Henry fought with Smith he could hear scuffling behind him, but before he could turn to see, a loud blast ripped through the air freezing everything. Everything that is, except for the sound of someone slapping against wood. Henry turned around to see Leadtooth up against the livery stable wall, looking wide-eyed and terrified. Elmer was standing in front of him shaking like a leaf with his monstrous Bowie knife to the criminal's throat, and his arm was shaking so bad that he was stabbing his neck full of tiny holes.

A few feet away was Soapy's henchman Mace who'd fired the shot, but Sam Steele had suddenly appeared and stood firmly planted with his giant hand gripping Mace's face. At arm's length he had the thugs head pinned to the wall as he flailed wildly against the building trying to free himself. Mace still had the gun in one hand but Sam already had a hold of the barrel.

"You know, it's a really nice day today." Sam said calmly as he tore the gun away from Mace, "and in a situation like this, one or all of us could end up dead in a heartbeat." Then he pulled the thugs head from the wall and shoved it hard so he landed in the mud beside Soapy.

With that Henry jumped up and snapped at Soapy "Gimme my money back!"

"You spent your money fair and square!" Soapy shot back while getting up from the mud, "The fact that you're unsatisfied with your purchases," he drawled, "well, that's absolutely tragic."

"Don't pee on my boots and tell me it's raining!" snarled Henry through gritted teeth, "I know a road apple when I see one!"

Then Sam interjected "I think things might work out for everyone if we all just turned and walked away."

Leadtooth's situation hadn't changed much, so he was all for it, but Soapy stood defiant, and shoving his thumbs into his vest pockets he said "Listen! I'm boss of this merry-go-round! And I'll not be goin' anywhere! If you can't get through Skagway in one piece, I'm doing you a favor. You're much too stupid to survive in the Yukon."

"You about the end of your blather!" growled back Henry, still wanting to attack him.

Then they noticed a crowd starting to gather a short distance away, and most of them looked like more of Soapy's gang. Soapy too noticed this and smiled back at Henry and taunted, "Interesting turn of events don't you think?"

Sam bent over and picked up Mace's mangled hat, then stepping up in front of Soapy and his man, threw the hat back in the mud beside the thug. Mace stayed motionless, fearing to get up and face Sam again without his gun.

"I'm gonna call this one a draw." said Sam, as he emptied the bullets from Mace's gun. Then he dropped the pistol into the mud and stepped on it. Elmer saw this, so he took Leadtooth's gun and did the same thing. Leadtooth was seething with hatred for Elmer now, almost consumed with rage.

As they began leaving, Henry railed at Soapy "You better stay in Skagway! For your own safety!"

"Begone!" ordered back Soapy, as he pointed the way out of town.

Making their way back toward the horses, they both thanked Sam numerous times for another timely bailout. Having warned them to leave town more than once, Sam couldn't help taking a poke at them. "So how long you guys stayin' in town for?" he asked.

"We're leaving right now!" assured Elmer, "I'm way too nervous to hang around Skagway now."

"I think that's a wise decision." replied Sam, "In fact I think it's your only option."

"You gonna leave too Sam?" asked Elmer.

"Not yet, but soon enough." he answered, "I'm sure I'll see ya on the trail though." Then he wished them luck and marched off toward the waterfront.

In the fall of 1897 Skagway mushroomed with people, and crime. Soapy Smith had arrived a few months earlier with the core of his gang from Colorado, where he'd ruled and terrorized both Denver and Leadville. Seizing control of Skagway his gang soon numbered in the hundreds, with no one knowing the total number but Soapy. Many were in disguise or undercover, like Charles Bowers posing as a priest, and every kind of crime was committed almost hourly. His subversive network extended onto the boats and every port to San Francisco, and everywhere Soapy's men would promote Skagway and the Klondike. They would regularly offer people help and assistance, while at the same time assessing their wealth and weaknesses. They'd read telegrams, open mail, eavesdrop, anything they could to determine ones property and purpose, and by the time many of the stampeders arrived in Skagway, they were already set up to be sheared by professionals.

Soapy continued to consolidate his power, and any new criminal element arriving in his town would be quickly absorbed into the gang or rode out of town on a rail. And with Soapy controlling the news and being an expert in propaganda, he managed to maintain the facade of a compassionate community leader, and his popularity actually grew.

When they arrived back at Charlie's, he was still tending his temporarily vacant bar. "I see you boys are still alive." he observed.

"Just barely." replied Henry while untying the horses, "I wasn't very successful."

"Well cheer up guys. You can use the horses for the first part of the trail… and good news from the Klondike today. They say the whole area runs at least 10¢ a pan."

"We better get goin' then." muttered Henry, still very depressed.

"I shouldn't be far behind you." said Charlie.

Then they wished each other luck and finally began their journey for real. Though under a lot different circumstances than they thought a few hours earlier.

Before long, Henry and Elmer found themselves deep in the giant trees of the pacific coast. The trail quickly turned muddy as they wound their way through the massive trunks, and people began to appear all around them. So many, that soon they'd become part of a long moving line. A few hours passed, and they emerged from the trees again to follow along the shoreline of the inlet. The mountains dropped steeply here, and left little room for the trail to pass. In many places it was darn right treacherous.

At the head of the inlet, they could see a large tidal flat covered with wooden buildings, all on stilts. As the line filed by it, they decided not to lose any time by taking a closer look, but rather to continue on. A sign by the trail said 'Dyea', and where it said population 2,000, it'd been crossed out and now read 3,000.

It was a whole town on stilts with raised wooden sidewalks joining all the buildings together. It was built of the same rough sawn lumber as Skagway, and the whole thing looked brand new. It was just as busy as Skagway too, with buildings being constructed all around the outskirts. Barely any closer to the Klondike, Dyea only existed for one reason, to bypass Skagway and Soapy Smith.

After Dyea, the trail began following a small river valley into the mountains. The next few miles were easy to travel, and along the way they noticed that any places to camp were already full of tents and supplies. They also passed the occasional portable bar. They weren't like Charlie's though. Most of them were little more than a board nailed between two trees, then decorated with a bottle and a few glasses. For a more genuine ambiance, some had a piece of canvas nailed to the board, which then hung fashionably to the ground.

There had been many small gambling operations along the path as well. Usually on a small table with some blocks of wood pulled around it for men to sit on. Most of them were operated by roguish looking strong-arm types, and Henry and Elmer were a little wiser since Skagway, and suspected that most of them were Soapy's men.

They'd moved up the valley a few more miles when Elmer said "We're making pretty good time! At this rate we'll be over this path in a day or two."

All day long the sun had been warm and bright, and there had been no wind at all. But here in the mountains, as soon as the sun disappeared it became very cold. Henry figured it was near freezing and it made him think how it was already mid-September, and to finish their journey before the dead of winter would sure be a lot better than not to.

They talked it over and decided that because of the large number of people, they'd better camp for the night in any place they could find. Their search became even more desperate, when the small valley they were in turned into an ever narrowing gap and the line snaked between canyon walls barely forty feet apart.

As they wound their way forward a camping spot began looking quite hopeless, until suddenly the canyon opened up to a large meadow where there were numerous camps scattered about, but still room for more. They didn't have much experience at building campsites, and with darkness falling fast, they didn't have much time to learn. So Henry took care of the horses and put up a quick lean-to, while Elmer gathered some wood and made something to eat.

Some of their new neighbors soon ventured over, and before long they were trading rumors and information. They didn't learn much though. No one seemed to know any more about where they were going than they did. One of them had started down the White Pass trail though, just as they almost had, but was smart enough to turn back after a week. He said it was a horrible trail, and an awful sight with dead animals everywhere. And that in some particularly bad places, animals were piled in heaps below the trail.

Some of their neighbors had met a kind and helpful Captain Smith in Skagway, who'd given them both guidance and assistance. Just about everyone else had also encountered Smith or his associates, and some knew exactly how much they'd been helped. Others didn't, and were shocked to learn of their useless and overcharged purchases. Most had sent telegrams, bought horses, mailed letters, wired money, or were clipped in one or more other ways.

They also learned Soapy had set up a phony recruiting station for the Spanish American war, and while men would receive physicals from a fake doctor, in an adjoining room their clothes were rifled through and stripped of possessions.

One man told how after sending a telegram, he was asked if he wanted to see the eagle. "They said they had a giant American eagle in a cage." he started, "So I following them into the alley, and was promptly whacked on the head and robbed. Kinda scattered my chickens." he added.

The same man was carrying about a hundred burlap sacks with him, 'for fillin' with gold'.

They woke in the morning a lot later than they intended to, so quickly folded up their camp to get going. Practically everyone else was already gone, off moving their supplies further up the trail.

After loading up the horses and putting on their packs, they tramped across the clearing to its edge. They were still about fifty yards from the trail, when Elmer noticed a bush beside him move as if it had been hit with something. When he looked towards it, he was shocked to see a hooded head with two eye holes cut in it. Suddenly the ambusher sprang towards him wielding a large axe raised up for striking! Elmer yelled "Henry lookout!" and frantically tried to get away!

Up ahead, Henry turned around just in time to see the axe drive down into Elmer's pack, with the momentum sending him crashing to the ground! Henry dropped his pack and ran towards him, as the hooded man tried to free his axe, which had become stuck in the canvas. Then a second hooded man with a large club sprung from the bushes and swung it hard at Henry, narrowly missing him and tumbling to the ground! The man over Elmer got his axe free just as a third man tackled Henry down, and before he could get back up the club bashed off his back so hard it knocked the wind out of him!

Then he heard Elmer scream in pain as he was hit with another chop from the axe! When the assassin raised up the axe up for a final blow, a deafening shot rang out that blasted the head off it! Then a second shot tore the handle from the thug's hand, sending it careening end over end into the bushes!

The attackers then quickly fled, leaving Elmer badly injured and Henry gasping for air! Unable to stand, Henry slowly turned around to see where the shots had come from, and some distance away stood Arizona Charlie, still holding up his long pistol with smoke wafting from the barrel.

Charlie quickly reached them, and holstering his gun said "What the hell was that you guys?"

Then he immediately began cutting long strips of canvas from the top of one of their duffle bags, to make a temporary bandage for Elmer's leg. The axe had sunk in deep just above his knee.

When Elmer could finally talk, he tried to put a brave face on how bad he was hurt, and gritted out "Hi Charlie....that sure was good shootin'."

"You fellas know who attacked you?" asked Charlie.

They did. The disguises were terrible. They recognized the badly dented hat that Mace wore, and the man with the axe may have had a hood, but from the neck down he was wearing all Leadtooth's clothes.

Charlie said "It doesn't seem like Soapy's work to me. You guys said you're nearly broke, and Soapy doesn't take a chance without gaining a profit."

Eventually they decided that it was probably Soapy's henchmen running their own revenge plot for the Skagway incident. Though Charlie figured they must've worked pretty hard to catch them alone out here, as there were almost always people around now.

Henry stood back up once his breath returned, and was basically uninjured except for a large bruise growing on his back. Elmer too was lucky, though he may not have felt that way. He'd recover from his wound once they sewed his leg back up, but he wouldn't be walking anywhere for some time. The cut was deep.

"My place is close," offered Charlie, "let's take him there."

Charlie had set up his bar where the field traffic joined the trail. So they helped Elmer to his camp, and after Charlie generously poured half a dozen drinks into him, Henry sewed up his leg doing an almost professional job.

Henry knew he'd have to decide what to do now, and he also knew that Elmer would want to continue on to the Klondike. But they'd have to lay up somewhere for at least a few weeks, and preferably somewhere hidden from Soapy's men.

They couldn't feed the horses for too long either. But the amount of work they could save was immense, so he had to figure out what to do with them too.

After thinking about it for a while, he decided to unload one of the horses so Elmer could ride as far up the trail as the animals could travel. Then he could come back for the things they left behind. They'd be further from Skagway that way too.

So Henry readied Elmer and the horses for the trip. Then in gratitude he bought two more drinks, having one himself and offering the other back to Charlie, as Elmer needed no more. The drinks cost fifty cents each now. His price had doubled since Skagway. But for as long as they'd been at his camp customers continuously stepped off the trail to drink, and some drank like it was water.

Soon they thanked Charlie again, though Elmer's attempt was pretty gibbled, and once more joined into the advancing line. After travelling for about a mile the trail began to rise up, and began winding it's way high into the mountains. Already the trees were smaller and only grew half way up each mountain, with jagged rock soaring a few thousand feet higher. Every half mile or so the path would get noticeably steeper, and it happened so regular, it was like the trail was divided into sections. It continued to become more difficult until finally they came to a place where the trail climbed over a wide rock slide made up of huge boulders. Suddenly the horses could go no further. People on foot could continue on through the rocks, but everyone with animals was forced to unload, and bear their own burdens from here on.

Henry led the horses and Elmer back down the trail a few hundred yards, looking for a place to camp. Level pieces of ground were scarce now, but he found a pretty good spot on the high side of the trail. He had to clear some trees out to make it useable, but it wasn't near the busy path, and he knew that given their circumstances, it was better to camp out of sight anyway.

Elmer was still in substantial pain, while at the same time drowsy with fatigue and alcohol. So Henry helped him off the horse, then up through the bush to where they were going to camp. After sitting Elmer down, he took a look around at what he'd have to do to carve out a campsite, and decided that the first thing to do was make a way for the horses to get up. To carry all their stuff through the bush himself would be a nightmare.

Then probably because it was a warm sunny day, he looked over and saw Elmer already sound asleep. So he got his buffalo coat and laid it over him like a large blanket, then began cutting trees out of the way to get the loaded horses up to their 'soon to be' campsite.

By early evening Henry'd put up their canvas wall tent in a fairly permanent fashion, and their stove was puffing white smoke into the air and heating the tent comfortably. He'd moved Elmer inside, and unloaded the horses, but it was too late to go back for the load they'd left at Charlie's. So he spent the rest of the evening cutting firewood as they were going to be camped here for some time.

When Henry woke in the morning it was colder than he expected, so after filling and re-lighting the stove, he built a fire pit outside so Elmer could go out and still be warm. It looked like it was going to be plenty warm again anyway though, as it was another cloudless sky. He knew this had to be rare weather. The size of the trees below, and all the creeks and rivers showed signs of heavy and probably frequent rainfalls.

He was making a temporary crutch for Elmer when he heard him begin stirring inside the tent. He went in, and wondering how his leg was asked "How you feelin' Elmer, hurt much?"

"It feels like someone opened up my head and poured in a bucket a glue." he moaned, "And there's a little mule in there kickin' the crap outta me."

He wasn't used to drinking alcohol, and his hangover was worse than his leg.

Before Henry went back down the valley to get the rest of their supplies, he was helping Elmer to the fire pit outside when the cigar case fell from his pocket.

"I forgot all about this!" he said. He hadn't been wearing his heavy coat much because of the balmy weather.

"Where did you get that from?" asked Elmer puzzled.

"Here" Henry said throwing it to him, "This should cheer you up a bit. It's Soapy Smith's. I stole it from him in the fight."

Elmer smiled in spite of his pounding head. He looked at the fancy engraving that decorated the case, and when he opened it, found it full with five paper tubes containing expensive looking cigars.

"Look." said Elmer, "There's initials on it, but they're not Soapy's. It says P.D.R."

"Somehow that doesn't surprise me." replied Henry as he sat down on a log.

The bruise on his back was still bothering him some, and when he leaned back to stretch his muscles, he saw the mountain tops across the valley, and a spectacular glacier he hadn't noticed before. "Wow! Look at that Elmer! he said.

Elmer's head hurt nearly too much to tilt that high, but when he did he saw that almost directly across from them was an extraordinary glacier. It seemed to be squirting out into space from between two towering peaks. It was lit up all pink from the sun, and because of a long deep split behind its face, it had the appearance of a giant precious stone reflecting its light. It also looked like the whole thing could break free at any time, and come crashing down into the valley. They both admired its beauty, and marveled at the precarious distance it seemed to be suspended.

When Henry left, his plan was to sell all but one of the horses at Dyea, for whatever he could get for them. Then use the remaining horse to carry the last load back, then sell it at this end of the trail for whatever he could get. Elmer's job was to keep a fire going under a pot of beans, and heal as fast as possible.

After a few hours went by, Elmer was sitting making coffee when he glanced up to see a giant dog standing about twenty feet away. It had a couple of huge packs on it with big hunks of moose meat sticking out of them. He'd seen a lot of dogs in his life, and this one was by far the biggest one he'd ever seen. It had to weigh over two hundred pounds, and it didn't look like it feared anything. After it stared at him a few more seconds it began walking towards him. Unable to run away, he would have been scared had the dog showed any sign of aggression. "Nero!" he heard a woman yell.

He turned to see a small woman walk out of the bush from the high side of their camp. She was a little over five feet tall, and she too was carrying a full pack of moose meat, and a very large rifle. She was a little older than Elmer, in her mid-twenties, and she had to be as tough as nails by the weight of her pack. He could also tell by the pine needles covering her, that she'd been traveling through some very thick bush. As she came near, she saw Elmer was injured and said "My dog wasn't showing his teeth was he?"

"No he didn't," answered Elmer, and then mumbled "thank God."

"I'm Belinda." she said with a slight Irish accent, "Belinda Mulroney."

"Elmer." he replied, "Sit down, have a coffee." he offered, hoping to have company for awhile and something to take his mind off his painful leg.

"So where you from Belinda?" he asked as she sat down.

"Pennsylvania." she answered, "Scranton. I'm your typical 'coal miner's daughter'."

"You don't seem typical." suggested Elmer, as he poured her a coffee, "How'd you end up here?"

"I was working on a steamship when I heard about the rush." she told him, "Since I was already on a boat heading here, I thought I'd try my luck."

"How's your luck been so far?" he asked.

"As good as anybody's." she answered, "But I was way off on how much money and food I was going to need."

"Us too." replied Elmer, "Way off."

"I camped here and been shooting moose to earn some money." she said, "You can just about see my place through the bush there." and she pointed up towards the direction she'd come from.

"Isn't moose hunting kinda dangerous?" said Elmer, thinking of her size.

"They're just cows with long legs." she calmly replied.

"I see you've had a bit of bad luck." she added looking at his leg.

"Yea, it wasn't an accident though." he told her, "We met the wrong people in Skagway."

"Well it's pretty hard to meet the right people in Skagway." she answered.

They continued talking as they drank their coffee, and Elmer noticed that she was a very proper woman with refined manners.

Eventually Belinda said she had to get back to work, and as she got up her monstrous dog jumped to her command. When she began to leave she turned back to Elmer and said "You best get healthy as fast as you can. You don't want to spend the winter here."

Throughout the day Elmer would glance up at the glacier once in a while, watching it change colors as the sun moved across the sky. It went from pink and yellow, to green and white, and was turning blue when Henry returned. He'd sold the horses for a mere $20, and that was after shopping them around awhile. After returning, he sold the last one on the trail below for ten cents. They really were a dime a dozen here.

In the following days, Elmer began moving around a little better, and he'd limp down through the bush to where he could sit and overlook the trail. He'd watch it for hours some days, as a constant stream of gold seekers passed by. They were every age, men and women, rich and poor, and they carried everything under the sun. Cowboys, sailors, maids, musicians, and everything else went by. Many in groups. A barber shoppe quartet, a platoon of bagpipers, even a women's temperance league. Every kind of animal that could walk and carry a load was also being used, from small dogs to teams of mules and oxen.

He saw some familiar faces go by too. The man they saw taking pictures in Seattle went by, with a loaded cart being pulled by a team of goats. He also spied the old woman they'd seen talking to Soapy Smith, with her six-gun still in her belt.

One morning he'd just arrived at his perch, when he saw Sam Steele disappear up the trail with about half a dozen men.

Most of them were in their twenty's, and they were all wearing buffalo coats like his.

It was almost hot that afternoon, and as they sat by the campfire Elmer decided to try one of his cigars. He took one of the paper tubes from the case and pulled the cigar from it, then lit it with a stick he picked up from the fire. He didn't smoke but he'd tried it before, and he knew enough to be cautious so as not to cough his guts out.

After taking a small puff, he leaned back to relax and blow the smoke out when the glacier caught his eye. "Look Henry, the glacier's all twinkly."

They both sat and watched it sparkle different colors, when Henry became confused.

"Wait a minute!" he said, "There's something wrong here!" Suddenly the face of the entire glacier fell forward, falling towards the valley floor. They sat awestruck as the colossal block of ice smashed into the valley bottom, blasting chunks the size of houses thousands of feet. A sound like hundreds of firing cannons soon reached them, and became more deafening as it continued. The massive lumps were then mashed into thousands and then millions of pieces, forming an immense river of ice that pushed a wall of rocks, trees, and debris down the valley, obliterating everything in its path.

They thought it'd come perilously close to the trail if not over it, but it swept around the base of the mountain and out of their sight. Some time passed before the river stopped moving, and a little longer for the thundering roar to fade. Still staring intently, Henry mused "I'll bet we never see that again."

For years, the few men that climbed over the Chilkoot had reported seeing a precariously poised glacier, dubbed 'The Pretty One', hanging over the pass. Now a sixty foot thick, three hundred foot high slab of ice had plummeted into the valley, sending down a flood of debris that wiped out part of the trail, and the belongings and camps of more than forty people. Because of the noise and location almost everyone had time to scramble to higher ground, but it did kill three people, and Arizona Charlie was one of those who had his belongings wiped out.

It was only a few hours before news of the victims arrived from below, but the most astonishing thing, was that the line never stopped. As soon as the river of ice stopped moving, with the persistence of ants the gold seekers picked their way over and around the debris, to continue the race for gold.

Soon the weather became much cooler, and they woke one morning to a biting cold. Emerging from their tent, they found Belinda outside sitting with her dog by a raging fire and sipping tea she'd made. She said she preferred tea to coffee, and as she spoke she presented them with a big slab of moose meat. She said she'd finally amassed the money and food needed to proceed over the pass, and was going to be moving on. She must've done quite well hunting, as she said she'd hired some men to carry most of her things. She didn't just have the usual supplies either. She possessed numerous cases of hot water bottles, and bolts of canvas she planned to sell in the Klondike.

They all sat sipping tea from their tin cups, and as the weather warmed and the fire slowed, they began talking of what they might do if they did find their fortunes.

"My mother and sisters got it pretty rough back home." said Elmer, "I'd like to have enough to take their worries away, and fix up the ranch too. Then maybe take 'em to Paris. They always imagined about going there."

"I'd like to travel." agreed Belinda, as she poked at the fire with a small stick, "Maybe travel the world on a sailboat."

"Would you go to Paris?" asked Elmer.

"Absolutely." she replied. Then she asked "What about you Henry?"

"I doubt if I'd go to Paris." he answered, knowing that wasn't what she meant.

"That's not what I was asking." she said.

"I know." chuckled Henry, then he said "I'd probably buy a ranch somewhere back home, maybe around Elmer's mother's place. I always liked it there."

"We're dreaming here Henry," said Elmer, "You're supposed to think big."

"Alright." he answered, "Then I'd get a really big ranch, with really big cows."

Belinda started giggling.

"See! You're mocking my dream." said Henry, then he added "Might I suggest that you'd already be in the Klondike, if you'd a just saddled up your dog."

Then Elmer started laughing.

They talked for a while longer but eventually it was back to reality, and Belinda bid them good-bye, then left for the Klondike with the behemoth 'Nero' at her side.

A few days later it snowed, and in the following weeks it continued to pile up. They discovered that camped high in the mountains where the trees were much smaller, didn't give them near the wind protection they'd hoped for.

Elmer continued to watch the trail every day, and found it agonizing to watch an endless line of men pass them by. He kept getting better though, and when it looked like he'd be okay in a week or so, Henry began moving their supplies about a mile up the trail to a place called Sheep Camp. Really it was a large log cabin built on the only piece of level ground there was, and all around it were tents pitched at odd angles. You could buy supper there for 75¢, which was an arm and a leg, but you were then entitled to sleep on the floor for as long as you wanted. They were full all the time.

When Elmer was well enough to travel again, his first few trips were difficult, as his leg muscles needed rebuilding. Like all the other sections of the trail, they barely got started when the pitch increased again, to the point where falling over backwards could be a dangerous thing. To make matters worse, the trail was becoming icy and quite treacherous in some places.

They were above the tree line now, and on rare occasions when the clouds would lift, they could see glaciers and jagged peaks all around them. And when the wind blew over the mountains and down onto them, it was extremely cold.

After one particularly arduous trip, they were overwhelmed by the scent of freshly baked buns. They followed it to the Sheep Camp cabin, where they couldn't stop themselves from buying a couple, at an outrageous 25¢ each. Then they sat inside with the other men that had succumbed to the irresistible smell, taking advantage of the well heated building.

There they met and talked to four brothers named Mizner. Edgar Mizner was the oldest and somewhat unfriendly, but the others were very sociable telling that Addison was an architect, and Wilson a piano player and gambler who hoped to clean up in the Klondike. And with them they had their youngest brother William. They all looked to be in their twenty's, except for Edgar who appeared to be an older bureaucratic type, and were all tall sturdy men. But even though they all dressed alike with their business suits and derby hats, they appeared to be quite different fellows.

Most everyone that wasn't sleeping was devouring the hot dinner rolls, when a man spoke up asking "Hey Hambone, how come these buns are brown today?"

"I gave Sweaty the job." he answered, "And he cut his finger pretty bad makin' 'em."

Everyone turned to the stove where 'Sweaty' was making a new batch of buns. The heavily perspiring man nodded politely, as they noticed he was still bleeding profusely through a dirty bandage. Henry couldn't take another bite, or swallow the one he had, but Elmer kept chewing his bun calmly.

The Mizner's couldn't eat anymore either. In fact Edgar choked so hard he sprayed soggy pieces all over the sleeping men. Then he quickly swilled down a couple of whiskeys as if trying to disinfect his mouth. By the time he finished coughing he too was perspiring heavily.

"You're startin' to look a lot like Sweaty." Addison told him as he laughed, "Maybe his blood is starting to mingle with yours.

A man had begun bothering Hambone for a free bun, which didn't seem very likely. He claimed that he'd begun his journey with more than sufficient funds, but upon landing in Skagway a saintly old priest had steered him to the 'Bureau of Information', where they lied to him about everything. But Hambone reasoned out loud, that if he fed him, he'd have to feed everybody.

When Henry and Elmer left the building to return to their camp, they saw that even this far up the trail, at least two of the tents crowded around the large cabin were devoted to gambling.

It took nearly two more weeks to pack all their supplies up to Sheep Camp, and by the end of it Elmer had his legs back. Their last trip was with the tent and stove, which they planned to carry far past the log cabin, and establish a new camp to pack to. They also had to bring their woodpile. Beyond Sheep Camp they were above the tree line, and there was absolutely nothing to burn.

Also beyond the cabin, the trail became steeper again. They weren't really walking or hiking anymore, but climbing, and over the next three miles the trail would rise up more than two thousand feet.

They climbed most of the day to advance two and a half miles, and with little daylight left and their tongues hanging out, they set up a quick camp in the snow.

They woke in the morning to yet another freezing day, and after talking about it, they decided not to light the stove in an effort to conserve wood. Instead, they'd warm up by walking down to Sheep Camp for another load. The moving line was crowded going both ways now, as everyone worked to shuttle their supplies up the trail. And because of the steepness, it was almost as slow and difficult descending the trail as it was to climb with a full load.

Eventually they arrived down at Sheep Camp again, and not far from their stack of goods they spied Arizona Charlie. He had a raging fire going beside his bar to entice cold customers off the trail, and he was talking to the old woman they'd seen in Skagway with the big gun in her belt. As they drew near they heard her say "I best be goin' Charlie, I gotta build a camp today." and with that she brushed by them on her way up the mountain.

Elmer's curiosity got the best of him, so he asked Charlie "Who's that old woman? We saw her talking to Soapy in Skagway. Is she part of his gang?"

"No, not at all." laughed Charlie, "Have you guys heard of Calamity Jane."

"Who hasn't?" replied Elmer, as he watched her find a place in line. "That's Calamity Jane?!" he asked again, completely surprised. He never thought he'd see a living legend.

"How come she knows Soapy?" he asked.

"Same as me." Charlie replied, "She's from Leadville too, and we both used to be in Buffalo Bill's Wild West Show."

"You were in Buffalo Bill's Wild West Show?" said Elmer.

"Yup, sharpshooter." he answered. Then he jokingly stuck his thumbs into his vest pockets, and posed as if being photographed and said "Why I'm a colorful character of the American West." Then he added "When I shot the axe from that guys hand, you didn't think it was a fluke did ya?"

Elmer then bombarded Charlie with questions, wanting to know more about his exploits, and Calamity Jane. His grilling ended when Henry noticed that Charlie didn't have his portable bar anymore, but rather a board nailed up on heavy sticks.

"What happened to your bar?" he asked.

"Lost everything but my wallet when the glacier came down." he answered. "Had to go back to Skagway and re-outfit. It wasn't cheap either." Then he went on to tell them about scrambling up the hillside to escape the flood of debris from the glacier.

Henry figured they still owed Charlie, and they had a bit of money again from selling the horses. So they bought two more drinks from him, despite the fact that his sign now read 75¢ a drink. The rising price hadn't affected his clientele much though. His business was still booming. They sat by Charlie's fire warming up for a while, then wished him better luck than he'd been having, and went off to pick up another load. They decided food and more firewood should be the next cargo packed, so they loaded up as much as they could carry on their backs, and began the slow climb back up to their camp.

As the days went by, they shuttled load after load up the pass, usually with a stiff north wind in their faces. The wind rarely stopped now, and the temperature kept dropping until most days were -15 to -20 below zero. Many of the hats the stampeders were wearing were completely inadequate for such temperatures, and as ears began to freeze, many were cutting wide strips of wool or other materials to tie over their heads and ears. Henry and Elmer were forced to do likewise and figured they looked pretty ridiculous. But it was at least tempered by everyone else looking much the same.

Many also had the wrong footwear, so feet were starting to freeze too. Passing a tent one afternoon, they heard a man screaming as a doctor cut off some of his toes. If frozen too badly, toes would turn black and start rotting, with gangrene to follow. The only remedy was amputation.

The biting cold was forcing many people to give up now. The badly dressed and ill-equipped were learning that they had little chance of going much further. At least not without considerable danger and discomfort. They were hardly missed though. Gold fever still was running rampant, and the army of men just kept pouring up the valley.

On one of Henry and Elmer's last trips down to Sheep Camp, there was much commotion when they arrived. A great mob of men were gathered at the front of a large tent, with many more inside. They were deciding what to do with two men that were thieves, if not murderers.

The men had arrived with a loaded sled being pulled by a large dog team, and when the ice that'd built up on the side of the sleigh fell off, it revealed the true owners name, and it wasn't them. There were men that knew the real owner, and the thieves couldn't or wouldn't explain how they came into possession of his outfit.

Normally the thing to do was to turn them over to the law, but the only law for hundreds of miles was Soapy Smith's law in Skagway, and everyone agreed, that was no law at all. Some thought that the thieves might even be part of Soapy's gang. It was generally decided that they couldn't just let the men go, as no one was willing to tolerate thievery of any kind. Everyone's belongings were vulnerable most all the time.

It was decided that a traditional miners meeting would be held. A court where a group of sober minded men would weigh the evidence, judge the accused, and decide on a punishment if necessary. It had been used by pioneers and prospectors over the decades as a method of dealing with criminals in extremely isolated conditions. It would also stand up in a court of law.

Everything went as expected at the meeting, until they got to the punishment part. Then while they were deciding on a sentence, the possibilities being forwarded rattled one of the men so bad that he quickly jumped up drawing a hidden gun and knife, then sliced a long gash in the back of the tent and squeezed through it to run off down the trail. The pursuing men quickly tore the tent wide open, and poured through yelling "Thief!-Stop!-Thief!" as they chased him down the trail. The thief quickly realized that he couldn't escape and suddenly stopped. Then promptly brought the gun up and shot himself in the face.

Poor Addison Mizner was plodding up the trail, just in time to first get splattered with the man's brains, and then get slammed backwards into the snow with the dead man landing on top of him. With the man's body draped over him, and a heavy pack on his back, Addison had to wait to be freed before he could get back up again.

The miners meeting then sentenced the other man to forty lashes with a bullwhip, but it too started to get pretty ugly after just ten lashes, and at fifteen, the Mizner brother's stepped in and put a stop to it. The man was then ordered back down the trail, but first they hung a sign around his neck that said "Thief", and he was told that if he removed the sign before Skagway, they'd find out about it and he'd get the rest of his lashes.

Soon, Henry and Elmer were advancing their camp up the trail to a new and further location. Their first trip up this new section, they found that they had a particularly steep part to climb. Struggling to the top of it, Elmer was following behind when he heard Henry utter the words "Oh my God!" then step out of the line. Elmer took a few more steps then got out of line with him, noticing that some other men had done the same. His attention quickly turned to what Henry was looking at, and then they both stood there stunned!

They could see the line of people winding ahead about a half a mile to the valley's end, where all the mountains descended steeply to form a large natural bowl. And in that bowl many hundreds of people were milling about. Then on the far side of the crowd they saw another line of people that seemed to go straight up until they became like a thread and disappeared into the clouds. It was 'The Golden Stairs', and at the top was the Yukon.

The longer they stared at it, the more formidable it became, so fearing discouragement they soon got back in line again.

As they continued forward they realized it wasn't looking any better, and by the time they reached the mass of tents and people, they knew it was going to take weeks of back-breaking work to carry their supplies over the top.

The Golden Stairs were narrow steps hacked into the ice, forming an endless staircase rising straight up and over the mountains.

Other than the solid rock above them, snow and ice was all there was now, and with the frigid cold and the intimidating staircase, Henry and Elmer for the first time contemplated quitting.

While they were discussing it, they learned something that really wasn't bad news, but depressed them all the same. Once people saw the Golden Stairs, many were unwilling or unable to go any further, and those that turned back would abandon most of their supplies right where they sat. Now the two tons of food that Henry and Elmer had paid dearly for in Skagway, then packed uphill for weeks, could be bought for a tenth the price.

They ultimately decided that they couldn't afford to turn back, and really had to continue. So after sitting depressed for some time, they resumed moving their belongings to the foot of the stairs. Eventually getting them stacked in a neat pile outside their tent, like the hundreds of other stampeders.

This was the staging area for everyone's attack on the summit. Where load after load would be packed up the stairs, until a person had all their food and supplies piled on top. The more you could carry the fewer trips it took. So everyone loaded themselves to their maximum capacity for every trip.

Professional packers could be hired here, if one had the money. Most of them were the local Chilkat Indians. They'd historically guarded the pass against unwanted intrusions into the Yukon, but now unable to stop this human tide, they took advantage of the situation by hiring themselves out as packers. Each trip they'd rent themselves to the highest bidder, usually between 40¢ and $1 a pound, a price completely out of reach for the ordinary man. But some of the Indians were getting very rich, very fast.

Henry and Elmer had to pack their own things though. So in the morning after a heavy breakfast, they loaded their packs with about sixty pounds each, and began moving forward to the bottom of the stairs. They shuffled along with many other heavy laden men, all funneling towards the bottom step. On the way they passed a large set of scales, where loads, especially food, could be quickly weighed. No one wanted to carry even one pound up the stairs that wasn't absolutely necessary.

It was almost three quarters of an hour before they reached the front of the stairs, and were glad to get there. Standing in line for so long, their hands, feet, and noses had begun to freeze. They knew that hard work would warm them up again though, and they were about to get their fill. Just before taking their first step onto the stairs, Elmer looked back at Henry and said "Well, let's get this over with." and they began their incredible climb.

The first thing they learned was 'The Chilkoot Lock-step'. The stairs were so crowded with packers, that there was literally a man on every step. So it worked out best, that when one man stepped forward, all the others did too, synchronizing the entire line. After each step the whole line would hesitate a second, allowing for any miss-steps to be corrected, then step forward again in unison, and repeat the process.

On the way up the mountain there were resting places trampled in the snow, and about a half an hour from the bottom Henry and Elmer found themselves in one, gasping for air and sweating under their heavy coats. Again they wondered if it was worth continuing, and soon came to the same conclusion as before, that they just couldn't afford to turn back. Then starting to feel cold again, they tried to get back in line.

It turned out to be much harder than they thought. Interrupting the line wasn't tolerated, so the only thing they could do was wait for a space. It took quite a while for one to appear, and as they would later learn could sometimes take hours. They rested three more times on the way up, and a little over five hours later stepped out on top exhausted.

Now they were in a small draw between two jagged mountains, and all around them lay hundreds of piles of belongings, all marked with tall poles, so as not to get lost in the many blizzards and deep snowfalls. There was also a biting wind and no real cover, convincing them to hurry up and place their load somewhere, and get back down the mountain. They didn't have to worry at all about their things being stolen here. At the far end of the draw just past the piles, was the 'Northwest Mounted Police Border Outpost', which from its position overlooked the entire draw.

The return trip back down to the scales wasn't on the stairs, but rather on a regular trail pounded deep into the snow, which seemed to zigzag endlessly down the mountain. It only took about half an hour to traverse back down to the bottom, but it had a huge cooling effect. After sweating all the way up the stairs, when walking back down, shirts, hats, coats, gloves, and anything else wet, would begin to freeze solid.

There was only one other way back down the mountain, and though it took less than a minute it rarely went without incident. Some men would try to slide straight down the mountain side, riding on the head of a shovel or some other suitable aid. Many of these attempts would provide much appreciated entertainment, as they would often end with spectacular cartwheel filled crashes, sometimes with injuries.

Within a week Henry and Elmer could pack nearly seventy-five pounds a trip, which was a little more than the average person's load of about sixty, and they were also a little faster than the average, usually taking five to five and a half hours to get to the top, when most people took six to eight hours. The trouble was, by the time they got back down the mountain, like most people they were too worn out to make another trip. Even though the constant packing was making them stronger than they'd ever been, to do the stairs twice in one day was too much.

A few men however, had become incredibly powerful. If a person never stepped out of line it was a little less than four hours to the top, and a very few were making two or even three trips a day, with a couple of them carrying two and three hundred pounds on their back.

Some men were gaining instant fame by the loads they carried. A man named Ballantine carried a piano over the stairs. A Chilkat Indian called 'Jumbo' regularly carried loads of 350 pounds, and sometimes made three trips a day. Tom Linville, who carried a man with a broken leg eleven miles from Sheep Camp to Dyea in only a few hours.

At meal times now, men's conversation often turned to feats of strength they'd witnessed, or odd loads they'd seen carried. For cast-iron stoves, boats, field plows, millstones, and practically everything else was being packed over the 'Golden Stairs'.

As the weeks went by, Henry and Elmer carried load after load up the icy staircase. It was such a grueling task that it was not uncommon to see men sitting in the resting places, still wearing their packs, and sound asleep at -20 or even -30 below. At first they'd sweat each time going up, and freeze coming back down. But as the temperature dropped even further, they were cold going up, and even colder coming back down.

Each time they reached the bottom again, they'd hurry straight to their tent and frantically build a fire in their stove. Then as soon as they had the tent warmed to a bearable temperature, they'd begin making something to eat.

They pretty much ate the same thing every meal, as did everyone else. It was called 'Bannock'. A simple dough made of flour, water, sugar, salt and baking powder, then cooked in a greasy frying pan. It would turn into a very heavy sweet bread that tasted good hot or cold, and could also be saved for later. But mostly it was quick to make, and no dishes or utensils were required, and if done properly, even the frying pan remained ready to go again.

One morning after a hearty pan of bannock, they were carrying their loads towards the stairs, when they heard some men arguing. It turned out that someone who'd already gone over the stairs, had paid the Indian packers with Confederate money, and now some of the Indians had returned from Skagway where they'd tried to spend it. They told the others, and unable to tell one kind of paper money from another, the Indians decided that they wouldn't accept any paper money anymore. Some of the stampeders were outraged by their decision, but the Indians wouldn't budge. From now on, only people who could pay in gold could hire the Native packers.

Henry and Elmer then saw another unrelated commotion, and they'd seen it before. A very large man they'd seen quite a few times had a huge wooden box as part of his cargo. That by itself wasn't unusual, but it had a hinged lid on top and he spent great amounts of time with the lid open, and fidgeting inside. People noticed this, and had become more and more curious to see what he was doing. He was adamantly against this and guarded the box jealously. He was of a good nature though, so they would regularly continue the harassment.

It seemed to snow all the time now, and despite the ferocious winds that usually blew over the summit, each trip up they'd find their pile of supplies buried even deeper in the snow. In fact, without their marking stick, sometimes they wouldn't have found it at all. There were other people who either had no marker or had them blow over, and some of them would lose their piles until spring.

Another result of the near continuous snowfalls, was that the path back down the mountain was now a pounded down trench through shoulder deep snow. But rather than protect them from the wind, the snow would blow along the surface and dump straight down their necks.

Then one morning they had a rude awakening when the temperature dropped again, and it was now more than -40 below. Henry quickly moved to light a fire, and stood in his long underwear stuffing the stove as fast as he could. In less than a minute he could hardly feel his fingers, and by the time he lit the match, he was shivering so bad he could barely hold it to the paper. When the fire got going, Elmer got up to put the frying pan on the stove, but as soon as he picked it up suddenly yelled "Holy Fingers!" and dropped it as fast as he could while grabbing his hand in pain. The frozen steel had instantly freeze-burned his hand, and though it had froze his skin, it looked and felt just as if it had been burned.

Circumstances that were miserable, had now become agonizing and dangerous, and making it worse was everyone's clothes were starting to wear out. Especially gloves, mitts and socks. Most had resorted to sewing thumbs on worn out socks, or wrapping their hands and feet in wool or anything else that would work. People were also becoming covered with rough made patches, and many other examples of bad sewing.

It was blizzard conditions, yet the relentless army of people still assaulted the stairs continuously. The wind slowed somewhat in the intense cold, but sometimes an icy fog blew over the summit and down the stairs, freezing everything exposed. The hacking off of fingers and toes was becoming common place, and typhoid, pneumonia, and other sicknesses had begun claiming the weak and worn out. On one particularly bad night, thirteen people died.

Henry and Elmer packed as hard and fast as they could. It was the key to getting out of this place and it was all they could think about now. Occasionally they would see and talk to the Mizner brothers, usually finding out things were just as bad for them.

Almost everyone knew how many times they'd climbed the Golden Stairs, and when Henry and Elmer finally got to their last load it was their thirty-seventh trip each, and had taken them more than a month. Knowing it was to be their last trip and they wouldn't be coming back down again, they took it easy that morning and ended up getting a very late start.

The last load to be carried was going to be a heavy one as it included their stove and tent. So after they bundled themselves up and loaded up their packs, they joined in the shuffle to the foot of the stairs for the last time. On the way there they saw the big man with the mysterious box again, and as usual, he was in it with both hands. As curious as everyone else, they continued watching the man as they slowly moved forward, hoping for some hint at what it might contain. Eventually they reached the front of the line and it was their turn to go. So after they each took a big breath, they started up the stairs and disappeared into the descending fog.

They carried their loads a little further than usual, and a lot further than they thought they would, before finally falling into a resting place. When they sat down, they found that though they weren't exactly warm, they weren't cold either. Elmer's buffalo coat that was at first a burden, and then practical, was now a well envied luxury.

As they sat resting, Henry thought about how they'd been packing for months, and were still less than twenty miles from Skagway. So far this race for gold had been no more than an agonizing crawl. He also remembered how quick both he and Elmer had made the decision to come north.

Suddenly Elmer said "Look, there's the man with the camera box."

Peering through the ice fog, Henry could see it was the same photographer that they'd seen in Seattle. They couldn't believe he had his camera set up in this weather.

"I wonder if we'll be in one of his pictures?" said Elmer.

Just then another man stepped out of the line to rest, and sat down beside Henry. He was a big powerful looking man in his late twenties, and as he loosened the straps on his pack he introduced himself as Clarence Berry, and said he had a wife back down at the scales. Then the three of them sat in the cold and watched the line of people struggle up the stairs.

Before long Clarence turned to Henry, and with his collar turned up as high as it would go said "I thought Hell would be hotter."

Elmer too had been thinking of his and Henry's start in Seattle, and leaning in front of Henry he proudly announced to Clarence "We're on a big adventure!"

Henry started laughing, and when he thought about how almost everything had been so far beyond what they'd expected, he just laughed harder. When he finally stopped he said "I'd be positive I was crazy for being here, except for all these other people."

"I wouldn't put too much comfort in that." replied Clarence, "Sometimes I think we all must be insane." Then he produced a bottle of whiskey. "I'm not really a drinking man." he said, "I got it from a guy that owed me money and I don't want to pack it anymore."

He figured it might help fend off the cold, and that maybe they could help him drink it. They figured they could maybe help him drink it too, as it seemed to be getting even colder with darkness falling, and they were all eager for any kind of fire.

Soon the three of them were taking turns drinking from the bottle, trying to heat themselves up from the inside. Henry guzzled freely for a few seconds and after passing it to Clarence said "At least this weather's gotta be making a few people quit."

After taking his turn, Clarence replied "I started out with forty other people....There's only three of us left now."

As the temperature dropped even further and the ice fog became thicker, a warm fuzzy feeling began to overtake them all. Before long they all sat quiet with just their eyes exposed, watching a surreal procession of people and cargo stagger by. With the snow and fog and the blowing wind, they could only see a few yards, and the heavy laden figures seemed to appear one at a time. They saw a man carrying a blacksmith's anvil, and another that struggled under a large metal bathtub. Then an old woman packing a sewing machine and a large rifle, and was singing a hymn as she passed by. Even the man with the giant box went past them. They saw the Mizner brothers too, but it was much too cold for anything but business, so they passed on by exchanging only nods and a bunch of muffled "Howdys"

The next thing Elmer knew Henry was waking him up. Clarence Berry was already gone, and with a little better visibility Henry had spied a couple of spaces in the line moving up the stairs. So they readied themselves to step in, and soon joined back in the long column of men doing the 'Chilkoot Lock-step' for the last time.

It was still a long way to the top, so they had to rest again. But after their second stop they began to get extremely cold, and by the time they reached the summit they were getting into real trouble. The wind was howling on top and driving the snow straight sideways. Much too windy to set up their tent. They had to do something quick though, or they'd be freezing very soon. Their fingers and toes had already been stinging for some time, and if the stinging stopped it meant they were frozen, and would probably have to be cut off.

It was a real emergency, so they did the only thing they could think of. They quickly dug a deep depression in the snow and spread in the end of their tent. Then they threw in their bedding and pulled the rest of the tent canvas over top of them. Under the canvas they lay down, and then stuffed their bedding and everything else tightly around and over them. Now they'd either get colder and lose body parts and maybe die, or start warming up again and be safe for some time.

Normally what they did would've froze them badly before too long, but the blowing snow quickly laid a thick white blanket over the canvas, and insulated them from the deadly cold.

When they woke in the morning, they pushed their way through the snow to see a bright sunny day that was calmer and warmer than anything they'd seen for a month. And the only effects they were feeling were that of a long, deep sleep. It took some time to dig out all their supplies, as some of the first loads they'd carried up the stairs were buried more than 8 feet deep in the snow. Then they began moving it to the Mounted Police Customs tent, where they'd each have their ton of food weighed.

It was such a nice day and with the stairs behind them now, their spirits began to soar again. Elmer even decided to smoke another one of Soapy's cigars. But by the time he finished it, he decided that he wasn't much of a smoker.

Once their things were moved, they lined up for the customs inspection by the North West Mounted Police. Everyone called them 'Mounties', and they'd been posted at the summit to enforce the ton of food requirement. They were also there to establish Canadian law and bar criminals from entering the Yukon, in particular Soapy and his gang. They were mostly young men in their twenty's, and were uniformed in bright scarlet tunics, underneath their buffalo coats.

When Henry and Elmer reached the front of the line, their entry into Canada went smooth and swift. The Mounties didn't have to ask them many questions, they already knew where they were going and why. So after giving their names and where they were from, they answered a few more questions about what they might be carrying, then their food was weighed and they were passed through, with a 'Welcome to Canada'.

Shortly after Henry and Elmer were granted entry, everyone's attention was drawn to another man in line. It was the big man with the mysterious box, and he still didn't want anyone to look in it. Not even the Mounties. But the Corporal in charge told him "Look! You can either let us look in the box, or you can pack it back to Skagway. It's your call."

The man knew that if he ever wanted to see the Klondike he had to relent. So appearing rather embarrassed, he opened the box and stepped back.

As one of the young officers stepped up to it, he said "How come there's holes in the lid?" Then he reached in and pulled out a handful of shredded newspaper. Suddenly he looked back up at the others in surprise and exclaimed "He's got a box full a cats!"

As everyone roared with laughter, the officer said to the man "I'll be back in a minute. The superintendent's got to decide on something like this." And with that he ducked out of the tent and into another a few yards away, and after a few seconds came out again followed by the superintendent.

It was Sam Steele!

Henry and Elmer were speechless as he walked by them in his scarlet uniform. He grinned at them and said "Glad to see you fellas finally made it out of Skagway, and ain't froze to death yet either." Then he looked at the man with the box and said "Now, what's a guy gonna do with a big box a cats in the Yukon?"

The man was big but still had to look up a little to Sam, and while he worked at keeping the kittens from climbing out of the box, he explained how he figured that a lot of miners in the Klondike would be lonely, and would pay handsomely for feline companionship, especially during the winter months.

"Do you ever let 'em out a there?" asked Sam.

"All the time." answered the man, "In my tent. But they been in there lots since they were little. They like it."

"Any of 'em sick?" asked Sam.

"Absolutely not." the man assured.

"Well I can't see any problem." said Sam, and passed him on through.

Henry and Elmer moved their supplies up past where the police Gatling gun stood. The Mounties manned it twenty-four hours a day, mostly as a deterrent for Soapy's gang. Also, handguns were illegal in Canada except by special permit, and some men were reluctant to give them up. The machine gun helped them decide. From its location it could sweep over the entire pass.

Since he arrived, Sam Steele was the top law enforcement officer in the Yukon, but he had very few men to enforce the law over the territory. So up until now his main priority had been to keep Soapy Smith and his gang from even entering the Yukon. He knew what the Klondike would turn into, if Soapy ran it.

After they passed through customs, Henry and Elmer found themselves at a vantage point where they could see miles down the pass in both directions. Looking back towards Skagway, they saw the long line of people winding up the pass to the scales, then up the Golden Stairs.

"I'll bet I remember these stairs till the day I die." reflected Henry.

"I'll bet everybody does." agreed Elmer.

"Looks like there's a lot more people at the scales now than when we got here too." added Henry.

It was then that Sam came up by them and yelled for one of his officers. One showed up right away and Sam asked "Anybody die on our side of the border last night?"

"No sir." answered the constable, "At least none we know of yet."

"Then I want you to take a couple of men and a sleigh down to the treeline. We're running low on firewood, and this is about as nice a day as we're gonna get." Sam then dismissed the officer and walked over a little closer to Henry and Elmer.

"Almost -50 below last night." he said, as he peered through binoculars down towards the scales. "You guys familiar with the term 'Parade of Fools'?"

They didn't think he expected them to answer, so they didn't. But they both hoped he was wrong.

When they turned to look ahead into the Yukon, it was beautiful. The sky was blue and the sun which was always low now, was casting a soft pink light on all the mountains. The Yukon was like Alaska, only higher, more rugged, and more mountainous. It was also more isolated and with fewer people. Up until the last few years, the only people living in the Yukon had been a few trappers and prospectors, and the resident Indian bands. It was also rumored that a number of mountain men had been driven north by the settling of the American west, and as many as fifty had slipped into the Yukon and disappeared into the wilderness. No one knew for sure, as they weren't the kind of men that drew attention to themselves.

The Yukon was changing now though, as the endless line of men stretched from Skagway to as far as they could see in front of them. Tens of thousands were struggling towards the gold fields, through some of the worst conditions on earth.

The first few miles on the Yukon side of the pass sloped down quite gently. So Henry and Elmer built a crude sled, as did most stampeders, and it seemed that no matter how high they stacked their supplies on the sleigh, a slight pull would skid the load down the slope with ease. In fact from now on, a sled pulled by dogs was the best transportation there was.

After traveling a few miles, the trail began to level out somewhat and they passed a small, snow covered lake. It was Crater Lake, and it was actually the extreme headwaters of the Yukon River. The river was very unique in that it began less than twenty miles from the ocean, yet the water in Crater Lake would travel over twenty two hundred miles through the Yukon and Alaska before mixing with the Bering Sea.

Before long, pulling the sled became much more difficult, so they were envious when they saw Belinda again. She was sitting in a basket sleigh being briskly pulled along by Nero.

A few more miles went by when trees began to appear, but so did rougher terrain, where more and more often they had to drag the sled over solid rock. Further down the trail where the trees began to grow thicker and provide some degree of cover, they saw Arizona Charlie again with his bar set up. He was charging $1 a drink now, and so many men were crammed around his board and fire that they couldn't really talk to him very well. They spoke briefly anyway though, and after taking advantage of his fire, they were beginning to leave when Elmer noticed one of the men was smoking a cigar. It reminded him of his own cigars and decided he should probably give one to Charlie.

So after fishing out the case, he was handing one of the tubes over to the old scout when he heard a man ask "Those for sale?"

Elmer hadn't thought of selling them before, but he liked the idea. He just wasn't sure what to charge for one. Then the man saw that he only had two left. "They look like pretty good cigars." he said, "Give ya $2 for one."

Elmer struggled quickly to get one out of the case before the man could change his mind. His fingers were still cold though, and he pulled one free only to fumble it and drop it in the snow. When he bent over to pick it up, it suddenly came to him that flashing Soapy Smith's cigar case in front of a bunch of strangers might not be such a good idea. So he quickly gave the man the last tube from the case, then put it away. He then scooped up the tube from the snow and shoved it into his pocket, as he looked around to see if anyone seemed overly-interested.

To his relief no one seemed to care at all, but he still realized that it was a dumb thing to do. He probably didn't have to worry at all now that they'd crossed the border, but more trouble they didn't need, especially serious trouble. After receiving the $2, they left to head back to their own camp to eat. They were hungry, and the bannock pan was waiting.

Henry had just flipped the bannock to brown the topside, when Elmer spied the photographer coming down the trail. He had skis under the wheels of his wagon, and it was still being pulled by his team of goats. They were remarkably well suited for the weather and terrain, and were one of the few animals that could make it over the pass.

Suddenly Elmer jumped up without saying anything, and ran over to the trail to meet him. After they talked for a few minutes, Elmer led him back to their camp and tied his goats to a tree. They could see that his wagon was loaded high with camera supplies, though they really didn't know what any of it did.

"This is Eric Hegg." said Elmer introducing him. Then he said to Hegg, "This is my uncle, Henry."

"Howdy." said Henry greeting him, "Can we offer you somethin' to eat?"

"That would be great." replied the photographer with a heavy Swedish lilt, "I must have lost a foot of belly since I started this trip."

So they sat and ate big wedges of bannock, and Hegg told them that he was from Bellingham, Washington where he had a studio. He said he saw what was happening with the gold rush, and thought that somebody should photograph it. So he closed up his business and came north.

As Hegg talked, Henry noticed a strange smile come over his face. Then he saw that across the fire, Elmer had set down his piece of bannock and was digging through one of their food boxes for a handful of raisins. While his back was turned, a half a dozen birds about the size of robins had swooped in, and were tearing his bannock to bits. They were gray birds with a little black on them, that everyone called 'Whiskey Jacks'. They seemed to live under the spruce and pine trees, and if you stopped to camp, or eat, or anything else, they'd show up almost immediately, regardless of the temperature. They were incredibly brazen, and for some reason seemed to be picking on Elmer. He finally turned back around, and screamed loud in disgust scaring them away.

"Camp robbers!" laughed Hegg, as they watched Elmer stare down at the few remaining crumbs.

They talked for a while after eating, then Hegg left when he realized it was getting colder again. It was still sunny most days, but it didn't do much to warm things up. People had been getting sick all along, but now the temperature dropped to around -40 below again, and again people were freezing their fingers and toes. And because people were walking greater distances now, badly blistered feet were becoming common, and some would have a foot covered with blood before they even knew they had a problem.

Henry and Elmer had thought for some time that it'd warm up as soon as the trail dropped down out of the mountains. But they'd slowly come to realize that the trail wasn't going to drop out of the mountains, and a long slow decent was the best they could hope for.

One day as they pulled and pushed their sled over the landscape, they came across a mound in the snow that was an obvious grave. Carved into a nearby tree were the words 'Bury me here where I failed'. They were later to learn that the man was unable to bear the continuous suffering of the journey, and had shot himself. Paradoxically, less than a mile away was a neat log cabin with a large woodpile outside, and a sign out front that read 'Sleep in a feather bed $10'.

After Henry and Elmer passed by the cabin, they ran into the man who'd shared his whiskey with them on the stairs. It was Clarence Berry and the big man was pulling his wife along in a sleigh. They hadn't spoken much on the stairs because of the blizzard, and it wasn't a whole lot warmer now. But they talked for a while anyway, learning that he was a fruit farmer from Fresno, California. And just like everyone else, he'd come north both on a whim, and as a last resort. He also admitted that like everyone else, the trail had become a nightmare that he just wanted to end.

They'd barely said good-bye to the Berry's, when things got worse for them too. The occasional smooth sections of bedrock they had to cross, had gradually become rougher and more frequent, until they had to abandon their sleigh altogether. From now on they had to carry everything on their backs again.

So each day they'd pack until the sun turned the mountains pink and purple, then with the following darkness, the northern lights would appear and dance throughout the night.

Mile after mile they slowly moved forward, until one morning as they walked along, they noticed many of the trees had been cut down. As they continued traveling, more and more of the trees were missing, until finally everything was gone. They knew then that they had to be very close to Lake Bennett and the end of the Chilkoot Trail.

Their pace quickened with excitement when they thought of it all coming to an end soon, and they continued to hike over the many small and now treeless hills expecting to see Bennett at any time. Eventually their anticipation began turning to frustration, until finally Elmer blurted out "Well, where is the damn place? It just goes on and on!"

"Your right." sympathized Henry, "It feels endless."

They kept on with their heavy loads, and in the end packed nearly two more miles before arriving at the lake.

The trail ended here, with about three thousand tents spread across the valley making up the town of Bennett. The Dead Horse Trail also ended here, and some of the stampeders coming off this path, had been so tortured that they were changed or damaged for life.

All along the shoreline there were boats in various stages of construction, and many of them were being worked on as Henry and Elmer watched. They too would have to camp and build a boat, and as they searched for a suitable camping spot, they noticed that beside every tent was a large woodpile for fighting the cold.

It was becoming obvious that even though the days of endlessly packing their supplies were coming to an end, their days of working till sundown were not. There was still lots of camping space though, so they quickly selected a site and began building their new camp.

It was another week before they had all their supplies off the trail, and were glad to be done with it for good. It was then time to build up a woodpile. But after making a few trips, they realized it was going to be much harder than they thought. Every stick had been cut for a couple of miles in every direction, and even further up the trails. So over and over they dragged their newly built sleigh out through the snow, then loaded it with as many logs as they could skid.

One day after they'd dragged the sleigh over a small hill they stopped to rest for a minute. Elmer said "I thought when we got off the trail things would get a little easier. Not harder."

"I know." answered Henry, "I wouldn't care if I never saw this sleigh again."

"Well at least we just about got enough wood now." replied Elmer.

"I'm half expecting we did this the hard way too." said Henry, adding "Boy, knowledge sure is the key."

"What do ya mean?" asked Elmer.

"Well look how much time, effort and money we spent getting our supplies up to the scales." said Henry, "When we coulda just walked up there and bought 'em,...and bought 'em a lot cheaper than in Skagway. Then we raced all the way here, and what do we get out of it? A better camping spot, that's it. If we would have known those things ahead a time, we sure could a saved ourselves a pile a work."

"But then we wouldn't have all the fond memories." answered Elmer sarcastically. Then he added "You know what they say,....gettin' there is half the fun."

Henry started giggling at how absurd Elmer's statement sounded.

"But your right." Elmer went on, "When we get back to camp, let's take it easy for a while."

"You convinced me" replied Henry, "When we get this load back home, let's take the rest of the day off and look around town.

When they got back to Bennett, they noticed more tents had been set up around them and one of them was the police headquarters. Sam Steele had left some of the Mounties to guard the pass, and brought the rest with him to oversee Bennett. And no one knew it, but he'd also left a couple of men undercover in Skagway. Their job was to learn who was in Soapy's gang and any plans they might have, so as to better keep the Mounties on the pass informed.

There were some great looking dogs over at the Mounties tent. The North West Mounted Police were usually mounted on horseback, but in the harsh Yukon winter, dogsled was the only way to go, and Steele's Mounties had some of the fastest teams in the country. Steele figured that with such a tidal wave of people and so few Mounties, he had to firmly establish the law, and part of his plan was 'No Getaways'.

When Henry and Elmer passed in front of the police tent, they noticed a row of bottles and jars sitting on a board. Elmer asked one of the officers what they were for, and the Mountie explained in detail that because they had no way of telling the temperature, they'd made a 'Yukon thermometer'. In each bottle or jar was a liquid that would freeze at a different temperature.

"See." he said, pointing out the glass containers, "Mercury -40, coal oil -50, extract of ginger -60, and Perry Davis Pain Killer -75 below."

The Yukon thermometer was saying -40 below, so they were beginning to move on when Henry saw a map nailed to a board. It was a vague map of the Yukon with the river marked through it to Alaska. There weren't many features, but they could see that Lake Bennett was followed by a series of large lakes, then after that the river wound much further north completely through the Yukon. There was a large X on the map where it said 'Dawson', and beside it in much larger letters was the word 'Klondike'.

"What's Dawson?" Elmer asked the Mountie.

"It's a town of tents kinda like this one," he answered, "only smaller. It's where you'll be getting out of the water."

Henry tried to measure some distances with his fingers but they quickly began freezing. "How far is it?" he asked.

"It's about five hundred miles," the Mountie replied, "after you get through the lakes."

They continued looking at the map for a while, but couldn't really glean any more information from it. So they left to explore the rest of Bennett.

They saw the Mizners were already camped and working on their woodpile. And Belinda too was already in Bennett and down at the lakeside piling up boards for her boat. They kept an eye open for Arizona Charlie, figuring he'd probably be camped in a prominent place. But they never saw him anywhere and decided he must still be out on the trail somewhere.

As they walked along the waterfront, they began discussing what to do about building their own boat. They had all the tools, tar, nails, and other materials for the job, but they'd never built a boat before. In fact, neither one of them had built much of anything before. After talking about it for a while, they decided that probably the best thing to do, was to find someone else building a sturdy craft, and copy what they were doing. They didn't have to make any quick decisions though, before they could build anything they had to make boards.

It was here that all the men traveling alone had to find a partner. It took boards to build a boat, and to make boards, logs had to be sawed length ways. This took two people, one on each end of a long whipsaw. It was also easier to build one big boat, than two smaller ones.

Henry and Elmer were almost back to their camp when they heard a number of gunshots. They detoured slightly to investigate and found Sam Steele and one of his Mounties questioning a rough looking man. They stopped to listen along with others already gathered and heard the man tell Sam "My gun fired accidently while I was cleaning it."

"That was quite a few accidental shots." replied Steele, "What were you cleaning it with?"

"I already put it away" the man sneered back, implying that Steele could go away now.

"It sounded like a pistol to me." suggested Sam, "Let's have a look at your gun."

"I already told ya, I put it away." he snarled again.

"You're a pretty obnoxious fellow aren't ya." said Sam, "Same attitude as Soapy's boys." Then Sam told a young Mountie to check his stuff, and he promptly found an illegal handgun and a deck of marked playing cards. As they continued looking through his things, two more Mounties arrived, and one of them identified the man as part of Soapy's gang. Steele then placed him under arrest and confiscated all his belongings. Then he ordered him back over the pass to Skagway.

"You can tell Soapy Smith there's no profit for him here." said Steele. Then he told two of his men "Fix your bayonets and escort this man back across the border....So he doesn't doddle or get lost." Then he stepped up to the thug and growled "Now step lively!" and the Mounties marched him off up the trail.

Henry and Elmer spent the following days sawing logs into lumber and trying to find a boat they liked the look of. Then not far from where they were camped, they finally saw a boat being built they wanted to copy. The owner was a man named Augustus Mack from Brooklyn, New York and he'd apparently been down the river before. He said he wasn't really a carpenter but was confident his boat would more than make it to Dawson, and he also seemed like he'd be helpful if they needed advice.

As they continued the back-breaking work of sawing logs into lumber, the weather began to warm up. First to -20 below, and then even warmer. And even though everyone always had work to do, people began to socialize, mostly to exchange horror stories of the pass and the Golden Stairs.

After they ate supper one evening, they saw a group of men sitting around at Augustus Mack's camp and Henry thought they should go over and visit for awhile. But Elmer said he was tired, and would rather stay behind and study the map he'd bought and dream of giant gold strikes. So Henry filled his coffee cup and wandered over to join the conversation.

When he was almost there, he heard one of the men yell "Hey Henry." It was Clarence Berry.

"Glad to see you're off the trail." he said as Henry stepped up to the fire.

"I'm glad to see I'm off the trail too." answered Henry, "How's it goin' for you Clarence? You start your boat yet?"

"Yea." he said, "I work on it whenever I'm not working on all the other stuff."

Henry agreed with him and sipped at his coffee as the men went back to talking about the price they'd all paid to get here, in time, money and effort.

The cost of sailing to Skagway kept coming up, as apparently so many people wanted to come north now, the price had tripled. One of the men said he was working in a gold mine in California when they heard news of the strike, and almost everyone quit to leave for the Yukon. In fact so many people were Klondike bound, many businesses on the west coast were having trouble keeping enough staff to operate. In many cases it was the leaders themselves, like Mayors, Judges, and company executives that were leaving.

There was a young woman sitting at the fire with them as they talked, but it was some time before Henry spoke with her. She was quite striking to look at and her hair appeared to be of all different colors and seemed to change as she moved. Even though she was wearing men's clothes like Clarence Berry's wife, she was drawing much attention from the men. She was treated with respect though, as all women were that had made it over the pass, and when Henry finally did get to talk to her, he found that it was her personality that was really attracting them.

Her name was Kate Rockwell and she'd been traveling with three other girls until they all turned back on her. She said she was a chorus girl who'd suffered the same hard times as everyone else and thought she might be able to find work in the Klondike.

Henry knew that there was no way a woman of her beauty would be allowed to starve up here.

An interesting story surfaced while they all talked of their journey. When Sam Steele's name was mentioned, a man claimed that when he was in Skagway, he saw some of Soapy's men fueled by alcohol bothering him in a restaurant. Until Steele finally ended it, when he reached into a bowl of apples and calmly took one out and snipped it in half between his index and fore finger. The man swore that though he wasn't wearing the red jacket, it was positively Steele.

It was almost -30 below again when they woke in the morning. So with frost pouring from his breath, Elmer lit a fire in the stove and continued adding wood to really warm up the tent. He also hung his socks over the stove to warm them up too. Then he moved over to the door flap of the tent to look out and see what kind of a day they'd be dealing with. Opening it just a crack, he peered out and saw Sam. He turned and said to Henry "Sam's out there choppin' wood." Then after a few more seconds, he looked back at Henry again and remarked "He's not even wearing gloves!"

Then Elmer smelled something burning and looked back to the stove just in time to see his socks burst into flames. Actually it was a fairly common occurrence amongst the stampeders, in Bennett and on the trail.

The time had come to start building their boat. So before long they had a fire going outside to warm up their bucket of tar. Elmer was sitting by it taking a last look at his map before they went to work, when Sam appeared. He was on his way down to the shoreline to check out some of the boats when he decided to take advantage of their fire for a few minutes. "Howdy Elmer." he said, "You guys building a boat yet?"

"Hi Sam." replied Elmer, "We're starting on one today."

Then Sam got distracted by Elmer's map.

"So you bought one of Soapy's maps eh?"

What do you mean 'Soapy's maps'?" said Elmer.

"There aren't any maps of the gold fields." replied Sam, "Soapy had a bunch a phonies made up to sell to people. I've seen a lot of 'em."

A now discouraged Elmer lowered the map and stared blankly into space.

"Don't feel too bad." added Steele, as he gazed around the area, "Some people bought claims from Soapy, and they're not gonna find out till they get there that they don't exist."

Elmer just sat expressionless staring into the fire.

Sam began to leave again and parted with "Build your boat good and strong. Don't wanna see no wooden deathtraps."

Elmer sat a few more minutes, then calmly laid his map over the fire as if covering it with a tablecloth, and watched as it burst into flames.

As Elmer took the bucket of heated tar away from the fire, he accidently got a little on his sleeve. "Aw darn." he spouted sarcastically, "I've ruined my best shirt."

Working hard for months in rough country, had worn their clothes out completely. Everything they had was worn, torn and frayed. And not just theirs, everyone else was dressed in rags as well.

Also affecting everyone's appearance was sunburn. The sun had been shining brightly almost everyday now and combined with the reflection off the snow, most people had become badly burned. The only protection available was to take the blackest ashes from their fires and rub it into their faces and necks. So now everyone appeared as if they slept in a coal bin.

Once they got started, Henry and Elmer worked everyday on their boat, along side hundreds of other stampeders. Most those who weren't, were usually sawing lumber. A job so miserable, that occasionally fights would break out. To saw the logs, they had to be elevated onto a high crib of wood so that one of the sawyers could work from underneath. As they worked, the man beneath the log would receive a face full of sawdust every time he pulled down on the saw, while the man on top would complain that he not only had to pull the saw back up, but all too often his partner as well. As a result, many of the new partnerships were being seriously tested.

Henry and Elmer usually took something to eat with them when they went to work at the waterfront, but quickly learned that if they didn't find a real safe place to put it, they'd lose it to the ravens. The large black birds were incredibly smart and very adept at both stealing food and opening containers. They also liked shiny objects and would steal watches, money, spoons and forks, anything left unguarded that they took a fancy to. Just venturing a few feet from ones food or valuables, was often to see them for the last time.

There'd always been some of them around ever since Skagway, but now with the stampeders camped in the same place all the time, the big birds were really taking advantage. They'd often work in pairs or groups to distract dogs or even people away from their food. And their sense of timing would infuriate some men, as they'd always escape with just a few feet or even inches to spare.

Not far from Henry and Elmer's boat, Belinda's vessel was beginning to take shape, so they'd visit her on occasion to talk with her and see her progress. She had a couple of men hired to help her, so she was actually building faster than they were.

Her big dog still guarded her continuously, and when anyone approached it would let out a very deep and threatening growl, more like a wolf than a dog. It would then move in front of Belinda and bear its huge fangs at the approaching person. If she didn't call Nero off and they kept advancing, Nero too would move forward, causing a deadly duel of nerves. But once she called his name, it was like they didn't exist to him.

A lot of men claimed that their dogs were part or even half wolf, but with most of them it looked very doubtful. Some were even laughable. But Belinda's dog may have been. When other dogs came near their hair would stand on end, and they'd appear very fearful and anxious to leave. Nero was more than double Belinda's weight, but they'd obviously come to some kind of arrangement, as no one else could get near him, nor wanted to.

Before long Henry and Elmer's boat was actually beginning to look like one, and while they were working on it one afternoon, a dog team pulling a sleigh came along the frozen lake towards Bennett. As they watched it get closer, they could see a man riding in the sleigh as well as the one driving it. When it arrived at the tent city and the stampeders learned that the men were from Dawson, they were immediately bombarded with questions of the Klondike. Especially gold.

The men told that scurvy had broken out in Dawson and the town was on the edge of starvation. And that unable to spare food for animals, many people had been forced to kill their dogs. It had also gotten down to -70 below in Dawson, and even colder in the surrounding areas, making the -40 and -50 below the stampeders had endured, seem mild in comparison.

There was some good news too though, at least good to the stampeders. The men said that Dawson had a shortage of everything except for gold and rich people, but that they too were dressed in rags.

Eventually they learned that the man in the sleigh was called 'One-eyed Riley', and he'd paid the dog musher $1,000 to bring him out of the Yukon. He'd gotten lucky playing Faro, and riding an incredible streak of luck had amassed a fortune of $28,000. Then not trusting himself to refrain from gambling until he could leave in the spring by riverboat, he arranged to leave immediately by dogsled, and even though the $1,000 fee was outrageous, he'd had to run behind the sleigh most the way.

The news of much gold and rich people in the Klondike, soon sent another wave of gold fever through Bennett, which now had a population of more than twenty thousand. The tent city was expanding continuously as people poured in off the trails, and now not hundreds but thousands of boats were being built. Most all of them by amateurs.

Spring was beginning to come now, and about the time Henry and Elmer were finishing their boat, the sun began melting the snow and ice. Then everyone came to realize that with four large lakes to cross in loaded down vessels, a mast and sail might be invaluable. So with the help of Augustus Mack, Henry and Elmer attached a sturdy mast to the center of their boat.

As Bennett had grown, so had the number of people doing business, and now that the weather had warmed, many more tents had signs on them advertising their services. Enterprises like Doctor, Dentist, Saloon, Restaurant, and many many more.

Walking back from the beach to their camp one day, Henry saw a new one that interested him. A man had a 'New York Times' newspaper that was less that a month old, and he was charging people $1 to read it. Inside his tent men sat reading and exchanging sections of the paper, and it was too much for Henry. He dug deep, and paid one of his few precious dollars to enter.

He decided it was worth it as soon as he walked in, and he got to sit in a real chair. He'd almost forgotten what it felt like. He had to wait a few minutes for the front section of the paper, but when he got it he was surprised to see that even as far away as New York, the headline news was of the Klondike, and the massive rush to get there.

It wasn't until he'd devoured most the newspaper that he fully began to realize the influence the gold rush was having on the outside world. The international news was of expeditions setting sail from around the world for the Klondike. While the business section told of booming transportation companies, and banks and investment companies forming consortiums to exploit the Klondike. Even the classified ads were mostly of people wanting a grubstake, or a partner for travel to the Klondike. The entire continent was being jerked out of it's depression by gold fever and it all made Henry wonder what kind of tidal wave of people there must be behind them.

When Henry finished the paper, he was heading back to their camp again when he saw an odd sight. A large group of people were gathered around a small thick-walled corral structure. It seemed a man from Seattle had learned of the food shortage in Dawson and of the astronomical price of eggs. So on the morning he was to leave for the Klondike, he gathered over three hundred freshly laid eggs to bring with him. Now from a fervent overzealousness to keep the eggs from freezing, he'd had over 260 baby chicks hatch out on him. The man thought he'd come to ruin, until it was pointed out to him that a live chicken in Dawson was going to be worth a lot more than an egg.

It didn't take long for the news from the man's New York Times to ripple throughout Bennett, making everyone even more anxious to get moving again. Once people had their boats built the only thing left to do was wait, and to Elmer and many others, it seemed to be taking forever for the ice on the lake to melt.

The snow slowly disappeared from the hills and was replaced by a thick carpet of purple crocus flowers, yet the ice on the lake still remained. As many people were going through the agonizing wait, many others were frantically trying to finish their boats before the ice went out. While all the time, more and more people flowed down from the passes.

Then one day the unthinkable happened. News came down the Chilkoot Trail that a huge avalanche had buried the Scales and Golden Stairs. In fact nearly a quarter mile of the trail had been covered with thirty feet of snow, burying hundreds of people alive in the process. It wasn't without warning though. The warm weather conditions had made the snowpack so dangerous, that the local Chilkat Indians had refused to carry any loads in the preceding days. However the drive for gold by the stampeders was such that they ignored the warnings and continued on at their own peril. Luckily most were saved by rescuers or managed to claw themselves out of an icy grave. But still, in the end sixty-three people died.

A few days later they learned that Soapy Smith had set up a temporary morgue to handle the bodies, but really they were being stripped of money and possessions.

It was the middle of May now, and the Yukon spring was in full bloom. The days had become longer until now there was light very late in the evenings, and the sun was rising earlier every morning. As a result, the hammering and sawing on the boats had become almost continuous.

With the sun beating down most days the temperature was now rising to seventy or eighty degrees, but still cooling drasticly at night, usually to near freezing. The ice on the lake was melting noticeably each day though, and a line of water had begun growing from the shoreline outward. This caused high anxiety for Elmer and most others ready to go, and absolute panic for late arrivals.

The entire waterfront was a frenzy of activity, with thousands working frantically to finish their boats. There was more fighting amongst the stampeders now too, as many late arrivals were forced to arrange quick partnerships, and were under huge pressure to finish in time. No one wanted to be left behind.

The cool evenings and cold nights were still requiring Henry and Elmer to have a fire, and nearly reaching the end of their wood pile they decided to go down and gather the leftover pieces from around their boat.

When they arrived at the shoreline they saw Belinda sitting over by her boat, and as they approached her they noticed she was holding a hand mirror and applying more black ash to her face. She gave them a slightly embarrassed smile as if she'd been caught applying rouge, then held out the mirror and a blackened stick to Elmer. "I think you could use a little more protection yourself." she said.

Henry agreed, saying "Especially your nose. It's pretty red."

So Elmer sat down and began smearing soot to his nose and face. Belinda turned away for a moment, and when she turned back towards them she held out a bag and asked "You guys want a cookie?"

"Yes, thank you." Elmer blurted out eagerly, having nearly forgotten he even had a sweet tooth.

They'd seen the sign on a tent advertising the cookies, but they were too expensive for them to consider. Henry took one, and then Elmer too, setting his down beside him until he finished putting the ash on his face.

"Mmmm, peanut butter." mumbled Henry after taking a bite.

Belinda then climbed in her boat and sat down, and picking up a large needle threaded with sinew, she began sewing some pieces of canvas together. They could see her boat was already finished, so Elmer asked "You making a sail Belinda?"

"No." she replied, "I already made one. If everything goes right this should be a tent when I'm done."

They both stood up and moved to the boat to see better, and Elmer asked "What are you gonna do with another tent?"

"Sell it in Dawson." she answered, "I should be flat broke by then."

Suddenly the sunlight seemed to flicker, and they turned to see a large raven snatch up Elmer's cookie and fly off towards the deep forest with other ravens in hot pusuit. Henry and Belinda both tried to control their laughter, while Elmer stared at the spot where his cookie used to be. He had a pretty dumb look on his face, a combination of disbelief and anger. "I swear! Every bird in the Yukon has it in for me!" he complained.

Still giggling Belinda asked "You want another cookie Elmer?"

Knowing they were expensive and not feeling he deserved one, he replied "No thanks, I'd probably lose it too."

She gave him one anyway, and they went on talking for awhile, eventually getting around to guessing how long it'd be until the ice went out. After all, it was the most popular topic in Bennett now. It's all everybody talked about.

They were just about to leave to go gather the extra pieces of wood from around their boat, when Belinda muttered "Curses, it never ends."

They saw she was looking at some approaching men.

"They come almost everyday." she said, "Trying to buy Nero. I tell 'em he's not for sale, but they keep coming anyway.... Maybe I'll make a sign." she added smiling, "Then let Nero run off the stubborn ones."

Henry and Elmer gathered up their left over wood and realized it wasn't nearly as much as they thought. In fact they ran out of wood the very next day. Then after thinking about it for awhile they decided to burn some of their tent poles next. They considered going for more wood, but it was miles from Bennett now before there was anything at all to cut. They figured that with any luck at all, the ice would go out before getting more would really become necessary.

So they cut out some of the extra poles stabilizing their tent, and woke the very next morning with the whole thing collapsed on top of them, probably blown down by a gust of wind. When they emerged from underneath the flattened canvas, they saw that one side of their tent had remained standing. It had been stabilized while they slept by a quick and shoddily built camp, that was so close to them they were almost touching. In fact much of it was secured to their tent poles.

It was easy propping up their tent again though, and as they finished the job they studied the new camp wondering who the occupant might be.

Suddenly a small man emerged that was a very curious sight. He seemed to be in direct contrast to everybody else in

Bennett. The little fellow was a little over five feet tall, and while everyone else's clothes were ragged and dirty, his looked to be brand new and spotless.

Most people seemed to be as poor as they looked, but this man was dressed as if he might be very rich. He was wearing a royal blue Prince Albert jacket and a frilly white shirt with a starched collar, and as he drew a little closer they could see a huge diamond pin stuck in his tie. He had long scraggly hair and a moustache to match, and Elmer thought that except for the stove pipe hat he was wearing, he kind of looked like a little pirate.

He didn't really walk towards them as much as he strutted like royalty, but he too had blackened his face to protect it, giving himself a somewhat comical appearance. When he got to them, he glanced back at the two camps practically tied together and said "Staked pretty close. Yea, pretty close. Sorry though. Not much room left."

He talked fast and his words were all broken and choppy.

"Not to worry." replied Henry, "We'll all be gone soon."

"Yes yes, very soon. I'm Bill" he said, thrusting out his hand.

"Oh, I'm Henry, and this is Elmer." said Henry.

"What do you do for a living?" asked Bill.

"I'm a logger from Washington," answered Henry, "Or used to be." then added "And Elmer's kinda suffered from his age and the depression."

"Yea." nodded Elmer.

"What about yourself?" asked Henry.

"I used to be a boat pilot." he answered, "Now I'm a gambler, a proficient gambler."

As Bill kept talking, they noticed he possessed abundant energy and seemed to have trouble standing still. He had the silver tongue though, and as he continued shifting around he began questioning them about any surplus firewood they might have. After they explained that they were down to burning their scraps, Bill said "Ice might go anyway. Looks like hot today."

Then he suddenly seemed distracted as if he just remembered something. "Oh, gotta see the girls." He said, "Yes....the pretty girls." and marched off towards another new camp about a hundred feet away.

Henry and Elmer both wondered exactly what he meant by 'pretty girls'.

Then Elmer said "Well he seems pretty proud of himself, that's for sure."

"He's right about one thing." said Henry, "It's gonna be hot today."

"Its hot already." replied Elmer.

Without much to do but wait for the ice to go out, Henry and Elmer spent most of the day wandering the waterfront. They studied the various types of crafts, and their construction, and wondered if some of them were going to float at all.

Sam Steele was examining boats too. He and his men were walking through the thousands of vessels being constructed, telling the stampeders to "Build them long and strong like the Yukon River." and usually following it with "The Klondike is big, and gold doesn't have legs." All in a vain attempt to convince people to take more time, and build safer boats.

When Steele would work his way through the already completed boats, he'd warn some of the men that their projects seemed woefully inadequate, and that if it was up to him, he wouldn't let them go in what appeared to be little more than floating coffins.

In fact it was serious enough that in the last few weeks Steele ruled that every craft be named or numbered. His Mounties went around listing all the boats with its occupants, and recording their next of kin. The voyage ahead was going to be perilous, and Steele knew they weren't all going to make it. This way, they could determine in Dawson most of those who were drowned or killed.

Henry and Elmer saw Sam arguing with a particularly stubborn man, who was refusing to paint a number on his boat. He instead, was claiming to be an expert boatman whose craft would stand up to anything. It seemed he'd taken having to number his boat, as criticism of his workmanship, and because he had two grown sons with him he simply didn't want to back down. Finally in anger, he grabbed the tar brush from its bucket and smeared a large and sarcastic 666 on the bow, then threw the brush hard to the ground coating it with a thick layer of gravel. Not wanting to argue anymore, Steele didn't bother to tell him the number was already taken, so wrote the number down in the ledger book with the word 'tar' beside it.

Most men however, were much more reasonable, and to those people Steele's men could be counted on for advice and some acurate knowledge of what they were going to encounter. In fact they randomly posted notices throughout the waterfront that listed the more serious dangers that lay ahead.

When Henry and Elmer nudged their way into a group of men to read one, they saw that it was a big list indeed, starting with flipping their boat or blowing onto rocks on the lakes, to Miles Canyon, Whitehorse Rapids, and Five Finger Rapids. To dangers like falling asleep on the river, or falling into the water itself.

After reading the list a few times, they decided to head back to camp for supper. It was going to take them some time though. Exploring Bennett's waterfront had led them around the lake to the far side of the bay.

While picking their way back through the legions of boats, they happened upon the Mizner brothers. The three younger brothers, William, Wilson, and Addison, were loading their boat with supplies, while Edgar seemed to be accounting for everything in a ledger. As there were four of them, their boat was practically a ship. Henry and Elmer talked to the brothers for some time, while Edgar abstained again, keeping his head firmly buried in the ledger.

As they spoke, Henry noticed that their pile of food and cargo was huge, and even though their boat was also big, he wondered if it would all fit. Finally he asked if they were sure there'd be room for everything, and Wilson told him that they planned on leaving some of their bulk food behind. Many of the stampeders were planning to do the same thing, mostly to make their boats safer and more maneuverable.

Henry and Elmer started towards home again, and some time later much closer to their camp, they saw their new neighbor Bill talking to a large group of people. From a distance he looked like a rich landowner that had come to speak with the peasants, but when they got close enough to hear, they heard him describing the perils that lay ahead on the river.

"Miles Canyon," he said, "Narrow, narrow place. River rips through it....Rips through it. Hundred foot walls. Black walls, on both sides, and nowhere to get out."

Bill seemed to relish the attention he was commanding, and in his gibbled manner of speaking, he continued to dispense his knowledge of the river and the Klondike.

It turned out that Bill was in the Klondike when the rush began. He claimed that he'd struck it rich, and was just returning from San Francisco to build a world-class cassino and dancehall. Bill's words to the growing crowd were causing considerable anxiety, and his descriptions of the obstacles ahead were frightening many. Finally some of the men reasoned that it just couldn't be that dangerous, or this many thousands of people wouldn't be willing to do it.

Balancing out their fear was Bill's assurance that the Klondike was all it was said to be, and that the gold practically did flow like water. Then some in the crowd openly accused him of exaggerating both the dangers and the riches, saying he was only trying to gain notoriety for himself. Not a far-fetched idea, after watching Bill gleefully absorb attention.

Later on as Henry and Elmer sat eating their supper, they noticed that Bill had aquired a few days supply of wood. As they tried to guess where he'd gotten it from, they heard arguing coming from Augustus Mack's camp. They looked over to see Mack and the much smaller Bill, in a wildly animated conversation. When the argument ended, they watched Bill march off towards the tent he'd visited earlier, where the supposed 'pretty girls' resided.

After they finished eating, Henry noticed that Mack was still alone at his camp, and still being curious about the conversation he'd had with Bill, he decided it was time to take another coffee over to his camp.

"Howdy boys." said Mack, as Henry walked towards him.

It was only then that Henry realized Elmer was following along.

"Didn't I see your tent trying to smother you this morning?" he joked.

"Yea." replied Henry, "It mighta got us too, except for that little fellow's camp holding up one end."

"Yea....Bill, he's a savior." chuckled Mack.

"We saw you talking to him earlier." said Henry "He grate you the wrong way?"

"Sometimes." replied Mack, "If he's not talking somebody out of something, he's bragging about his boatsmanship. That's why everybody calls him 'Swiftwater Bill', 'cause he's always bragging about his boating skills, but he still piled up in Miles Canyon."

They were still curious what Bill and Mack were fighting about, so Elmer asked "He said he was a gambler, and we saw you guys arguing before, does he owe you money?"

"No." started Mack, "I was heading to Skagway last fall to sail south for the winter, when just down the lake from here I went snowblind in a blizzard. It was about a week before I could see good enough to travel again. But after just a couple a days Bill came by. He was on his way to San Francisco to get the furnishings for his dancehall, and his packers had quit on him. He wanted to borrow one of the native packers that I'd hired, so I let him take a man named Charlie, assuming that he'd leave him in Skagway for me. Instead, Bill took him to San Francisco and put him in a hotel room while he did his business. But after a few days when he went back to check on him, he was gone. Of course Bill has no idea what happened to him, and to top it off, Charlie only speaks his native language. No English at all! And he's afraid of white people. Lord knows what happened to him. Anyway, that's what you saw us arguing about."

As they talked, they noticed that down at the camp Bill had gone to, a couple of girls had emerged from the tent. Pretty girls.

"He does have pretty girls!" grinned Elmer.

"Yea." said Mack, "Dancehall girls from San Francisco. The best looking ones he could find. He's been keeping them hidden to avoid a pestering crowd."

"Let's go see!" urged Elmer, kind of hoping that Henry would come up with the rest of the plan.

Elmer also hoped to get his friend back in the game again. Henry never talked about it, but he'd been married before, to his childhood sweetheart. The marriage started off well enough, but then one day he came home from work to find out she'd run off with a lawyer from St. Louis. Only Elmer and a few of Henry's friends knew how badly he'd been blown out of the water. But now Elmer figured he just needed a little push, or something to get him going again.

Elmer needed Henry's help too. He hadn't been around girls much, and would become awkwardly shy when he was. If a girl was pretty, and he tried to look at her and talk at the same time, there was a good chance his speech would deteriorate to gibberish. As he often told Henry, around girls he could speak in tongues.

"I think we should go ask Bill how to properly pilot our watercraft." said Henry standing to his feet.

Elmer eagerly jumped up to follow, but Mack said he was still angry at Bill for losing Charlie and was staying home. Then before they could leave, Kate Rockwell suddenly appeared and right on her heels was Clarence and Ethel Berry. So they instinctively sat down again, as did everyone else.

The Berry's hadn't left San Francisco to begin their journey, until Henry and Elmer were well on their way up the trail, and Clarence said that before they left, the newspapers had been full of stories of the Klondike.

"And Swiftwater Bill too." added Ethel.

"Sure was." said Clarence, "They called him 'The King of the Klondike'." then he added, "There was always stories about him, renting whole floors of hotels, and gambling huge amounts of money. They said he was even riding around in a fancy coach with footmen, and with a plaque on the back that said he was King of the Klondike."

"Don't forget he was having baths in champagne." added Ethel again.

"Yea. How 'bout that." said Clarence, "He doesn't drink, but sometimes he baths in champagne."

"Right now, I'd bath in just about anything." suggested Kate, causing the rest of them to laugh.

As they all kept talking, Henry and Elmer once more fell under Kate's spell. She'd completely charmed them again with her beguiling personality.

It seemed like only a few minutes had passed, when suddenly Henry realized how late it actually was. They'd forgotten all about going to check out the pretty girls, and now it was much too late.

Walking back to their camp Elmer said "Oh well, maybe we can see them tomorrow."

"Yea." replied Henry, "They're not going anywhere."

It'd been a long busy day, and both of them were tired, so within a few minutes of laying down they were both snoring loudly.

Henry was first to wake in the morning, and after crawling out from under a heap of crumpled canvas again, he saw that this time the wind had blown their tent down. A light breeze was still flapping some of the canvas around. Over the sound of the flapping, he could hear men yelling at each other, and when he looked towards the lake he saw men running all over the place. The ice was gone! He couldn't believe it! He'd been waiting with the patience of Job, yet now it was catching him by surprise.

"Elmer! Get up! The ice is gone!

Poor Elmer tried to jump up and run out of the tent, but with the tent already down and being half asleep, he just stood up and fell forward cocooning himself in the canvas. When he finally struggled out the end, he watched with Henry as the entire tent city went into a frenzy.

They became even more excited, when they realized that all they had to do was fold up their tent and pack a few loads to their boat, and they could leave too. Already they could count dozens of boats well on their way, and it spurred them on even more to get moving. As everyone in Bennett could see, the race was on.

It was going to be another hot day, and by the time they made it to the beach with their first load, they had sweat streaming off them. The city was bustling with activity and the waterfront was near chaos. They felt sorry for the people with unfinished boats, as they too were caught up in the excitement, and were now working feverishly to complete their vessels.

"Look." said Elmer, "It's Swiftwater Bill."

He wasn't far from their boat, and they could see that a huge barge they'd been watching men build, actually belonged to him. Now they were loading it with rugs and fancy furniture, large crates, and many more dancehall supplies. Somehow they'd dragged ten foot long mirrors over the pass, and kept them in one piece.

Bill and his men weren't in any hurry though, having already struck it rich he didn't have to be part of the race, so he wasn't, and his knowledge of the Yukon had enabled him to show up at the last minute, and not have to idle around Bennett going stir crazy, like everybody else.

The last load Henry and Elmer had to move was their tent, and they folded it up in such a hurry, it ended up a large awkward lump that took both of them to carry.

When they arrived at the beach for the last time, they saw thousands of people racing to launch their boats. Like many of the vessels, Henry and Elmer's boat sat on logs with more placed behind it so they could quickly roll it down into the water, and after throwing their tent in, they both started prying at the bow to try and get it moving.

They could hear the Mounties among the frantic stampeders. Yelling at them to "Go slow!" and "If you fall in the water and can't get out, you die!"

Their words were falling on deaf ears.

Upon entering the water, some of the overloaded and shoddily built boats began floundering immediately. A few had already turned over.

Suddenly Henry and Elmer's boat began rolling towards the water, and Henry quickly jumped in. Elmer thought he'd push a little more to make sure it kept moving, but before he knew it the boat took off and he was scrambling to catch up. As the boat plunged hard into the water, it heaved up and down with Elmer dangling from the bow.

"Oh God!" he yelled loudly.

Henry could only see his head and hands, and his face had a look of shock, as if perhaps he'd been cut in half.

"H-help me get outta here!" he yelled again. He thought he could climb into the boat by himself, but his wet clothes had become so heavy they were actually pulling him down.

With Henry's help he managed to pull himself up into the boat, and already he'd learned a lesson on how much trouble could be had in the blink of an eye.

"I don't think you could drown this close to shore." grinned Henry.

"Actually, I think you could." replied Elmer, shivering and soaked from his chest down. "Besides, I wasn't worried about that. I was worried about freezing to death. That water's unbelievable!"

The whole waterfront was pandemonium now. Vessels and debris were everywhere, and when Henry and Elmer saw men in other boats frantically bailing out water, they quickly checked their own boat for leaks or cracks. They found nothing, and it seemed that with Mack's help they'd built a very sturdy craft.

It was quite wide and worked best with one of them on each oar to row, but like most the other stampeders, they had no experience at all. They had a lot of trouble maneuvering at first, but before long their oars hacked at the water sometimes in unison, propelling them slowly and crookedly away from shore.

They were surrounded by thousands of watercraft of every kind now. Whalers, skiffs, doreys, Chinese junks, and every kind of barge, canoe, and raft you could imagine. They were constructed of every kind of material, and most all were built and piloted by complete rookies.

In direct contrast were the French-Canadian voyageurs. When it came to building boats for carrying large loads on rivers, they were absolute professionals. They showed up late, built their boats effortlessly, and sang the entire time they did it.

Now they were singing again as they streaked past everyone, all paddling in perfect unison, and in only a few minutes they were so far away, all that could be seen were their red toques and flying paddles.

Many of the business people had taken the advertising signs from their tents, and nailed them to the sides of their boats. It was obvious they intended to do business on the dangerous journey ahead. There were doctors and barbers and such, but they also saw 'The Midnight Sun Newspaper', 'The Bank of Commerce', and 'Harpers Bazaar Magazine'.

It wasn't long 'till Henry and Elmer realized that rowing their heavy boat down the lake was going to be very hard and very slow. But the breeze was still light, so they decided to hoist the sail and begin their sailing experience while it was still safe to do so.

When they stood up to rig the large canvas square, they could see that Bennett had become a virtual ghost town. Where thousands of tents had been, there were now just a few left among thousands of abandoned wooden frames. Bennett would never be as large again, but it wasn't going to die yet either. The army of goldseekers was still arriving continuously, and the line still stretched unbroken all the way back to Skagway.

As they gazed back at the near empty town, they saw a couple of familiar figures. Eric Hegg the photographer had set up his camera box on a small hill, and was taking pictures of the massive floatilla, and not far away on the beach stood Sam Steele flanked by two of his officers. The three of them were staring out into the lake and talking.

Suddenly Elmer said "Hey! Isn't that Mace over there?" remembering Soapy's man from Skagway and the attack on the trail."

He was becoming afraid even as he pointed him out.

They stared at the lone figure standing on the shoreline, as he seemed to look over all the boats repeatedly. Henry strained to see better, but he couldn't tell whether it was him or not.

"I don't know." he finally said, "It could be him. The guys profile looks right. I just can't tell for sure."

Henry saw Elmer was becoming increasingly worried and although Sam was some distance away from the suspicious character, Henry said "Well one thing's for sure. If it is Mace, in a place as empty as that Sam'll have him rounded up in an hour."

"Yea" said Elmer hopefully, "and he'll surely recognize him." Then he pondered, "If it was Mace, do you think he was looking for us?"

"Don't know." replied Henry, "I can't really believe we're that important....More likely is, he's lookin' for who ever just left him behind to rid themselves of his company."

Henry's words worked, and with so much happening, Elmer's mind soon moved to other things. They went back to raising their sail again, and never having done it before were pleasantly surprised when it reached the top of the mast. The wind suddenly filled it with a loud 'whump', and their boat began plowing through the water much faster than they could row. Henry quickly crawled over their cargo to the back of the boat, and grabbing the long arm of the tiller slowly began steering them back and forth.

He soon became fascinated with sailing their craft, and began tinkering with everything he could trying to go faster. They were still nervous though. They'd never been on moving water before, and were very glad that the lakes came before the river.

Back on shore, Sam Steele was nervous as well. He knew that except for the boat swallowing canyon that Swiftwater Bill had warned them about, all these new argonauts were sailing into the unknown.

It was May 29th when the ice went out at Bennett, and in the following hours, Steele and his Mounties counted the remaining boats. As they stood on the shoreline watching, the floating mass of vessels stretched as far as the eye could see. A corporal compared their count to the one taken earlier before the ice broke, and over seven thousand boats now covered the surface of Lake Bennett. He wrote 7,134 into the official record book.

In the middle of it all, a few miles down the twenty mile long lake, were Henry and Elmer. Henry's mind was still racing along faster than the boat, though both were beginning to slow down, and the wind continued to dissipate until early in the evening, when it completely stopped and ground the great race to a standstill.

With the sun low in the sky again, everything became cast in a now familiar gold light. The day had been scorching hot, and it was still probably around eighty degrees. So when the blue-green water turned to glass, the exhausted stampeders began basking in the sunlight, all content that they'd soon be citizens of the 'Promised Land'.

A faint haze grew over the lake and everything became silent. Then while Elmer laid himself over the tent canvas and closed his eyes, Henry sat in the back gazing around at the amazing spectacle.

"This is the strangest sight I've ever seen." he finally said, "Even more than that glacier last fall."

Just as he thought the ragged floatilla couldn't look any stranger, he peered through the haze to see a boat with a very odd cargo. It was the guy with the box of cats, and now that they'd been liberated they seemed to cover every square inch of his vessel.

Henry continued to marvel at the incredible scene, eventually musing that "This place might be cold and dangerous sometimes, but it sure is pretty. In a really strange way too. Kinda haunting."

Elmer lay motionless but still answered "That's cause it's trying to kill us."

Soon a faint melody could be heard wafting over the water, emanating from a lone but happy harmonica. Before long it was joined by an accordian, and then by a fiddle, then virtually every instrument that could be loaded on a boat blended in. When the singing started practically every boat on the lake was involved, and a choir of twenty thousand was cheerfully belting out 'Ode to Joy'.

Suddenly Elmer popped up declaring "I still have a cigar left!" and began digging under the canvas for his buffalo coat. When he pulled the silver case from its pocket, he opened it up and was surprised to find it empty. Then he remembered quickly hiding it from the men at Charlie's bar weeks earlier. So he dug in his coat a second time to search the other pocket.

"Yes!" he remarked, holding up the paper tube. Then he flopped backwards onto the canvas again, making him self comfortable to light up.

But after flipping the cap off the tube, he found it difficult to get the cigar out. "This thing's stuck in here." he said, "Looks kinda funny too." Suddenly it pulled free, showing itself to be a tightly rolled piece of brown paper. Elmer became a little excited as he realized it could be something important. "Gee Henry, we might have something here."

Henry had been watching and sat up straight to see better. Then he leaned forward to watch Elmer intently, as both of them became keenly interested in the contents.

It opened up to show a crude hand drawn map with only two words written on it. Up in the right hand corner it said

'Tombstone', and near the center in small letters was the word 'Gold'.

"Can this be real?" wondered Elmer out loud.

They became riveted to the paper as they tried to decipher its secret. The markings were easy to read, indicating hills, valleys, creeks, and a lone jaggedly drawn mountain. The word 'Gold' appeared at the base of the mountain, and from one of its many valleys, a creek ran downward and off the map. Some distance from the mountain, the creek was joined by two others, one merging in from each side.

There were two odd features about the map. All three creeks joined at exactly the same place, and the mountain in the middle had been drawn with a very high peak.

There were lots of things the map didn't show as well. No names, no scale, no paths marked, or anything else helpful, only a small arrow pointing off the page, probably indicating north.

Meanwhile the song 'Ode to Joy' had ended, and when attempts to begin a new song failed, the gigantic choir broke into hundreds of smaller ones each rendering their own tune.

"Do you think it's real?" asked Elmer again.

"I think it probably is." replied Henry, "It was kept hidden, and it's not one of Soapy's phony ones either. We know what they look like."

Suddenly a shiver ran through Elmer as he realized the map was Soapy Smith's. "This is Soapy's map!" he exclaimed.

"We better keep our voices down." suggested Henry.

"That probably was Mace back there on shore." added Elmer, "Lookin' for us and this map."

He spoke quietly but appeared to be quite panicked.

"We can't be sure of that." answered Henry, "Look" he said, pointing at the initials P.D.R. engraved on the case, "Those aren't even Soapy's initials. He mighta stole the case and didn't know the map was in it."

"They both thought for awhile trying to figure things out, then still looking at the map Elmer said "Do you think we could find this place?"

"I don't know." replied Henry, "We probably won't find out 'till we get to Dawson."

"I just thought of something." said Elmer, "Remember when we stopped at Charlie's bar back on the trail, and how I just about sold this tube to that guy that wanted to buy one of my cigars."

"That's right!" remembered Henry, "You dropped it in the snow."

"Sure glad I fumbled it now." said Elmer.

They continued studying the map until another boat began drifting near, then they put it back in the tube, and the tube back in the case. They decided it'd be wise to keep the map hidden and not talk openly about it to anyone. Especially since they didn't know exactly what the situation was. They also figured the safest place to keep it was back in the case.

The jumbled music radiating over the lake went on until the early morning, as no one cared if they slept anyway. There was no point in going to shore so the whole fleet just sat motionless on the water.

Night was barely night anymore, but rather a long pink and purple twilight that ended only briefly just before the sun rose again, and as it slowly climbed from behind the mountains, a new breeze swept over the lake stirring the fleet to action. Countless sails filled with wind again and the entire flotilla began skidding forward. Once more the race was on.

Before long the wind became strong enough to smear the ramshackle fleet down the entire length of the lake. At first Henry took the helm and resumed trying to make the boat go faster, but after awhile they took turns steering their craft, while the other studied their new found map. Actually it wasn't so much studying, as looking at the map and dreaming of what could be. But as they approached the end of the lake and the beginning of the river, the map was put away and they nervously looked ahead, searching for the moving water.

Having never done this before, their hearts pounded with anticipation as they readied themselves to take down the sail and man the oars. The water was a bit rough and it was hard to distinguish any differences ahead, other than the lake narrowing drastically.

Then suddenly the waves began to smooth out and they could feel the boat being tugged around from beneath. So Henry quickly pulled down their sail, as Elmer sat ready to row out of any emergency.

The river was only about fifty yards wide, and though it moved briskly along, it didn't seem to hold any danger. They carefully stayed out in the middle though, and just as they began to relax a little, it dumped them into another giant lake.

"That's gotta be the shortest river in the world." remarked Elmer.

"I know." answered Henry, "What was it, a hundred yards? Maybe a little more?"

They could see ahead on the lake, and there were hundreds of boats spread all over this one too. Henry raised their sail again, and though they knew they were supposed follow along the left side, they soon found that they too were being pushed further and further from shore.

This was 'Tagish Lake', and as the waves and water became rougher they had to be careful of where exactly they were heading. Far from shore it was easy to become mixed up on which arm of the lake to take, and the arms were long, one of them over a hundred miles. If you took the wrong one, and some did, it could set you back days or even weeks.

The wind had become very erratic now, at times even blowing at the front of their boat. Then suddenly a fierce wind came raging out of the mountains and began driving huge waves into them. Henry quickly pulled their sail down again, but it only slowed them down a little and didn't help at all with the waves. Even with one of them manning each oar, they still had very little effect on their vessels direction, and as their loaded boat heaved around in the frightening conditions, they watched themselves get blown past the bay they were suppose to turn in to, and much further up the lake.

Then the gale blew harder sending even larger waves at them, with some sloshing up over the sides. They gave up trying to control the boat now and both began bailing out water to try and keep from sinking. The wind was sounding like a freight train but Elmer could still hear Henry yell "I think we might go down! We have to lighten the load!"

Henry didn't have to wonder whether Elmer heard him or not, wide-eyed and terrified, he immediately dropped his bailing bucket, and began flinging anything and everything over the side.

As Henry joined in, he couldn't believe how fast they'd gotten into trouble, and on such a nice and sunny day.

"Hey! There was a boat over there before!" yelled Elmer, as he pointed to a spot out on the lake.

Henry too noticed the boat had disappeared, but saw that Elmer was already scared enough, so hadn't mentioned it. He'd been watching fairly close and was pretty sure he'd seen other boats disappear as well. But it was the one Elmer pointed to that convinced him that they better do whatever they could to stay afloat, and right now!

Within a few minutes they'd thrown nearly a ton of supplies overboard, and their plan worked well. They began riding much higher in the water with the waves barely threatening the boat at all. At least not threatening to swamp it.

As they bailed out the water, they realized they were again being pushed towards land and might still be in serious peril. The upcoming shoreline was mostly made up of jagged rocks and large outcroppings. They couldn't tell if there were any good places to beach, and were still too far out to know where they'd strike land anyway. They thought about throwing more supplies overboard, but decided it probably wouldn't help and only blow them towards shore faster.

A few minutes later they were much closer and could see only a few small places where a boat could land, and some of them already had boats in them. Other less fortunate vessels had already been smashed on the rocks, and a couple were being broken up as they watched. They quickly decided on a place to at least try and land the boat, then began rowing for their lives! The spot they were trying for already had a boat and people in it, but still looked the most promising of the few they might be able to reach.

As hard as they rowed, it soon became obvious they weren't going to make it, when suddenly the wind nearly died, and allowed them some much needed time. They ended up landing fairly easy, with the boat plowing through a line of wood and debris, then grinding to a stop in the rough gravel. They quickly jumped out and secured the bow line to a big rock, though they probably couldn't have pried it back off shore if they'd wanted to. At least not until the waves got smaller.

"What's your cargo boys? Horseshoes and rabbit feet?" It was Arizona Charlie and he sat sopping wet on a small pile of soaked supplies. He'd seen how lucky they'd been, first with being reprieved by the wind, and then with hitting the beach. "You boys got the luck of the Leprechauns." he said.

He was probably a little envious. He'd lost nearly everything again and his boat was smashed to pieces.

"Did lots a people hit the rocks?" asked Elmer.

"I think more sank out in the lake than hit the rocks." he replied.

Henry thought about how Charlie didn't seem to have much luck at all, but that maybe now wasn't a good time to mention it.

"Boy Charlie, you sure got crappy luck." blurted out Elmer, "What are you gonna do now?"

"Well, right now I'm watching for more of my stuff to float by." he said, "But I've cut a deal to travel with this fella." and he pointed to the boat beside theirs.

"Where is he?" asked Elmer.

"He broke his mast." answered Charlie, "He's out in the bush cutting a new one."

As they talked with Charlie the wind and waves continued to slow, until only a light breeze blew over the water, producing an effect like shimmering silver. It was time to go again, so once more they wished Charlie luck, and then pushed themselves back off the beach to begin rowing their much lighter boat back down the lake.

At first they were fairly nervous of being ambushed by the wind again, but after a few hours it became very calm and they relaxed enough to study the map again.

It was late in the evening now and with the sun settling on the mountains, the whole scene was incredibly beautiful. The only sound they could hear was the warbling of various loons, and Henry and Elmer could hardly believe this was the same lake that almost drowned them a few hours earlier.

In fact so many people did drown that a graveyard was started on shore, and the arm of the lake that the wind had come blasting out of was thereafter called 'Windy Arm'. A name that over time proved to be very appropriate, becoming well known for its sudden and ferocious winds.

By morning they'd crossed the lake back to where they should've been and entered the next section of river. They anxiously prepared themselves for the unknown again, only to find themselves drifting into yet another large lake. It was longer and wider than Lake Bennett, but they were going to have to sail its full length just the same.

The huge floatilla had been straggling apart for some time now, but as the wind blew Henry and Elmer down the lake, they could still gaze out over hundreds of other boats.

By the next afternoon they'd crossed the lake without incident and were starting into the river again, but this time it was different. It was the real beginning of the Yukon River and it was already big, at least 50 yards across, deep and moving quickly.

They were nervous again at first, but the huge current churned the river slowly about, giving it a calming, lazy effect. So it wasn't long before they were both laid back watching the forest and marshlands go by. They figured out that as long as they were in the middle of the river, it didn't really matter much which way the boat pointed.

The hot weather they'd been having had produced a number of forest fires in the area, and as they sailed along everything began to appear in various shades of blue.

They drifted downstream for a few more hours, when the banks of the river suddenly began to grow higher. Then rounding a sharp bend, they came to a huge rock in the middle of the river with a sign on it that said "Stop" and an arrow pointing to the right. They manned the oars to obey the sign, and had just started rowing when hundreds of boats came into view. They were all beached on the right hand side, anywhere and everywhere they could fit.

They saw that just past all the boats the land rose up everywhere except for a deep black crack. An eerie sight through the smoky haze, and it had to be where the river flowed except that it didn't look possible.

"This must be the canyon we heard so much about." said Henry.

They landed their boat and tied it to a mangled little spruce tree, with the ropes of at least a dozen other boats already tied to it. Hundreds of people were milling about here, most walking one way or the other along the river bank. Henry and Elmer joined in the crowd, knowing instinctively that they were off to see the canyon.

After walking on a path of near solid rock for some distance, they found themselves on a flat plateau, split in half by the ominous gorge. As they carefully walked up to the edge, they could see it was only sixty to seventy feet across but very deep, and they were going to have to look almost straight over the rim to see the water.

So they cautiously stepped up to the lip to peer down. They couldn't believe it. The black walls on both sides were straight up and down for a hundred feet, and in the bottom, the river was almost pure white.

Even so, they could see that the water was splashing over and off a good many rocks and obstacles. Unable to gauge the depth of the water, Henry was trying to figure out how a strong deep river more than 50 yards across, could fit through this crack.

"That Swiftwater Bill wasn't lying at all." said Elmer partly in shock.

"I know," replied Henry, "I can't imagine what it's like down there."

Suddenly they saw a boat appear, then after that a raft. Watching from above, it was almost impossible to tell how little, or how much trouble they were in, but often they could see water spray completely over them. They were also riding sideways and backwards sometimes.

Just as Henry and Elmer began to figure it must be pretty bad, they saw the raft slam to a stop and the mast break off. Yet they still heard nothing but the roar of the water. The raft continued hitting rocks, spinning this way and that, until it finally went out of their sight.

Only grasses and a few trees grew along the edge of the cliff, making it easy to walk beside. So they travelled more than a mile along it, mingling with the hundreds of other people also trying to assess the dangers.

By the time they got back to their boat things were turning chaotic. More boats were arriving all the time and the canyon looked frightening, and from what Henry and Elmer were hearing, it didn't get any better for at least five miles down the river.

Most people didn't know what to do. Some had begun packing their supplies to the bottom of the rapids, while others started building camps. Many more were bustling about asking everyone else what they were going to do. There were men sitting around as if waiting for something to happen, while some just sat in their boats depressed.

Still others, burning with gold fever weren't stopping for anything or even slowing down, but sailing straight into the crack and the complete unknown.

The Mounties had arrived at the canyon ahead of most the stampeders, having sped past them in their small and light canoes. Now some of the officers were arguing with people trying to convince them to lighten their loads, or explaining that a boat didn't have to chance the canyon with eight or ten people in it, that most could walk to the foot of the rapids. A young Corporal named Dickson said that already over a hundred boats had been sunk or smashed.

Henry and Elmer got back in their own boat and sat down. They too had to decide what to do.

Then suddenly Sam Steele appeared.

He'd just returned from evaluating the entire length of the dangerous water, and was walking towards the boats with nearly a thousand people crowded around him. There was total confusion now, with many looking to Steele to straighten it out.

To Steele, the gold rush had become a constantly moving train wreck, and as he neared the boats he stepped up onto a mound of bedrock and motioned for everyone to be quiet. Then he addressed the crowd. He said that everyone must agree that they were all part of a very unique set of circumstances, and that for their own safety he was going to enforce a few of his own laws.

Most people knew about Steele by now, and he'd gained a reputation for being tough but fair, but even though he had their respect, for many it left a bitter taste to have someone tell them what they could, or couldn't do.

"You ain't Moses!" someone yelled from the crowd.

"No." he answered, "But I'm the only law in the Yukon, and if you have a complaint you can either write a letter to Ottawa or wait for a judge to get here. But for now, this is the law. From now on no women or kids go through the canyon and rapids. If they could make it over the Passes and Golden Stairs, they can certainly walk an easy five miles downhill." Then he said "So far, about 130 of the boats that went into that canyon came out kindling. We can't dig the graves fast enough. So from now on, no overloaded boats, and every boat's gotta have an experienced pilot on board."

Then he told them that any infraction of these rules would be $100 fine.

When Steele finished talking, he faced about a thousand questions.

Henry and Elmer began discussing what they should do again, and quickly realized that somehow they had to hire a professional. Not long after they heard a weak voice behind them ask "Anybody need a boat pilot?"

Henry instantly noticed that no one else had heard the timid question and quickly yelled back," Over here!" hoping to cut the man off from speaking again.

They stood up as he came over, and he said "Hi, my name's Jack."

When Henry saw him up close he became skeptical. He was looking at a skinny kid that didn't look like he should even be outdoors.

"How old are you kid?" he asked.

"Twenty-two" Jack answered confidently, "but more important, I've been through this canyon five times."

Henry thought at least the kid was older than he looked, and this was probably as lucky as they were going to get. Besides, he did seem to be confident enough. He sure didn't look the part though.

"Where you from?" asked Henry.

"San Francisco" he replied, "The poor side." Then he told them that he'd arrived in Dawson the year before, but was too late to prospect and nearly starved to death during the winter. "I got Scurvy and spent a month in a little log hospital" he told them, "By spring I was skinny and broke, so I came straight here to try and make some money piloting boats."

"How much do you charge?" asked Elmer.

"Same as the others." he answered, "$20 for a boat, or $25 for a barge or raft."

"Oh." said Elmer, "We have a boat, but I don't think we have $20."

Actually he knew as well as Henry they didn't have $20.

"Well, there must be somethin' you need that we got." offered Elmer, starting to barter with him.

Henry was surprised that Elmer had taken over negotiating with Jack. It seemed that without him noticing, Elmer was becoming a more confident guy.

Sure enough, Elmer had soon cut a deal to have Jack pilot the boat, and they were getting along pretty well too. The deal was for Elmer's bowie knife, and all the money that they did have. So after digging the money and knife from their belongings, Elmer was stepping out of the boat to let Jack take it, when Jack said that he wanted to show them some things about the canyon first.

So they walked down the trail again, and up to the canyon's edge to where they'd been before. From there they traveled along the cliff, where all along people peered into the gorge to try and determine their odds of surviving.

When Henry, Elmer and Jack stepped up to the lip and looked down, they saw Belinda going through the canyon. As she steered the boat and the two men she'd hired rowed for their lives, Nero lay stretched out over the cargo as if bored or asleep. The river was so fast, it seemed only seconds before she was nearly out of sight. Jack was watching too, and momentarily forgetting about the canyon he remarked "Did you see the size of that dog?"

"It's even bigger up close." answered Elmer.

Then getting back to business Jack pointed into the gorge and said "We can't touch the walls down there. It's like hitting a giant cheese grater. And if we do crash, there's no way to get out."

Then Elmer noticed that just downstream on the other side, the river had eaten into the wall creating a large horseshoe shape in the canyon. "Maybe if we have to, we could rest in that bay over there?" he suggested.

"No!" answered Jack adamantly, "Whatever we do, we have to stay out of there. It's a horrible whirlpool that keeps boats in there. Even swamps some of them. Earlier two Swede's got caught in it, and they didn't get out again for six hours."

After examining the river a little longer, they began heading back to their boat. On the way Jack said "Oh yea, I forgot to mention something. You see that boat down there?"

Henry and Elmer both looked over the edge to see a boat floundering down the river with no one in it at all.

"That's another option." said Jack, "You let the boat go through with no one in it. Then when it comes out below the rapids, you chase it down with canoes. But that's if it comes out."

They watched the boat below bash its way through the canyon, and it seemed to be taking on water. It also still had a long ways to go.

"How many make it through?" asked Henry.

"Well, not a lot." replied Jack, "They do it 'cause it's free."

Henry and Elmer thought about it, but discarded the idea by the time they got back to their boat. They needed the supplies and property they still had left, and didn't want to put them at any more risk than they already were.

The whole area was becoming very crowded now, with still more boats arriving all the time. Thousands of people were now bottlenecking at the mouth of the canyon.

Jack climbed on the boat and made his way back to the stern, then sat down at the tiller making himself comfortable to steer. "Might as well get going." he said.

Elmer climbed on the boat to grab his coat, just in case Jack sunk somewhere, when suddenly Henry pushed the boat back out in the river and jumped in the bow with a handful of rope. Elmer hadn't seen him untie it and was shocked to find himself in the boat and drifting towards the canyon. Instantly he yelled at Henry "No! No! What are you doing! We're not supposed to be in the boat! We're suppose to be walkin' ....aren't we?"

He'd seen the change on Henry's face.

"The more oars in the water the better." replied Jack.

Both Henry and Jack started grinning. They hadn't realized that Elmer thought just Jack was going through the rapids.

The smiling didn't last long though, directly in front of them lay the mouth of the gorge, where the river went from yards to only feet across. As Elmer struggled to adjust to his new situation, Jack told him again how it was better to have a man on each oar, as well as one on the tiller. He also began telling them what they had to do when they got into the canyon.

"We have to stay in the middle for the first couple a miles." he said, "Until we get to the rapids. There's some rocks to watchout for, but we'll see them coming. The most important thing is to not hit the canyon walls. Loaded boats only hit once or twice before they start tearing apart. Oh yea, and we have to stay out of that whirlpool!"

The current began picking up speed and Jack began talking faster. He also started yelling as the roar from the water was becoming deafening.

"White water has air in it!" he shouted, "The whiter the water, the deeper we sink into it! Aim for any blue water you see!"

They were right in the mouth now with the cliffs rising straight up beside them. Then the river itself seemed to rise up before dropping them into the crevice. Henry yelled back to Jack, "What do we do when we get to the rapids?"

"Pray!" yelled Jack, and they slipped into the canyon.

For the first few seconds they rode in on swift blue water, which then seemed to slide under a thick layer of white. The layer turned out to be a wall, and they blasted through it losing sight of everything.

They seemed to be getting sprayed and splashed from every direction as they heaved up and down in huge swells, and about all they could do was to try and keep the boat pointed forward.

When they could see again, they saw they'd made it past a good many rocks by pure luck. The river was faster than they thought, narrower than they thought, and rougher than they thought. One thing was for sure, if they were going to make it through, it wasn't going to take very long. They were absolutely tearing through the canyon now.

Elmer was scared stiff and concentrating hard to survive.

"Aim for the blue water." he mumbled, "Aim for the blue water.".... "There is no blue water!" he yelled. The whole river was white.

The water was moving so fast, that the middle of the river was four to five feet higher than the edges along the cliffs, and they found themselves constantly and frantically rowing from one side or the other trying to get back to the middle. At times they'd blister along only inches away from the jagged walls, while regularly dodging large rocks. Some with boards and boat parts already pressing against them.

Then they saw a group of rocks that had men stranded on them. As the boat shot passed, the men looked quite desperate, but there was nothing they could do for them. Their best chance of rescue was probably to wait for a vessel to happen close by, and try to dive into it.

The whirlpool was coming up now, so Henry and Elmer rowed hard as Jack pointed the boat towards the opposite side of the canyon. They passed by at a safe enough distance to keep from sliding into it, and as the river was a little wider here, it allowed them a few seconds to rest.

They could see boats in front of them, and behind, and three more caught in the whirlpool. At eye level, the giant swirling pool looked horrific. Though it was huge, it spun fast enough to raise the water up higher on the outside edge, and looked extremely hard to get out of. On one of the boats circling around in the pool, the people on it were bailing frantically. There was nothing anybody could do for them either.

Henry remembered looking down from the cliff up above, and when he glanced up saw, hundreds of people watching them. "Look! There's Hegg with his camera again." he yelled to Elmer.

Elmer looked up and saw Hegg and the camera standing out on a large and precariously shaped ledge. They could only imagine the photographs he was taking from there.

"He's not afraid to go where he has to to get the pictures, that's for sure." said Henry.

"I wonder if he took any pictures of us?" replied Elmer.

"Let's hope we get a chance to ask him." yelled back Henry.

The gap between the cliffs began to narrow, and as the flow quickened, they began ripping through the canyon again. Now the worst part lay just ahead.

The river that had been more than 150 feet across, and then narrowed to sixty to seventy feet wide through the canyon, was now going to fit through a thirty foot slit in the rock. It was said that watching it squirt through from the other side, was like watching a giant bucket being emptied on to rocks.

"Head for the far right!" Jack yelled.

The roar coming from ahead was the loudest they'd heard yet, and once in position, there was very little they could do but drift reluctantly into the gap.

Shooting through the hole it felt like the boat went into a free fall, with Henry and Elmer both holding their oars in a death grip. Then the canyon suddenly disappeared, leaving the river in front of them to tumble down as if on a giant staircase. Ahead huge shards of rock were sticking out of the water, spread across the river like a giant set of claws.

"Row!" yelled Jack as they slipped over the first step into the all white water.

Beneath the foam, the current seemed to pull at them like some unseen monster. It'd pull or push, or spin them around, with their efforts amounting to little or nothing. They careened down the giant staircase, missing some rocks by luck and others by hard work.

After sweeping around one of the giant stones they were suddenly pulled sideways to face the next. They struggled to avoid a collision, and at the last second Elmer pointed his oar towards the rock hoping to deflect them away. But the oar was still attached to the boat through the oarlock, so when it struck the boat jerked violently and the end of his oar snapped off. When they crashed into it he was still trying to fend it off with the broken stub of his oar, and it quickly jammed into the mass of broken boards already being held there by the current.

The boards were from already destroyed boats, and one of them had '666' painted on it in tar.

Then their boat began sliding along the rock while at the same time slowly turning over on its side. All three of them thought they were done for. The boat tipped to within a hair of filling with water, and then the current just held them there. But after a few terrifying seconds, they suddenly popped free again and continued their wild ride towards the bottom.

They watched some of the boats in front of them sink into swells so deep they could only see the people's heads, and on some occasions seemed to swallow them up completely. In fact, some of the heavier boats were being swallowed, and would come up later in pieces.

When Henry and Elmer dropped into the rapids, they were struck at how big they really were. The Indians called this stretch of water 'Whitehorse Rapids', because the large white waves resembled the flowing mane of giant white horses.

Elmer yelled to Henry "Where's the extra oar!"

"We messed up!" Henry shouted back, "We put it in the boat first, and then piled everything else on top of it!"

They both thought they might sink, but soon realized that the first of the swells was the worst, and each one following was a little smaller. Still they spent much of their time speeding along sideways or backwards, as Elmer could really only splash at the water with his broken stub.

They rode out the swells until they slowly dissipated and the river widened out again, then they all laid back to take in some big breaths. They'd made it through.

"We have to land on the right hand shore." said Jack, "It's where everybody else is."

Elmer reached back for a paddle that belonged to Jack, then leaning over the side of the boat he began paddling as if it were a very large canoe. Slowly making their way towards shore, they floated by newly dug graves, with men digging more as they passed.

On the side of the river, signs began appearing that were messages to people. Short notes like "Cecil-Stop ahead" and "Bob-We made it".

They were nearly to shore when they began passing a long line of people that were obvious survivors of crashed and sunken boats. Many were spread along the bank, sitting by their gear and supplies drying in the sun, and most had a look of complete ruin on their faces.

With Jack's help they landed the boat, and then promptly talked him into eating some bannock with them before starting his hike back up to the head of the canyon again. It wasn't hard to pursuade him as they were all famished, and Jack said that since wintering in Dawson he was always hungry. None of them wanted to spend much time though, so Elmer began making the meal as Henry built a fire, and Jack wrote things in his journal.

Soon they were sitting by a fire and enjoying the hot heavy bread, while they laughed and talked of their trip through the canyon. And even though they were sitting in the midst of a crowd that had lost nearly everything, their spirits began to soar. It began sinking in that they'd not only survived the canyon and rapids, but the most feared obstacle of their journey was now behind them. They still had five hundred miles to go, but there were few dangers ahead now, and only one more lake to cross.

"We sure had a foot in the grave for awhile back there." laughed Jack.

"Yea, and the other on a slippery rock." added Elmer.

As they talked, they conversed with some of the other people around them, hearing of their successes and failures. It was then that they learned of a very lucky few that had merrily bounced and bashed their way through the canyon, piling into everything they encountered, yet somehow remained blissfully unaware that they were in any danger at all.

Something else that seemed to be happening repeatedly was the whittling down of rafts. They were almost impossible to control in the current, and many that weren't destroyed were often reduced in size. After striking an object, frequently the outside logs would be torn free, and some rafts were emerging from the canyon much smaller, and carrying much less cargo.

They finished eating and thanked Jack before he left, and he said that he hoped to see him again in Dawson. He was going to pilot boats for another month or so, but that he wasn't done with prospecting just yet. Henry and Elmer both thought he was crazy, going through the canyon when he didn't absolutely have to.

Soon their minds were pulled back to the race for gold again, and it took them little time to pack up and leave. A few miles down river from the canyon the land flattened out some, and they became surrounded by low and rolling hills. The river was wider now, and almost tranquil compared to what they'd been through. In fact, with a belly full of bannock they soon began to have trouble staying awake. They remembered what the Mounties had said about sleeping on the move, so after fighting it as long as they could, they reluctantly decided to stop and sleep somewhere.

Seeing a suitable strip of beach approaching on their left, they began rowing towards it. Already being on the left they thought they had plenty of time, but the river was moving faster than it appeared, and after a burst of hard rowing they watched helplessly as they slid past it just out of reach.

They rowed back to the middle again, and saw that far down the river on the other side was a very long landing place. Ten minutes later, they watched again as the end of it went by while they were only yards away. They were in too good of mood for it to frustrate them, but it was obviously taking longer than they thought to row anywhere in the current. So they decided to stay on the one side and just wait for a place to show up. One did and they beached quickly, discovering that to completely stop the boat, Elmer had to jump to the shore with the bowline and act as brakes.

He tied up to a small pine tree and Henry too hopped out. Then they walked up the gravel beach to where it met with a small meadow. "We could sleep here for awhile." suggested Henry, "It's not going to rain so we shouldn't have to build any cover."

He could say it with confidence, as they were still gripped in the heat wave and knew they'd be warm and dry.

Suddenly a boat hit the beach in front of them, then started drifting downstream towards theirs. It was Arizona Charlie, and he made no attempt to jump to shore, but passing by their boat he simply lassoed the tiller and when his boat swung in behind theirs, he stepped out on the beach. "Howdy boys. Glad to see you're still alive." he said greeting them.

"You too Charlie." replied Elmer, "How you doing?"

"Lotsa close ones." answered Charlie, "But I survived with what's left of my things for a change."

"Where's your new partner?" asked Henry, remembering that he used to have one.

"Well we were so happy about making it through that God forsaken canyon," said Charlie, "we celebrated with a few drinks. Uh.....he's sleeping in the bottom of the boat."

Henry and Elmer both looked over, but couldn't see him. He was indeed in the bottom of the boat.

"I been following you guys for awhile." said Charlie, "I was just goin' to pull off and snooze when I saw you start zigzagging all over the river."

"We were lookin' for a place to sleep too." said Henry. "But we're not very good at landing yet."

So the three of them pulled their rolled up beds from the boats, and brought them back up to the meadow to sleep. But before they unrolled them, Charlie said "How 'bout a toast to surviving?...and something to help us sleep." Then he pulled a bottle of whiskey from the center of his bedroll. "My treat." he added.

"You bet Charlie ...Thanks." said Henry, sitting down on his own bedroll.

Elmer quickly did likewise, while trying to appear calm and controlled like his older companions.

Charlie chuckled a little, noticing he looked more like a kid waiting for ice cream. Then he held up the bottle and said, "This is the last one to survive." and pealed the seal from the cork.

Intending to only have a couple of shots, they took turns drinking from the bottle as they sat and watched other stampeders drift by. It was very late now, and they were tired. But underneath the fatigue, the exhilaration of the canyon was still there and the alcohol seemed to be fueling it back to life. So soon they sat laughing and lamenting the events of their journey.

The forest fire smoke was a little hazier here, causing a screaming pink and red sky that seemed to raise their spirits even more. The whole river reflected the glowing sky off their hands and faces, and before long Henry and Charlie were laughing hysterically, as Elmer stood in front of them wildly animating his battle with the rock, and how he'd rowed with the broken oar.

They continued on with their giddy conversation, forgetting all about going to sleep, with their attention occasionally being drawn to debris floating down the river, sometimes taking turns trying to guess what it was. Even an empty boat drifted by, causing them to speculate on the circumstances behind it. They also stopped talking once in a while, to marvel at the strange sunlight.

Eventually, Elmer became quite drunk. He stood in front of them demonstrating his expertise with an invisible fly rod, while professing to be, probably the best fisherman in all of Oregon.

Suddenly he stopped, and just stood motionless.

Then his eyes seemed to wander independently, and Henry and Charlie both knew he was going to be sick.

As fast as he could, Elmer slurred out "I gotta go thig for a midut.", then stumbled a few yards toward the boat before falling to his hands and knees and throwing up all over the rocks.

Both Henry and Charlie started laughing again, before Charlie stopped to say "I believe that Elmer's hurried declaration may have been little more than an elaborate ruse."

They listened to Elmer throw up for awhile, when Henry finally said, "Geez Elmer, you're gonna turn inside out!"

They heard him mumble "Oh God!" a couple of times, then fall over. A few minutes later he began snoring, so Henry and Charlie walked over to where he lay, and each took an arm to pack him up to his bed.

Elmer woke up a few hours later with a terrible headache and Henry kicking at him. Henry'd tried subtler methods first to wake him up, but with no results.

Finally Elmer opened one eye, and gradually looking up said "You look terrible Henry, you should probably get some more sleep.....Don't worry. I'll come get ya." Then his eye closed again.

"Ha-ha" said Henry as he kicked at him again, "Get up! The dream is dead. It's time to go."

When Elmer staggered to his feet, he saw a half a dozen ravens hopping around on the beach. Charlie was walking by with his bedroll, when Elmer, still staring at the birds grumbled "What are they doin' here?"

Charlie looked back at him with a look of surprise, like he should already know. "Why, eating your puke." he replied, as he too glanced over at the big birds, "You left a hell of a mess over there."

Elmer recoiled as he tried to get the sickening thought out of his mind. Then he accidentally peeked back and saw one of the birds eating heartily. His throat quickly tightened, and he began throwing up again, and this time because of his pounding headache, the sound of him getting sick was peppered with a great many "Oh Gods!"

Charlie was down at the boats with Henry now, and laughing again yelled back at Elmer "You're goin' to make 'em fat!"

Then Henry took a shot himself yelling "Ya! Those are smart birds Elmer. If you keep feedin' them, they'll follow us all the way to Dawson."

They were getting ready to leave by the time Charlie's partner finally woke up. Having slept in a boat that never quit moving, the poor man was in worse shape than Elmer. When Henry saw him he joked "Hey Charlie! What'd you do to your partner?"

Charlie looked at the man for a few seconds, then smiled back and answered "I think he's seasick."

The man complained of a very turbulent stomach, so he and Charlie stayed behind to cook a breakfast. Henry and Elmer pushed off again though, and were soon drifting down the middle of the river again.

The river was smooth and serene now and almost effortless to navigate, yet they still moved swiftly along. As time went by, the haze from the forest fires became much thicker and though they could still see well enough, everything appeared a very pale blue, and the distant mountains almost invisible.

Henry sat in the back, and lazily watched for animals along the shoreline. He'd quickly realized that because the boat floated along in basic silence, often the animals didn't notice them at all and would continue about their business, sometimes only a few yards away.

Elmer had already become bored, and sat on the bow with a leg dangling over each side as he poked at the water with a stick.

Eventually he saw a patch of trees up ahead with the river splitting to flow on each side of them. "Look Henry, here comes an island."

At first it seemed as if they might run right into it, but as they drew closer, the current pushed them off to one side just in time to keep them from having to row.

The island was wide and long and had a group of men camped at the front of it, and they passed by near enough that one man waved, while another simply nodded his head.

This close to land the trees seemed to be speeding by, and before they knew it, they'd glided almost to the far end of the island.

Suddenly Henry violently threw himself to the floor of the boat, urgently motioning Elmer to do the same!

Instantly Elmer saw that only ten or fifteen yards away on the bank of the island, stood Mace, Leadtooth, and a couple of other thugs gathered around a fire! So far they hadn't been noticed and Elmer quickly dove to the bottom of the boat like Henry hoping to keep it that way!

They couldn't believe the bizarre situation, and were terrified they were going to be spotted. From down by the floorboards they could still see the tips of the trees going by, and now they seemed to be moving at a snails pace.

Finally they couldn't see the trees anymore, but knew that Soapy's men would still be able to see the boat for awhile, so they both continued to lie motionless.

When they eventually sat up again, they'd waited plenty long and were far out of sight of their camp.

"What the hell was that?" gasped Elmer still in shock, "How did they get here?"

"More important," replied Henry, "What are they doing here?"

Elmer looked back to the island and said "I wonder if they saw us? Do you think they saw us Henry?"

"I didn't hear anything." he replied, "But damn, we were so close. I don't see how they could of missed seeing the boat."

"They probably don't know what our boat looks like." suggested Elmer.

But they both remembered seeing what could've been Mace back on the shore at Bennett.

"Maybe they're not even lookin' for us." suggested Elmer hopefully.

"Yea....maybe." said Henry, knowing that they were probably after the map.

Really Elmer knew too, but said "Maybe they don't even know about the map, and they're just on their way to the Klondike like everybody else."

"Or maybe they know more about the map than we do" said Henry.

They traveled almost continuously after that, hoping to put both time and distance between themselves and Soapy's criminals. They also kept talking trying to determine what they did or didn't know, as Elmer kept a nervous watch behind them.

Miles later the river dumped them into the last great lake. Lake LeBarge, and it still had countless chunks of ice floating around in it. The haze from the fires had slowly become thicker, until now they couldn't see the mountains at all, and the dozens of boats spread out in front of them appeared fainter and fainter as they faded with the distance.

There was very little wind at first, so like most the other vessels, they left their sail up while occasionally using the oars to push away lumps of ice. Then well into their crossing, the light breeze turned into a strong one, and fending off the ice became much more difficult. Before long they were completely surrounded and being pushed helplessly along with the frozen lumps. Then the ice blew into a long line, trapping them on the wrong side of the lake.

Most boats they could see had successfully escaped their predicament, but an unlucky few had become trapped just like they were. The ice wasn't terribly thick but they still couldn't push their way through it. It'd have to stop moving around first. So they decided to row to shore and eat, and hope for the wind to stop.

The boat landed easily, and they'd almost finished cooking when the wind began to slow. So they sat and ate while the water became smooth again, allowing the ice to drift and separate.

"Let's have some coffee too." suggested Elmer.

"Might as well." replied Henry, "Without any wind, we got a lot of rowing to do when we get back out there."

Before long they'd finished eating and sat drinking hot coffee. And with the thick haze over the lake, the scene took on a very eerie appearance. They couldn't see any other boats now, they were all deep in the smoke somewhere.

Then they heard "Dinner's over boys." and when they turned around their blood ran cold! A few yards away stood Mace pointing a gun at them!

"You saw us float past." said Henry.

"Yup." replied Mace, "How could I miss ya? I coulda pissed in yer boat."

Henry noticed he was alone and sarcasticly said "Didn't you have some friends awhile ago?"

"I decided I didn't need that many friends," he answered, "to deal with you anyway,... or to get to Dawson."

It was obvious he'd left them on the island with no way to get off.

Then he said "Now, Soapy wants his map back."

Beneath the fear in Henry and Elmer, an anger was growing at having a gun pointed at them. Neither of them said anything though, they just stood there.

Mace waited a few seconds then said "Fine! Let's go." and cocked the gun, waving them towards the boat.

After he climbed in the back and sat down, he made them push off, then sit down and row.

It took a little while to poke through the lingering ice, then as they rowed further out in the lake, Elmer said "You're the guys that ambushed us on the trail. Aren't ya?"

"Boy! There's no flies on you." he sneered, "Woulda got ya too, except for that sharpshootin' bastard."

Far from shore, they really started to worry at what was about to happen.

Elmer said "You just gonna leave your boat behind?"

"It's no good anymore." he said, "I was followin' you guys when the ice pushed me up on the beach. I'll be ridin' in to Dawson in yer outfit." he grinned.

"You're gonna keep the map for yourself!" blurted out Elmer.

So much for pretending they didn't know anything.

"Stop rowing." he said, "That's far enough." Then he looked and pointed the gun at Elmer. "Yer red hot." he said, "Can you guess what happens next?"

Elmer just stared at the bottom of the boat and didn't answer.

Then Mace said "Okay, here's the deal. You hand over the map, and I'll put you off on the next island. Otherwise, we see how far you can swim from here."

Neither Henry nor Elmer believed him. He could've made the same offer on shore and left them there if they gave him the map. The only reason to come out here first, was to take advantage of the icy cold water and no other boats around. He was going to kill them.

Their minds raced as they searched for options, but couldn't find any. Then seeing no move to accept his offer, Mace glared at Elmer and growled "Get out!"

"No!" protested Henry, "We'll give you the map."

Elmer had no problem with that, and began digging for his buffalo coat.

"Careful there kid." warned Mace, "Don't be grabbin' for just anything."

Elmer found the coat, and cautiously removed the silver case as Mace nervously supervised. Once out, he began opening the case to extract the tube, when Mace yelled "Just give it here!"

So Elmer closed the case again and lightly tossed it to him. It was a perfect throw, but Mace bobbled it anyway and dropped it in the bottom of the boat. They could tell he wanted to blame

Elmer, but it was entirely his own fault. He tried to retrieve it quickly, but bending over to pick it up he had to look away for just a split-second, and when he did, Henry sprang to his feet while raising up the oar to whack him on the head!

Henry knew he'd probably be shot, but figured if he did nothing, he was going to be shot or drowned anyway. He was hoping Elmer would follow his lead, but even better, Elmer had done his own thinking and jumped up at the same time.

Mace had almost straightened up again before Henry brought his oar down to strike, and as he did Mace fired! The bullet missed Henry but tore the end off his oar! Mace quickly turned away to avoid Henry's descending blow, and with the boat shifting around from their momentum, he fell down in the back. Then because of his now shortened oar, Henry missed with his mighty swing, throwing himself off balance so that he too fell in the back beside Mace. Before he could move Elmer's oar came smashing down, missing Mace, but striking close enough and hard enough to kill either one of them!

Mace jumped up first, but before he could point the gun he had to dodge another life threatening blow from Elmer, and as he did, Henry jumped to his feet beside him and pushed him overboard!

He hit the water with a splash, and as Henry fumbled to pick up his oar again, Elmer leaped into the back trying to hit him again!

Henry sprung back up yelling "Get him Elmer! Get him!"

Once more Mace aimed the gun but before he could fire, Elmer's oar came crashing down grazing his head and smashing onto his shoulder!

Mace let out a loud groan, and shot a bullet that whizzed by between them!

The frightening chaos was now causing the boat to jerk violently around, and when Elmer raised up his oar again, he too fell down in the boat. Then once more Henry swung and missed with his shortened oar, hitting only a part of Mace's submerged arm. As Mace fought to point the gun again and Henry struggled to raise his oar, Elmer's oar came smashing down on Mace!

It was kill or be killed, and over the next few seconds the battle to survive became alarmingly gruesome. Finally, with a solid whack from Henry's broken oar, Mace slipped below the surface, taking the silver case with him.

They watched a few nervous seconds for him to resurface again, then tired and winded, they collapsed back down in the boat to breathe.

"Damn!" gasped Henry, "That was awful."

Suddenly a bullet ripped through the bottom of the boat between his legs! Then another tearing through his hat! They panicked for what to do! Elmer scrambled on top of their supplies, while Henry jumped up pulling his feet together and leaned over the side. He peered down through the water and saw Mace about four or five feet down, and he seemed to be pointing the gun straight up at him! He quickly ducked away as another bullet split the surface, but already spent, it simply paused in the air before falling harmlessly into the boat.

"Wow Henry! Did you see that?" gasped Elmer!

"Yea...I had a pretty good look." answered Henry.

It was the end of Mace.

Henry and Elmer were frozen with shock at the horrifying turn of events. But soon realized that the boat was filling with water through the bullet holes. They weren't going to sink though, they could easily bail it out faster than it was coming in.

But they had other problems. There was no wind at all, and they'd broken their spare oar, so now they only had the one.

Elmer stood on the holes as they tried to solve their problems, but with the incident hardly over, they could barely breathe or think.

They were also starting to feel guilty of even having taken part in such an awful event. They hadn't murdered Mace, but it sure felt like they did.

The ripples from the boat were fanning out in every direction now, seeming to scream "Look over here! Look over here!" They both just wanted to get far away.

Suddenly Henry said "I know what might work." and began digging through their cooking utensils. A few minutes later he had their frying pan tied to the broken end of the oar.

"Wait." said Elmer, "Let's tie a string through the handle ...we don't wanna lose it." Then they jammed twisted pieces of canvas into the bullet holes, and started rowing for shore.

Soon a breeze blew over the lake, thinning out the haze and revealing many not so distant vessels. They had to wonder if any of them had heard the gunshots, as well as the commotion.

They raised up their sail again to take advantage of the wind, and decided that because the plugs in the bullet holes were working so well, they'd just keep going for awhile.

So they sailed along in silence, neither one of them feeling inclined to speak.

Finally Elmer said, "Well I guess Soapy knows we took his map."

"Yea, I'm sorry about that." regretted Henry, "I shouldn't a stole that damn thing in the first place. It's brought us a world a trouble."

"Naw ...I woulda done the same thing." replied Elmer quickly, "Besides, it hasn't done Soapy a lot of good either. And now that it's gone, it's kinda like we got even with him. I'll bet not too many people can say that."

"That could be a problem." said Henry, "They might end up thinking we still have it."

"I wonder if Leadtooth and those other guys know why Mace and their boat went missing?" said Elmer.

"They gotta suspect." answered Henry, "I reckon they'll keep heading for Dawson too."

"How long do you think it'll take 'em to get off that island?" asked Elmer.

"As fast as they can steal a boat." replied Henry, "And I saw guys camped on the other end of the island, so they're probably already off it."

"If we stop to camp or eat, we should probably do it out of sight." added Elmer wisely.

"I guess we'll have to tell Sam about killing Mace too." said Henry.

"Well he should understand, that's for sure." replied Elmer, "After fighting with Mace himself."

"I wonder if we should leave out the part about the map?" said Henry, "It might just complicate things."

"Yea, probably." answered Elmer. But was really thinking like Henry, that the map could make them appear responsible for the whole incident.

"At least if Sam does find out, he's our friend." added Elmer.

"Do you think that'll make a difference?" questioned Henry.

"....No." muttered Elmer, like he should've known better.

Boats following behind made them nervous now. So after crossing the lake at what felt like a terribly slow pace, they were both glad to get on the river again. Fewer eyes could see them now, and as long as they kept floating along, they weren't in any immediate danger.

After a few hours of always seeing the same boats behind them, they eventually began to relax a little. They were actually becoming quite comfortable again, when suddenly the boat ground to a stop. To their astonishment, they were stuck on a sandbar hidden just below the surface.

"Damn!" cried Henry surprised, "We're almost in the middle of the river!"

They quickly surveyed their situation and became somewhat dismayed. They were going to have to get out of the boat and push it back upstream about fifty yards to get around the bar.

The instant they jumped out, their worn out boots filled with the icy water and they both let out a shudder. It was very slow going pushing the boat against the current, and it quickly turned into a torture test. The cold water on their feet became excruciatingly painful, and if they hopped back in the boat again, it swiftly started drifting back to where they began.

Before long they'd forgotten all about Leadtooth, and as they pushed up stream with their teeth grit tightly in pain, they watched boat after boat drift by with the occupants smiling and waving at them. It never occurred to them that from a distance, their grimacing faces appeared to be smiles of embarrassment.

It would have been embarrassing too, if not for the agony.

Once on the move again, they figured Leadtooth could be closer than ever behind them, so they drifted continuously until the next day. They passed very few islands and really no places to stop discretely, at least none they could reach before the current swept them on by. So they ended up traveling a great distance, more than a hundred miles.

They'd begun traveling through the thickest forest fire smoke yet, when their last obstacle appeared. It was a set of rapids called 'Five Fingers', named for five giant pillars of rock spaced evenly across the river.

Because of the smoke, they were already very close when they saw the columns rising up in front of them. They looked terribly ominous, but Jack had told them not to worry, that they were only a few hundred feet long, and were no where near as formitable as the Whitehorse Rapids or Miles Canyon. He said if they kept themselves to the right they should be okay, but he also told them to be careful, that there was still "Plenty of opportunity for disaster."

Just like at the head of Miles Canyon, a good many boats had pulled over to shore before reaching the pillars. There wasn't as many as at the canyon though, only about a hundred or so. So Henry and Elmer decided to trust in what Jack had told them, and plunge straight into it.

It was probably too late to get stopped anyway.

The water quickly sped up as they slid between the giant rocks, and again they could see people watching from the cliffs up above.

In just a few seconds they'd passed between the tall columns, and were heaving up and down in the huge swells. They quickly diminished though, and they were out of danger in no time.

When they gazed around at the boats that had landed after negotiating the rapids, they were sure one of them was Belinda's. There was already nothing they could do to stop and talk though, it would mean rowing back upstream, an almost impossible task even along shore. But they were glad to see she'd made it through the canyon.

Over the next few hours the smoke continued to thicken, eventually becoming so dense that they could barely see twenty or thirty yards. They thought about stopping and waiting for it to improve, but for all they knew it could be weeks clearing off, or might even get worse.

The next thing they saw coming at them was land. It was one of the countless islands strung along the rest of the way to the Klondike. Not knowing which direction to row, they let the island approach until just as before, they slipped off to one side and then skimmed along beside it only a few yards away.

The islands came in all sizes, from just a mound of gravel, sometimes with a tree or two on it, to wide and well treed islands, stretching two or three miles downstream. Often in the haze it became so confusing, that they couldn't be sure whether they were looking at the riverbank or the side of an island.

But there was one thing that had become very clear. Other streams and tributaries had been continuously adding themselves to the river, until now it had grown to many times the size it had been back at the canyon.

Something else that had become obvious, was that living in near constant daylight had made 'What time it was', almost irrelevant. It was the middle of the night now, and it meant nothing.

Then Elmer said "What the heck is that?" He was staring forward into the smoke, at a very thick and obscured horizontal line. As Henry too began to study it, Elmer said "I think it must be the other bank of the river." A few more seconds passed before he yelled "Holy Crap!"

The dark object had suddenly revealed itself to be a giant tree. It had tipped over completely until it hung just above the river, with many of its branches brushing into the water.

The high water levels from each spring run-off would erode some of the rivers banks, tipping many of the trees into the water, and creating a lot of these hazards. They were dubbed 'sweepers' and were incredibly dangerous, as often the current would cause the vessels to roll underneath the fallen trunks.

It was too late for Henry and Elmer, all they could do was wait for the deadly mishap to occur! They frantically tried to figure the outcome as they swept into it, until finally just ducking down in the boat.

The bow hit first, then the boat suddenly jerked and twisted, then they heard a loud crack! It was quickly followed by an even louder crash, and then nothing.

They rose back up, to happily see they'd managed to fit under the log, and the crack they'd heard was their mast being snapped off.

"Damn! That was close!" exclaimed Henry. He felt a little better than Elmer to have survived, as the mast had crashed down directly over top of him before it tore away from the boat.

"I thought we'd get pushed under for sure!" said Elmer, still surprised the boat had fit under the log. He looked back to see their mast and sail hooked on one of the trees branches, with the broken end bobbing back and forth in the water. "Didn't do our sail much good." he added.

"Oh well." replied Henry, "We didn't need it anymore anyway."

Suddenly 'Thud!', and the boat stopped violently again, this time knocking them both over. Then they continued to drift on in silence again.

They'd struck another toppled tree, only this one was completely submerged and they never saw it coming. Henry reached for the rudder arm to pull himself back up again, but it was gone. "Rudder too! We gotta get away from shore quick!" he said urgently, "We can't afford to lose anymore boat parts."

They manned their oars and as they began to row, decided that they had to stop somewhere and do some boat repairs. Their mast and sail had been torn off, the rudder was gone, they had bullet holes in their bottom, and a frying pan oar.

Eventually the smoke thinned somewhat, enabling them to see a few hundred yards ahead and making things much safer. So they finally beached themselves on a long well treed island, after purposely traveling down a narrow channel on the back side, hoping to remain well hidden.

After landing, Elmer took the butcher knife and began carving plugs to fit in the bullet holes, while Henry took the axe and went into the bush to cut a piece of wood for a new oar.

About ten minutes had passed, when suddenly Elmer could hear Henry yelling and screaming! "Leadtooth!" he thought, and jumped up to run out and help! He took the butcher knife with him, and as he ran across the gravel bar towards the woods he realized that though Henry was still yelling, he was also coming towards him!

Elmer listened to him crashing through the bush and then heard him scream "Launch the boat! Launch the boat!" Elmer took his word for it and ran back towards the boat, totally confused at what was happening.

Suddenly Henry shot out of the bush running full bore and completely shirtless! Then a few yards behind a large snorting cow moose blasted free from the brush charging hot after him!

This panicked Elmer too, and upon reaching the boat he barely slowed down before ramming his shoulder into the bow and driving it backwards into the water. And no sooner had he jumped in the boat, when Henry dove in behind him.

The moose too was close enough to breathe on them, and ran into the river up to its knees, before piling headlong into the bow and driving them out even further.

As they began floating away, they looked back at the moose still standing in the water snorting and staring at them. "That was no cow with long legs!" gasped Henry, "That thing tried to kill me!" He'd never been so out of breath before.

"It sure looked like it wanted to." agreed Elmer, and then added "What happened to your shirt?"

"It charged out of nowhere," answered Henry, "and when I started to run away it tried to bite me on my neck, but it only got me by the collar. Thank God my shirt was worn out. Then I fell down and it tried to stomp me to death. The only reason I got away was 'cause I got lucky. When it was trying to finish me, it tripped and fell down too. Anyway," he added still out of breath,

"I think we should stop on smaller islands from now on. Ones we can check out for moose."

They didn't know it, but it was a wise decision. In the spring and early summer many of the larger islands had moose on them. They would swim out to birth their calves free from the threat of wolf and bear attacks. And while on these islands, they had a particularly aggressive nature.

They were more discerning now about choosing places to stop. So much so, that it was nearly two more hours before they landed the boat again.

For the first hour Elmer occasionally burst into laughter, repeatedly picturing the moose ripping Henry's shirt off. And it didn't help that he was still wearing the cuffs. "Well at least you only lost a couple a tailfeathers." he finally teased.

Then Henry took off the cuffs and put on his other shirt, mostly to try and stop Elmer from laughing.

They only floated about twenty more miles, when they encountered another wrecked boat.

Some of the 'sweepers' overhanging the river were much more dangerous than the tree they had hit. After tipping over, some of them had thick branches that stuck down into the water. The current would pull the branches down and back, then suddenly let it all go. The whole tree would then spring back up, and teeter high above the water before crashing back down again. These ones were called 'preachers', because of their up and down praying motion. They'd repeat the motion continuously, until either the water level dropped or the tree fell in completely. To be underneath a descending preacher was to be swamped or smashed to pieces.

The wreck they saw was a mast, a sail, and the front end of a boat, all hooked on a large preacher still plunging up and down in the river.

After they landed the boat again, Elmer resumed making plugs to fit the bullet holes, when he noticed that Henry seemed a little reluctant to walk into the woods again. Once more Elmer chuckled at him, then took the axe himself to go cut another oar.

A few minutes after Henry took over carving the plugs, he suddenly heard Elmer begin yelling and screaming. "Moose!" he thought instantly. Then considered "Maybe it's Leadtooth!" So he started running towards the bush, only to have Elmer suddenly emerged from the woods still shrieking and running right by him. Then he suddenly stopped and stood staring at the ground.

Henry too stopped, and continuing to look for his assailant called out "What's happening Elmer!"

Elmer still had his back to him, but slowly turned around and looked up.

"Geez Elmer! What happened? Your face is all ripped up!"

"I got attacked by birds!" he yelled, "Falcons!" He was both angry and embarrassed. "They dive at you!" he said, "And when they shoot past, you turn around to see where they went, and they're right there!"

"How many was there?" asked Henry.

"Just two.....I think, they musta had a nest."

His face wasn't as bad as it looked. It was mostly scratches, though some were fairly deep. His worst injury was a slightly torn ear.

"Didn't ya fight back at all?" smirked Henry. For he'd obviously lost the battle.

They were both afraid to go into the woods now, but Henry figured that if he was going to search for gold in the Klondike, he was going to have to walk in the bush all the time. So as Elmer washed out his wounds in the river, Henry picked up the axe and marched into the trees again. When he returned, he had a crudely fashioned replacement oar, and Elmer had finished pounding new plugs into the bullet holes.

They should've slept awhile before resuming their voyage again, but Elmer said his face still stung, and it probably would for awhile. So they pushed off anyway, and soon after Henry was sound asleep in the boat.

He woke up some four hours later with rain pounding down on him, and found that he'd stiffened right up from his race with the moose. "How long's it been raining?" he asked.

"Five minutes." replied Elmer.

As Henry slowly sat up, he tried hard to hide his grin at seeing Elmer's face again. It wouldn't be the last time either.

It was only about another twenty minutes before the rain stopped, but it was enough to soak everything and thin out some of the smoke. Then because of the wet ground, they saw something they'd heard about, but never seen before. It was an otter slide. As they drifted by in silence, the animals paid no attention to them, and would run straight up a steep hillside about sixty feet, then turn and slide headfirst on their bellies down a well worn trench. Without fear they'd splash down into the water at an incredible speed, only to scramble out of the river and back up the hill to do it all over again. They counted at least five otters on the slide, and there seemed to be no reason for their behavior other than the sheer fun of it.

The weather had become unpredictable now, in fact darn right erratic. For a whole day the sun shone frequently, but only for short periods of time, while both white and black clouds sailed overhead, occasionally sprinkling or dumping rain on them.

Then Henry and Elmer made another bad mistake. They both fell asleep in the boat. They'd been taking chances for some time, continuing to travel when one of them fell asleep and the other was nearly as tired. Now suddenly the boat lurched and they both woke up to a loud crunching noise. They quickly jumped up to see that they were in the middle of a swift moving ocean of ice. Some of the chunks were huge, and they tumbled and turned in the current, grinding into each other and anything else with them. They were in terrible peril, with a great possibility of their boat being crushed.

The ice was the fault of the 'White River'. Less than 150 miles to the south, stood the St. Elias Mountains, containing some of the largest ice fields in the world. The White River flowed out of them, and brought its icy payload to the Yukon River.

Henry and Elmer had seen many other large rivers add themselves to the Yukon, but they were both sound asleep for this one. At first they had to fight for their lives to keep the ice away, but as the miles went by it began breaking up into smaller and smaller pieces, until eventually turning the entire river a dirty brown. They never talked about falling asleep in the boat, but they both knew it wouldn't happen again.

There was no telling how long they'd slept for. It could've been two hours or ten. The only sure thing was that they'd drifted long enough to finally escape the forest fire smoke. The broken clouds were still overhead and for the next whole day it rained more often than not.

They were sitting hunched over in a dull drizzle, when they began hearing noise from up ahead on the river. At first they thought it might be more rapids, but soon discovered it was a large crowd of men on an island. There was much commotion and they seemed to be having a party. But as they drew closer, they began to realize it was pretty much the exact opposite.

Many of the hastily formed partnerships that had been born out of necessity back in Bennett, were now coming apart at the seams. Henry and Elmer had seen tempers boil over frequently back at the rapids, and now some of the relationships had become incredibly bitter and could last no longer.

There was a sign on the front of the island that read 'Split-up Island'. 'Fair Arbitrators-$1'. There was even a couple of Mounties mediating disputes.

They could see many arguments and shoving matches, and men dividing up their property. The hatred of some was such, as to cut everything in half. Tents, candles, even bags of flour were being hacked down the middle. Then to their disbelief, they saw men sawing their boat in half.

They decided it best to avoid the place, figuring at the very least it'd be bad luck to stop. So they let the current push them on by, towards their now fast approaching goal.

A few hours later a sign appeared on the bank that read "Dawson Around Corner'-'Stay Right'.

The river was a giant now and they were in the middle, so they knew they had some serious rowing to do. Even so, it still took longer than they thought, but eventually they neared the bank on the right hand side. Then Henry suddenly jumped up and yelled "Behold! The Klondike!"

Elmer quickly spun around to see a long line of tents on the riverbank ahead. They were still a half mile away, but they could see much activity amid the dwellings. "It looks just like Skagway" lamented Elmer. He'd pictured the 'City of Gold' in his mind many times, and this wasn't it.

"Look at the bright side." said Henry, "It only took a year and everything we had to get here."

It was very early June, and it had taken them almost 11 months to reach the Klondike.

Closer to shore, they realized that the river was actually moving very fast and the tents of Dawson were already upon them. Before they knew it, they were passing by frantically looking for a place to land. But there was nowhere. A continuous row of boats lined the shore, some with other boats tied behind them.

As the town swiftly passed by, they finally became desperate and did what they saw others doing. They just piled headlong into the already beached vessels and Elmer roped one randomly with their bowline, then when the slack tightened up they again smashed sideways into other boats.

Many people watched but no one cared. None of these boats would ever sail anywhere again.

They could see other less fortunate vessels still out in the river that were much too late to reach shore in time, leaving their owners to face a very arduous trek to move their belongings back up river.

Meanwhile, Henry and Elmer tied their boat up securely, then crawled over someone else's boat to step out on shore. They were finally here.

The City of Gold

The river was swelled high with the spring run-off, making it easy for Henry and Elmer to climb the few feet up the bank and stand on top. Before them lay the large treeless flat that was Dawson.

At the front facing the river were a few rough sawn board buildings, mashed together with many others that were half boards and half tent. Some were brothels and boarding houses, but most were saloons and gambling houses. Behind this street, stretched the huge sea of tents that made up the rest of Dawson.

Both Henry and Elmer could feel a strange excitement growing in them, as if gold could be under the very ground they were standing on. They decided to look around a little, figuring their stuff would probably be okay unattended. Even though there were thousands of people everywhere, all were deeply involved in doing their own business.

They spied a large board building not too far off, with a sign on it reading 'Monte Carlo Dance Hall'. As they instinctively began heading towards it, they realized that even though they'd heard that the streets of Dawson were paved with gold, they were actually paved with mud. It was far worse than Skagway, and a full foot deep.

For an entire week before the stampeders began arriving, Dawson had lain under five feet of water. Ice had jammed up the river just below town, and hadn't broken free until a couple of days before the boats began arriving, leaving the whole place a giant bog.

It was shoulder to shoulder on the crowded street, and as Henry and Elmer stumbled through the muck with everyone else, men were continuously asking them if they knew this person, or had seen that person, all searching for someone specific in the huge throng. Henry and Elmer decided that if they lost track of each other, they'd meet back at the boat. Actually, Henry probably could've found Elmer rather quickly, as everyone they passed was noticing his clawed up face.

Everyone they passed also seemed to be in very high spirits, as virtually all the stampeders were feeling the optimism of Klondike gold. A few people were feeling disappointed though. Expecting to see rich men, fancy buildings, and a city of gold, they instead saw tents, mud, and ragged looking people.

It was taking Henry and Elmer a long time to get anywhere, and not having thought out what they were really doing, they soon turned around to plod their way back to their boat.

On the riverbank, thousands of piles were growing as more and more people arrived and unloaded their boats.

When Henry and Elmer got back to the beach, they saw that Belinda too had made it to Dawson and was standing by her boat. As they approached her, she took a 50¢ piece from her pocket and threw it as far out in the river as she could. Then she turned to them and declared that she was now flat broke and tired of living that way. From now on she swore, she would never need change again.

Elmer was kind of shocked at this, and still staring at the disappating splash said "That was half a days work."

"Look at those signs over there." she replied, "It's not even a cup a coffee around here." Then she asked "What happened to your face?"

There was no way around it. He had to explain.

The stampeders with merchandise to sell were already setting up shop right there on the riverbank. Most had quickly made signs advertising their wares and prices, and the prices weren't cheap, or even reasonable. But it didn't matter. When One-eyed Riley told everyone in Bennett that Dawson was running out of everything but gold, he wasn't lying. In fact there was so much gold in Dawson, that during the winter months much of it had been put in piles on Front Street. There were no safes in Dawson, and the gold wouldn't have fit if there had been. So many people reasoned that the safest place to put it was where all could see.

Most of the previous 2500 residents of Dawson could be considered wealthy to extremely rich. Now these same people, with hunger in their bellies and holes in their clothes, absolutely swamped the newly arrived merchants ready to buy almost anything.

A small Italian man that had managed to skid sixteen thousand pounds of candy over the pass, was now selling it for $4 a pound and taking in the gold as fast as he could move. Henry and Elmer saw a man selling eggs for $18 a dozen, and who knows how old they were?

"I don't think we can afford to eat here." said Elmer.

"We don't have to worry about that." answered Henry, "We brought a ton of food with us, remember?"

Actually, $18 a dozen for eggs was a huge drop in price from a few weeks earlier. The last egg in Dawson had sold for $100, as the town had gotten down to its last exhausted chicken.

Then they saw the big man with the box of cats, and he was definitely going to have the last laugh. He was selling his cats for $150 each, and had a long line of men waiting in front of him.

Belinda hadn't even waited until her boat was unloaded. As soon as she saw the crowd of potential customers, she began selling her tents and hot water bottles immediately.

Hundreds of people an hour were pouring into Dawson now, and one of the next to arrive was Swiftwater Bill. He was riding onboard a huge freighter canoe being paddled by a dozen hired men. Bill stood proud in the middle of his boat, surrounded by stacks of whiskey cases, and the most beautiful dancehall girls San Francisco had to offer. The rest of his cassino supplies were arriving on barges behind him. He appeared as a flamboyant swashbuckler, here to save the day. Some of the crowd thought so too, throwing up a huge cheer when they saw his cargo.

He was gathering a lot of attention as he landed his boat, and then another crowd began to grow. Most everyone in Dawson knew Bill before he left the Klondike, and they'd not only been hearing of his escapades in the south, but they also knew he'd borrowed Charlie the packer from Augustus Mack, and were angry about how he'd lost him in San Francisco.

Bill never skipped a beat. He stepped out of the boat, then faced the annoyed crowd saying "Flattered I am. Half the town comin' out to greet my return. And bearing torches too."

The crowd began to berate him, when suddenly a much angrier man pushed his way through. His name was Dr. Wolf, and he was a disgruntled business partner of Bill's. Bill had gotten him all fired up with tales of gold and riches, then borrowed $20,000 from him with the promise to pay 100%

interest. Wolf hadn't met Bill before their agreement, and when stories of him renting whole floors of the best hotels, and bathing in champagne reached Dawson, poor Wolf started coming apart at the seams.

Now he was telling Bill that he could keep the interest on the loan, but he wanted his $20,000 back, "And right now!"

"I'll have it in less than an hour." answered Bill.

"Well start getting'!" grumbled Wolf.

Bill left, and returned in less than half an hour with all of Wolf's money.

Bill's barges had begun arriving now, so he had the men start packing the cargo up to his casino. The casino he owned was the Monte Carlo, and it was about to receive a very expensive upgrade.

It took Henry and Elmer awhile to move everything from their boat to the top of the riverbank, and as they continued to empty their vessel, they started to realize they were going to miss their beat up little craft. They'd built it themselves, it had kept them alive, and carried them hundreds of miles.

Suddenly Belinda appeared, "I'll give you a dollar for your boat." she said.

"Sold!" answered Elmer quickly, hoping it might be the first dollar of a mighty empire.

"Oh pudding," she replied smiling, "I paid too much. Bested again!" she added, as she flipped Elmer the dollar.

Really she didn't have to offer them anything for their vessel. Most all the boats had been abandoned now and were considered worthless.

It'd only taken Belinda four hours to sell all her tents and hot water bottles, and now she was working on a new enterprise. She'd hired men that at best could be called temporary labour, to pull boats out of the water and saw out all the useable lumber. Then she was piling it in her business tent.

Henry was trying to figure out what to do with most of their food now. It was impractical to drag it all around prospecting. So he ended up selling all the food that they couldn't carry for $10. Not a bad deal, as many of the piles were being outright abandoned while their owners raced off to search for gold. Most of the excess food was eventually gathered up by store owners, to be sold back to the stampeders later in the year.

Henry and Elmer were practically asleep on their feet now, and finding it difficult to form a plan. So again they challenged the mud of Front Street, and went looking for a place to sleep.

Stumbling along with their heavy packs, they began passing the crudely built casinos and dancehalls where hoards of men were gambling and spending their gold freely. There was Bill McPhees Pioneer Saloon, The Northern Saloon, and of course Swiftwater Bill's Monte Carlo, The Bank Saloon, and the M&M Saloon and Dancehall that advertised 'A dollar a Dance', and many others.

Some of the poorer establishments had dirt floors, which had now turned to mud. But the larger buildings like the Monte Carlo had floors of rough cut lumber, with purposely built spaces between the boards, which sucked up spilled gold like water into sponges.

Music could be heard coming from most the places, with happy fiddles and banjos, and honky tonk pianos plunking out ragtime. However they were all competing with the hammering of a dozen men, building a wide boardwalk along the entire street.

As they plodded along in the crowd taking everything in, Elmer straggled behind a few yards, when suddenly he felt someone grab him by the arm and firmly pull him to a stop. He turned around to see a large rugged looking woman.

She quickly moved in beside him as if she were a close friend, then only inches from his ear she whispered "I can help you sweetheart." Then she gave him a stiff push in the direction she wanted him to go, with the momentum of his pack helping move him along.

"I can fix everything." she rasped trying to whisper again. Then she bit his ear and gave him an even bigger push to keep him moving.

Everything was happening fast, and Elmer was confused and starting to panic. "Henry!" he yelled looking for help.

He tried to plant his feet hard, but she was extremely strong and quickly adjusting, she pushed him on a few more yards. Suddenly he realized he was in front of her tent, and with no help in sight.

She looked to be in her mid-thirties, and was a few inches taller than Elmer and very sturdy. She wasn't very attractive either. Along with her rugged features, she had both a glass eye and some missing teeth.

"I gotta go!" protested Elmer, while turning to get away.

She quickly put a hand in the middle of his chest, then practically ordering him inside said "Let's talk." then violently shoved him over backwards into her tent.

Now Elmer really panicked. He rolled over as quickly as he could with his heavy pack on, and had crawled most the way back out when she got a hold of his legs. He fought for all he was worth to get free, until finally running out of breath, when she began dragging him back inside like a giant spider.

Now Elmer was looking to anyone for help, and got the attention of a man walking across the street. "Hey Mister! Help me!" he begged.

The man saw what was going on, and laughing loudly he squatted down in front of Elmer and asked "Would you like a hand kid?"

"Please!" replied Elmer "She's like a vice!"

The man laughed again, then grabbing on to him, pulled hard back forcing the woman to let go. Elmer quickly got up and hurried to move away from her tent.

"I'm Elmer." he said to the stranger, "Thanks a lot for helping me."

Just then the woman stuck her head back out of the tent and yelled to Elmer "Aw, come back baby! I don't care about your face!"

"That woman's dangerous!" insisted Elmer.

"She's been there for two days." answered the stranger. Then he said "I'm Tex. Tex Rickard" and he shook hands with Elmer, while trying not to get too much mud on himself. Elmer was nearly covered from head to toe now. "They call her 'The Siren.'" added Tex, "And look, she's camped right in the middle of the street. There's been a lot a complaint's about her."

"Yea, well they can add mine to the list." replied Elmer.

"They say she has a silver tongue," said Tex, "and if that doesn't work she'll prostitute herself, and as a last resort, she simply overpowers and robs you."

"That doesn't surprise me." said Elmer, "She's like wrestling a bear."

Instead of wandering off through the crowd to look for Henry, Elmer thought it'd be wiser to just wait for Henry to come back. So he asked Rickard where he was from and if he'd come over the Chilkoot. Tex said that like his name implied he was from Texas, and used to be a sheriff, in fact a Texas Ranger, and that he'd come over the pass three years earlier in '95.

Elmer quickly realized that he must have some knowledge of the Klondike, and said that it'd sure help him out if he could tell him what he'd do if he was in his shoes. "You know." said Elmer, "Where would you look for gold? And where's everybody else going?"

Just as Tex began to answer Henry returned. He looked at Elmer with bewilderment and said, "Where'd you go to?" Then noticing he was covered with mud asked "And what happened to you?"

"I fell down." replied Elmer, "I'll tell ya about it later."

"Come on inside." laughed Rickard, "I'll draw you a bad map." Then he motioned them towards the Bank Saloon.

Once inside, they saw that even though it had the same rough board floor as the other saloons, it had very comfortable looking furniture and nice tables for playing cards. It also had a long bar with a lanky looking cowboy standing at the end. He was well dressed, and when they passed by him to sit at a table, Tex said "How do, Sam?"

The man was tall like Rickard but had a much thinner build. "Howdy Tex." he answered, "I bought some coffee today. Wanna try a cup?"

"Absolutely!" replied Tex, "I barely remember what it tastes like."

It'd been months since Dawson ran out of coffee.

"Sit down boys" invited Tex, as he picked up a paper and pencil from the bar. "I'll show you the road out of town, and where everyone else goes. But keep in mind, I'm not a prospector." Rickard then showed them on paper, the trail everyone used through the Klondike valley, following the river to where Bonanza Creek flowed in.

"Then everybody just follows it up." he said, "That's where the gold comes from. Not just Bonanza Creek though, there's lots of 'em. Eldorado, Hunker, Sulpher, Dominion, and over here's Bear Creek."

Tex drew a new line on the paper with each name he spoke. "Everywhere they found gold's been staked though. You have to find somewhere new."

"This'll help a lot." said Henry, and then asked "How do we stake a claim?"

"Boy, you guys are green!" answered Tex. Then as he explained both staking and panning, his friend Sam came back to the table with three cups of coffee.

"Not playin' cards tonight Sam?" asked Tex.

"Couple a guys over there wanna play. We're waitin' for Goldie."

Henry realized that three cups of coffee meant that two of them were for him and Elmer. He wanted to save what little money they had, so quickly told Sam "We don't really have any money."

Sam was already walking away towards the bar again, and just said "Yer with Tex."

They were curious how Tex knew Sam, and when Henry asked him he said "He's a gambler like me. He gave me a job when I was broke."

Then he went on to tell them "When I first came north I was depending on my partner, but he turned back on me on the Chilkoot. Don't blame him though, that pass almost killed us. But when I got down the river to Circle and ran out of money, Sam gave me a job dealing cards in his gambling joint. 'Silent Sam Bonnifield's Saloon and Gambling House'. He actually gave me the place when he moved up to Sixty Mile."

"You mean he gave you a saloon?" asked Elmer, not sure he'd heard him right.

"Yea, we were pretty good friends by then." answered Tex, "It was a good business too, The biggest saloon in Circle. But it instantly turned worthless when they found gold here. The place became a ghost town overnight and I couldn't sell it for anything. So I just gave it to two guys sitting there having a drink, and joined the rush to get here."

When Rickard left Circle, because of the goldrush sled dogs cost more than anyone could afford. So at -40 and -50 below, he dragged his own sleigh 220 miles up the Yukon River. Once he arrived in the Klondike he did very well, buying two claims on Bonanza, and then re-selling them for a $60,000 profit. With that he built the Northern Saloon on Front Street.

"Then my luck at the tables took a turn for the worse." he said, "Cards dried up and I lost it all." Then after taking a sip of his coffee he added "Now I'm a dealer at the Monte Carlo."

"Swiftwater Bill's?" said Elmer, "We know him."

"Yup. Swiftwater Bill's." aswered Tex, "Now there's a guy that can walk between the raindrops."

They were nearly finished their coffee when Tex said "Well, there's Goldie. If you boys'll excuse me, I'm gonna get in on this game for awhile."

"Where?" said Elmer, "I don't see her."

Tex laughed and said "That's him over there, Louis 'Goldie' Golden. He's a proffesional gambler too. Has a regular game with Sam. For pretty high stakes too."

Henry and Elmer thanked Tex for his help, and Sam for his coffee, and then headed off to a nearby boarding house that Rickard told them about. On the way there, Elmer finally told Henry about the awful man who'd tripped him in the mud and tried to rob him, and then how with Rickard's help, they ran him off.

When they arrived at the boarding house they found out it was going to cost $10 each for them to sleep. But after they told the manager they only had $10, he didn't seem to want the money to leave.

After thinking about it for a minute, he said that the place was practically empty because all his regulars were still off mining. So for $5 each he'd let them sleep until every other bed was full, then they were out. They were dead on their feet, so handed over their money and were led to a couple of bunks inside. It was a large room where about sixty beds were crammed into a space where thirty should have been.

It wasn't dark out, and they could hear all the hammering and sawing coming from outside. But it didn't matter. They flopped down on the beds and were asleep.

A little over six hours later the manager was waking them up and telling them to get out. As they stood up and stretched, they noticed the place was now completely full of snoring men.

"Look Henry." said Elmer, "Look what they're doing."

As they looked around the room, they saw that some of the men were jiggling or waggling their arms about, while completely sound a sleep. Others just lay there wiggling or twitching their fingers, but even that looked pretty strange. Before they were out of the room, Elmer asked the manager "Why are they doin' that?"

The man watched their behavior himself for a moment, then looked at Elmer and said matter-of-factly, "They're panning for gold."

Elmer, still half asleep, stared back at the manager for a second and replied "I think something bit me."

The man just walked away saying "Only one?"

Soon they were standing out in the sunshine again, getting ready to head out to Bonanza Creek and start their prospecting careers. Not far from them was a group of men having a conversation, and they overheard one of them say "The Cheese Sandwich Mine. It's laid in there between bedrock and the gravel like a slab of cheese!" Then another said "I know for sure that three Scotts up on Eldorado are gettin' twelve ounces to the pan."

It was very encouraging talk. Twelve ounces a pan was a forune. But they heard some discouraging talk too. Some of them were complaining that all the good ground was already staked. Undeterred, they left to follow Tex Rickard's map to the goldfields.

Walking by the waterfront, what they saw was unbelievable now. Supplies were stacked absolutely everywhere, and all along the shoreline there were boats, tied to boats, tied to more boats.

Then they saw another unique vessel arrive. Somehow a man named Cal Miller had conquered the Pass, the winter, and the Yukon River, with a milk cow, when few other animals had survived at all. Now he was floating into Dawson with the cow standing in the middle of his boat chewing its cud. A memorable enough sight, that from then on in Dawson the man was referred to as 'Cow' Miller.

More boats were arriving behind Miller too. In fact with no darkness or night at all now, the boats never stopped, and the population of Dawson was exploding with the people pouring in from up river. Boats were beginning to arrive from downstream as well. The big riverboats however, had to wait in the ocean until the ice completely cleared the river, and wouldn't be arriving for another couple of weeks.

As Henry and Elmer stumbled through the mud passed the Bank Saloon, they heard Tex yell to them. When they'd made their way over to him he said "I found a couple of guides for ya. Frank and Joe here are heading out to Swiftwater Bill's claim on business." Then he said "Frank here's The Champ."

Rickard introduced him as Frank Slavin 'the Heavy Weight Boxing Champion of the British Empire'.

"I coulda been World Champ too." added Slavin.

"And this is Joe Boyle his sparring partner, and bouncer at the Monte Carlo." said Tex, "Frank helps him out sometimes."

Henry thought how Swiftwater Bill had sure hired men capable of dealing with his tough clientele. These were two more huge guys, as tall as Tex and Sam Bonnifield but much wider.

Henry and Elmer shook hands with the two sets of giant paws, and then the four of them struck off for the gold fields.

It was warm and sunny as they wound their way up the Klondike River valley. They followed the river through a forest of spruce and pine trees, broken up occasionally by meadows and stands of poplar and aspen. Boyle and Slavin talked to each other much of the way, appearing to be as good a buddies as Tex and Sam.

Eventually they reached the tributary that was Bonanza Creek, and to Henry and Elmer it looked like any other stream. But as they began to follow it into the small mountains, their stomachs began knotting up with excitement. Not only could the very land they were walking on be hiding untold riches, but to a world hungry for gold, the valley ahead had become almost sacred ground.

Upon entering the narrow valley, they began to see small log cabins dotted along the creek, obviously belonging to miners working their claims. As the four of them hiked further into the hills, a man caught up to them on a horse. It was a thin scraggly looking beast, bearing a man with the same appearance. He was also quite drunk.

"Howdy Dick." said Boyle, "Goin' back to the piggy bank?"

"Yea." the man answered, and then he slurred out "And some guys from Goldbottom wanna see."

Then Boyle asked "If yer gonna take a couple a pans, maybe these guys could watch. They could use some inspirin'."

"Sure Joe! You and Frank should come up too, have a drink."

"Like to Dick." replied Boyle, "But we got business and we're on the clock."

After Dick rode on ahead, Joe filled Henry and Elmer in about Dick Lowe. He'd been a mule skinner working for the government when they surveyed all the new claims. Then when they found there was a small fraction of unstaked ground where

Bonanza and Eldorado creek met, no one wanted it because of its size. Finally Lowe decided to stake it. He spent the next few months shafting to bedrock, but didn't find a single speck. Discouraged, he tried to sell the claim for $900, but with no takers.

Finally he decided to try one more time, and struck gold richer than anyone had ever seen, or heard of. He'd been drunk ever since, and just seemed to come out to his claim once in awhile to replenish his gold supply. He had a penchant for gambling and the ladies, and spent most of his time in the casinos and dancehalls. He'd also bring anyone and everyone to his claim, to show off how rich it was.

Suddenly Boyle and Slavin stopped walking. "Well good luck boys." said Joe, "Keep your wits about ya. Up here a guy can get roughed up pretty fast."

"Oh I see." said Henry, "This is Swiftwater Bill's claim."

"Yup. Thirteen Below." replied Joe.

"What's thirteen below?" asked Henry.

"On each creek, the first claim staked is called the Discovery Claim." he explained, "Then the first one below it is called One Below, and the fourth one above it is called Four Above, and like that." He finished by saying that Dick Lowe's claim would be easy to find, that it was right beside the trail. So they continued on up the valley alone.

When Henry and Elmer got there, Lowe was standing in front of his cabin with three other men. They walked over and introduced themselves, and after talking a few minutes, they watched Lowe pick up a pan and shovel. A few yards away was his shaft to bedrock, and beside it a pile of dirt from the bottom part of the hole. He stabbed the shovel into it and heaped the pan with gravel, then carried it over to the creek to be washed. Everyone peered down to watch him slosh the water back and forth in the pan, and it seemed to Henry and Elmer that he was being much too reckless.

But Lowe looked up smiling and said "Hang on to yer drawers boys!"

A few seconds later the pan was only half full of the washed gravel, and he shook it back and forth a few times to scrape off a couple more inches with his fingers. Then Dick tilted it slightly, and with a single strong swirl of the water all the visible dirt moved away showing nothing but yellow. Lowe quickly poured the water out, then drug his fingers through the pan leaving deep yellow trenches behind. It was all gold, and they were all stunned! "Sheeeesh! Look at that!" said Henry. It was spectacular!

Finally one of the other men asked "How much do you think is there?"

"I don't know," answered Lowe, "fifty-sixty ounces."

They all stood mesmerized as Lowe pushed his hand around in the golden heap, exposing nuggets, bigger nuggets, kernels and flakes, and all lying on a thick bed of dust. Actually there were many claims that could produce pans like this, but occasionally Lowe would get seventy or even eighty ounces.

When Henry and Elmer left Lowe's claim they were still jarred by what they'd seen, and for awhile hiked up the trail without forming any plan at all. They were having trouble thinking.

Eventually they decided that since they were between the Klondike and Yukon rivers, they'd head south. That way when it was it was time to come back, the rivers would funnel them back towards Dawson and they wouldn't get lost.

They also planned to travel far enough, that they'd distance themselves from all the other prospectors, and all the well trampled creeks.

So they walked down the valleys making their way southward, and when the valley they were in would veer off in a different direction, they'd climb over the hill and down into the next. Each valley would contain a small river or creek, which they'd always try panning, but each time only finding a few specks. Also each time, it felt like they'd freeze their fingers right off in the frigid water.

The heat wave was back on them again, sending the midday temperatures up to near a hundred degrees. It made it more difficult to travel and work at that time of day, but with the continuous daylight they began to ignore time, and simply slept when they were tired. In fact without darkness, dead tired was the only way they could sleep.

They'd walked for nearly three days before trying a large creek where they found a lot of specks in the pan. It wasn't enough to make a living, but it was worth exploring further. So they followed the creek upstream panning occasionally as they went, but with only slightly better results.

Finally in a fast moving part of the creek, the pan showed much better, with many specks and a few small flakes. They were encouraged by the findings, and thought it might get even better further up the creek. But almost as soon as they started they ran into the back of a beaver dam. It was about five feet high and not very wide, but they still had trouble getting around it.

They had to fight their way through thick bush for awhile, but when they got back to the water above the dam, they found themselves standing on the grassy bank of a large scenic beaver pond.

They stared at it for a few minutes before leaving to pan their way up the creek, but after some time, when none of their showings were as promising as below the dam, they decided to move back down and test it further.

"We have to dig to bedrock," said Henry, "that's where the gold's supposed to be." Then he took their pick and began digging a hole.

They took turns picking and shoveling while the other panned the results, until picking at what sounded like solid rock, Elmer said "I think we hit bottom."

Henry quickly took a pan hoping for better showings, but soon found it was no better than the others they'd taken.

"Maybe let's try the other side of the creek." suggested Elmer.

Henry agreed, and sometime later announced that he too had hit bedrock. A pan from the bottom of their new hole showed to be the best one yet, but it still wasn't good enough, and they couldn't go any deeper.

When Elmer hit bedrock in a third dig, Henry became suspicious. He scraped the bottom of each hole, and noticing they were all exactly the same depth said "This isn't bedrock, its frozen!"

They'd discovered permafrost.

Tex Rickard had told them how to melt their way down by building fires, but it was cold ugly work, and they hadn't panned enough to make it worthwhile.

A little discouraged, they decided to get some much needed sleep before figuring out what to do next. There was no flat ground where they were working, so they took everything up and set it down by the edge of the beaver pond.

They sat down quietly on their packs for awhile, and watched as the beavers swam around not far in front of them. The animals seemed to be curious and appeared to be checking them out as well.

After resting a bit, they cooked and ate some bannock, then smeared black ash on their faces again to protect from sunburn.

Then they took their blankets a few yards back from the water, and lay down on the grass to sleep.

They woke up hours later dumbfounded. Water was lapping at their feet, the pond was a lot bigger, and their packs were gone!

The beavers wern't the dumb critters they thought they were, and had simply build their dam a little higher to flood out their unwanted visitors. Elmer jumped up, and splashing up to the previous shoreline, stared at the dam for a moment and yelled "Oh no!" Their packs had been chewed to pieces and strategically stuffed into the dam along with their contents. "The little buggers chewed it all up!" he yelled back to Henry. Even their axe and shovel handles had been gnawed off and inserted into the structure.

"We're finished." said Henry, "We can't do anything now. And not only that, we're three days from Dawson without any food."

Elmer was still trying to figure out their true situation, when he said "At least we don't have any packs to carry now."

"Yea," replied Henry, "but it's gonna be a rough trip back anyway."

There really was nothing they could do but start walking back. So finally Elmer said "Well ...I guess we might as well get started."

"This could be embarrassing." suggested Henry as they walked along, "I mean we can't exactly tell people we were attacked by grizzlies."

"Which embarrassment do you mean?" replied Elmer, "Failing in three days, or getting whipped by a bunch of rodents."

After they'd walked for two days and it felt like they were starving to death, they ran across a porcupine. Henry still had matches and his pocket knife, so they quickly reasoned that they could cook and eat parts of the prickly beast on sticks over a fire.

They'd caught it out in the open, but as they searched for something to club it with, the porcupine noticed his peril and waddled directly towards thicker brush.

Elmer quickly found a suitable stick, but before he could hit the animal with it, it pushed its way even deeper into the willows. He hurried in after it, but the further in he went the thicker it got, until finally he couldn't swing his club at all, or even keep up with the animal. "I can't even move in here!" he yelled back to Henry, "These things are smart too!"

Before long Elmer emerged from the willows again, still without anything to eat. Once again they'd been beaten by a giant rodent.

Then suddenly Henry shouted "Look over here Elmer!" He'd found a patch of low bush cranberries and last years mossberries growing on the ground. They weren't as filling as porcupine, but they ate until their mouths were stained red and purple anyway.

They had no choice but to resume their long trek back towards town, and after travelling for almost another full day, they walked into Dawson down Front Street, carrying just two blankets and a frying pan.

It'd been less than a week since they left Dawson, but it had changed a lot since they left. The wooden boardwalks down Front Street were all finished, with the crews now building down the side streets. And the walkways were much wider and proper than the ones back in Skagway. But even so, they were so crowded with people that it was a tough call whether to fight the crowd on the boardwalk, or the mud in the street.

Most of the stampeders from Bennett were in Dawson now. So the number of boats arriving was down to a trickle, only about a half dozen an hour, and with the population of Dawson swollen to about thirty thousand, it had quickly become Dawson City.

A great many businesses had sprung up while they were gone, both on Front Street and down the side streets. Most of them were tent establishments, advertising everything from barbers, dentists, and newspapers, to banks, lawyers, and restaurants. One of them was Eric Hegg. His sign read "E.A. Hegg-Photographic Studio".

Wooden buildings were also going up all over the place, and many were of the rough lumber type. But some were of much finer materials, as numerous casinos and dancehalls were replacing their original tent structures, with large stylish buildings with extravagant interiors to draw in customers. Dawson was changing by the hour.

Belinda had moved her tent to a lot she'd purchased, and now had men working for her fulltime. They were building cabins from the lumber she'd salvaged from the boats, and she was selling them for $1,000 each as soon as they were finished.

Sam Steele had also arrived in Dawson, and began establishing the law immediately. The first thing he did was move 'The Siren' from the middle of the street. And because he'd be the law until the courts and a judge arrived, he called a meeting of all the casino, saloon, and dancehall owners, plus representatives from all the other major business. Everyone knew he was fair, but also a stickler for the law, so they were quite apprehensive as to what he was going to say.

Steele told them that though he was going to enforce the law, he could also see the reality of the situation. Gambling, prostitution, and the sale of alcohol was all illegal in the Yukon, but he said that he and his Mounties would turn a blind eye to the pleasures of the flesh, but only with a few iron-clad conditions.

The owners had no choice. Just being allowed to stay open was a bonus.

He told them that any violent crime, or any type of stealing, wouldn't be tolerated at all. Especially in the drinking and gambling establishments. And if any of them were caught cheating their customers, they'd be jailed, and everyone else closed down permanently. No second chances.

The Mounties compound had been established in plain view of the booming town, and out front for all to see were the prisoners working on a growing pile of wood. A $10 or $20 fine in the Klondike was almost laughable. Even $50 and $100 fines meant little to many. So more serious sentences tended to be two or three months working on the woodpile, or taking the first available riverboat back out of the Yukon. Either way, anyone convicted would pretty much miss out on the race to find gold.

Steele had also moved most of the obvious prostitutes when he moved 'the siren', and now they resided down a side street dubbed 'Paradise Alley', which was actually King Street.

Many signs designating the side streets had appeared while Henry and Elmer were out exploring. With names reflecting the Canadian and American roots of most the stampeders, like Queen, Princess, Broadway, and Wall Street.

Looking around, Henry noticed from the business signs that prices were still as high as ever. $4 for a meal, 75¢ a drink, and $1 for a dance. 'Cow' Miller's milk was for sale now too. $5 a mug.

They also noticed the many huskies running around. Not used nearly as much in the summertime, many often escaped to explore Dawson, and now Elmer was marveling at the ones with blue eyes, and others with a brown eye and blue eye both.

As Henry and Elmer continued down Front Street, they remembered that with Steele's arrival they had an obligation to tell him about Mace, and Soapy's cigar case. Besides, it was probably only a matter of time before they encountered Leadtooth again.

They talked it over and decided that though they'd have to tell Sam, they'd do it later some time. In their minds they weren't dodging the issue, they were just putting it off for awhile. After all, Sam was awful busy, and they had pressing problems of their own, like finding something to eat.

The streets were still very crowded, though not with the same mayhem of a week earlier, then suddenly appearing in front of them was about a hundred or so men gathered around a raised platform. They found themselves passing by the corner of it, where there was a set of stairs leading up the back. It was obviously a quickly built and somewhat shoddily constructed stage, erected to attract attention by one of the many new entertainment establishments, which were also being raised up as fast possible.

Suddenly a half a dozen dancehall girls appeared, and began climbing up the stairs to the stage. As many of the men, especially the drunk ones, began to cheer, the last girl to scale the stairs caught her dress on a protruding nail on the handrail. As she jerked repeatedly trying to free it, the flimsy handrail wobbled back and forth, pulling her dress tightly around her. She was very shapely and attractive, and when the light breeze caught her hair in the low sunlight, Henry was smitten. She was perfect. He stood dumbfounded and smiling, at least smiling as well as one could with an open mouth.

Elmer too had watched the girls climb onto the stage, and when he turned and saw Henry he said "What's a matter Henry? You look like a billygoat starin' at a new fence."

Henry tried to pull himself back together, but he couldn't take his eyes off her.

With the dress still wrapped tightly around her, a drunken man descending the stairs decided to strike a match off her rear end to light his cigar, and when she whirled around to smack his face, she hit the cigar straight on driving it into the back of his throat. "Light it now, ya walkin' vomit!" she growled, as she pushed him down the rest of the stairs.

All Henry heard was the voice of an angel, which seemed to sparkle when she talked. He couldn't believe how he was feeling towards the girl.

In the mean time, she tore her dress free again and caught up with the other dancers up on the platform. They'd just begun dancing to the music, when suddenly the whole end of the structure collapsed. The girls all fell, then slid down the platform and off the end into the mud, landing in a heap in front of Henry.

A roar of laughter went up, and Henry realized that if he thought fast, he could be the first to help her. Besides, he'd watched her land, and she might even be injured.

He quickly stepped forward to tell her that he could carry her anywhere she needed to go. But when she looked up and their eyes met, his mind turned to jelly, and he found himself picking her up before he'd said anything at all.

Rushing to regain his confidence he blurted out "I can carry you anywhere. I mean ... I can take you."

She seemed both confused at Henry, and in pain.

Henry couldn't believe the crap coming out of his mouth, but quickly reasoned that he could take her across the street, and set her on the boardwalk out of the mud.

Holding her in his arms now, he continued to deteriorate. "I see wood over there." he said, adding to the impression he was already making, then began stomping confidently through the mud.

It was an act. It almost felt like he had no bones at all.

Suddenly he heard a wagon coming, and at the same time heard the driver yell "Get out of the way!" The horses were running hard trying to pull the wagon through the mud without getting stuck. So Henry tried hard to hurry, but everything conspired against him. Stumbling forward in the slop with the now terrified girl, he barely escaped them from being run over.

But he ended up leaning too far forward, and as she rolled from his arms and landed face down in the quagmire, he crashed down on top of her, mashing her in even deeper.

A huge roar of laughter erupted from the watching crowd, and when Henry got off the poor girl, she came up spitting flames. "You're not helping!" she screamed, "You're making it worse! Now I'm stuck in the middle of the street!"

Henry took it as if she thought he was going to abandon her there. "Oh no!" he said scooping her up again "I'm not done yet." But he only carried her a few more yards, before his hungry, worn-out body collapsed again.

This time when she emerged from the mud berating him, Elmer too was standing beside them. All Henry's confidence was gone now, leaving him with nothing but a stupid smile.

Elmer had a look of utter disbelief on his face, and as she saw the remnants of his falcon scars, and the ash still smeared into their faces, and the purple stains from the berries they'd eaten, she suddenly quit yelling. Then in a much calmer, almost apologetic voice, she said to Henry "I'm sorry, are you simple-minded?"

"Oh my God!" thought Henry "She was serious! Even worse, she thought they were idiot partners!" He hurried to interject, "No! We're smart guys!" but it was hardly out of his mouth before he realized, that it was exactly what an idiot would say.

They were only a few yards from the boardwalk now, but before he could dig his hole any deeper, about a half dozen men arrived all offering to save her. Mostly from Henry. One of them picked her up and lifted her to another man on the boardwalk, then they all headed off in a herd looking for a doctor.

It was only then Henry noticed, that everyone around was still laughing so hard they could barely stand. He sat down on the boardwalk and watched as the girl went out of sight, then turned to Elmer and said "Well I think that went pretty well."

Elmer quickly realized that Henry was scrambled now, and not really sure what to do, he figured that maybe eating something could change his mood. They had to find something to eat soon anyway. So Elmer said "You wanna wait here for awhile Henry? I'm gonna try and rustle us up some grub."

Henry didn't even hear the first part of what Elmer said, and answered "Naw, I'll just wait here."

It was about twenty minutes later when Elmer returned. He'd found a kid working in one of the tent restaurants willing to stake them to a meal. His name was Sid, and he was only about seventeen but had a job as a waiter. He and Elmer had struck a deal, where by he'd give them a meal, but when they got any money or gold they had to keep him in mind, and pay him back double for his taking the chance of not seeing them again. Elmer also had to give him the dollar he'd gotten from Belinda for their boat. The deal was a little steep for them, but Sid was gambling on their character.

So soon they were wolfing down a heavy stew of potatoes, carrots, onions, garlic and moose meat. And it had flavour, lots of flavour, and it wasn't their own cooking either, which made it taste even better. It would have been a treat even if they had money. And when you consider the fact they were almost starving, had anyone tried to take their bowls away, they'd have certainly lost an arm.

Sid sat with them awhile, partly just to visit, but partly to gauge their character too. He was a pretty smart kid, and seemed to get along with Elmer quite well.

Before long they'd stuffed themselves to capacity, and were sitting back sipping on very good coffee. They were trying to determine their next move now, but it was slow going as Henry was still trying to forget his earlier disaster. He knew that when it came to the girl, his ship had not only sailed, but sank, and the best thing to do was to try and forget it.

They knew they still wanted to look for gold, but they needed money to re-supply themselves. So they had to get jobs. They shouldn't be too hard to find though, the place was booming.

"I wonder if we could get jobs working on someone elses claim." said Elmer.

Because of the one claim per person law, there were already hundreds of men owning extremely rich ground, and this was the season to mine as much as possible. Men were needed to work the claims, build roads, transport supplies, and work in sawmills, which were turning out to be gold mines in their own right. There was work everywhere. Such demand, that the usual dollar a day men earned, had ballooned up to $10 a day or more.

Sid was just getting up from the table to go back to work, and suggested "Maybe you guy's could work building the boardwalks around town. They tried to hire me yesterday, and I was only walking down the street."

After Sid had gone, Henry said "That won't work for us. For sure Leadtooth's in Dawson, and he's going to know about the map. I bet we'd run into him the first day building boardwalks."

They decided first to get some sleep, and then head back out to the claims on Bonanza. It was warm out, so with no money and no better place to go, they went down and layed in the tall grass by the river at the edge of town.

They woke some hours later to a large commotion far down the shoreline, directly in front of town. It was the first riverboat to arrive, and it looked as though half of Dawson had gone down to meet it. They too didn't want to miss out on anything, so hurried along the beach until they reached the cheering crowd.

All eyes were on a very small steamship called the 'Mae West'. Its only cargo was sixteen barrels of whiskey, which would be selling for $1 a glass within an hour of the boat landing. It had spent the winter trapped in the ice just a few hundred miles downstream, so the citizens of Dawson already knew of its precious cargo, and now nearly seven thousand people lined the shore to greet the tiny ship.

Henry and Elmer could see a few familiar faces in the mass of people. Swiftwater Bill was easy to spot, and they also saw Tex Rickard and Sam Bonnifield in the crowd. In fact all the saloon owners were present, and eager to bid on the valuable barrels onboard.

Frank Slavin and Joe Boyle were also in the middle of it all, not far from Swiftwater Bill. At second glance, they noticed that Bill had a young attractive dancehall girl on his arm.

They saw another face too. It was Augustus Mack. So he too had obviously made it back to the Klondike.

Most the crowd however, had gone down to the river solely to greet the first riverboat of the season. It was a very big deal, after talking about it for the entire winter.

After awhile the crowd began to dissipate, and Henry and Elmer began their trek out to the claims on Bonanza and Eldorado Creeks. Passing by the edge of town, they heared Belinda yell to them "Hey guys! Where you off to?" She'd noticed they were heading out of town without packs on their backs, and were empty handed.

She'd started yet another business. A rough lumber restaurant that appeared extremely busy. "She's doing something different every time we see her." said Henry.

As they walked towards her, Elmer added "Maybe we should hitch our wagon to Belinda's." Before Henry could answer they'd reached the restaurant, and Belinda asked them again where they were off to.

"We're heading out to the creeks." answered Henry, "We had a bit a bad luck, so we're gonna need jobs for awhile." He didn't want her to know about their embarrassing loss to the beavers.

"I need guys." she said immediately, "Work for me!"

"We can't." replied Henry, "We'd like to, but we kinda want to stay out a Dawson for awhile."

"That shouldn't be a problem." she said, and went on to tell them of a plan she had. She'd decided to build a store out on the creeks, roughly where Bonanza and Eldorado met.

Many of the business owners in Dawson had gotten wind of her plan, and were openly ridiculing her. Saying that Dawson City was where the people were, and where the riverboats would be landing, and so the obvious place to do business. However Belinda reasoned, that though the people and cargo were arriving in Dawson, the gold was coming from the creeks. In fact she'd already begun hauling building materials out to the fork of Bonanza and Eldorado. "I need men to move supplies out there." she said, "You'd rarely have to go into town."

"That would suit us just fine." answered Henry. And so they began working for Belinda.

Their first job, was to go straight back into Dawson. Belinda had bought an old mule named 'Gary' to help move her supplies out to the creeks, and it had a habit of going missing. The thing was, Gary had a drinking problem. Early on, for some reason the old mule had walked into a saloon and pushed its way up to the bar. It appeared as if it wanted a drink, so with the crowded establishment laughing loudly, the bartender obliged and gave Gary a drink. Then just as if someone had taught him, the mule took the glass in his lips and threw back his head and the drink both, and then stood as if waiting for another. So with the crowd now roaring with laughter, the bartender again obliged, and then again, and soon everyone was buying drinks for Gary.

Some hours later Belinda found Gary passed out in an alley, and it took her some time to prod him back to her camp, only to find he was much too hungover to work. This angered her enough, that she stomped back to the saloon and berated the bartender in front of his customers, until he promised not to get Gary drunk anymore.

She thought the problem had been solved, but found that the very next night, Gary's expertise at escaping had gotten him free again, and she found him leaning against the Monte Carlo with whiskey on his breath.

Again she went to the saloon to confront the bartender, but the man swore that when Gary came in again, he didn't give him anything to drink, until he finally relented and gave him just one, and then one more to lure him outside to get rid of him.

"You know how hard it is to move a mule when he doesn't wanna go." said the bartender.

Belinda realized he was telling the truth, when some of the patrons said that they'd seen Gary the night before, but drinking in a different establishment.

It wasn't long before she'd torn strips off Gary's new supplier, and had the mule back home again.

Gary had learned how to push over, break down, chew through, and unlatch whatever it took to escape, and now he'd gone missing again. And Belinda wanted Henry and Elmer to go find and retrieve him. So they soon found themselves venturing back into Dawson again, trying to find out where Gary ended up.

One of the first places they came to look was the Monte Carlo. They entered the building, to find both business and construction going on at the same time. Swiftwater Bill was talking to a group of dancehall girls, and Tex Rickard was dealing cards at one of the tables. Honky tonk piano music filled the air, and when they looked to its source, saw Wilson Mizner banging away at the keys.

They walked over to him, and when the song ended they said their greetings, then asked him how he'd been doing since he got to Dawson.

He said he was doing great, that he both worked and gambled at the Monte Carlo now, and that his brother Edgar had also gotten a job, working for the Alaska Commercial Company.

When they asked him about Belinda's mule, he said it had indeed been there, but after one drink had been kicked out, so as not to raise the ire of Belinda.

They said good-bye to Wilson, and then on their way out the door they ran into Joe Boyle and Slavin on their way in. "Howdy fella's." greeted Joe, "How'd your prospectin' trip go?"

"Not well." answered Henry, "We didn't find much."

"You weren't gone long." replied Joe, "What happened?"

There was no way he was going to tell them about the beavers. "Everywhere we looked we hit permafrost." explained Henry, "And we didn't find enough gold to wanna start diggin' through that stuff."

"Yea, you need pretty good showings for that." answered Boyle. Then he asked "So have you given up on prospectin', or you gonna try again?"

"We'll be going back out." said Henry, "But we gotta gather some money first, so right now we're working for pay." Then he asked them if they'd seen Belinda's mule. Joe said they hadn't, but he wished them good luck in their search.

Their next stop was Silent Sam's Bank Saloon. Sam was deeply engrossed in what appeared to be a high stakes poker game, so they talked to the bartender instead. He confirmed that the mule had been there hours earlier, but it was the same story. He'd been encouraged to leave after a single drink.

When they left Henry said "I hope we find that mule soon. I mean, this can't be a good idea. How far away could Leadtooth really be?"

"I'm sure we'll find him around the next corner." replied Elmer sarcastically.

"Which one?" said Henry, "Gary or Leadtooth?"

"Both." answered Elmer.

They rounded the next corner to actually find Gary standing in front of them, with all four legs spread wide apart.

"Wow, that was easy." said Elmer, as they walked up and slipped the rope around the mule's neck. Then to their surprise, even though Gary was staggering a bit, he began following along as if he wanted to come with them.

As they trudged through the streets with Gary in tow, they kept their eyes open for Leadtooth. Then coming towards them on the boardwalk, they saw an incredibly attractive woman. In fact, most the men on the street were stopping what they were doing to stare as she past. It was Kate Rockwell, and she wasn't wearing men's clothes anymore. In a stark contrast to everyone else, she had on a bright yellow dress, with a matching hat and parasol.

"Hi Kate." said Elmer as she passed.

When she saw them she immediately stopped and turned to talk. "Henry, Elmer, How are things going for you?"

They were flattered she even remembered their names. "We're still alive and hoping to do better." answered Henry.

It seemed as though she was glad to see familiar faces.

"How's it going for you Kate?" asked Elmer. Then he added what he was thinking, by saying "You sure look great."

"Thank you Elmer." she answered with a smile, "I'm doing quite well."

She said she'd found work as soon as she arrived in Dawson, and both Henry and Elmer thought "What a surprise."

"I'm performing at the Opera House." she said, "But other places want to hire me too."

She said she was just on her way to work, and as she wished them luck and began to leave, Henry called out, "Break a leg, Kate."

She smiled back at them and left, then Elmer quickly turned to Henry and said, "Why'd you say that for?"

"That's what you're supposed to say." replied Henry.

Elmer still looked sceptical.

"Really," added Henry, "That's what you say."

"She sure is fun to talk to." said Elmer.

They managed to lead Gary back to Belinda's without incident, though they did see Steele and a couple of his Mounties straightening out some kind of altercation.

Then after a cup of coffee, Belinda began helping them load up Gary for the trip out to the creeks. But before they were even half done, it became obvious that the mule was too sick to work again.

"I guess it's just you guys this time fellas." said Belinda.

So they loaded themselves up with as much as they could carry. Henry with saws, axes, hammers, and other tools Belinda had purchased, and Elmer with a keg of nails. And so began their new job as pack animals.

For the next week they carried load after load out to the spot Belinda had selected. A place where Bonanza and Eldorado, the two most gold-laden creeks in the Klondike conjoined. This would put her square in the middle of the richest claims in the entire Yukon.

During this time Henry and Elmer stayed completely out of Dawson, in an effort to both duck Leadtooth and to save money. An unexpected benefit was a much quieter and sounder sleep, at least as much as could be expected without any darkness.

Even though they stayed out of town, news traveled to them anyway, and they learned that a couple more small riverboats that had spent the winter frozen in ice downriver from the Mae West had arrived. Each one cause for another celebration.

They were also hearing news of Kate. Her singing and dancing, and all-round attractiveness was completely charming the population of Dawson, causing a great number of men to become quite enamoured with her. With her personality, how could they not?

There was also a lot of talk circulating about Edgar Mizner. The company he worked for had a policy of grubstaking prospectors for an equal share of any gold they discovered. But Edgar had an extremely strict policy, hurting many men that even had excellent claims in the process. Now some of them could barely feed themselves as they worked their way down to bedrock. This action, along with his arrogant nature, was quickly turning Edgar into a hated man.

Then another morning came when Henry and Elmer were about to travel out to the creeks, when Belinda told them Gary was missing. Most days he'd been carrying loads of lumber along with them. But just like many of the men in the Klondike, Gary preferred the high life of Dawson. Bartenders weren't getting him drunk anymore, but he'd learned to be just pushy and stubborn enough, to get one or two drinks from each one of them, and then move on, travelling from bar to bar.

Henry offered to go in alone to find Gary, but Elmer knew, and rightly so, that if they were going to run into Leadtooth, it'd be better if they met him as a team. So they decided to start looking for the mule where they'd found him the last time, and upon reaching the centre of town, were surprised to see that not only were the muddy streets drying into firm ground again, but much of Dawson was becoming a city of wooden buildings. It was still surrounded by a sea of tents, but the town was continuing to change at an incredible pace.

"Hey! There's Swiftwater Bill." said Elmer, pointing across the street. It was Bill alright. He was strolling along the boardwalk with a very pretty girl on his arm. Her name was "Gussie Lamore", and she was one of the dancehall girls Bill had brought over the pass with him.

She was nineteen years old, and was already well known in town as "the Little Nugget". Bill's intention was to marry her as he'd fallen in love, and now he was showing her off to the whole population.

Henry's attention was suddenly drawn to a wagon parked in front of a nearby store. He looked curiously at the woman sitting on the board seat. Then just as a man climbed up to take the reins, she turned her head to talk to him and Henry could see her face clearly. "I knew it!" he exclaimed. It was the same girl he'd fallen head over heels for, in the now somewhat famous mud incident. The man snapped the reins a couple of times and they began leaving.

Henry quickly turned to Elmer and said, "I gotta see where she goes."

"Looks like she already has a guy." suggested Elmer, worried about a repeat of the embarrassing scene from a week earlier.

"I just wanna see where she goes." said Henry again, as his feet were leaving anyway.

Elmer realized the futility of trying to stop him. "You go ahead." he said, "I'll find Gary...I'll meet you back at Belinda's!" he yelled, as Henry was already some distance away.

Henry found himself following after the wagon as it made its way down Front Street, and by the time they reached the edge of town, he was beginning to feel like an idiot again. Girl or not, it wasn't a feeling he could stand for very long, so he stopped following and just watched as the girl began to leave Dawson.

But she didn't! The wagon suddenly turned off the road and started through a meadow towards the river. Henry knew where they were going. It was a place just upstream from Dawson, where catwalks were built out on the river to anchor fish traps.

It was all hidden by a thick grove of poplar trees. So Henry moved to where he could see clearly down to the river, and watched as the wagon stopped in front of a large wall tent. Then a man walked up and took the girl in his arms as if to carry her. "Lucky bugger" Henry mumbled to himself.

Then the man set her down and handed her a couple of crudely made crutches. Now Henry could see that she really had been hurt when the stage collapsed, and he badly wanted to apologize to her for the entire mud incident.

He also wanted to show her that he wasn't a lunatic, but he knew that to even get her to listen to him would be a tricky dance indeed. She was surrounded by at least a half dozen men, so he certainly couldn't apologize now.

So he decided to return tomorrow and see if he could catch her alone. It'd also give him time to think. He was concerned about once again losing the ability to string words together and make sentences.

Across town, Elmer had been searching the side and back streets for Gary, eventually ending up in the Paradise Alley section of King Street. There he was delayed for some time by a young dancehall girl named Belle Mitchell, as she worked hard to seduce him while holding on to him continuously, and persistently talking the sweet talk.

When he finally escaped Belle, he couldn't help thinking how she was a little like the siren, only a smaller, younger, prettier version.

When he resumed his search, he hadn't walked far before he found Gary again. The mule was down a narrow alley laying on his side, and at first looked as if he might be dead. But as Elmer got closer, he realized that not only was Gary still breathing, he was snoring quite loudly.

He slipped the rope around Gary's neck, and pulled on the rope to lift the mule's head up, but once up, Gary saw who it was and pulled back hard to lay his head down again, nearly yanking Elmer down on top of him.

The second time Elmer pulled, Gary was ready for it and nothing happened. The mule wasn't near death that was for sure.

So Elmer bent over to shorten his grip on the rope to pull even harder, when "Whack!" he felt a stunning blow to the side of his face, and a wave of pain rush across his head as he tumbled to the ground! He knew without looking it was Leadtooth, and as he hurried to get back up, he received another devastating blow! Rolling across the ground but still conscious, Elmer struggled to get to his feet again, just in time for Leadtooth to attack him again!

This time they both fell to the ground, with Leadtooth driving Elmer's face into the dirt. His face skidded a few feet before stopping, when the more powerful thug growled, "I outta make you eat a ton a this dirt!" Then he pulled Elmer back to his feet and ramming him up against one of the wood buildings, put a large knife to his throat and said, "I'm only gonna ask once! Where's the map?"

Elmer felt some blood run down his forehead, and had dirt in one of his eyes blurring his vision. By now he figured Leadtooth was going to kill him anyway, and answered defiantly, "It's in the silver case."

They both knew that wasn't the answer Leadtooth wanted to hear, and as he raised up the knife to finish him, Elmer suddenly blurted out "Mace took it!"

"And where's Mace now?" asked Leadtooth sarcastically.

"I don't know! He took it from us back on the river." answered Elmer.

"And then what?" said the thug.

"I don't know!" answered Elmer again, "He sunk our boat and left us stranded!"

It was a believable story to Leadtooth. After all, Mace had left him stranded too. "That ugly bastard!" he grumbled while trying to think.

"Yea, you're much prettier." mumbled Elmer.

That was it for Leadtooth, and he lunged forward trying to stab Elmer in the neck. But Elmer quickly moved his head to the side while trying to grab the arm holding the knife. He missed, but deflected the knife so it instead cut into his shoulder. Leadtooth brought back the knife again, and this time Elmer knew he was done.

Suddenly a gun barrel appeared in Leadtooth's ear, and a loud voice said, "Freeze right there less you wanna hear a freight train through yer head!"

Elmer turned to see a blurry vision of a Mountie's scarlet tunic. Wiping the blood and dirt from his eyes, he saw that it was one of Steele's sergeants.

It was Belle Mitchell that had heard the commotion and summoned the nearby Mountie. His name was Sergeant Fury, and though the Mounties were known for rarely drawing their guns, Fury realized that he was dealing with a real animal in Leadtooth, and wasn't going to leave anything to chance. He forced Leadtooth to drop the knife, and keeping the revolver pointed at his head, blew on his whistle for assistance.

Help arrived almost immediately in the form of Steele and two of his constables. Steele took one look at Elmer, and then Leadtooth, then said "Well, look who's here. One of Soapy's boys, lost in a whole other country." Then he asked Elmer, "What happened?"

"I was trying to fetch Belinda's mule when he attacked me from behind." explained Elmer.

Steele then turned back to Leadtooth, "I don't suppose you wanna tell us what yer up to?"

"I don't know nothin' about nothin'." he shot back angrily.

"Yea? Well this ain't Skagway." said Steele. "Here we have jobs for natural-born criminals that don't know nothin' about nothin'." Then to Elmer's delight, Steele said "'Till a judge gets here, I'm going to see to it you cut enough wood to heat Dawson for most a next winter." "Look at it this way," he added, as he gave the thug a big push towards the police compound, "at the end of it all, you get a free boat ride to a nice warm prison down south."

Elmer received many looks of astonishment as he led Gary back to Belinda's. In a strange way it looked as if he may have lost a fight with the mule. His face appeared to be a real mess again, but just as before when the falcon attacked him, it was mostly deep scratches and minor cuts.

He was in sight of Belinda's place, when he saw Henry coming from the other direction. Henry couldn't believe his eyes. He knew instantly what had happened, and his mood quickly descended to extreme guilt. He knew he should've stayed with Elmer.

Belinda too saw Elmer approaching, and quickly set out a chair for him at the back of her building. Henry immediately took the mule from his partner, saying "Damn, Elmer! It was Leadtooth wasn't it?"

"Yup. Caught me in an alley. But Steele's got him now." grinned Elmer.

Belinda grabbed him by the arm and sat him down on the chair, then began cleaning his wounds with water and a cloth. As she worked, Elmer told them everything that happened, except for the part about the map. He'd tell Henry about that later when they were alone.

"I shoulda been there." regretted Henry.

"Don't worry about it." said Elmer. "I lost a couple o' buttons, but I'll be okay."

Elmer's face didn't need any stitches, but his shoulder would need a few. So after Belinda finishing cleaning his face, she poured a drink into him and proceeded to sew his shoulder closed. It only took five stitches, and by the time she was done, Henry noticed that not only was Elmer in a much better mood than before his encounter with Leadtooth, but he too was beginning to feel uplifted, knowing that Soapy's thug was in Steele's hands.

They woke early the next morning to another sunny warm day, and after eating they loaded both Gary and themselves for another trip out to the creeks. Belinda then came over and lightened Elmer's load, knowing that he had to be ailing somewhat from his struggle the day before. Normally she was a fairly tough taskmaster to her employees, but it was becoming quite evident that she was more their friend than their boss.

Their spirits were still high as they began this trip, though every time they passed someone, Elmer stared at the ground so as not to have to answer questions about his face again.

When they arrived out at Bonanza and Belinda's growing pile of supplies, they were surprised to see that she already had men building a new store and restaurant out of them. And at the speed they were building, they were going to be finished in no time.

Their trip back was uneventful except for Gary locking up for awhile. 'Till they realized that he only wanted a drink of water, probably to aid his hangover.

Once they got back in Dawson, Henry wasted no time in cleaning up and putting Gary away. He was still thinking of catching the girl without a large crowd around her. So as Elmer waited for his supper, Henry hurried off towards the fish traps to where he'd seen her last.

When he arrived at the river, he saw that she was there alright, but so was another large group of men. He stopped in frustration again, then seeing an old man walking past, he decided to ask the old guy about the woman. "S'cuse me, mister," he said, lightly grabbing the man by the arm, "Do you know who that woman is over there?"

The old man looked at Henry, then started grinning, knowing exactly what he was thinking. "Sure kid" he said, "She's a wounded dancehall girl. She's mending clothes now, and minding the fishnets. Ya can't dance on a bad stick?" He added.

"I think I saw her before." lied Henry, trying to pretend she was just a fleeting curiosity.

"Ya, she sure is pretty." laughed the old man as they both looked back at her.

Then when the old man started to leave, Henry suddenly yelled to him "Wait! You don't happen to know what her name is do ya?"

"It's Rebecca." he answered as he continued walking way, adding "Good luck kid."

'What a great name!' thought Henry.

He stood watching her for awhile longer, before finally figuring maybe he could tear his shirt and then take it to her for repair. Of course he'd have to find a time when no one else was around, if that was possible.

By the time he began making his way back to Belinda's, he figured his plan just might work. Upon arriving he sat down and ate supper, and as Elmer watched him eat, he told him of his plan to approach her in the morning, before the other men came around.

Then Elmer spoke of his own immediate plan. "Let's go into Dawson." he said, "Have a look around."

"Good idea." answered Henry. It had been awhile since they could travel around without the fear of encountering Leadtooth, and it was still early in the evening.

As they made their way up Front Street, they could see that the near continuous party that was Dawson City, was just beginning to heat up. The cheerful atmosphere was infecting practically everyone.

In fact, during their entire walk-about they only encountered one angry person. Swiftwater Bill. His sweetheart Gussie Lamore had jilted him. Jilted him twice. First she'd promised to marry him if he brought her to the Klondike, which he had. Then he found out that she was already married to one "Emile Leglice". Bill then lavished her with a great many expensive gifts to win her over anyway, including giving her her weight in gold.

But then he'd woke that very morning to head to his favourite restaurant for breakfast, where he saw Gussie out with another man, eating her favourite meal of toast and eggs.

Enraged at the sight of her on another man's arm, Bill spent the rest of the day buying up every egg in Dawson, despite the fact that they were the most expensive item on every menu.

When Henry and Elmer saw him, they stood mingled with a large crowd of people on the street, all watching as Bill sat in the restaurant and was having the eggs fried up one at a time.

He sat with a stoic demeanour that was suppressing his obvious rage, and as each egg arrived at his table, he'd fling it through the open window to a pack of eager huskies waiting in the street. Barely any of them hit the ground.

After this event, Bill had a new title added to his name. He was dubbed "Swiftwater Bill – Knight of the Golden Omelette".

Henry and Elmer were working hard to save their money for prospecting again. But Dawson was becoming a very exciting and expensive place, especially in the evenings when it was very hard to resist. So soon after Bill ran out of eggs, they forced themselves to return to Belinda's, calling it a night.

Henry woke early the next morning to the sound of a steamboat whistle. Another small riverboat had inched its way up the Yukon, and it wasn't long before he realized that it could be a real blessing. Many of the citizens up early would probably go down to see what people and cargo it carried, as well as learn any news it may bring. It could distract men from heading for Rebecca's.

So he started off toward the fishnets immediately, heading straight across the road and down through the meadow. He was about half way there when he suddenly thought, "Damn! What if I start talking gibberish again?" He slowed his pace a little, but within a few minutes could see her through the trees. She was out on the catwalk. Alone!

"Okay! What's my plan?" he thought, as he slowed down even more. He didn't have one. "She already thinks I drink kerosene, and I gotta do better than last time."

Then he thought how he really couldn't do worse than last time. He also knew he couldn't dawdle all day thinking about it. Then he remembered what the old man had said about her sewing clothes, so he quickly tore the side of his shirt up almost a foot.

"Crap!" he instantly thought. He didn't have the necessary spare. "Okay, this is better." he reasoned, "Now it's an emergency."

The girl Rebecca was approaching the deep end of the catwalk, checking each net for fish as she went. As she peered into the last net, she saw a dark object moving about not yet caught in the webbing. So she bent over for a closer look, but couldn't really see much better. It looked like it could be lost cargo from some unfortunate vessel. Whatever it was, it was nearing the surface again, so she knelt down as close to the water as possible, getting ready to reach in and grab it.

When she plunged her arm in, the distortion of the water caused her to miss, and she only hit the object. When it turned over, the current pushed it quickly upwards again breaking through the surface. It was part of a gruesome corpse, and it lunged up towards her as if trying to give her a kiss!

She shot backwards trying to escape, but with her long blonde hair getting wrapped on the cadaver's extended arm! It then fell back under again taking her hair and head with it! She clung to the boards of the catwalk, but couldn't pull her head back out of the water!

She fought hard and eventually managed to pull up enough for a quick breath, but the river was strong and the corpse heavy, pulling her under again as she fought for her life!

Henry reached the other end of the catwalk, and before stepping on to it he looked up and saw her, then quickly looked away. "Darn it." he thought to himself, "She's washing her hair."

He knew he shouldn't look back, but she was so beautiful to him he couldn't help himself. Then taking another peek, he immediately realized something was wrong, and began running over the boards of the walk as fast as he could!

He got to her just as she came up for another breath, and could see she was entangled in something. He immediately grabbed on to her, but her head went back under again anyway. He quickly realized he'd have to pull whatever it was completely out of the water if he was to save her.

They both pulled against it until her head came out again, then with lightning quick reflex, Henry let go of her and plunged both arms deep into the water, and grabbing the remains with both hands, heaved up as hard as he could, pulling the corpse completely out of the water and onto the catwalk. Then suddenly realizing what he was hanging on to, he let go as fast as he possibly could.

Rebecca couldn't get away from it fast enough either, and took little time unravelling her hair from the human mess. Then after reeling backward a few feet herself, ended up on her hands and knees trying to get her breath back.

Henry too was kneeling on the catwalk trying to breathe, when he glanced over at the cadaver and noticed it was missing limbs and body parts, and how its shredded jacket was wrapped and knotted tightly around what was left. "Oh my god! It's

Mace!" he suddenly realized, and the bulge with the cigar case took away any doubt.

Henry had too much to think about. How did Mace get here? What did it mean? What about the map? He couldn't tell the girl. "Oh yea, and the girl."

He looked over at her still trying to regain her breath, and when she looked up he could tell she recognized him. "Its okay." he quickly assured her, "I'm not crazy."

He couldn't believe he said it calmly and actually sounded reasonable.

She still seemed a little unsure but said, "Even if you are crazy, believe me, I'm really glad to see you."

When she began to get to her feet, Henry saw her crutches lying on the walk. He quickly stepped over Mace and scooped one up, while she picked up the other. Then he helped her the rest of the way to her feet.

"I wonder what his story is?" she said, looking down at Mace.

Henry didn't know what to say. Too much had happened at once. The only thing he knew for sure, was that he couldn't get the map without her knowing about it. But then he thought, if he could involve her in things that might not be bad. In fact, that might not be bad at all.

The feeling he got when his hand briefly held hers to help her up, or when he had his arm around her waist just for a second to hand her the crutch, convinced him to go for broke.

"I think I might know that guy." he finally said, and bent down to untangle the jacket, working towards the silver case. When he got to it and removed it, he realized it left a telltale shape in the worn fabric, showing that something had been there. So he thought better of it, and took the tube with the map out, then placed the case back in the pocket.

"I have to show you something." he said, holding up the tube in front of her.

"I'm not sure what to think." she replied. "You don't seem dangerous."

"No, I'm not." answered Henry, "But that guy sure was." he added looking down at Mace. "I'll try and tell you the story before a crowd gathers down here."

He looked back toward the trail to see that no one was coming yet, then began to tell her the true story from the beginning, while at the same time helping her along the catwalk. By the time he was telling her about seeing Mace and Leadtooth on the island below the canyon, they'd made it to shore and were standing in front of a large tent.

She trusted Henry enough to ask him if he wanted a coffee and he immediately answered, "Yes, thank you." knowing he would've drunk cod liver oil, if that's what she was offering.

Then she walked into the tent. "Come on in." she said smiling back at him.

He couldn't believe it as he walked inside. His best hopes for the day had already been far surpassed.

"I'm Rebecca Wilson." she said, beginning to pour the coffee.

"Henry Browning." he quickly replied, then almost added a "Glad to meet you." but quickly reasoned that would bring up the mud incident, and he did not want to go there.

"Sit down." she said pointing to a table and chairs.

Henry sat down while looking around the place. Her large tent was divided, with her residence in the back, the kitchen, table and chairs in the middle, and a business counter near the front.

She noticed him looking around and said, "It's not really my place. I just rent it."

"I should probably finish the story about the map before people start showing up." said Henry.

"Yes." she agreed handing him the coffee. Then she sat down with him to listen, saying "Call me Becky." She knew too that they didn't have much time. Someone would surely show up before long.

Henry told her the rest of the story, and then they sat and studied the map together. Becky saw as Henry and Elmer had, that they could probably find the place on the map, if they could learn where Tombstone was. Henry also hastened to point out that Mace and Leadtooth were both gone now, and there wasn't likely any danger surrounding the map anymore.

She thought for a few seconds, then asked, "What's this Elmer like?"

He assured her that he was a good man, and that when she'd first met them, they were on the tail end of a very bad week.

"Someone's coming!" she suddenly said, and stood up for a better look. "It's Belle." she added.

"What should I do?" said Henry. It was the same Belle Mitchell that had tried to seduce Elmer.

Rebecca looked at Henry and said, "I'll send her for the Mounties. I'll meet her outside too, she doesn't need to know you're here."

Then she walked on her crutches out to meet Belle, and Henry heard her say, "Belle! I'm glad you're here. I need someone with two good legs." Then she told Belle about finding some poor stampeder in the nets.

Belle had kind of befriended and attached herself to Rebecca, partly because her injured foot made her too slow to escape. Belle's circle of friends had decreased drastically the previous winter, when in the cold of November she left a burning candle on a block of wood in her room, starting a great fire that burned up most of the wooden buildings in Dawson.

Rebecca finished explaining to Belle what she needed her to do, then Belle turned around and hurried back towards town. Rebecca then returned into the tent and sat down again. "I'll be partners in this with you," she said to Henry, "but with a couple of conditions."

"What are they?" he asked.

"I don't get around too well right now," she answered, "so I want to keep half the map."

"That's reasonable." replied Henry. "What's the other condition?"

"If we find out where Tombstone is, I go too, even if you have to carry me."

"That too is only fair." answered Henry, secretly relishing the very thought of it.

With that, she dug out a large pair of scissors, but before cutting the map, they got caught up again studying and theorizing on many of the map's markings.

Before they knew it the Mounties arrived with Belle. Steele wasn't with them, but they did bring along a couple of prisoners to do the dirty work. By the time Becky and Henry looked out to see, the prisoners had already been directed to the end of the catwalk to gather up Mace. So Henry hadn't seen that one of them was Leadtooth.

Then while one of the prisoners stopped short of the end to set down a stretcher and unravel a large canvas bag, Leadtooth continued to the end of the catwalk where he recognized the corpse and its jacket immediately. Squatting down beside it, in a low voice he said, "Lookin' good Mace, bin travellin' lately. So how'd stealin' our boat pan out for ya?" Then he saw the cigar case, and quickly shoved it into his own pocket, then flattened the bulge it made in Mace's jacket.

"What's that ya said?" replied the other prisoner.

"Nothing to you." snapped Leadtooth glaring back at him.

"Hey! What are you doin' there?" yelled the Mountie arriving behind. "I said not to touch nothin' 'till you were told!"

"Not a problem." said Leadtooth standing up again and stepping back. "This guy's a mess."

Back in front of the tent, Becky and Henry finished telling the other Mountie how they'd found the dead man's corpse, while Becky was checking the nets for fish. Then as the Mountie headed out on the catwalk, they went back in her tent where she and Henry quickly cut the map in half, then both folded and put away their part. They also agreed to do their best to learn the location of Tombstone.

Just as Henry finished explaining to Becky that he and Elmer were staying over at Belinda's camp, Belle Mitchell entered the tent. Becky then looked at Henry and said, "I better start sewing this pile of clothes. I still have to feed myself."

Then as Henry stood up she added, "I'll let you know if I hear anything."

"I will too of course." assured Henry.

Then as he was leaving the tent, she spoke again. "Henry," she said smiling, "I could sew that shirt for you next time you come."

"That'd be great Becky." he answered. He'd forgotten all about it.

Henry felt so good leaving her place, he didn't notice Leadtooth, or his murderous stare. But Leadtooth had noticed that Mace, Henry and the silver case had all been alone in the same place.

As Henry walked back through the poplar trees, he felt about as giddy as a grown man could. He couldn't believe how his morning had turned out. He'd completely redeemed himself for the mud incident. He'd saved her from drowning. He even got the map back. And not only that, he could make up reasons to talk to Becky whenever he wanted to. Even talk to her alone.

"What a day!" he thought as he took a big kick at an imaginary rock. "What a day!"

He arrived back at Belinda's to see Elmer sitting alone drinking coffee. He was seemingly deep in thought as he sat leaning back in his chair, with the fingers of both hands interlocked on top of his head.

"Does it seem harder to you to work for a living since we saw Dick Lowe's claim?" he asked.

"Frequently." answered Henry. "But I found something this morning that might make it a little easier." Then he pulled the cigar tube from his pocket and threw it to Elmer. "I'll bet you never thought you'd see that again." he added.

Elmer recognized it immediately. "What the...! How in the world did you get this?" He stared at Henry in complete bewilderment.

"I took it from our good friend Mace." answered Henry.

Elmer looked even more confused.

"That's right." added Henry, "He made it to the Klondike after all."

Henry went on to explain the entire morning, including completely redeeming himself for the mud incident. He also had to explain why there was only half a map in the tube, and how he had to cut a deal with "Becky".

After that he got sidetracked talking about her, finally saying, "You shoulda seen it Elmer. I was talkin', words came out, the words made sentences. It was a thing to behold."

"Ah, yes," replied Elmer pausing for a moment, "as opposed to our regular gushing of gibberish to the ladies." Then teasing sarcastically he said, "Your story is good sir. Yet I remain sceptical, in that I have not yet seen this animal."

Henry chuckled for a moment, knowing it was true.

Then Elmer changed the conversation to the next obvious subject. "Now we're gonna to have to find out where Tombstone is."

"Becky's gonna try and find out too." added Henry.

Elmer sat thinking for a couple of minutes, piecing together everything Henry had told him. "How did Mace get here?" he finally asked.

"I don't know." answered Henry. "But the cold water seemed to have preserved him pretty good. He was awful banged up though, and missing a lot of parts."

"Well, he did travel quite a ways." added Elmer. "He must a got caught up and pried loose once in a while too."

Over the next few days they asked almost everyone they knew about Tombstone, even questioning strangers if they could casually slip it into the conversation. But no one knew anything.

Also in a couple of days, Henry figured he'd waited the minimal amount of time to take his torn shirt back to Rebecca. But when he did, even though he went early not only was Belle there, but so was most of the torn shirt crowd. He did get a chance to ask her if she'd learned anything, but she'd had no better luck than they had. He figured it hopeless to try and separate her from the crowd, so he left frustrated and disappointed.

They continued to haul freight for Belinda, but even though she was paying them well, the money didn't go very far in Dawson. They'd been saving, but it was accumulating slowly. It was frustrating for them to see all around, the wealthy, the rich, the extremely rich, and all the gold flowing like water. Then one day they carried a load out to the creeks when everything changed.

Dropping the load where they always did, they noticed that not only was Belinda's building nearly finished, but right beside it she had men beginning a new one. As they stood admiring the new structure, they noticed another man approaching who was looking for something on the ground. When he got close, he too stopped to look at the new construction. "Howdy." he said, "You guys work for Belinda?"

"We do." answered Elmer, "In fact we packed most of this building out here."

"She sure doesn't waste time gettin' things done." he said. "Tom. Tom Lippy." he added.

As they introduced themselves, they noticed that he was not only a big man, but looked to be as solid as granite. After talking with him a few minutes, they learned he was an iron moulder and physical training instructor from Pennsylvania. He was also a man with a very cheerful disposition.

"I was just waitin' here for my wife." he said. "Thought I'd smack around with the ol' mashie. You haven't seen a little yellow ball have you?"

"No," answered Elmer, "What's a mashie?"

"It's a golf club." replied Lippy, holding up the wooden club he had with him. "I've lost my ball around here somewhere." He started looking for it again, so Henry and Elmer began kicking around in the grass, helping him look as they continued to talk.

"I'm surprised you guys aren't out prospecting." He said, "You know, with the new strikes and all."

"What new strikes?" asked Elmer just a little quicker than Henry. They both quit looking for the ball as soon as they heard what he said.

"Up in the hills, above Bonanza and Eldorado." he said, "The White Channel."

"You're gonna have to fill us in." asked Henry eagerly.

"Well, it's not really new strikes as much as a new realization." he said, "A few guys found gold high up on the hills. Then a few more struck it yesterday, and by this morning everyone realized that it was all coming out of the same white gravel."

"We were told that gold was as low as it could get, like in the bottom of creeks." said Henry.

"That's what everyone thought." said Lippy. "In fact no self-respectin' old timer woulda been caught dead searching the tops of the hills. They would've been a laughing stock. It took beginners that had no idea what they were doing to discover the White Channel."

"How come you're not up there lookin' for a claim?" asked Elmer, who'd been slowly learning to be sceptical.

"Got lucky." answered Lippy. "I was prospecting down river when the first strike was made on Bonanza. I got here just in time and staked #16 Eldorado, and it's a good one. And in the Klondike you're only allowed one claim."

Actually Lippy's claim was proving to be spectacular, one of the best in the Klondike. Talking further about how he came to the Yukon, he said that he'd had a very vivid and convincing dream, that if he went to the Yukon he'd strike it rich. And that was before any gold had been discovered. He also said that he too had piled up and wrecked his boat at the foot of Miles Canyon.

When they saw Lippy's wife approaching on her return trip from Dawson, Henry asked him "If you were a couple a guys like us, how would you go about exploring this white channel?"

It was a very wise move by Henry, as Tom Lippy was both knowledgeable and experienced.

"Well, you only need the basic equipment." he said. Then as he drew on the ground with his mashie, he pointed out the direction of Bonanza and Eldorado creeks, and which of the hills around them that had been found to have the white gravel running across their tops.

"If I were you guys, I'd follow along this line here 'till I found something."

When Lippy's wife walked up to the three of them carrying a heavy pack, Tom introduced her as "Salome". She was small, young, tough, and quite attractive. A lot like Belinda Mulrony.

After exchanging pleasantries, Henry said "Well, we gotta get back to Dawson and change professions."

"I think that's a good idea fellas," said Tom, "at least for the time being. But I wouldn't dawdle if I was you, these hills are gonna get staked fast."

They thanked him repeatedly for his knowledge and advice, and had only walked a few yards when Elmer suddenly bent over and picked up the lost ball. "Hey Tom! I found yer goff ball!" he then lobbed it to Lippy, receiving a "Thanks partner." and they quickly left for town.

"I bet it costs us all the money we saved to go prospecting again." said Henry as they hurried along.

"At Dawson City prices, we might even have to go without some things." suggested Elmer.

"Let's hope it doesn't come to that." said Henry, adding "It's too bad those beavers beat us up so bad on our first trip, they never left us anything we could use again."

"I still wonder what they did with our gold pan." replied Elmer.

"Me too" said Henry, "Now let's never speak of them again."

As soon as they were back in town, they had to stop at Belinda's to tell her they were quitting their jobs. They thought she'd be upset or even mad, but were pleasantly surprised when she understood completely, even saying, "After all, that's why you came to the Klondike in the first place isn't it?" Then she added, "If you don't find anything, you can always come back here."

They thanked Belinda for her understanding, and she wished them luck, then with time being important they headed towards town to buy a couple of weeks food supply for themselves.

As soon as they entered the dry goods store, they realized that with the sky-high prices, they weren't going to have money for much else other than food. They'd still need shovels, gold pans, a pick, an axe, canvas, and much more, all essential for living in the wilderness. They were going to have to eat no matter where they went though, so they went ahead and bought the food anyway.

When they left the store they instinctively began heading towards the Monte Carlo. To them it was the centre of activity in Dawson, and offered them the best chance of encountering people that could give them advice on what to do. They'd gotten so excited about going prospecting again, that they hadn't really thought things through. They knew they'd be going anyway though, even if they were lacking some things. Besides, the last thing they wanted to do was ask Belinda for their jobs back after just a few hours.

As they walked down Front Street lugging their sack of food, they heard, "Hey, Henry! Elmer!" It was Arizona Charlie.

"Hey Charlie" said Henry, "You didn't drown after all."

"No. In fact since I saw you guys last, I haven't even got my feet wet." he boasted.

"Are you still selling whisky?" asked Henry, wondering what he was now up to.

"No, ran out." he answered, "Besides, there's way too much competition around here."

"You must be doin' something else for a living then." said Henry, "'Cause with the prices around here, a guy can only be income-free a couple a days before starvation sets in."

"We found that out." added Elmer, as he set down their sack of food and pointed at it as if it ate their money.

"I been selling stories of the Klondike to publishers." said Charlie. "I wouldn't a believed it, but it's like owning a paper gold mine. The publishers tell me they eat it up in the outside world." Then Charlie started to leave.

"Where you goin'?" asked Elmer, wondering why he was in such a hurry.

"I'd like to hang around and talk more guys," he answered, "But I gotta go. I'm in the middle of buying a couple of smashed up riverboats. Not all of them make it to Dawson." he added. "I'm gonna use the wood to build the fanciest theatre in town." Then still walking away and almost yelling back to them, he said, "I hope to see you opening night!"

"We'll be in the front row!" shouted back Henry, not expecting it to actually happen.

Reaching the Monte Carlo, they stepped off the boardwalk and through the brand new saloon-style doors, and then set down their sack of food. Frank Slavin and Joe Boyle were the bouncers at the door, so their bag was certainly going to be safe. Then gazing throughout the establishment, they saw that many magnificent renovations had been done, with many more in progress. The most obvious being very ornate balcony suites, extending completely around the perimeter.

Amid the sounds of the refurbishing, was Wilson Mizner still singing and playing the piano, and to overcome the unwanted background noise, he was really belting it out.

"Wow, he's pretty good." remarked Elmer.

They'd guessed right about there being some people there they knew. Tex Rickard was weighing out gold at a poker table, and then filling large pokes with even amounts. It was gold he'd taken in exchange for poker chips, from men who promptly lost most of the chips straight back to him, at the very same table.

Swiftwater Bill was at the bar entertaining dancehall girls with his silver-tongued conversation, while sipping from a very ornate tea cup. The cup seemed to suit him well with his immaculate clothing, newly accessorized with huge diamond cufflinks, a watch chain weighted with many giant nuggets, and a diamond stick-pin even larger than the one he was wearing when they first met him. And he was still the only man in the Yukon with a starched collar.

Henry and Elmer decided to talk to Slavin and Boyle, not just because they were the closest and the only ones not busy doing something, but because they'd been around the Klondike awhile, and seemed to know what they were talking about.

After they told them of their predicament, the only thing Slavin and Boyle could think of, was to try and get a grubstake from the Alaska Commercial Company. But the odds were slim with Edgar Mizner in charge, and his strict policy of turning down virtually everybody.

With no other apparent options, Henry and Elmer soon found themselves down at the company store, lined up with about a dozen other men. In just a few minutes they saw that it probably wasn't going to work. Edgar was indeed in charge, and they watched him reject a couple of men outright that owned claims right in the middle of it all on Bonanza Creek. Realizing they didn't have any chance at all, they left the line-up to make their way back to the Monte Carlo, trying to conjure up a new idea as they walked.

"Elmer! Henry!" It was Tex Rickard. He'd left the Monte Carlo and was standing in front of the bank saloon. "Come on over!" he yelled, "Step in a minute."

When they approached the building, he walked into Silent Sam's establishment ahead of them. They followed along and just inside the door he stood waiting. He wanted to talk to them without anyone else overhearing.

"Have you guys heard anything about new strikes out in the hills?" he asked, "I been dealin' all day, and all day I can see something's startin' to happen."

Henry and Elmer looked at each other.

"Well, you helped us." said Henry. So they told him what they'd learned about gold running along the hills above Bonanza and Eldorado, and how they were urgently seeking a grubstake to try and get in on it.

"A lotta people get 'em from Big Alex." suggested Rickard. "You might be able to catch him at home."

"We don't know who that is." said Henry.

So Rickard went on to tell them who Big Alex was, and how to find him.

He was a big Scotsman that didn't actually stake his first claim, but bought #30 Eldorado from a Russian immigrant for a side of bacon and a bag of flour. It was one of the richest claims in the Klondike, and before long he began buying other claims and shares of claims, becoming the richest man in the Yukon.

Now he owned more than 30 claims and a great many businesses in Dawson, yet remained benevolent and generous, and was probably the humblest miner in all the Klondike. He talked agonizingly slow, appearing to be not that bright, yet actually the reverse was true and he had an incredible head for business. He kept many complicated business deals straight in his mind, in fact so many that he'd become the biggest employer in the Yukon. In San Francisco, Swiftwater Bill might have been the king of the Klondike, but up here it was Big Alex McDonald.

Rickard assured them that he was very approachable, and told them how to find his room at his own "McDonald Hotel".

"He's made a lot a money grubstakin' prospectors." added Rickard.

Henry and Elmer found his room easy enough. They'd been by the McDonald Hotel often. So after spending a few minutes readying themselves to ask the stranger for money, they knocked on the door and waited.

Nothing happened.

Then they heard "...C'mon in" slowly drawled out.

They opened the door to walk into what was a very nice but somewhat small hotel room, with McDonald sitting on the side of his bed holding a newspaper. He was huge, with a big black moustache.

"What's yer interest, fellas?"

To Henry and Elmer he looked to be nearly a giant. "Well, sir," answered Henry, "The long story is we need a grubstake."

"I see." he finally answered, "A lotta guys been in today." Then he just sat there, eventually asking them their names.

He continued to ask them questions, speaking very slowly, and with painfully long bouts of silence between each one. Until finally he stood up, and moving about as fast as he talked, walked a few feet to a dresser and took out a couple of sheets of paper from the top drawer. "Lookin' for a piece a the White Channel?" he asked.

He'd already heard about the new findings in the hills, and had been grubstaking prospectors all day. He showed the papers to them and they were grubstake agreements. He would finance them, and in return would own half of any claim they staked, and half of any gold they found. They agreed, and both signed one of the forms.

Then he said, "Take what you need out o' the bowl." and motioned behind them. They turned around to see a large bowl on a table in the corner of the room, absolutely heaped with nuggets. As they stepped up to it and stared, they turned to McDonald as if they weren't sure they'd heard him right.

"Go ahead." he said, "Take some big ones, be sure you got enough."

Being honest, they took exactly what they thought they'd need, even though paying it back wasn't part of the agreement. Then they thanked McDonald for trusting them before they left, promising they'd be honest and try their best to make it pay.

After leaving McDonald's room, Elmer could still see the large bowl of gold in his mind, and finally said, "There musta been forty–fifty pounds in that bowl."

"At least." answered Henry, "A picture of it would sure make a nice lookin' postcard."

When they looked around now, they could see Dawson buzzing with excitement. The race was definitely on again, so they hurried off to supply themselves.

While looking over new picks and shovels, they saw that the store was sold out of gold pans, so they'd have to get them somewhere else. Then they saw Jack in the store. "Hey Jack!" said Elmer getting his attention, "What are ya up to? Piloting boats or prospecting?"

"Neither." he answered, "I found good colors on Henderson Creek so I'm gonna build a cabin. But I need an axe." He was purchasing a very large one. They didn't say anything, but Jack hadn't gained much weight since they last saw him, and they both thought that maybe he should be buying a smaller axe. One easier to swing.

They were on a mission now, so only talked to Jack until they'd made their purchases, then quickly headed out of town towards Bonanza Creek. On the way, Henry talked about acting a little wiser on this prospecting trip than they had on their last. They both remembered what the beavers had done to them on their first expedition.

"Damn." exclaimed Elmer suddenly. "We forgot all about payin' Sid back for the meal we got from him. You probably had other things on your mind." he said to Henry, "But I shoulda remembered."

"Your right." answered Henry. "It wouldn't make much sense to go back now though. Besides, we're nearly broke again anyway. We'll have to see him when we get back."

Suddenly Elmer's head shot back and his hat flew off, as an object ricocheted hard off his head! Leadtooth had hit him with the silver case from the edge of the woodpile he was now working on. And as quick as Henry and Elmer saw what was happening, they dropped to the ground narrowly dodging a large piece of cord wood flying end over end! When they looked up, they saw

Leadtooth standing with both hands clenched in hard fists. But he'd run out of time. A rifle butt drove into his back and down he went. One of the Mounties guarding the prison workforce now stood glaring down at him and said, "What's wrong with ya stupid? Your not workin' long enough hours now?"

Henry and Elmer jumped to their feet quickly, with Henry grabbing the silver case as he got up. Feeling both safe again and seething with anger, Elmer yelled "Good luck in hell! Ya road apple!" Then he suddenly grabbed the case from Henry and holding it up, yelled "Thanks for the silver! And you be sure and cut lotsa wood, I don't want to be cold next winter!"

Henry thought Elmer had said it pretty well, but he couldn't help tipping his hat to Leadtooth and half yelling, "You have a good summer now!"

Then the Mountie yelled at them, "No talkin' to the prisoners! Move on!"

So they moved on. But they wouldn't walk by the woodpile again without looking for Leadtooth, and they wouldn't walk so close to the pile at all.

They traveled at a fairly quick pace with their packs and equipment, continuously talking about why Leadtooth threw the case at them. Did he just not care anymore? Was he letting them know he knew they had the map? Or was it just pure anger and hate?

It wasn't long before they were half way to Bonanza again, when Henry suddenly stopped, and without saying anything stepped off the road and sat down on a rock. Then looking depressed and rubbing his forehead with both hands he said, "We might as well rest awhile before we head back to town."

"Why? What for?" asked Elmer. He was confused.

"We forgot gold pans." replied Henry. "Remember the store was sold out so we were going to get 'em somewhere else. You'd think we'd a been more careful when you consider how many tail feathers we already lost in this country."

Elmer sat down too. They had no choice but to go back. They couldn't prospect without them. They watched a few men walk past who were obviously going out to prospect themselves, and it quickly began to look as if they were going to lose this race too.

Then along came Clarence Berry. "Hi Clarence" said Elmer, trying to appear upbeat. "You goin' out to prospect?"

"Naw," he answered, "I been here since the beginning. You boys look kinda down though. Whatsa matter?"

They told him about their predicament, and he began laughing. "Come on up to my claim," he said "I'll give you a couple a mine. I got lots."

Their mood quickly improved again as they followed along with him up to his claim. It was then that they realized for the first time, that when they saw Clarence on the Chilkoot Pass, he didn't have a ton of food to carry, only a pack and the sleigh he pulled his wife in.

Berry's claim was the fifth one on Eldorado, and when they arrived, they saw that he had a log cabin pretty much like everyone else's, with a sod roof and a single window. His was one of the classier ones though, in that most cabin windows were nothing more than a small hole with a piece of moosehide hung over it to keep the cold out. His window was much larger, with the glass being rows of empty pickle jars chinked with moss.

"Nice lookin' cabin there Clarence." said Henry.

"Yea, it's okay." He replied, "Shoulda peeled the logs though. The woodpeckers drive us nuts."

When they walked around to the front of his cabin, they saw his wife Ethel sitting by a fire with Tom Lippy and his wife Salome. Clarence began to introduce them, when Henry said

"Actually, we've already met. In fact, Tom's the one who told us about this new rush."

Tom's claim was about a mile further up Eldorado, and he and Berry had become good friends over the past year, as their wives had been about the only women in the area, and always wanted to visit each other.

On both their claims, the gold in the pans could be measured in pounds. They had two of the richest in the Klondike.

"Sit down. Have a coffee before ya go." said Clarence. "I'll get a couple a pans for ya." They had no choice as the women were already pouring. Besides, they wouldn't be here at all without Clarence and Tom's help.

As they sat down Tom jumped up saying, "I'll get the pans for ya Clarence." and took off to get them practically running.

Clarence sat back down again saying "Tom never gets enough a work." And then turning towards him with a smile on his face, he said in a much louder voice "And he likes doing everything the hard way!"

Tom was back almost right away and handed them the pans. Then he poured himself a coffee and sat down, just as Henry asked "If you guys were us, where would you start lookin' for a claim?"

"Hard to tell," answered Clarence "Up here gold seems to be wherever you find it. Maybe on any of these hills that aren't staked yet. If there are any."

"Look for the white gravel that I mentioned before." added Tom.

"Do you think there'd be spots in any creeks left?" asked Henry.

"I doubt it," answered Clarence, "There's a lot of men running around in the creek beds."

The women hadn't really quit moving around since they'd poured the coffee, and now they came out of the Berrys' cabin and stood in front of Clarence and Tom. "We're going to go into town for supplies." said Ethel.

Both were still dressed in men's clothes, as they both laboured beside their husbands to work their claims. So they walked a few yards away to the pile of dirt that'd been brought up from bedrock, and began poking and kicking at the frozen lumps, picking out the larger nuggets as they'd see them.

Henry and Elmer both thought about how rich a claim had to be to be able to do this.

Suddenly Clarence jumped up and said, "Hey! We don't need any supplies! Yer goin' shopping!"

They both just grinned back at him, and continued gathering nuggets.

Clarence looked at Henry and Elmer, saying, "Can't really blame 'em. They been workin' like dogs and living on bare essentials since we got here. And now Dawson's fillin' up with all kinds a things to buy."

With the girls leaving, Tom said he'd better get back to work again, and left for his claim up the valley. Henry and Elmer decided they'd better get going themselves, and insisted on giving Clarence the last of their gold to pay for the gold pans. But he wouldn't hear of it. In fact he said, "Just a minute." and quickly left to return brandishing two sticks of dynamite. "Don't use 'em unless you find good colors on the surface." he said. "Then they'll help ya dig."

From the very start, their prospecting trip became difficult. There was no reason to stay on the trail along the creeks anymore, as the new discoveries were all high in the hills. So they began thrashing their way up the nearest slope. The grade was steep and covered with small trees and thick willows that continually slapped back in their faces.

Eventually they reached the top and stepped out into a small clearing. It had been hacked out with an axe, by a man who was squatting beside a small hole he'd dug. "Already staked boys." he said, "And it's not bad."

They could see that he'd dug straight into the bleached gravel of the White Channel.

Up here the trees and willows were a little shorter, only to their shoulders, so they could see well enough to spy out the next hill to tackle. They could also tell that all the hills around were covered with these horrible willows, and nothing was going to get any easier.

Thus began a long miserable trek of stumbling down hills, then staggering across muskeg and swamp, and then fighting their way back up the next hill. And on the top and sides of each slope, they'd find claim posts. Many of the hills were long on top, where they'd encounter one claim after another, with the posts often tied back to back. The only encouraging sign was that every so often they'd encounter someone with a hole already dug, and a few of them had struck white gravel.

So they figured they were traveling in the right direction, and finally descended one of the hills to find a small creek flowing in the bottom with some gravel showing in it. It wasn't white, but it was a place they could explore further, so went to work with their pans and shovels.

They started digging small holes and loading up their pans for washing, but each time would get the same results, nothing. After digging about a dozen holes in various places, their moods began to sink. "I don't think there's anything here." said Elmer.

"Yea," agreed Henry, "Let's make something to eat."

So Henry built a fire while Elmer made a frying pan full of bannock, and they both ate without saying much. Panning for gold was hard work, and they could both already feel their backs getting sore. Then Henry noticed that Elmer was feeling even lower than he let on, so he decided to try a couple more holes.

"I'm going to dig these ones as deep as I can." he said, hoping to boost Elmer's spirit again.

Elmer didn't move or say anything. He'd obviously explored this creek all he was going to. Henry dug a couple more holes down to the now familiar permafrost, and again had the same results. Not even a speck.

Elmer sat staring into the fire, which from neglect was now lazily wafting smoke back and forth from a single piece of wood. Opposite Elmer, a couple of whisky jacks pecked at the leftover bannock in the now cold frying pan, while a few yards away more of the birds ate from the open bag of flour.

"Hey Elmer, there's birds in the flour bag." said Henry.

He slowly turned around to see, as if he didn't care at all. Then suddenly jumping up in frustration he yelled "That's 'cause every kinda bird up here steals from ya!" Then throwing the leftover bannock at the open bag, he shouted "And they never sleep either!"

Despite their luck they had to continue, so packed up everything and began climbing the next hill. It wasn't as high as the others had been, and upon reaching the top, they found themselves looking out over a very wide valley. This was the last hill in the line. It wasn't long on top either, but rather came to a point like a Chinese hat.

"I guess we should dig a hole." said Henry.

They proceeded to cut the willows out of the way, then shovel and pick their way through the topsoil. It was extremely tough going, with the tangled root systems of the willows spread everywhere, so soon Elmer came up with a better idea.

"Let's blast it with a stick of dynamite." he said.

They hadn't found any colors yet, or even dug through the topsoil, but Henry agreed. "Might as well." he said, "It's the last hill there is anyway."

So they buried one of the sticks in the hole they'd dug, and then lit the fuse. Berry had told them it would take about five minutes to burn down, so they scrambled down the hill to where they'd eaten and had their fire. They'd never used dynamite before, and found their hearts pounding with anticipation as they waited for the blast to occur.

Ka-boom!! They both flinched badly. The blast was much louder than they expected. Then as they jumped back up to race up the hill, it began raining rocks all around them. They hadn't run far enough away!

They immediately realized the danger they were in, and both quickly made themselves as small as possible, while holding the gold pans over their heads. It continued raining down rocks for another few seconds, with one loud "bong!" ringing off Elmer's pan.

After it stopped, they waited a little longer to make sure, and then slowly getting up Henry said, "I guess we could'a done that a little better."

Gazing around where they stood, they saw that many of the new rocks lying around were white in color. This sent them charging back up the hill to see what they had.

Elmer was first to reach the top, and very excited yelled "The dirt's all white!"

They'd blasted into what appeared to be the White Channel. In fact they'd blown the top right off the little hill. They both dropped to their knees to examine the ground as best they could, when Elmer said "I don't see any gold."

They continued staring, while occasionally brushing the ground with their hands hoping to turn something up. "Hey! I think this might be gold." said Henry, pulling a small lump from the ground. It was hard to tell, as it too was covered with a fine white dust, but as soon as he brushed it with his fingers, it revealed itself to be the precious metal.

"It is!" he exclaimed, "It is!"

Their eyes quickly began scouring the ground for more. Almost immediately Henry said again, "Look, here's another one!"

Then Elmer answered, "Look, here's a big one!" holding up a nugget the size of his thumbnail.

"Let's try panning some." said Henry. "That'll tell us what we're lookin' at here."

They both picked up their shovels and tried to stab them into the gold-bearing gravel. They only went in an inch or two, so they tried again. But it was the same thing. "It's that lousy permafrost." said Henry.

Still managing to pick and scrape their pans full, they rushed down to the creek to wash them out. Then saturating the gravel with water they began a cycle of shaking the wet dirt back and forth, then stopping intermittently to scrape the top couple of inches back into the creek. As their pans contained less and less dirt to slosh around, they'd never been so excited.

When they had it reduced to a couple of pounds of dirt in the pan, they had to be more careful, scraping off only small amounts. They both finally scraped off about a half inch from their tilted pans, then added more water, and with a couple of big swirls of the sandy gravel that remained, it caught with the moving water and left a heap of yellow on one side of their pans. They looked at each other with big grins on their faces. "We're rich!" said Elmer.

They dumped out the remaining water and sand, and then began plowing through the gold with their fingers, revealing dozens of nuggets hidden in the gold dust. "It's so heavy." said Elmer. "There must be at least a pound in each of these pans." Their lives were going to change drastically now, and they both knew it.

"I can't believe it." said Henry, "We actually hit it."

Their minds flooded with optimism as they pondered their futures, until finally Elmer could contain the fantastic feeling no more, and jumping up on a nearby rock he declared "I'm rich!!"

Henry too was feeling giddy, and jumping up on the rock beside him, he elbowed Elmer aside saying, "For your mother's sake, find some confidence man." Then yelled "For we are – the kings – of all – we – survey!!"

"Yes!" added Elmer, "And the owners of Little Knob Hill! That's what we'll call it."

"We better make sure it isn't already staked." said Henry. They hadn't seen any claim posts, but they had to be positive.

So they began a thorough search, and after looking for some time and not finding anything, they knew it didn't belong to anyone so put up their own posts, staking it in Henry's name.

Then as hard as they tried they couldn't really mine any more from their frozen little hill, at least not until the permafrost melted. So with their pokes almost full anyway, they decided to leave for town. The best part was, that in the days they'd be gone to file their claim, it could easily melt down another foot.

So they gathered up their gear and began their trip back. They should've been too tired now, but because of their new-found fortune, they traveled a few miles over the willow-covered hills before building a fire and lying down to rest. Even then, they still talked for awhile about what they would do now that they were men of means.

When they woke in the morning, they again began thrashing their way through the willows and small trees towards Dawson. At first as they crossed the hills, they'd occasionally see men working their newly staked claims, but as the day wore on, they realized that they hadn't seen any men or claim posts for some time. They continued on until finally Elmer said, "Do you think we're lost?"

"Yes, I do." replied Henry, "As we been walking along, I was thinking how hard it was going to be to find the same place we crossed the valley to get on these hills. Now I'm not even sure we're in the same valley."

"What do ya think we should do?" asked Elmer.

"I don't know." replied Henry, "One thing's for sure, it's still uglier traveling down in the valley than it is up on these hills."

"We might as well keep going then." said Elmer, "We're probably still heading in the right direction anyway."

So they kept on going, until they came down a hill and found a decent sized creek and a small clearing at the bottom. They decided to stop and rest for awhile, so took off their packs, and got out a bag of raisins to chew on.

After he ate some, Henry leaned against his pack so he was half sitting and half lying down, then folded his hands together across his stomach and closed his eyes for a better rest.

Elmer wasn't quite as tired, so after a few minutes of staring at the fast-moving creek, he decided he might as well try panning it. "I'm gonna see if there's any gold here." he said. "After all, we walked all this way."

After a few minutes of shovelling and sloshing water around in his pan, he said "Cheez Henry, you should come and look at this. There's not bad gold here."

Henry got up immediately and walked over to where Elmer was to look in the pan. "Wow! You're right." he said, "It's not Little Knob Hill, but there's at least two or three grams in there."

"And I didn't even dig down!" replied Elmer.

"Let's dig a hole and see what we get." suggested Henry. So they dug down a couple of feet and filled up their pans again. This time when the gravel was gone, they both had about a half an ounce in the bottom of their pans. "This is a good creek!" said Henry, "We should stake it."

So Elmer went up the creek about 250 feet, while Henry went down the same distance, and they staked it in Elmer's name. "With two good claims, we're riding the gravy train now!" said Henry.

"Yup! With great big biscuit wheels!" grinned Elmer. They both wanted to pan some more, so they stayed and filled their pokes to capacity, then struck off for Dawson again.

They hadn't gone far at all, when they ran into a man coming from the opposite direction. They told him they'd been wandering the hills for a few days, and had become disoriented at how far it was to Dawson. Then they asked if they were heading in the right direction. He said he'd been wandering the hills for a few days himself, but figured it was ten or twelve miles to Dawson, and that they were indeed heading in the right direction. Adding that if he was wrong, he too was in trouble.

They thanked him for his help, then set off again, finding that they were now in an even better mood. "What should we do first when we get to Dawson?" said Elmer.

"Register our claims." replied Henry.

"Yea, I know." said Elmer. "We have to pay Sid for the meal too. But I mean after that."

"Well, that meal he gave us went down pretty good." said Henry, "I think we should eat there again."

"That's a good idea." answered Elmer, practically drooling at the thought of it. "Then let's buy some new clothes. Everything we got is pretty much shot now." It was true, thrashing through the willows for days had basically finished off their worn out clothes.

"We need new boots too." added Henry, "And some hats would be nice."

"Its fun figuring out how to spend money you actually have." said Elmer.

It was still hard travelling through the bush, but it had gotten somewhat easier since they staked the creek. Then just as they started wondering if it was ever going to end, they stepped out of the bush onto the trail not far from town. It was then they realized that they'd probably taken the most difficult route there was back to Dawson.

They passed a newly posted sign at the edge of town, that read 'No more digging for gold in the city limits' "I gotta good idea." said Elmer, as they approached onto Front Street. "Let's get a room in one of the fancy hotels for the night, where we can shave and have a bath in a real tub."

"That's not a good idea," replied Henry, "That's a great idea!"

Dawson was extremely busy again, as now the big riverboats had begun arriving. A dozen of the large ships were now beached along Front Street, and brought with them the finest things in the world. They were loaded down with carpets, mirrors, fine art and paintings, Tiffany lamps, Chippendale furniture, and the newest Paris fashions for the ladies of the Klondike. Swiss watches, Belgian chocolate, Napoleon Brandy, and every other fine thing a person could want or think of.

And people, lots of people. A great many women were arriving now, along with men of every profession, and of course many more goldseekers as well. The boats also carried news. The people arriving on the boats said there were only two kinds of people in the world now, those in the Klondike, and those wishing they were in the Klondike. In fact, some of the riverboats were having trouble leaving Dawson, as many of their crew members were abandoning their jobs as soon as the boats hit the beach.

Then Henry and Elmer noticed that they were almost the only ones raggedly dressed now. Nearly everyone else, no matter what their profession, was wearing new clothes. Henry really wanted to go and see Becky now, but realized he should probably improve his appearance first.

They continued walking towards the Claims Office, knowing that filing their claims was the most important thing they had to do. The Claims Office was no more than a tent with a large wooden table out front, where a couple of government clerks tried to deal with an absolute onslaught of people trying to file claims. Hundreds of people formed two long lines, and at the front of one of those lines was Big Alex McDonald, sitting in a chair, and slowly drawling out what was probably a complicated staking issue, to a completely exasperated clerk.

"We could stand here for what might end up being days." said Henry, then added "I guess we could take turns."

"Let's hire someone to stand in line for us." suggested Elmer.

"Wow, you're just full a good ideas today." said Henry. "Maybe it's because you're a rich man now."

"Oh, I sure hope so." said Elmer, "That could change everything."

"Anyway," said Henry, "Let's go pay Sid and eat again. Maybe we can find somebody there."

When they walked into the restaurant, they saw that Jack was sitting alone at one of the tables. Which was a good thing as every other table was full. So they went over and sat down with him. "How's your scribblings coming along?" asked Elmer, seeing that he was again writing in his journal.

"Scribbling's all it is at this point." he replied while closing it up, "How you guys doing?"

"Great!" said Elmer, showing him his stuffed gold poke, "How about you?"

"Well, I haven't found much gold yet." he answered, "And I'm starting to regret beginning a cabin before I actually found anything."

"Do you know if Sid's working right now?" asked Henry.

"Yes he is." replied Jack, "He's busy though, with the place being full and all."

As Henry looked around for Sid, Elmer was sensing that Jack might be broke. "Hey Jack," he said, "I was wondering if I could buy my Bowie knife back from you?"

"You bet." replied Jack. Just then Sid showed up at the table. So as Elmer paid Jack for his knife, Henry paid Sid handsomely for the meal they'd already gotten from him, plus more for another meal for themselves and Jack.

While he was paying Sid out of his poke, Henry asked him if he knew of anyone that could stand in line at the Claims Office for them, adding that they'd pay well for the service.

"I'll do it." said Sid.

"It might be for a day or two," replied Henry, "Don't you have to work?"

"No, I don't." added Sid, "I gotta work a couple more hours, but then I got two days off, so I can do it."

"Deal." said Henry. And Sid headed off to the kitchen to get their food.

After they finished eating, they decided that the first thing they should do was to go buy some new clothes. So they went to one of the newly built clothing stores to pick out some quality things to wear. Then they got them wrapped up to go, so they could put them on later after they got cleaned up.

Then just as they were leaving the store, Henry ran smack into Becky in the doorway. "Hi Becky" he said, partly in shock, "You don't have your crutches any more. What are you up to?" Immediately he thought "What a pathetic way to greet her."

"I was just picking up some things Belle wanted." she answered, "She wanted me to go out with her tonight, with it being Independence Day and all."

"It is?" said Henry, "We didn't even realize it." Then he thought to himself, "That's right, just tell her yer stupid." Then he added, "I did notice a lot of people about town."

He didn't want to tell her that as soon as he got cleaned up, he was coming straight to her place to ask her out for the evening. "Well, we were thinking of going to the Monte Carlo tonight." he said. It was the nicest place he could think of. "So if your plans aren't real firm, why don't you come by."

"I don't think we have any actual plans." she said, "So we very well may."

They were blocking the doorway for other people now, so Henry said, "Great! I'll see you later then." and again they began to leave.

"See you Henry." she said with a shy smile.

The smile burned right through him.

"Did you see that Elmer?" he said as they walked down the street. "Even though I was surprised to see her, I didn't get too flustered, and I only sounded a little like an idiot."

"What did she say when you told her we struck it rich?" he asked.

It was only then that Henry realized he hadn't mentioned it at all. "…I forgot to." he confessed.

"You mean you forgot to tell her about the biggest thing that ever happened to you?" said Elmer, "…yea, not flustered at all."

Then Elmer said "Look, there's our place." They were looking at the Aurora Hotel, and the sign over the door said 'Baths $2.50' and 'Sheets – 240 threads per inch'. "That's it." agreed Henry, and in they went.

The shaves and hot baths alone made them feel like different people. Then they put on their new clothes. They'd both bought shiny new black boots, black pants, and very good embossed leather belts. Then Henry put on a very high quality blue flannel shirt, and a dark leather coat that was top of the line. His new hat was the same, and looked as if it was designed specifically for looking good in the Klondike. He looked great.

Whereas Elmer had chosen an expensive white cotton shirt, then added cufflinks that were little gold pans with a tiny nugget in them, then a bowtie, and a fancy claw hammer jacket that was practically a tuxedo. His hat was a top-of-the-line 'Gambler', with a very decorative band.

"You look like one of the richest men in the Klondike." concluded Henry, which of course was the point. Then he added "You don't want to work in those clothes,"

"I'll get new work clothes tomorrow." replied Elmer.

Then they hung their fat yet slightly depleted gold pokes from their belts, as everyone with any money did, and after slicking down their hair with tonic, Henry said "Well, let's go wag our tails."

Starting off down Front Street towards the Monte Carlo, they were already envisioning what it would be like to be kings of the Klondike. Of course, they weren't anywhere near that rich yet, but they had two extremely promising claims to mine.

Walking through town, they saw a lot of people already celebrating the holidays. The Canadian Independence Day was July 1st, and the American on July 4th, and Dawson was probably the first and only city ever, to take the Independence Days of two separate countries and mash them together into one long party.

There were other ways too that Dawson was different than most, if not all other cities in the world. For one thing, Dawson was virtually a gun-free town, with practically no crime at all. Then there was the population. At thirty to forty thousand people, it truly had become Dawson City, and with the extreme distances, obstacles, and conditions that people had to overcome just to get there, most the population was intelligent, courageous, adventurous, and optimistic by nature.

Also, because of all the conditions that Dawson had begun under, it was the only city in the world without children. And Dawson City was rich, unbelievably rich, and now with the arrival of the riverboats and all the fine things they brought, Dawson City glittered. People were referring to it as "The Paris of the North', and 'The Funest Place on Earth'.

"Look." said Henry, "It's Hegg again." Hegg was on the roof of one of the buildings, taking pictures of everything. As Henry and Elmer continued walking, they noticed how the music from banjos and fiddles and the like, had been replaced by professional bands and small orchestras. Nearly every hundred feet, great new music flowed out the casino and dancehall doors to the street.

"You notice there's a lot more women around now." said Elmer.

It was true, women had been pouring off the newly landed boats, arriving in the Klondike to seek their fortunes like everybody else. Some came to prospect, while many more came looking for work or to seek husbands, and still others to parade around town offering female companionship.

When Henry and Elmer approached the Monte Carlo, they saw Frank Slavin and Joe Boyle laughing hysterically. They were both looking over to Bill MacPhee's Pioneer Saloon, and witnessing a huge battle of wills. Gary was trying to force his way in for a drink, while a half a dozen waiters and bartenders tried to block the door. "Who's winning?" asked Henry, as he and Elmer joined in watching the spectacle.

"It's been pretty even so far." replied Boyle. "That's one determined mule."

"He'd probably have a lot better luck if he had some money." suggested Elmer.

Boyle cracked up. "Elmer! That's a true statement!"

Then Boyle noticed their new clothes and fat pokes. "Being Independence Day," said Joe, "Bill wants us to keep out anybody too drunk or too poor. But you boys don't look either. You musta struck it good."

"We dug into the White Channel." replied Henry smiling.

"Good for you guys!" he said, vigorously shaking Henry's hand up and down. "Good for you!" He seemed genuinely glad for them. Then he shook Elmer's hand while patting him on the back. "Come on in." he said, "There's always room for another gold baron."

As soon as they stepped through the door, they were caught up in what could best be described as a whirlwind of joy. The party had obviously started without them.

The Monte Carlo was incredibly opulent now, right down to the furniture and hardwood floors. Though a little sawdust was still thrown down in strategic places to soak up any spilled gold. The walls were now made of extravagant panels with intricate designs on them, and huge mirrors and paintings hung everywhere.

The place was full of boisterous people, with many of them merrily dancing to the music. All the women were wearing brightly coloured dresses, and most of the men had heavy pokes of gold hanging from their belts. "There's nowhere for us to sit." said Henry. "All the tables are full."

There was one table, a very large one in a prime location up front, and it was obviously reserved for Klondike kings and other important people. Swiftwater Bill was there, sitting with his new girlfriend Nellie Lamore. She was the sister of his last girlfriend Gussie, and both were very attractive dancehall girls. Clarence Berry and Arizona Charlie were sitting with them, and as awkward as it may have been, Wilson Mizner was sitting with his new girlfriend, Gussie Lamore. And Wilson wasn't playing the piano anymore, he'd been replaced by a large professional band.

Then a voice said "You guys struck it, didn't ya?" It was Tex Rickard, and he too had noticed their new clothes and pokes.

"We sure did." answered Elmer.

"Where'd you find it?" he asked.

"We think we hit the end of the White Channel." replied Henry.

"Well congratulations." he said shaking their hands. Then asked "How come you're standin' way back here?"

"Nowhere to sit." confessed Henry.

"Well, don't stand here lookin' like hobos!" he said, "Come and sit with us." and he began leading them to the head table.

Etiquette said you didn't go near this table unless you were invited, so they couldn't believe their luck. When they arrived at the table, Rickard loudly announced, "Look everybody, Henry and Scratchy struck it big!" and while everyone congratulated them, Arizona Charlie poured them glasses of champagne.

"A toast. To your new found wealth." he said, and everyone lifted their glasses and drank. Of course Swiftwater Bill toasted them with his tea cup, and then introduced them to the Lamore sisters and Arkansaw Jim Hall, another filthy rich claim holder.

Then Elmer, even though he was sure he already knew, asked Tex "Why Scratchy?" Before Tex could speak, Clarence answered for him, "Because not too many people know who you are, but half the town knows the guy that always has the scratched up face."

"A toast!" said Wilson Mizner, "To Scratchy's fame!" and everyone laughed as they held up their glasses and drank again.

After a few more toasts, Wilson and Gussie got up to dance, and Nellie left to gamble some of Bill's money on the roulette wheel. Bill seemed unconcerned about any potential losses, and for good reason, he owned the place.

That's when Tex took the opportunity to take a friendly shot at Bill's love life. "Bill, how do you lose one girl, then just a couple a weeks later, catch the girl's own sister?"

"Passion and gold, Rickard," Bill answered truthfully, "Lotsa passion and gold. Of course, it's still not that Dawson City mud love that some of us are famous for." he added, glancing at Henry with a big smirk on his face.

The whole table erupted with laughter.

As soon as it began to quiet down, Henry answered "You flatter me sir, and might I add that it's high praise indeed, coming from the one and only 'Knight of the Golden Omelette'."

The entire table erupted again. "Touché sir," replied Bill holding up his cup again, "Touché."

To Henry, they'd just been accepted into Klondike royalty. Then Bill said "I guess in hindsight I could've handled the situation with Gussie a little better. But oh well, it's all blood under the bridge now."

Wilson and Gussie returned from dancing, and while they sat down Henry turned to Elmer and said "Maybe it's true, maybe we can think better rich." In any case, he felt so good now that he ordered three more bottles of champagne for the table.

Then Elmer said "Hey Henry, when we dig up more gold I wanna get watch chains like all these guys." Every other man at the table had a watch in a vest pocket, with a chain hanging across their stomachs to the opposite pocket, and hanging every two or three inches on the chain was a huge nugget. When Arizona Charlie noticed them looking at his, Elmer said "We wanna get watch chains like yours, and I wished I'd gotta coat like yours too." Charlie was wearing a very fancy buckskin leather coat with fringes, overtop a fine dark suit. "I got this one hoping to attract some ladies." added Elmer.

"Yours is great." said Charlie. "When you're dressed like you or Bill, it sends a message. It says you got money to spend." Elmer noticed that he'd put him in the same league as Swiftwater Bill. "You didn't really need it though." added Charlie, "You're rich now, and dancehall girls can smell gold. Really! You coulda come in here wearing nothin' but a barrel and they'd still be attracted to you."

It wasn't long before the first girl came up to the table and asked Elmer to dance. Up till now he'd been intimidated by them, as they were all so beautiful. But with his new found confidence and Charlie's encouragement, Elmer headed off to the dance floor.

Then Kate Rockwell arrived at their table. "Do you have room for me fellas?" she asked. She didn't know how stupid her question was. Kate could pretty much have anything she wanted. Just having her sit at their table would give them all some extra status. She was known as Klondike Kate now, and was famous all over the Yukon. She'd also become a pin-up girl, yet kept a good reputation and was still respected by everyone.

Tonight she had on a stunning dress from Paris that gathered her even more attention, if that was possible, and she was also accessorized with a lot of gold. She wore a belt made of $20 gold pieces with a matching bracelet, and her necklace was a solid gold chain with a nugget about every six inches. The nuggets weren't as big as the ones on the men's watch chains, but her chain was a full eight feet long and wrapped around her neck many times. Kate was so popular now, men were paying $750 or about four pounds of gold, just to buy her dinner and talk to her for the evening.

As Kate's looks and personality began drawing everyone in, Elmer returned from dancing. Not so much to sit down, but just to tell Henry how much fun he was having. It turned out, that unlike most of the miners, Elmer was chock-full of rhythm. And being young and rich, the girls all thought he was one of the best catches in the place. He'd been dancing up a storm, and between dances was buying himself and the girls drinks at the bar, mostly champagne.

Then Henry noticed a couple of girls walking towards them. It was Rebecca! He tried to stand up so fast, his new boots skidded a couple of times before they grabbed and he got to his feet. "Becky! I was hoping you'd come. Boy, you sure look good! Here, sit down." he said while pulling a chair out for her. "You too Belle."

Before she could say anything, Henry ordered three more bottles of champagne. Then he introduced her to the people she didn't know, and she sat down. Belle already knew everybody.

Becky said "What's happened Henry? I mean you look great, but a lot different than when I saw you earlier today."

"Me and Elmer struck it big!" he said as he poured them both a glass of champagne. "I forgot to tell you in the store today."

Everybody was starting to feel the bubbly drink now, and suddenly Tex said "Hey Scratchy, let me buy you a sourdough cocktail. Available only in the Klondike."

"A special drink." replied Elmer, "Sure I'll try it." Belle was already sidling up to Elmer, just as she had before. He didn't mind too much though. The way he figured it, Leadtooth probably would have killed him in the alley if not for her getting help. So he poured her a glass of champagne and said, "I hope you like dancin'."

When Becky heard what Elmer said about dancing, she pulled closer to Henry and wrapped one of her arms through his and quietly said "Henry, my foot's still giving me some trouble. So if I think someone's going to ask me to dance, I'm going to grab on to you like this to try and deter them. Okay?"

"I think you should play it safe," replied Henry, "And just stay close like this." He finished talking and she didn't move her arm at all.

What she didn't know, was Henry was practically melting to her touch. But what he didn't know, was that she wasn't telling him the truth. Her foot was still bothering her a little, but she could dance if she wanted to. Once again Henry couldn't believe his luck, first to have Becky so close to him, and then to have her see him with wealth and social status. It was more than he'd even hoped for.

Then Elmer's sourdough cocktail arrived. He knew that sourdough was the bannock bread that everyone constantly cooked and ate coming over the Chilkoot. In fact, it was so common that the people were often referred to as 'Sourdoughers'. So it didn't surprise him that you could only get the drink in the Klondike. Henry was curious as to what it might taste like too, so watched Elmer as he gulped down about half the drink. "It tastes like whisky." he said looking around at everybody. Then he tipped it up and drank down the rest of it. As the last of the drink went down, he felt something touch his lip. He looked into the glass then up at Henry in shock! "There's somebody's toe in here!" he yelled.

Everybody burst out laughing, but Tex and Charlie lost it completely. Tex could barely speak when he said, "Did I say sourdough cocktail? I'm sorry, I meant to say 'sour-toe' cocktail.

The drink had been invented as a joke, but had stayed popular enough that it was still ordered regularly. Some people drank it on a dare, but many were tricked into it, and sometimes the toe was swallowed completely. It was easily replaced though, as there'd been no shortage of people freezing their toes off in the Yukon.

Then Elmer stood up, and taking Belle by the hand said, "If you'll all excuse me, I'm gonna go dance it off." and they left for the dance floor, just as Nellie Lamore returned from dumping Bill's money at the gambling tables. She didn't sit down though, but instead said to Gussie "We should go get ready now, we have to go on stage pretty soon."

When Gussie stood up so did Kate saying "And I have to go on even before they do. I'll see you later my friends."

All the men stood politely when the girls left, and when Henry sat back down, Becky grabbed his arm again and said "Did you notice anything odd about Kate's belt and bracelet?"

"No." he answered, "What about it?"

"Well look." she said, and Henry looked at Kate's bracelet as she walked away. "Notice how one of the gold coins is missing?"

"Oh yea," replied Henry.

"It's on purpose." said Becky, "It makes some of the men think that it's fallen out, and they keep giving her new ones to replace it."

"Wow, that's pretty smart." said Henry.

Then Becky asked "So how did you and Elmer strike it rich?" Henry just started to tell her when the entire place began laughing and cheering. When they turned to see what the commotion was all about, everyone was watching a man on the dance floor. The man would throw one foot forward and plant it on the floor, then with his back hunched over, and timed to the music, he'd lunge forward and straighten up a little, then throw the other foot forward and repeat the process.

It was a dance almost everone recognized, as they themselves had done it countless times. It was the 'Chilkoot lock-step' used to get over the golden stairs. The cheering and laughter grew, until half the people in the place were doing the familiar dance, with some of the men even sticking their thumbs through their braces to simulate carrying a heavy pack.

When the joyful moment began to subside, Henry again turned his attention to Rebecca, to continue telling her how he and Elmer had found gold. When he finished, and told how Sid was standing in line for them down at the Claims Office, she said "Dance with me Henry."

"Absolutely." he replied, then "Wait, I thought you couldn't dance?"

"That's only partly true," she said, "I'm good for a couple of dances. Besides, this is a slow one."

So they finished their glasses and began heading for the dance floor. "What if other guys want to dance with you now?" asked Henry.

She wrapped her arm tight around his again and said, "I'll just stay close to you from now on."

When they started dancing Henry said "If your foot breaks down and you wanna fall into me, that's okay too."

Even though it was crowded, they could still see better from the dance floor than they could from the table, and when Henry looked over to the bar, he saw Elmer surrounded by Belle and a few other girls.

Then he saw a sign over the bar that stunned him. It said 'Champagne $80 a bottle'. He figured the numbers, and with the gold in his poke worth $16 an ounce, he'd already spent three full pounds of it on champagne. A few more bottles and his poke would be empty. He didn't really have to worry, as everyone else at the table was constantly ordering more bottles. But it was still a concern.

When they finished dancing and returned to the table, it wasn't long before Elmer and Belle came back and sat down. They both appeared quite drunk now, and instead of Belle sitting beside Elmer, she sat on his lap, seemingly to guard him from the other girls.

Then Henry turned to him and said "Hey Elmer, I noticed things are pretty expensive in here. You might wanna watch your money."

Elmer immediately held up his near empty poke and said, "I think that train has sailed!"

The dancehall was getting louder now, as most everyone in the place was intoxicated to one degree or another. Then Augustus Mack appeared. He'd been making his way to the bar when he saw them and stopped to say hi. "I see you guys made it after all." he said.

"Yea, we struck it good." said Henry.

"Yea, I can see." replied Mack. "Congratulations." Then he added, "But I meant you and your boat made it here after all." He was the man whose boat they'd copied back in Bennett.

"Yea," replied Henry, "The boat got whittled down some on the way, but we made it."

"We got whittled down some too." added Elmer.

"But you're doin' better now." said Mack. "And that's the important thing."

"Sit down." said Henry, inviting him to stay and talk.

"Naw, I gotta go." he replied. "There's people where I'm sitting that think they're dyin' of thirst."

"Well it was good talkin' to ya Mack!" yelled Elmer as he headed off into the crowd.

Soon another cheer went up from the boisterous crowd. This time because a man had walked out to the centre of the stage to speak. Then with top hat in hand, he started "Good evening ladies and gentlemen! Tonight the Monte Carlo Dancehall and Casino is extremely proud to present the most exciting and popular act in the Klondike! Now here she is!, The Jewel of the North!, The Flower of the Yukon!, and The Belle of Dawson City! Miss Klondike Kate Rockwell!"

The crowd cheered as a hoard of men raced to the front of the stage to be as close as possible. Then the curtain went up to show Kate standing in the centre of the stage, wearing nothing but two hundred yards of tightly wrapped transparent chiffon. The men cheered even louder as it was so thin and tight it still revealed her exquisite form. The only other thing she had on was a crown of twenty-four small lit candles that forced her to hold her head high, like a proud queen or a girl learning how to walk with books on her head.

When the music began to play, she began singing a slow love song. And Kate could sing! As the song went on, many of the men pressing against the stage began to take on the appearance of love-struck children. When the song ended the music kept playing, and Kate dropped the end of her chiffon wrap to the floor and began slowly turning.

The men began cheering again. They cheered for her song, and they cheered for her dropping the chiffon, and they gleefully showed their appreciation by throwing nuggets on the stage.

Then the music slowly began to quicken and Kate began to dance as she turned. And Kate could dance! The men marvelled at how seductively she could move, even with chiffon wrapped to her ankles and a crown of candles on her head.

Slowly she danced a little faster, and turned a little quicker, and with each turn another wrap of chiffon fell to the floor. For awhile as the dance sped up, each turn would reveal more of her bare legs, and just above the last wrap to fall would become transparent. As the wraps came off, the men became more and more excited, until nuggets were bouncing all over the stage. Then, when it appeared that if just a few more wraps came off she'd be left naked or in complete transparency, she'd continue to slow down more and more until barely turning. The men didn't want her to stop, so to encourage her on, they threw even more gold. For the last few turns Kate did, it absolutely rained nuggets around her.

As she walked off stage, she smiled and waved flirtatiously back at the men, causing a bunch of them to charge to the same side of the stage, to try and get back to meet her.

Before the cheering and applause subsided, two men with large push-brooms quickly came out and pushed all the gold into a pile, then plowed it off stage. While they were sweeping, the music continued to play, and a dozen costumed dancehall girls streamed onto the stage lining up near the back, and slowly began dancing back and forth with their hands on their hips.

Then the M.C. took the stage again, and yelling loudly to be heard over the music said "And now! For the new dance rage! Direct from Paris, France! The Can-Can Polka!"

Suddenly the girls formed a razor straight line, and as the orchestra began to really blast the music out, the trumpets, coronets, and trombones seemed to descend a scale getting ready to explode, and when they did, the girls came bouncing and kicking their way forward in perfect unison seeming to shake the entire building. No one had seen anything like it, and the whole place cheered wildly! When the girls reached the front of the stage, they held their arms out straight linking up shoulder to shoulder. Then continuing to bounce in the same perfect unison, they all held one knee high while twirling their ankles in small circles, then suddenly kicked their legs higher than the men thought possible. The loud cheering then became a deafening roar and the place went crazy! Nuggets, hats, poker chips, bowties, and everything else landed on stage, and pandemonium reigned!

With Belle still sitting on his lap, Elmer looked at Henry with a big smile on his face and yelled "What a night! ...What a night!"

Henry sat with his arm around Becky and a contented smile almost as big as Elmer's. "Yes!" he agreed, "What a night!"

Henry woke the next morning with a pounding headache. And as he got up to get a drink of water, Elmer began to stir. When he looked over to Elmer's bed, he saw that he hadn't even gotten in it to sleep, but instead had flopped down on top of the covers, still wearing his jacket and boots.

"Do ya want drink a water Elmer?" he asked.

"Yes, please, don't yell." he moaned.

Henry handed him the glass saying, "It smells kinda rank and stuffy in here, I'll open the window." He walked over to it and reaching for the latch, suddenly pulled his hand back saying "What the heck?" Elmer had thrown up all over the window, the latch, the sill, and the wall.

"Oh,...yea," he said remembering, "I couldn't find the latch in time."

"Well, we better pull ourselves together." said Henry, "We gotta go to the Claims Office." Then he grabbed his gold poke to see what was in it. "You got any money left?" he asked Elmer.

"Not a speck." he answered, "Don't even have to look."

"I only got a little bit left." said Henry, "Maybe a couple of ounces. It should be enough to file our claims though. It's a good thing we paid Sid up front."

It soon became apparent that as bad a shape as Henry was in, Elmer was worse, so Henry said "You can stay here and rest some more. I'll go down and see where Sid is in the line."

"I have to come." replied Elmer. "If he's near the front, we each have to file one of the claims."

"No,..we don't." said Henry, "I never thought of it 'till last night, and I didn't wanna tell you then."

"What?" asked Elmer concerned.

"We can't file the claim that you staked because we were lost at the time." said Henry, "We can't point it out on a map. It should be okay though, even if someone else finds it, they'll see our posts and figure they're too late. But this time when we go there, we'll figure out where we are." And with that, Henry left for the Claims Office.

A couple of hours later he returned. "I filed the claim." he said, "They gave me metal tags we have to nail on the posts. We got lucky too. Sid was almost to the front of the line. He said that a little while ago, it took three days to reach the front of the line."

"I figured out something too." said Elmer, "I shoulda bought work clothes before we went to the Monte Carlo. Now I gotta find more gold to get 'em, and once we leave town, I'm gonna blend in like a fish in the desert."

"Yea, that place sure sucked the money out of us." replied Henry.

So they picked up their packs and began the trip back out to Little Knob Hill. As they reached the outskirts of Dawson, Elmer asked "Are you going to tell Becky you're leaving town?"

"She already knows." answered Henry, "I told her last night, and I'd like to refill my poke before I see her again. I seem to talk better."

It was fourteen miles out to Bonanza, and for the first five miles they drank from pretty much every creek they came to. When they eventually arrived, they saw that Belinda had the beginnings of a little town coming along. In fact, they could have eaten at her new restaurant if they'd had any money left. She also had a bar, a hotel, a store, and cabins to rent. And she was also building a post office as there were now a good number of people living at Bonanza. Even so, many of Belinda's friends in the business establishment, still thought of it as sure folly to invest in buildings outside of Dawson.

Henry and Elmer didn't stop though, they didn't want to dawdle on this trip. So they followed the trail to the same place as before, then crossed over to the hills and thrashed their way through the hated willows and small trees until finally reaching their claim on Little Knob Hill.

"I guess we better nail these tags on the posts first." said Henry. So they each took a tag and nailed it to one of the posts, then grabbed a pan and shovel and headed up the hill to start mining. But when they reached the top and looked at where they'd worked, it didn't look right.

It seemed pretty much the same, but there didn't appear to be any of the white gravel in it. "Where's the white rocks and gravel that was here?" wondered Henry.

"Maybe it's dirty or something and we're just not seeing it." suggested Elmer.

They both stared at it with growing concern, until Henry said "Let's hope so." and stabbed his shovel into the ground. "Well, it's melted down like we hoped anyway." he added, continuing to dig a hole.

"At least we know that no one else came and dug it up on us." said Elmer.

Henry dug down about a foot and a half before hitting the now familiar permafrost. Then they took a pan full from the bottom of the hole, and another from the surface, then moved down to the creek to pan them out.

When they were finished, both pans showed the same results. Almost nothing. "What happened to our gold?" asked Elmer.

"I wish I knew." replied Henry as he sat down. Elmer sat down too. It was as if the strength to stand was being drained out of them. For a few minutes they sat switching their gaze from the pans, to the top of the hill, and back again. Finally Henry said "We have to try again." So they picked up the pans and headed up the hill again.

This time when they looked at where to dig, Elmer saw a small bit of white gravel, so put it in the pan along with the dirt surrounding it. Henry filled his pan from a new hole, and they again went to the creek to find out what they had.

When Elmer had finished sluicing his dirt out he said "I gotta couple of ounces this time."

When Henry finished he said "I got the same as last time. Nothin'."

They were confused now, so went back, and again they both got nothing. Elmer said "I'm gonna try a new place not quite on top of the hill."

"I'm gonna sit down and think about this." said Henry, "Maybe light a fire." It bothered him that he couldn't figure out what had happened.

By the time Elmer returned with his pan full of dirt, Henry had a small fire going, so he watched as Elmer filled his pan with water to try one more time. He was extra careful washing the dirt out this time, but when he finished and stood up, he said "Not even a speck."

"I think I know what might a happened here." said Henry, as Elmer sat down by the fire. "You know how the hills we walked along to get here were all staked because of the White Channel."

"Yea, and ours was the last hill in the line." replied Elmer.

"Yes, but all the other hills were higher than ours." said Henry, "And I think when they dig down on those hills they hit the top of the White Channel. But because our hill is so short, when we dug down we hit the bottom of the channel. That's why it seemed so good, 'cause the bottom of the channel has the most gold, and we were scraping off the absolute bottom"

"Well, that'd explain why digging deeper doesn't find us any more gold." answered Elmer, "And one thing's for sure. There's no more gold."

It'd been a really long day so far, especially considering how it started out, and with just a thin layer of cloud in the sky, it wasn't going to rain any time soon, so they decided to eat and sleep before moving on to find their other claim.

When they woke the next day, it felt as if they'd each gotten a long, deep sleep. But because of thicker cloud cover, they really couldn't tell what time of day it was. They were still pretty dogged from yesterday's disappointment, so were a bit slow getting started. But eventually they gathered themselves together and began plodding their way through the bush, determined to follow the exact same course as before.

It was easy at first, simply following over the hills until the claim posts ran out. But then it became trickier to head the direction they thought Dawson was in, while at the same time following the path of least resistance. Their plan worked though, and eventually they descended a hill to again pop out on what looked to be the right creek.

"Do you think this is the right place?" said Elmer.

"Yea I do," replied Henry, "But it doesn't look right. We're not in the same spot."

They looked around for a few seconds, then "Down there." said Elmer pointing down the creek. A couple of hundred feet away was the hole they'd dug the previous trip.

As soon as they got to it Elmer dropped his pack, then grabbed his pan and shovel and began filling the pan with gravel. It was as if he wanted to make sure the gold hadn't gone anywhere. It wasn't that strange when you consider what had just happened to them.

He'd relaxed by the time they'd finishing panning though, as they'd both found very good gold again. "We should fill our pokes, then figure out exactly where we are." said Henry, "Then get back to Dawson to file this claim"

"It'd be quicker if we used our other stick a dynamite." said Elmer.

"That's a good idea." replied Henry. So they buried the stick in the hole they'd already dug, and this time when they lit it and ran, they ran much further away, having learned their lesson at Little Knob Hill.

After hearing the explosion, they quickly made their way back up the creek, to find that their hole was about three feet deeper and had filled with water. It didn't matter though, they could still easily reach the bottom with their shovels.

As they tried to lift the dirt through the water, they had to move their shovels very slowly or the current they created would leave them with nothing. It took a few tries, but they got better at it and eventually filled their pans. They couldn't wait to see what they had. Taking the dirt from much deeper down should produce much better gold.

Suddenly a disturbance in the bush caught their attention, and Clarence Berry stepped out on the gravel bar. "Hello Henry," he said nodding his head. Then noticing Elmer's clothes, he tipped his hat chuckling and added, "Yer Lordship." then he asked "What are you guys doin' way up here? I thought ya dug into the White Channel."

"We did….Briefly." answered Henry, "This is our other claim. What are you doin' out here?"

"I was on my way to Lippy's cabin when I heard the explosion." said Clarence. "Thought I'd check it out."

So, did you guys stake this claim?" he asked.

"We staked it but didn't file it." answered Henry again, "We're not quite sure where we are."

"Well I can tell ya." answered Berry, "This is the headwaters of Eldorado. You're on Tom Lippy's claim."

"What!" said Henry, "We were lost when we found it, but we checked for claim posts and we didn't find any!" Then he remembered how they hadn't checked that well and just assumed they were in the middle of nowhere.

"One of his posts is right over there." said Berry, pointing about fifty feet upstream and to the other side of the creek. "Where'd ya put yours?"

"We went about two hundred and fifty feet each way." said Henry. "So part of what you staked is on the 'Lucky Swede's' claim." said Clarence. "He has the next one up from Lippy."

"Eldorado?" said Elmer, "That explains why the creek is so good."

"You guys better come with me to Tom's cabin." said Berry, "He's gonna want to know who blasted into his claim. You better knock down your posts first too, the Swede could already be in Dawson trying to find out who's cross-filing on him. Whose name did you put on the posts?"

"Mine" said Elmer.

"You'd both probably get credit for it, but you'll be the one known as the claim jumper." said Berry. "And you don't want that. If Steele even thought for a minute you'd done it on purpose, he'd probably hang you on Front Street."

They both knew it was serious, and left immediately to take down their posts. When they returned they dumped the dirt from their pans and began following Berry to Lippy's place. "This should be fun." said Clarence, getting a kick out of the whole situation.

"Ya, a real hayride." replied Henry sarcastically.

"I wouldn't worry too much." said Clarence, "Tom's a pretty easy goin' guy." It was true. If you were going to get caught mining someone else's claim, of all the men in the area Lippy was probably the best natured.

As they approached Tom's cabin, they saw him out front hitting golf balls towards an empty bucket. "I'd rather he wasn't holding a club." said Elmer.

When Lippy saw them coming, he stopped hitting balls and walked towards them and his fire pit. "Howdy fellas." He said, "Sit down. I heard you struck it rich."

"Well,..sort of," answered Henry as they sat down, "And we're feelin' mighty bad about it."

"How does that happen?" asked Tom.

So they told him everything. How they'd followed the advice that Tom himself had given them, to finding Little Knob Hill, then getting lost on the way back to Dawson and stumbling on to his claim.

After hearing how it all happened, Tom actually seemed kind of amused by it. "I guess no harm done." he said.

"Well, we did blast a hole in the creek." said Henry.

"What...?" exclaimed Lippy. "When I met ya, you were packin' things for Belinda. Where did you get the dynamite?"

"Clarence gave it to us." they both replied together with Elmer pointing at him.

"What!" exclaimed Lippy again looking over to Clarence, "You helped!"

"Well I didn't know they were goin' to blow up your claim with it!" he replied, while trying to keep from laughing.

"You bastard." said Tom picking up a small stick and throwing it at him.

Clarence was laughing openly now, and as Lippy looked for another stick to throw, Clarence jumped up and backed away about twenty feet to make himself a harder target. "Really Tom. Sorry." he giggled as another stick flew by.

"Yea, I can see yer distraught." said Lippy. "You owe me a steak dinner!"

"Okay! Okay! conceded Berry, "You and your wife both."

As Tom and Clarence sat back down again, Tom turned to Henry and Elmer and said, "And you guys owe me a steak dinner too."

"Deal!" said Henry, just glad their penalty was so light. Then he said to Clarence, "I guess we should give you your gold pans back too."

"Naw, you guys had enough hard luck," he replied, "And you might be able to use 'em again"

"I got coffee on the stove." said Lippy, "You guys want some?" Henry and Elmer gladly accepted, hoping to use it like a tonic on their troubles. Clarence too accepted, and when they were just about finished Clarence and Tom's wives appeared. They were returning from Dawson with a small amount of supplies. Clarence's wife Ethel was carrying a lightly loaded pack, while Tom's wife carried a packboard with a new window for their cabin tied to it. "Well, I gotta go back to work," said Tom, "The only reason Salome went to town was to get a real window for the cabin. There'll be hell to pay if I don't put it in today."

"I'll help ya." said Clarence.

So Henry and Elmer apologized to Lippy again, then said goodbye to everyone and left for Dawson.

They were barely out of sight of the cabin, when the depression they'd been fighting hit them like a train. They'd hidden it well talking to Tom and Clarence, but now they were becoming extremely distraught, and were just putting one foot in front of the other, not caring when or if they ever got to Dawson.

They didn't speak much at all for a few miles down the trail, when Elmer said, "Let's pull off somewhere and eat, then figure out what we're gonna do when we get to town."

"Yea." replied Henry, "It'll be better than wandering around Dawson trying to think."

So the next small creek they came to, they turned off the trail and went about a hundred feet in the bush to a small clearing. There they lit a fire, but rather than prepare something to eat, they both just sat down. They were too depressed to eat.

Once more they didn't talk for awhile, but just sat thinking about not having any money again, and the embarrassment they were going to feel back in town. Finally Henry said, "Well Elmer, we really pooped our pants on this one."

"Yup." agreed Elmer, "Crapped 'em in public."

"Prospecting for gold sure has its ups and downs." added Henry.

"Yea," replied Elmer, "but whenever we do it, it turns into a real train wreck."

"Oh,..no!" remembered Henry as he flopped back on the ground. "I'm gonna have to tell Becky." Then rubbing his eyes with both hands he said, "I'd rather tell her my brain was damaged as a child."

"You know," said Elmer, "people might make fun of us, but at least we know what it feels like to be rich, even if it was for just one day. Most people never will."

"Yea, but we acted pretty stupid." suggested Henry as he sat up again. "I been thinkin' about it. We walked into town with about a thousand dollars each. It'd take a full three years to make that much money back home, and we blew it in one night in the Monte Carlo."

"But Dawson just sucks it out of ya." replied Elmer, as if it wasn't all their fault.

"Most of it we spent on booze." said Henry, "Swiftwater Bill didn't drink, I don't see why I had to. Besides, I felt like crap the next day."

"Well that's true." agreed Elmer. "I coulda done without ol' John Barley-corn. In fact, I didn't wanna tell ya, but when you went to the Claims Office the next morning, I threw up again… and I had a case a the green apple splatters."

"Anyway," said Henry, "I plan on doing things different next time. If there is a next time."

"Yea, me too." agreed Elmer again. "But I sure wish I wasn't dressed like a carpetbagger."

"Maybe out here you are," answered Henry, "but for town you're just dressed kinda flashy."

"With money, I'd be flashy," replied Elmer, "without money, I'm more like a rat with a gold tooth. And now to top it off, I'm Scratchy the Klondike Claim Jumper."

"Don't try and grab all the glory," said Henry, "remember, I'm the famous Dawson City mudlover."

Elmer got up to get more wood for the fire, and still angry with himself over his clothes, as he walked away he began waggling his head back and forth and talking like a child, saying "I'm Scratchy the Claimjumper and I'm a big boy."

He returned in a couple of minutes with an armload of wood, and after placing a few pieces on the fire, sat back down again to resume trying to figure their next best move.

The clouds had been thickening all day, until now the gathering gloom matched their own, and it began dropping rain on them. It didn't budge them at all. For almost an hour they just sat absorbing the rain with indifference, until finally Henry stood up and said, "Well, let's go ask Belinda for our jobs back."

"Do ya figure?" said Elmer.

"Yes," replied Henry, "the White Channel will be all staked by now, and anywhere else left would be a real crapshoot. So until a new place is discovered, I think Belinda is our best bet. She'll probably hire us, and hopefully she'll pay us seventeen dollars a day like before."

"I think your right." said Elmer getting up. "Let's go."

So they left for Dawson again, and again didn't do much talking until they reached the Klondike River. Then as town came into sight Henry said, "We have that couple of ounces from Little Knob Hill, so let's get something to eat at Belinda's. That'll give us a chance to ask her for jobs."

"Good idea." said Elmer.

Then Henry added, "If it works, there should still be enough money left for you to buy a work shirt and a light coat."

"That'd be great," replied Elmer, "then I won't look like a guy who's just lost a fortune."

When they arrived back at Belinda's restaurant, it was very busy. She'd hired plenty of new people to work in the place, and a few of them were women, mainly because they were more available now, but partly to attract more business.

Belinda was working hard along with her new staff, but when she saw Henry and Elmer she came straight over to them.

"I heared you guys struck it big." she said, looking at their clothes. "Come back and tell me about it." and she led them into the back of the restaurant, past the kitchen to where she lived.

On the way, she told one of the girls in the kitchen to bring three coffees back to her, and by the time they sat down at her table, the girl set the coffee down and went back out to work.

"We didn't exactly strike it rich." said Henry. "We thought we had for a couple a days, but then it all went horribly wrong."

They went on to tell her the whole story, even with the embarrassing parts, and finished with Elmer saying, "And that's why I'm dressed for a wedding."

"Do you guys want work?" asked Belinda.

"Actually that's why we're here." answered Henry.

"It'll be a little different than last time." she said, "For one thing, you guys won't be working together most of the time. Here's my situation. It's easier to find workers now than it was before, but some of them aren't, let's say of the same calibre as people who came over the Chilkoot. Some don't know what they're doing, some are lazy, and some are just plain useless. I sent a couple of guys out to Bonanza with some things, and they couldn't find the place."

"How is that possible." replied Henry.

"That's what I said!" answered Belinda. "Anyway, I need you both to be foremen. Elmer, I'm gonna want you to lead men out to Bonanza and back, keep track of what gets transported, talk to the foreman at Bonanza, he'll have lists of things he needs, that sort of thing."

"And I've decided to build the best and most extravagant hotel in the Klondike. In fact, I've already started it down on Front Street. I'm gonna call it the 'Fairview'." she said. "But I've got the same problem, guys keep quitting, some don't know what they're doing, but mostly I need someone I can trust." Then looking at Henry she said, "Somebody to list materials, purchase things, transport them, keep track of everything, all the whatnots. If you want the jobs, I'll pay you twenty dollars a day plus room and board."

"Of course we'll take the jobs." said Henry with Elmer agreeing. "But we'd like to buy a meal now." added Elmer practically starving.

"I'll spring for it." she laughed, "Call it a hiring bonus." Then she got up and went to the doorway and yelled to the kitchen staff, "Two steak and eggs in here!" then she turned to them and added, "I'll go get a room arranged for you. You can start tomorrow."

As soon as she left Henry said, "This is better than I hoped, twenty dollars plus room and board. We might even be able to save a chunk a money if we try."

"Plus we haven't eaten a steak in about two years," said Elmer, still thinking about the food.

Belinda returned and visited with them, until they finished their extraordinary meal. Then Elmer went to settle into their new accommodations, before heading off to buy clothes more suited to his new job. At the same time, Henry decided to get his dreaded but unavoidable meeting with Becky over with. He badly wanted to see her but feared what she might think of him being broke again What worried him even more, was that she might think he was stupid like before.

When Henry left Belinda's, the rain had stopped and the sun was out again, so when he arrived at Becky's place at the catwalks, she was out sitting and talking to Belle in front of her tent.

He sat talking with them awhile and was trying to figure out how to get her alone, when to his surprise, she suggested they go for a walk along the river. As soon as they were alone, she put one hand on his arm and wrapped the other through his, just like she had in the Monte Carlo. When Henry looked at her, she smiled and said, "In case we see somebody and they want me to dance."

Henry was really messed up on the inside now. She made him feel like a million dollars, and at the same time thought he was worth a fortune, while he had to tell her he wasn't worth anything at all. It took a few minutes to work up the courage, but he finally came clean, telling her of their misadventure and how it all went bad.

"Well, it's not the end of the world." she said. "Besides, we still have the map."

He couldn't believe her attitude and how she thought about him. Then she said, "It seems like almost everyone else is getting rich. Why not us?"

All Henry could think about now, was that she hadn't moved her arms away from him at all, and she used the word 'us'. He was in love.

As they strolled along the river, he had a look around for other people. He'd decided to try and kiss her but he didn't want to damage her reputation. He saw no one, so stopped walking and pulled her close to steal a quick kiss, but when she wrapped her arms around his neck and pulled him close too, the kiss lasted much longer than he thought, or even hoped.

On the way back to her place, he remembered that he actually had things he could tell her that weren't bad, like having a great paying foreman's job in town. By the time he was saying goodbye to her, Becky kissed him again, this time in front of Belle. This caused him to walk home just as he had the first time he came to her place, kicking imaginary rocks the whole way.

The next morning Henry and Elmer began their new employment with Belinda, and quickly found that their jobs were the best they'd ever had. Rather than work like dogs, they held positions of authority where they facilitated things, recorded, planned logistics, and did general troubleshooting on Belinda's projects.

Over the next week they settled into their new occupations, but they both kept Tombstone in mind, and continuously questioned anyone who might possess knowledge on the subject. Henry also took any and every opportunity to go see Becky, with her occasionally meeting him at Belinda's when he got off work.

While Henry's relationship had grown, some of their friends situations had changed as well. Swiftwater Bill had married Nellie Lamore, and a week later their marriage and relationship were over. Very soon after, Bill had a new girl. Her name was Grace, and she was the younger sister of Gussie and Nellie, and she was quickly known as 'The Queen of the Monte Carlo'.

Kate Rockwell's situation had changed too. She was still wearing thousand dollar dresses and was by far the most popular person in the Yukon. But now other dancehall girls were gaining fame and notoriety as well. Bombay Peggy, Sweet Marie, and all three of the Lamore sisters were known as queens of the dancehalls. And Blanche Lamonte, Cad Wilson, and Diamond Tooth Gertie who had a diamond fixed in one of her front teeth. Practically all of them sported huge nugget-laden chains like Kate's, and slender bejewelled gold pokes.

Kate was now receiving many gifts, love letters, and marriage proposals every day, and she'd fallen in love with a man named Alexander Pantages. He'd apparently been a prizefighter at one time, but was now a waiter, and because of his lack of money, Kate spent lavishly on him, including silk shirts and fine suits and jewellery. She also used her influence to get him into a vaudeville act at the Orpheum Theatre.

The biggest surprise to everyone had been Wilson Mizner. He'd almost thrown his reputation as well as his future away, with an ill-conceived robbery attempt. In a decided effort to impress his new girlfriend Gussie, he planned to make her a gift of a large amount of chocolate. But with gold practically everywhere, when he broke into a popular restaurant, he found that it was the chocolate that was locked in the safe. Upon being spotted and unable to crack the safe, he quickly ran off to a nearby theatre, where he'd been singing and playing the piano during the evenings.

So with his co-workers providing an alibi, and only one witness and nothing actually stolen, and also because it seemed very out of character for Mizner, Steele didn't lay any charges against him. Though he did receive a stern warning accompanied with a frightening glare.

As Dawson City grew, Sam Steele was also gaining fame and popularity. With so much money at stake in every aspect of life in the Klondike, many attempts were being made to bribe both Steele and his Mounties, but both were proving to be absolutely incorruptible. Almost inconceivable when you consider that they only made a dollar a day like people in the south.

A story was also circulating in the city, about a man in Steele's court charged with cheating men in a card game. When Steele began reading his sentence, he said "A fifty dollar fine," and before he could finish speaking the man cut him off, blurting out "Fifty dollars! I got that right here in my shirt pocket!" Then Steele finished, saying "And sixty days on the woodpile. You got that in your other shirt pocket?"

With the continuous influx of people arriving in Dawson, people were demanding that Steele establish some control over the prostitution. The entire city and all its businesses operated twenty-four hours a day, and the prostitutes were no different. Accurate numbers were impossible to obtain, but somewhere between a hundred fifty and four hundred 'ladies' walked the streets or operated from brothels. So Steele forced them to move from King Street or 'Paradise Alley' to a place on the outskirts of town that was quickly dubbed 'Lousetown' or 'Hell's Half Acre'. He also stopped them from plying their trade from eight o'clock in the morning until four o'clock in the afternoon.

Their new place of residence was basically built over a swamp, so had highly elevated boardwalks running throughout, causing some of the extremely drunk patrons to take spectacular tumbles into the mud and swamp below.

Anyway, business flourished, Dawson boomed, and the ships kept arriving one after another. The gold kept flowing, and many a miner strutted into town sporting a fat poke on his belt, only to stumble home hours later, carrying an empty moosehide sack.

As good as Henry and Elmer's jobs were, the first thing they had to do each day was to walk past Leadtooth, then at least once again when they returned home from work. There was usually a fair amount of traffic to blend in with, and Leadtooth was always a busy guy, but on occasion they'd undergo a smouldering glare from the criminal, and twice Elmer had to dodge pieces of cordwood. Fortunately, the thug was powerless to become any more of a threat, so all they had to do was keep their wits about them.

At Henry's job, he was watching Belinda's Fairview go up fast. He also saw other buildings nearing completion. Just off Front Street they were putting the roof on Arizona Charlie's 'Palace Grand Dance Hall and Theatre', which Charlie was promising, would be the most opulent in the Klondike.

Meanwhile, Elmer was watching the population of Bonanza soar into the hundreds, with the rate of its growth actually increasing. So to speed up her building, Belinda purchased more animals. And now Elmer was leading a string of more than a dozen mules and horses back and forth to Bonanza, as well as a half dozen men. On occasion even Gary would join in the procession.

One day returning from Bonanza, Elmer encountered Swiftwater Bill at his claim with a bevy of dancehall girls. Bill regularly brought groups of them out to let them try their hand at panning, and to show off the richness of his claim. He said to Elmer, "You wouldn't believe it. For the first pan they're complete novices, city girls, worried about breaking a nail, or getting dirty. But when they see how much gold they find in the bottom, by the second pan they become absolute professionals."

Then Elmer noticed Big Alex McDonald walking towards him. The gigantic man had travelled out with Bill and the girls to check on some of his own claims, but as long as there were pretty girls all over Bill's claim, he thought he might as well stay and visit awhile. "Hello kid." he said, "Elmer, isn't it? I'm guessing we're not partners anymore."

Henry and Elmer hadn't gone back to tell him what happened to his grubstake money. "Sorry Mister McDonald," replied Elmer a little scared. "But it didn't pan out, and we forgot to come and tell ya."

It was only partly true. They were actually worried that he wouldn't believe them, especially after they bought new clothes and spent a fortune in the Monte Carlo in front of all to see. So Elmer explained to him how it all happened.

"That's okay kid." he drawled out. "It was worth the money just to hear how ya blew up Lippy's claim. Funniest thing I heared all summer."

"Yea" agreed Bill, "I spilled half a cup a tea when I heard that."

Elmer didn't much like that everyone had heard how he blew a hole on Lippy's claim, but he was glad that Big Alex knew. Actually it turned out that Big Alex didn't care about gold at all. He loved searching for it, but once in his possession he gave it away by the bucket load, considering it nothing more than yellow dirt. In fact, he openly called it "nothing but trash". A strange irony in that he was known to everyone as the bona fide King of the Klondike, and made regular deposits to the bank of a thousand pounds or more.

Back in Dawson at Belinda's restaurant, Henry sat having lunch with Becky and Belinda. As Belinda sipped her preferred tea, they talked of the big news to hit Dawson. Soapy Smith was dead. Just a few days after Independence Day, he got into a shootout with a man and both men were killed.

The people of Skagway had realized that their town's infamous character had become well known in the Klondike and southern cities as well, and it was costing them a future. Whether people were travelling to or from the Klondike, most had begun using the riverboats to avoid Skagway completely. Whenever the citizens of Skagway tried to have a meeting to discuss the issue, spies from Soapy's gang would gather around to listen, intimidate, and break up the meeting. In desperation, the townsfolk finally decided to hold their meeting down on Skagway's dock, where they could guard against unwanted intrusion.

When Soapy heard what was happening, he heavily armed himself and proceeded toward the dock to break up the meeting. A tactic that had worked before. This time however, a fed-up citizen named Frank Reid had had enough, and confronted Soapy and some of his gang at the end of the dock. A shootout then ensued, leaving Soapy dead and Reid to die a couple of days later.

Within minutes of Soapy's death vigilante groups began to form, and most of the gang were rounded up in a few hours, with the rest ferreted out over the next couple of days. The lengthy crime wave conducted by Soapy and his gang was over.

"Well, I for one don't mind seeing Soapy and his gang go down in flames." said Belinda, "You probably don't either." she added looking at Henry. "Wasn't it his gang that got Elmer on the Pass?"

"Yup" replied Henry, "They got us for a few dollars in Skagway too." Then Henry asked "How did they get you?"

"They didn't" answered Belinda, "But I got a big shipment of goods coming from Skagway any day now. Valuable stuff too. It's the guts to the Fairview. Fine crystal, bone china, mahogany furniture, that kind a stuff. Now I don't have to worry about Soapy and his boys clippin' part or even all of it. I heared it was getting pretty bad there lately. That if you shook hands with anybody, you better count your fingers."

"I can't imagine it getting worse than when we went through." said Henry. "It'd be hell on earth."

Henry and Rebecca finished eating, and Becky said "Let's go for a walk Henry."

"Sure" he replied, "Where should we go this time?" Henry didn't have to walk miles every day like Elmer did, so didn't mind going for walks, especially with Becky.

"Let's go down river to that big bluff." she said. "See what Dawson looks like from up high."

Then Belinda asked, "If you guys are going that way, could you check on how things are going at the Fairview? Like I said, the interior and all the furnishings should be coming from Skagway any day now, and I'm hoping to have the building finished when it gets here."

"Sure Belinda. No problem." answered Henry. He had the afternoon off, but was going to be walking right by it anyway.

As they began their walk through Dawson, Becky held on to Henry's arm as she always did. It was one of Henry's favourite things about their small excursions. He also liked the fact that she enjoyed wandering the hills and waterways around Dawson. For if she'd rather have been entertained in the city, he would have certainly obliged, but it would also just as certainly have kept him broke.

As they strolled down Front Street towards the Fairview, they came upon a large number of people massed in front of Silent Sam's Bank Saloon. Regularly held poker games in Sam's gambling house were often played for very high stakes, sometimes reaching the extreme. But right now a huge crowd of people had gathered to witness unheard of levels.

One of the players at the table was Silent Sam himself, or 'Square Sam' as he was often called, because he always ran a fair game. Another of the players was Sam's best friend Lois Golden, or 'Goldie' as everyone called him. They had actually come north together before the gold rush ever started. But right now they were adversaries in a huge hand of poker, where the pot had reached over fifty thousand dollars.

Then a man standing in the doorway of the packed saloon, relayed to the people outside "Sam just raised twenty-five thousand dollars!" and as the crowd on the street buzzed and speculated, the man yelled again "Goldie called, and raised another twenty-five thousand!" Then he looked back inside for a few seconds and yelled "And Sam calls!"

An open gasp went through the crowd as the bets were in gold, and the pot was now an incredible ten thousand ounces. In fact more. Then the people went quiet, waiting to hear the result of the incredible hand. The man yelled out "Goldie, four queens!" and then after a moment "Sam, four kings!" The crowd cheered and applauded, some as if they'd won the pot themselves.

When Henry and Rebecca resumed their walk again, Becky said, "One thing about coming to the Klondike, is I'll never forget some of the things I've seen up here."

After making sure all was well at the Fairview, they continued through town and out to the many paths and meadows that surrounded Dawson. It was mid-July now, and the fireweed flowers were in full bloom all over the Yukon. Most grew two to four feet high, with some growing as high as a person, and the top foot or two of all of them was covered with hundreds of light purple blossoms. Some of the wild meadows were completely blanketed with them, and when Henry and Rebecca crossed through such a field, Becky stopped to pick a few, and when Henry saw her with them growing up past her waist, and the afternoon sun beaming down on her, it burned into his mind like a photograph. If it was possible, he was now even more smitten with her. When Becky saw Henry looking at her she smiled back at him, and Henry said, "One thing about coming to the Klondike, is I'll never forget some of the things I've seen up here."

For the next week, everything went well for Henry and Elmer, as well as Rebecca. But Belinda was becoming increasingly concerned about her shipment from Skagway. Then one morning while Henry was working at the Fairview, he overheard a disturbing conversation. He immediately left for Belinda's, and a short time later was standing in her establishment waving her over to him.

"What's up Henry?" she asked curiously, "Something wrong?"

"I think maybe there is." he replied, "We should probably talk alone."

They stepped outside and Henry followed her away from the door. "What is it?" she asked.

"I was sitting in the Fairview doing some paperwork," started Henry, "and some guys came walking along the boardwalk. And when they got in front of the place they started talking. One guy mentioned how the Fairview was just about finished, and it probably wouldn't be long before it opened. But one guy was Bill McPhee, and he said he just got back from Skagway, and that the Fairview wasn't going to be opening for awhile. And that you had a surprise coming. Then when one of the others asked him what he meant, he said his saloon was running low on whisky, and that he had a big shipment on its way to Skagway, and wanted to get it here as fast as possible. But he couldn't find a packing outfit. So he paid some guy named Brooks that was packing your stuff, to dump it on the side of the trail, and then move his outfit back to Skagway to carry his whisky when it arrived."

Belinda looked in shock. "Are you sure that's what they said?" she asked.

"Yup." replied Henry.

"Are you sure it was Bill McPhee?" she added.

"Absolutely." said Henry.

"And they didn't know you were listening?"

"Not unless they could see through walls." he assured her.

Then Belinda paced for a few seconds thinking. "Was Elmer still out back when you came in?" she asked.

"They were still loading the animals." replied Henry. Then she hurried around back, with Henry following behind.

When Elmer saw them coming, he stopped what he was doing and walked towards them. "Belinda, I wanted to see you before I left." he said. "A couple of guys in my crew said some of the town is laughing at you. They said your cargo for the Fairview is layin' on the trail somewhere."

She was angry now. She said to Henry and Elmer, "You guys come with me." Then she yelled to Elmer's crew, "You guys! Don't go anywhere! Just stay here until I get back!" Then she marched off with Henry and Elmer to McPhee's Pioneer Saloon.

When they reached the entrance to his establishment, she said "You guys wait out here." Then she pushed through the doors to confront McPhee.

A few minutes passed before the doors flung open again, and Belinda stomped across the boardwalk and started down the street. Then McPhee appeared in the doorway and yelled out "It's just business!"

Belinda spun around as if she'd been shot. "Fine!" she raged back at him, "Then you can watch me do a little business of my own!"

With that she turned to Henry and said, "I want you to go to the shipping office and buy two tickets on the first boat going upriver, then come back to my place." Then she turned to walk away but yelled back "And passage for a dog too!" Then she marched off towards her place with Elmer at her side.

When they arrived back at Belinda's, Elmer's crew was still waiting. "Don't go anywhere Elmer." she said. "Wait for Henry to come back." then added, "I've got some organizing to do." Then she disappeared inside.

Soon Henry was back, and told Belinda that he'd booked the passage on a riverboat leaving in about three hours. There were ships sailing upriver to Miles Canyon regularly now, and more boats operating on Lake Bennett and the river above the Canyon.

Then Belinda said "Henry, I'm going to need you to take Elmer's crew to Bonanza today."

"What do ya want me to do?" asked Elmer.

"Pack your stuff." she said, "You're coming to Skagway with me." Then she said to Henry "We should be gone about a week or so. I want you to concentrate on the Fairview. If they need anything at Bonanza, you can send Elmer's crew by themselves. But if they come back with a list, you'll have to buy what they need and get them ready for the next trip. Oh, yea, and tell everyone who works for me, that if I find out they were in McPhee's saloon after today, they're fired."

Three hours later Elmer, Belinda and Nero, all stood on the deck of a large paddlewheeler as it began to churn its way upstream. Elmer had always enjoyed the Yukon scenery, at least when he wasn't worried about dying, and now he was about to see a lot more of it.

But as the miles went by, he found himself becoming more and more concerned with this Brooks fellow they were going to confront. Finally he had to ask Belinda, "So what's this Brooks guy like?"

"Well, he's pretty rugged." she answered.

"How rugged?" asked Elmer.

"Well, you know how cold the water is up here?"

"Yes, I do." he replied, "Very well."

"And you know how when the ships get to Skagway, even though they're still a quarter mile from shore, they dump everything overboard, including the animals?"

"I remember." said Elmer.

"Well, when they dumped Brooks' mules in, he dove in and swam to shore with them with all his clothes on."

By the next morning, the sights and scenery had changed a lot, as the sternwheeler had already taken them over one hundred miles. The boat only stopped at a few tiny communities, whose only reason for existence was to replenish the ship's dwindling wood supply. The instant the boat would beach itself, a number of waiting men pushing giant wheelbarrows piled high with cordwood, would run up a narrow gangplank onto the bow, then through a large set of doors into the heart of the ship. In just a few minutes the boat was filled with a new fuel supply, and was ready to sail again. Then with the giant paddlewheel put in reverse, the big blades would push a huge swell of water onto shore, gently raising the bow off the gravel for an effortless escape.

By the following morning the scenery had changed again, and Elmer saw the giant columns of Five Finger Rapids ahead.

It looked to him as though the ship could barely fit through, and the nearer they got, the worse it looked. By the time they squeezed between the granite pillars, Elmer felt as if he could reach out and brush them with his own fingers. A few riverboats had already piled up and sunk here, along with a good number of stampeders, but their boat managed to make it through unscathed. And once through the rapids, they continued on their voyage until very early the next morning, when they arrived at the Whitehorse Rapids.

A small but bustling community had sprung up since they'd come through on their way to the Klondike. It was called Whitehorse, named after the rapids at the foot of the canyon. The ship pulled to shore in front of the little town, and when the gangplank came down, Belinda and Elmer were among the first few off. The boat didn't have that many people on it, and even less cargo, but they could see it was going to be full or close to it, heading back downstream.

Obviously a great many people were still walking over the Chilkoot and White Pass trails. Only now if a person had the money, it wasn't necessary to build a boat anymore. There were riverboats operating above Miles Canyon too, moving stampeders from the end of Bennett Lake through the Tagish and Marsh Lake system, right to the head of the canyon. In fact, the boats on both ends of the canyon were scheduled to arrive at the same time, so that in just a few hours they could virtually trade passengers and cargo. For this reason Belinda and Elmer didn't spend any time in Whitehorse, but began walking up the canyon right away.

They could've ridden if they'd wanted to. A man named Macaulay had built a tram beside the canyon. Basically it was horse-drawn cars on wooden rails that stretched the five miles of the rapids. At each end the wooden tracks were laid right down into the water, enabling Macaulay to lift boats out of the river with cargo intact, traverse the entire canyon, then settle them back down in the water again.

For a fee people could ride on the tram, but for two hearty souls like Belinda and Elmer, a five-mile walk after a long boat ride was just a chance to stretch their legs.

Once at the head of the canyon, they had to wait awhile for the boat to sail, but when it did the journey was mostly on lakes, and without fighting a current it was only a few hours to the end of Lake Bennett.

When they arrived, Belinda again wasted no time, and rented a couple of horses so they could ride quickly to meet Brooks. "I'm hoping he's still in Skagway." she said to Elmer, "But if he's not, he'll be moving his outfit up the White Pass. It's no better than the Chilkoot, but he can use his mules on that trail."

"We're going to be able to move fast with good horses and light packs." said Elmer.

"We'll go as fast as we can without wearing out the horses." replied Belinda.

They finishing tying on their packs, and a couple of meals for Nero and the horses, then mounted up. "Well, let's go." Belinda said, "Come on Nero!" And they rode off down the trail.

For hours they hurried the horses along, mostly at a quick trot, but occasionally walked for awhile to rest them. Belinda was true to her word, they never did stop so she could rest, but only when the horses needed it, and as soon as they were ready, on they'd go again. Closer and closer they came to Skagway, with Belinda remarking how glad she was they hadn't met Brooks yet.

They steadily climbed up into the mountains until reaching the summit, then crossed over and descended the steep coastal side down towards the ocean.

Finally about five miles out of Skagway, they came around a corner and up ahead was Brooks, with a train of seventeen mules and about two dozen men, all heavily loaded with barrels and cases of alcohol. "Joe Brooks!" exclaimed Belinda, then added, "Brooks even has McPhee's favourite horse loaded down. He musta wanted this stuff pretty bad."

They kept riding for a few more minutes until they met up with Brooks, when Belinda stopped and turned her horse sideways across the trail, bringing the whole pack train to a stop.

What do you want?" said Brooks.

"I just came to check on my things." answered Belinda sarcastically, "I see you got it all packed into little boxes and magic barrels."

"Yer load's huge." answered Brooks. "I decided to move McPhee's stuff first."

"No. You're going to move my stuff first." snapped Belinda angrily.

"I already told ya I'm not." replied the stocky man. "So what are you goin' to do about it?"

"Well, I could wait 'till you get back to Dawson and sue your ass off." replied a now enraged Belinda. "But I can do better than that." And with that she rode past him with Elmer following, still heading for Skagway.

They travelled as fast as possible now, occasionally frightening some of the people packing towards them, and sure enough, about three miles down the trail they came across Belinda's mountain of cargo piled on the side of the trail under large tarps. Belinda didn't say anything, probably to keep flames from shooting out of her mouth, but after slowing down for a moment, they again sped towards Skagway.

It was only a couple of miles away, so they soon arrived to find that the town had changed a lot since they'd last seen it. Skagway had real law now, since the demise of Soapy Smith. Many of the crooked business establishments were closed, and most of the thugs and shady characters were gone. Elmer continued to follow Belinda as they road straight through town and up to the ocean front.

As soon as Belinda assessed where the largest concentration of newcomers were gathered, she proceeded to the middle of them. Then after dismounting her horse, she stepped up on a large packing crate and yelled, "Attention all men bound for the Klondike! If any of you need money, and would like to arrive at Dawson in less than a week instead of over a month, I may have a job offer for you!"

Then she waited a few minutes for the word to travel along the waterfront and a crowd to gather. "I'm a business owner from Dawson City!" she started. "And as many of you may already know, to cross the Canadian boarder you have to carry a list of food items that weighs about a ton. This is in addition to your other belongings. However! If you have gainful employment, this is not necessary! I'm offering you that employment, as well as all costs incurred to get you there.

So what do I want...no, what'll I demand? First. You'll be packin' things for me, so the only things you can take from here are the clothes you're wearing, and whatever you can fit in your pockets. Next. Here's the situation. I hired a packing company to transport cargo from here to Dawson City, but a few miles out of town they decided to dump my stuff, and take a better offer. Whoever I hire is going to come with me, we're going to catch up to the packing company, then we're going to convince them by whatever means necessary to honour their original contract! So I only need strong men, men who don't mind mixing it up if they have to! For that, I'm willing to pay better wages than you've ever made before! You'll get a token amount of your wages here, the rest when we land in Dawson."

"Okay, the most important part of all! You'll be expected to take orders from me, from now until the job is finished! Any deviation means you're cut loose on the spot, and you don't get paid! That means you'll probably end up trying to build a boat, without money, without tools, without food, and without friends! So decide wisely."

"Now, I'm not going to take anybody's word for anything! So you're going to have to try out for the job, but I'll pay you for that, too!"

With that, Belinda pulled out a big bag of gold, then sat down and paid the men to fight. For hours, Belinda, Elmer and Nero sat and watched the fights. Belinda was not only assessing the strength and ability of each man, but also their character. Sometimes she'd accept a man, and sometimes she'd reject both.

Each fight only lasted until she told them to stop, and after one battle when both combatants complained of rejection, she pointed at one and told him "You're not as tough as you think you are," then pointed at the other and said, "The only reason you're fighting is because I paid you to, and the very first instruction I gave you was to stop fighting, but you ignored me, and fought for almost half a minute longer, showing an inability or unwillingness to follow direction, the exact thing that I told you was the most important part of the job. I can't use you."

Eventually Belinda had thirty of the toughest men on the waterfront hired, and made the most capable one of them all her foreman. Then she gave them all a down payment in gold and, mounting her horse said "Let's go men. The sooner we get started, the sooner you get to the Klondike." The goal they'd all been dreaming of.

Belinda moved her small battalion of men through Skagway at a brisk walking pace, raising a few eyebrows along the way. When they got to the White Pass Trail, she slowed down a little. The trail was nowhere near the living hell it'd been the previous winter, but it was still a formidable path, and Belinda was wise enough to not wear the men out.

It took hours to catch up to Brooks and his team, so they stopped and rested a few times on the way, and when Belinda finally saw her nemesis up ahead on the trail, she stopped again. This time not only to rest the men, but to give instructions. "Elmer," she said, "when we get to them, you stay with me."

Then she told her foreman, "When we catch up to them, I want you to string the men out alongside the pack train, with yourself and a couple of others up front behind me. Then if I give you a nod, I want you and the men to start unloading their animals. If they resist, well, you know what to do. But only do what's necessary."

Then the foreman went and gave all the men instructions, and after resting a few more minutes, it was time to move up and catch the packing company.

As they overtook Brooks and his crew and began to pull even with them, Belinda suddenly bolted forward and turned her horse sideways as before, and once more brought the packing train to a grinding halt. Then just as Elmer pulled his horse up beside hers, she said "Hello Joe, I see you're still confused about the right thing to do."

"I already told ya what's gonna happen." growled Brooks, "Now get outta my way woman!"

"Not this time Brooks!" shot back Belinda, "You can do what you want. But I didn't just contract you and your men, I contracted for these animals as well, and they're coming with me!"

"Yer drunk!" he replied, "Now you and yer girls get lost!"

Hearing that, Belinda nodded to her foreman, and he and the men stepped up to unload the mules. Brooks yelled "Stop 'em, boys!" and the fight was on!

As soon as the mêlée began, Belinda quickly moved back a few feet, to separate herself from the giant brawl. Elmer moved with her to stay at her side, but wasn't sure what his job was now.

He felt useless just sitting there, and was plenty tough enough to join the fight, so he began getting off his horse.

"Elmer!" yelled Belinda, "You stay with me!"

He figured she must be using him for a bodyguard. But when a man at the edge of the battle started towards Belinda, Nero met him with a huge growl and a display of his massive weapons, convincing the man to go back to the fray again. And again Elmer wasn't sure what his job was. But he did figure out that Belinda was actually protecting him.

The fight didn't last long. As soon as it became clear that Belinda's men were going to prevail, Brooks' men gave up. Apparently they were unwilling to take a beating for their boss, when there was packing jobs practically everywhere. Brooks' foreman however, was not so like-minded and ended up taking quite a few lumps.

When it was all over, Belinda had her men unload all the mules as well as McPhee's horse, and stack all his cargo on the side of the trail. As her men covered it with canvas, she told Brooks "If you show up in Dawson, I'll not only sue you for the money I already paid you, but I'll sue you for lost income for every day the Fairview opens late, not to mention telling everyone how unreliable you are."

Then she went to the men who'd been packing for Brooks. "I bear no animosity towards you men," she said, "and you all know about my pile of goods back down the trail, and know that I need a lot of packers. If you'll come to work for me, I'll pay your wages, but I'll also pay you the money I would've paid Brooks when we get to Dawson. I'll divide it equally between all who take the job."

It was an easy decision for them. They could either go to the Klondike with Belinda and get paid more than double, or they could work for a very angry Brooks without the animals, and endlessly relay the backbreaking loads up the trail.

They all took the job except for Brooks' foreman and the man Nero threatened, and a few minutes later Belinda had Elmer at her side and a small army behind her, as she headed back towards her pile of goods.

Meanwhile back in Dawson, things were happening that would affect Elmer when he got back. As the riverboats continued arriving, one of the things they brought with them, was the Yukon's first judge. That meant Leadtooth would be seeing his day in court, and Elmer too would probably have to testify.

People were still arriving in droves off the incoming boats, partly because of Arizona Charlie's newsletters and stories of the Klondike, which were being widely published all over North America.

In fact, the Klondike was so popular now that fashion houses were coming out with Klondike fashions, Klondike boots and shoes, Klondike perfumes, and anything else they could think of. And after they learned about the discovery of the White Channel, the entire outside world went Klondike crazy. They even had a name for it, 'Klondicitis'. Mining companies began looking for new mines as well as opening old ones, people began looking for gold in their back yards, and many donned buttons that said, "I'm going to the Klondike."

A good number of people arriving in Dawson now, only stayed a short time before deciding that the place to be was out in the goldfields. As a result, Belinda's little town of Bonanza was quickly growing into the thousands. On Henry's first trip out with Belinda's packing crew, he couldn't believe how the town had grown since he'd last seen it.

Then later that evening after he'd returned to Dawson, he was on his way down to check on the Fairview, when he saw another surprising situation. Ahead of him on the street stood Joe Boyle, Rickard, Big Alex and others, and they'd been approached by a group of Native Indians, in the hopes of getting some questions answered.

An amazing thing had happened that day, that some considered practically a miracle. Charlie the Indian packer, the man Swiftwater Bill had lost in San Francisco, had found his way back home again.

Some of the Natives spoke pretty good English, but very few had ever left the Yukon, and the ones that did had only ventured a short distance into Alaska. So all they knew of the white men's culture came from what they'd seen in the Klondike.

Now Charlie was back from the outside world telling of the many strange sights he'd seen. Strange enough if you'd actually seen them for the first time, but bordered on unbelievable to just be hearing about.

The Natives wanted to know if what Charlie was saying was true, while the white people wanted to know how he'd found his way back to the Yukon.

So with the Natives questioning the white people, and they in turn questioning Charlie, who now spoke some English, they managed to piece together what had happened to him since Swiftwater Bill lost him.

It turned out Bill had left him in a hotel room, on or about the third floor up from the lobby. The room didn't have furniture or any windows, and when Bill didn't come back for three days, Charlie thought he'd been put in jail.

He finally decided to escape, and though he didn't speak any English yet, he knew that white people responded well to a smile. So having come up in the elevator and not knowing there was stairs, he headed down the hallway towards the lift, catching a glimpse in some of the other rooms on the way. Seeing windows and furniture in them, he decided that these were people's homes, and when he told his fellow Natives about it, he explained how some white people had all their homes stuck together and piled high on top of each other, and that they had a small house in the middle that would travel up and down and visit the other houses.

So hoping he wouldn't be noticed escaping, he rode down in the elevator and walked through the lobby with a big contrived grin on his face.

Once free, he wasn't sure where to go, but knowing that he didn't live near the ocean, he began heading inland. Afraid of people seeing him and being put in jail again, he stayed in the wilderness whenever possible, and proceeded to walk most of the way across America while snaring rabbits, eating from orchards, and stealing the odd chicken along the way.

He told how white men had tamed an animal that was like a moose with short legs, but only had a single antler on each side of its head. And he described seeing huge iron beasts that belched black smoke and pulled long lines of boxes on rails, and in the boxes were people, wood, animals, and all kinds of other things.

Then he said he got to a place on a huge lake where a great many of the iron beasts came, and there were too many houses and people to count, and too many of the animals with single antlers to count.

After Charlie described the place a little more, everyone agreed, that with the lake, the stockyards, the trains, the cable cars, and other landmarks, the only place it could possibly have been was Chicago. It was there he said he ran into a good Samaritan, someone who fed and housed him for the winter while teaching him English, and when they learned where he was from, they actually taught him how to read the stars to find his way back home again.

When he left Chicago in early spring, as he told his fellow Indians, it took him almost a month just to walk along one side of the lake, which would've been the full length of Lake Michigan and half of Lake Superior.

Then he said after a few more weeks, it took him almost that long again to walk across a huge flat land covered with grass, but had no trees growing on it, and that the people who lived there made their houses out of the grass, obviously describing the Canadian Prairies and the 'sodbuster' farmers who lived there.

Eventually he made it north to the headwaters of the Teslin River, where he finally recognized where he was, and then he built a raft to take him downstream to the mouth, and into the Yukon River. From there it was only a couple more days until he floated into Dawson.

The white citizens of Dawson then assured the Natives that everything Charlie had told them was true, though they could hardly believe it themselves, and from that day forward, he was referred to by everyone as 'Chicago Charlie'.

Once the Native Indians had their questions answered, they headed off to their village, to tell the others that Charlie had been telling the truth. This left Rickard, Henry and the others still talking about Charlie's incredible journey.

Then Rickard said he'd just heard from a nurse he knew, a story about one of the patrons of Dawson's drinking establishments. He was the Kansas City Kid, a lovable but hopeless drunk who had endeared himself to the employees of the Monte Carlo. They let him eat at the free buffet, and for months he'd been sleeping underneath the craps table. Then one day he became deathly ill so they carried him off to the hospital, and while there, the nurses decided to wash his clothes. That's when they discovered that from sleeping on the floor of the gambling house, he'd ground almost four ounces of gold dust into his clothes, along with a good deal of sawdust.

After Rickard finished telling about the Kansas City Kid, Henry continued on towards the Fairview with Joe Boyle walking with him. As they passed the Opera House, Arizona Charlie came out of the casino part of the establishment and yelled, "Hey you guys! You should come in here for a minute. You might wanna see this."

When they entered the building, they saw a large crowd gathered around watching Edgar Mizner, who was standing at the roulette wheel in a cold sweat. Hours earlier he'd lost his job at the Alaska Commercial Company, and decided to leave the Yukon. But before he left, he decided to buy his co-workers a drink. The bill came to less than five dollars, and even though he didn't gamble, he laughingly decided to win it back on the roulette wheel. Egged on by his friends, he laid his bet, they spun the wheel, and he lost. So he doubled his bet on the colors, and lost again. Then he continued doubling his bets and losing, until he was placing hundreds of dollars on each spin.

As he kept losing, word spread throughout Dawson and a large crowd began to gather. Most people new of his arrogant nature, and hearing that he was gambling for huge stakes, they came in the hopes of watching him lose.

He was down $15,000 now, and as Henry and the others looked on, Mizner decided to risk it all. He made four more bets of $1000 each, and lost every one. The pope of Alaska was broke. He would leave the Yukon with no more than he came with.

With the demise of Edgar Mizner, most everyone that watched began to walk away. And as Henry left the building with Boyle, he remembered to ask him "Hey Joe, have you heard of a place in the Yukon called Tombstone?"

"Can't say as I have." he replied, "Why you ask?"

"Me and Elmer heard there might be gold there." answered Henry, "But nobody seems to know where it is."

"Well keep askin' around." said Boyle as he began to leave, "Somebody must know where it is."

A couple of days later Henry was returning from the Fairview, when in the doorway of the Monte Carlo he saw a fight going on. A huge bully named Bill Hoffman had picked a fight with Frank Slavin, and had punched him in the face a number of times before knocking him to the floor. Slavin was boxing champion of The British Empire, but was also quite drunk. Tex Rickard and Wilson Mizner broke up the fight, while Slavin yelled "You might be able to knock me down when I'm drunk, but you wouldn't be near so lucky if I was sober."

"You'd get the same and worse!" barked Hoffman, "Especially without your friends to save ya!"

Both Rickard and Mizner suddenly realized the same opportunity. Tex said "Okay it's agreed, you'll fight in a couple of days."

"We'll find a fair place." added Wilson.

What they didn't know, was that Hoffman had come all the way from Australia to beat up Slavin. Hoping to increase his reputation on the world stage. As both men went their separate ways, Rickard said to Mizner "We have to stage it somewhere that'll hold a lot a people"

"I wonder what we should charge for admission?" added Mizner.

We should make posters to advertise it too." said Rickard, "And we should put up some prize money. It's more professional that way."

Then they looked at Henry, "Do you want a piece of this?"

"Naw, no thanks." answered Henry, "My plates already kinda full. I'd like to see it though."

Before leaving, Henry took a minute to glance around inside, looking for familiar faces. Then his jaw dropped wide open. It was Becky. She was dressed in dancehall attire and was talking to men at one of the tables. Then she opened up a slim decorated gold poke, that all the dancehall girls carried from their belts, and one of the men dropped in a couple of large nuggets.

Henry was in shock. He didn't know what to think. As she left the table and began heading toward the bar, he quickly walked over to meet with her. "How come you're working here again?" he asked, "Are you dancing?"

"Not on stage." she answered, "My foot's still not good enough for that. I'm just a bar girl."

Henry knew what that meant, and he didn't like it. Bar girls didn't just serve drinks to people. When men wanted to dance, they'd buy tokens from the bar. Then when they picked a girl to dance with, they'd give her one of the tokens, then later on she'd cash them in back at the bar for half the money. "Well this is no good." said Henry, "Now all those guys with torn shirts will just come here. Only now they get to hold on to you while they talk." He shook his head "This is no good at all."

"Don't worry Henry." she said grabbing on to his arm like she always did, "I didn't want to do it either, but I was only making enough money to get by down at the river, and I want to leave the Klondike with more than I came with. Just like everyone else."

"Let me help you." offered Henry, "I make good money." He was grasping for any alternative he could think of, and it wasn't a very good one. The fact was, she was probably going to make more money than he did.

"I thought about that," she answered, "but then we'd both leave without any money...and that's no good either. Look at it this way Henry, I really didn't want to do this, so I'll be asking everybody I see where Tombstone is."

"So will I." Henry assured her.

Henry left the Monte Carlo completely frustrated. If he was going to lose Becky to someone else, it was practically set up to happen now. The more he thought about it the worse it got. Then he realized that while he worked during the day, Becky would be working more in the evenings. He'd be seeing her less than ever. "This is bad," he said to himself, "This is really bad."

For the next few days, Henry worked hard and tried not to think of his predicament with Becky. It didn't work very well though. At night he could barely sleep, and just lay there trying to solve his problem. He even considered taking up gambling to try and restore his situation. But he didn't really believe it'd work, and thought he'd only come off looking irresponsible. Besides, he'd seen what happened to Edgar Mizner.

He found out that going down to watch Becky work wasn't going to help either. It just made it worse. Yet on occasion he still couldn't help himself. Eventually he cheered up a little, when he learned that Becky didn't work on Sundays. So he could still see her then if he planned ahead.

Then one day while walking towards the Monte Carlo to secure Becky's time for the following Sunday, he ran into Jack, who was looking a little depressed. "Hey Jack, how's your claim panning out?" he asked.

"Not that well." he replied, "I seem to have staked a gravel mine.

"You're on Henderson Creek aren't ya?" asked Henry.

"Yea, for the time being." answered Jack again.

"Sounds like you might have a new plan." said Henry.

"Well, I'm tired of diggin' in the dirt." he complained, "I decided to go back south again. I'm actually building a boat now to float down to St. Michaels. I'm thinking when I get there I can get a job on a ship heading south."

Jack was obviously as broke as Elmer had thought he was, when he bought his bowie knife back from him. "So how's your boat coming along?" asked Henry.

"Oh it's coming along fine." said Jack, "A couple of my friends have thrown in with me, so there's three of us working on it. Actually I just came from down there." he added, "I see Elmer's back from somewhere up river."

"You saw Elmer down there?" asked Henry as if to make sure.

"Ya." answered Jack, "He's down there with Belinda."

Henry thought about going down to meet them, but when he looked towards the river, he saw they were already coming up the street towards him.

Most everyone in Dawson had heard about Belinda's cargo being dumped on the side of the trail, with many snickering or even laughing openly about it. They'd also heard about her confrontation with Bill McPhee, and how she subsequently left town in a fit of rage. So as word spread up and down the street that Belinda was back in town, people began flowing out of the buildings to see the circumstances of her return.

Now they all looked on as Belinda slowly made her way up Front street. She was mounted on Bill McPhee's horse, and leading a lengthy caravan of men, animals, and her entire shipment of goods.

Actually it was Nero that led the way. His territory was wherever Belinda was, so with his head slightly lowered, he walked out in front taking slow purposefull strides, suggesting he'd take on any who thought otherwise. He rarely even glanced to the side, implying that all who stood there were insignificant. All the other dogs, even the ones from the south, knew enough to either get off the street, or at least not make any eye contact.

Jack was as impressed as anyone at seeing Nero, and said to Henry, "I can't believe that dog's personality! He just claims whatever ground he's on."

Henry had been watching Belinda as well as Nero work their way up the street, and replied "I think they're both staking some ground."

When Belinda reached the front of the Pioneer Saloon, she stopped her entire caravan. Then as Bill McPhee looked on from the boardwalk, she dismounted his horse and walked over to him. Then handing him the reins she said "Your horse Mr. McPhee."

"Where's my goods?" he snapped back angrily.

"Why on the side of the trail." she answered, like he should already know. Then as McPhee began to fume she added, "It's just business." Then she went back to leading her train of men and cargo off to the Fairview. From then on, no one made fun of Belinda again.

That evening over supper, Elmer told Henry all about his trip to Skagway. About Skagway being all cleaned up, and how Belinda got men to fight on the beach. Then about the fight on the trail, and how there was a town growing at the foot of Miles Canyon, and everything else that had happened.

Then Henry told Elmer about the things that had happened in Dawson since he left. All about Chicago Charlie coming back, and Edgar Mizner losing his job and all his money, and how they washed 4 ounces of gold out of the Kansas City Kid. Then about Jack deciding to leave, and how Frank Slavin got beat up, with another fight to come, this time while he's sober.

Then he told him about the most important things to happen. Becky working at the Monte Carlo, and how a judge had come to Dawson, and he was probably going to have to testify against Leadtooth.

"Love to" said Elmer.

"Yea" replied Henry, "but I been thinking, what if the silver case comes up? I mean who knows what he'll say."

"Well he can't claim it's his." said Elmer, "Those aren't his initials on it."

"But he could say it belongs to a friend of his and we stole it." suggested Henry, and then he added "But then maybe we could say there is no case. Or maybe we couldn't. It gets all mixed up. I don't know what to think."

"I guess we'll just have to wait and see what happens." replied Elmer.

The next morning, not only Henry went to work at the Fairview, so did Belinda, Elmer, and all of Elmer's crew. Belinda wanted to get it finished and open as soon as possible. When they started putting the inside together, they quickly realized that Belinda had told them the truth. It was going to be the most lavishly appointed hotel in all the Klondike. It was three stories high with just thirty large rooms, so it wouldn't be the biggest hotel, but it was going to be the most opulent in every way, including steam heat and Turkish baths.

After finishing work that day, Henry and Elmer decided to treat themselves. It was the night of the big fight between Frank Slavin and Bill Hoffman, and Henry had a plan. With Hoffman pounding on Slavin in the Monte Carlo, the betting odds on the fight had been put at even. But Henry figured that from everything they'd been told about Frank, and knowing the robbing power of alcohol, that Slavin had a much better chance of winning. It cost $25 for a ringside seat, so even though Henry wasn't really a gambling man, he was willing to risk a $50 bet in the hopes of him and Elmer getting to see the fight for free.

When they arrived at the venue it was extremely crowded, proof that Mizner and Rickard had done a good job promoting it. Even so, they still managed to buy their tickets and squeeze on in to ringside.

Both fighters were in their corners making themselves ready, with Slavin only a few feet away. So before Henry made his bet, he stepped up to the ring and said "Hey Frank! I was gonna bet on ya! Are ya gonna be able to beat this guy?"

"Bet the house Henry! I'm gonna hand him his ass on a platter!" answered Slavin. So Henry made his bet.

Before the fight started, Tex Rickard sat down beside them. "Hey Tex" said Henry, "How you and Wilson gonna make out on this fight?"

"We did great." answered Tex, "It's already done. And it didn't even take much work."

"Sounds like you had fun doin' it." said Henry.

"We did." replied Tex, "And we made a killing. In fact I think when I head back south I'm gonna keep doin' it."

Rickard and Mizner had rented the fire bell from one of the landed riverboats for a few hours, and when the timekeeper hit it with a hammer, the fight began.

Immediately both fighters started from their corners. Hoffman quickly came out a few steps to the middle of the ring, and bounced back and forth ready to begin sparring. While Slavin came out a few steps, then quickly took another large stride while throwing a huge overhand right smashing into the middle of Hoffmans face. Hoffman flew over backwards landing on his back on the canvas, out cold. The fight was over.

The crowd went quiet for a few seconds, and then a huge roar went up. Actually it was more of an uproar. Some cheered for their winning bets, others howled about not seeing a fight, while a few who'd lost their bets, began yelling "Fix!"

Rickard was disturbed at hearing the word "Fix" being yelled about, and looked at Henry and Elmer and said "Fix? What are they stupid? Who'd fix a fight like that!?"

"They don't actually believe it." assured Henry, "They're just sore they lost their money so fast."

Of course Henry's plan to see the fight for free didn't work out so well either. He'd won his bet, so got to see the fight for free. He just didn't get to see a fight.

For the next few days, Henry, Elmer and Belinda, worked to get the Fairview finished, and Sam Steele came with a summons for Elmer to testify in court.

Also during that time, Henry began to hear rumours that Rebecca had taken an interest in another man. He heard it from Elmer first, and knew that he wouldn't even have mentioned it unless he was sure.

Even though it distressed him severely, he didn't want to appear desperate by confronting her about it. So whenever he could, he discreetly questioned people he knew about her situation. Learning to his dismay that the rumours seemed to be true. She'd apparently met a Duke or a Lord or something. No one seemed to know for sure exactly what the man's title was, but to Henry this meant that he probably had money. How could he compete with that? So his situation with Rebecca just kept getting worse.

Something else happened in town that absolutely everybody heard about. Almost everything in the Klondike was still owned by ordinary men, and since the beginning, things were often changing hands on the flip of a card, or the roll of the dice. And in one such game, Swiftwater Bill lost the Monte Carlo. He hadn't gone broke like Edgar Mizner and a good many others, for he still had his claim on Bonanza. But it hurt just the same.

The day the Fairview opened was a special day for Belinda, and she'd prepared for it accordingly. The entire city was anxious to see the inside of the opulent establishment. So as the honoured citizens of Dawson streamed through the doors, they were greeted by Belinda herself, dressed in a white silk blouse, a short skirt, and knee-high leather boots. Behind her a skilled orchestra played their way in, as everyone gazed upon the ornate features. Fine hardwoods, crystal chandeliers, silver and brass fixtures, the best of everything.

In the dining room one could order anything from Delmonico steaks and Oysters Rockefeller, to French pastries and the finest of wines and champagne. The bar alone took in over $6000 the first night, with the rest of the business filling to capacity. The Fairview was a raging success.

Not long after the opening of Belinda's Fairview, came the opening of Arizona Charlie's Palace Grand Theatre and Dancehall, and like Charlie promised, it too was the grandest in the Klondike. He modelled it after the finest opera houses of Europe, with horseshoe shaped balconies and private seating.

He featured Klondike Kate as a performer, and he himself took the stage, displaying his skill as a superior marksman. He'd brought his wife to the Klondike, a woman as beautiful as any of the dancehall girls. And as she stood on stage with her hands held high, from forty feet away with a gun in each hand, Charlie shot glass balls from between her fingers. Charlie was one of the few people allowed into the Yukon with handguns, as they were one of the tools of his profession as a showman.

Once the Fairview opened, Elmer and his crew went back to freighting loads out to Bonanza, while Belinda got Henry to look after her businesses in town, as she now spent as much time in Bonanza as she did in Dawson.

Henry and Elmer couldn't figure out why she'd want to do that, until on one of his trips, Elmer learned what she was doing. In fact she told him.

He arrived at Bonanza with a load of supplies, so stopped at her saloon to deliver whiskey and cases of champagne. When he went inside, he saw that the place was crowded with Bonanza and Eldorado claim owners, along with some of their crews. All of which were drinking and spending money freely. Even Clarence Berry and Big Alex were there.

Then he saw Belinda waiting on tables. When she came outside with him to check on the load, Elmer said "Belinda, do you mind if I ask you a question?"

"What is it Elmer?" she asked.

"Well, people call you the queen of Bonanza now, and I was just wondering why the queen of Bonanza would rather wait on tables in a saloon, than live at the Fairview and work in Dawson?"

"There's opportunity here." she answered, "When I first opened this place, I noticed that the guys who own claims, and the men who work on them, would come here and talk, especially after a few drinks. They talk about the amount of gold coming off each claim, who spends it faster than they get it, who's mining wrong, everything."

"Are you going to buy a claim?" asked Elmer.

"I already went partners in a couple." said Belinda, "I bought half of #40 Bonanza yesterday. But yea. If the price is right, or someone gets into trouble, I'll be making an offer. That's why I'm here."

Neither one of them knew it, but Belinda was already the richest woman in the Klondike.

They finished unloading the cargo to the saloon, then Elmer delivered the rest to Belinda's hotel and restaurant. The last stop was delivering a desk to her new Post Office building, a little more than a block away.

When they got there, Elmer saw a man in a unique predicament. The guy had carried a package all the way back from Dawson, and then set it down on the porch before entering the Post Office. His parcel was a very large beef roast wrapped in wax paper, and while he was inside, Nero found the abandoned package and claimed it for himself. He'd carried it off a short distance, and then laid down with one leg slung over it as a guard. He hadn't torn into it yet, but the man couldn't figure out how to get it back. He didn't want to ask Belinda for help, and appear to be subservient to a woman, and to just walk up and grab it could mean losing some fingers or worse.

Of course shooting Nero was the worst idea of all. Not only would Sam Steele be coming to visit, but everyone knew what happened to Joe Brooks and his crew. So killing Belinda's friend probably wouldn't pan out at all.

"Hey!" the man said to Elmer, "Yer Belinda's friend. You could probably get it back for me."

"Yea I'm Belinda's friend." replied Elmer, "But I'm not stupid enough to try and take anything away from that dog."

Then the guy noticed a few other people had gathered to watch his dilema, so he said "I'll pay $10 to anyone who can get my roast back for me." A few men puzzled over it, but no one could think of anything. Then he said to the guy beside him, "You got any ideas?"

"I don't." replied the man shaking his head, "I really don't."

Then an old man happened by, and hoping his experience would provide the answer, he asked him, "How 'bout you old timer, ya wanna try?"

The old man said, "That's Belinda Mulrony's dog isn't it?"

"Yep. Ya wanna do it?" he asked again.

The old man thought for a few seconds, then answered "I'd rather slow dance with a grizzly."

Unable to solve his problem, the guy finally relented and went to ask for Belinda's help. She didn't get his roast back for him, but she did pay him for it.

Before delivering the desk, Elmer remembered to ask the people standing there, if any of them knew of a place called Tombstone. "The one in Arizona?" somebody asked.

"No, a place in the Yukon." answered Elmer.

None had, so they delivered the desk to the Post Office, and then Elmer started his trip back to Dawson. On his way out of town, he noticed there was now a huge amount of buildings going up in Bonanza. There had to be thousands of people living here now.

Meanwhile back in Dawson, Rebecca had been working at the Monte Carlo for over a week now, and Henry decided that it was time to go talk to her. He had to find out who this Count or Lord guy was. He figured he'd ask her about Tombstone first though, that way it wouldn't look like he just came to confront her.

However when he got to the Monte Carlo and went inside, he stood in the doorway a few minutes watching her work, and after seeing how much attention she was attracting from the other men, he chickened out. He could easily see his plan blowing up in his face. He still wanted to talk to her, but decided he had to come up with a better plan.

As he turned to leave, Swiftwater Bill and Joe Boyle came in. "Howdy Henry." said Joe greeting him, "How's it going for ya today?"

"Not bad." replied Henry. Then he decided to ask them, "Say, have you guys heard about Rebecca seeing some guy, a Count or a Duke or something?"

"Oh yea," said Bill, "Lord Chaybee."

"No, that's not it." replied Boyle.

"Well its Sir Somebody." suggested Bill.

"I think it's Achebee." replied Joe again.

"Yea, that sounds right." answered Bill.

All three of them were watching Rebecca now, as she served drinks to a table of enamoured men. "I think the rumours are probably true." suggested Joe.

"Why do you think that?" asked Henry quickly, hoping not to hear anything too bad.

"'Cause I heard her say it herself." replied Joe.

"Okay." said Henry, "That makes it much worse." He was near to distraught as he left the Monte Carlo. Maybe it really was over for him.

The next day was court day for Elmer, and Henry went along too. Not just to watch, but to be a witness in case anything from Skagway or the trail or even back in Seattle came up. On their way over to the courthouse, they noticed that Leadtooth was missing from the woodpile, and were glad they wouldn't have to worry about ducking any more pieces of cordwood.

When they got to the courthouse they found it wasn't a very big building, but it didn't need to be. Pretty much everybody in Dawson had something better to do than sit around watching court cases. Besides, serious cases were rare anyway.

Leadtooth's trial didn't last very long. It was pretty straight forward, and he didn't bother taking the stand to defend himself. The first witness called by the prosecution was Superintendent Sam Steele. He testified that Leadtooth was a well known accomplice of Soapy Smith, and told of his attempted attack on Elmer on the gangplank of the ship back in Seattle, thwarted by Steele himself.

Then Elmer was called to the stand. He confirmed Sam's testimony about Seattle, and then told how he was sure that Leadtooth was one of the men who attacked Henry and himself on the trail. Then he testified how Leadtooth had tried to kill him in the alley off King Street, and probably would have if not for Belle Mitchel summoning a Mountie so quickly.

The prosecutor called Belle to the stand next. Her testimony only took a couple of minutes, with her stating that she saw Elmer being attacked by a large man, so summoned a nearby Mountie. When asked if she knew who the man was, she pointed to Leadtooth and said, "Him. That's the man."

The last person to be called as a witness was Seargent Fury. He told how he was called to the scene of the crime by Belle, and when he arrived saw Leadtooth about to kill Elmer, so promptly arrested him.

It turned out that Henry's testimony wasn't needed at all. Anything he could substantiate, Steele already had.

Neither Henry nor Elmer could figure out why Leadtooth didn't try to use the silver case as some kind of alibi. But

Leadtooth knew that it would only make him appear more like Elmer's attacker on the trail. It could also lead back to the old man he'd stabbed in Seattle, and if the old man lived he could witness against him, and if he died, it could mean a murder charge and getting hung. The one thing the silver case wouldn't do was get him out of the jam he was in now.

In the end the Judge sentenced Leadtooth to twenty years, plus the time he'd already spent in jail and on the woodpile. He was to be shipped out on the first available riverboat, which basically meant right away. This was something Elmer wanted to see, so when they led him down to the boat, both Henry and Elmer were there to wave good-bye.

They took Leadtooth onto the bow of the ship and handcuffed him to a ring on the flagpole. Once secured, he turned to Elmer and yelled "When I get out I'll be comin' for you!"

Elmer quickly shouted back at him, "Well that's gonna seem like about a hundred years to you! Ya turnip!" Then he laughed adding, "And my future has a 'silver' lining!"

Henry laughed too and yelled, "Ya! You really got sent down the river this time!"

A few minutes later the gangplank was reeled up, and the giant paddlewheel pulled the boat back out in the river. Then it began its long journey to the outside world.

"I'm hungry." said Elmer, "I'm gonna celebrate with a drink and a steak."

"I thought you quit drinking." replied Henry.

"I did." answered Elmer, "This one would only be to celebrate, and to wash down the steak."

Henry was hungry too, so they headed off to the nearest restaurant. As soon as they sat down Sid came over to their table. "Hello fellas." he said.

"Hi Sid." replied Elmer greeting him, "I'll have a steak and a shot of whiskey. I'm celebrating a successful trial."

"You too?" answered Sid, "Steele and one of his Mounties just had a steak and a drink, for the same reason."

Then Sid left for a few seconds to return with a bottle, and pouring Elmer a drink said "And what'll you have Henry?"

"I'm partial to your moose stew." he answered, "And I'll have a couple a slices of bread too." Sid left the bottle on the table then went to fill their order.

Elmer finished his drink, and then poured himself another while waiting for his steak to arrive. When Sid happened by again Henry said "Steele must a come straight here from court if they're finished and gone already."

"They didn't hang around long after they ate." replied Sid, "They said they wanted to catch some guy before he got too far out of town." Steele and his Mounties were fast getting a reputation for always getting their man.

"How long before we got here did they leave?" asked Henry.

"Just a few minutes." answered Sid.

Suddenly Henry jumped to his feet. "Hold that stew 'till I get back! You go ahead and eat Elmer, I'll be back in a few minutes. I got an idea!" Then he hurried out of the cafe.

Tombstone

As he ran down the street towards the police station, Henry couldn't believe that out of all the people they'd asked about Tombstone, the one person most likely to know, they hadn't asked. He just hoped he could catch Sam before he left town.

He was nearly out of breath when he reached the station, and practically stumbled through the doorway. "Is Sam still here?" he gasped to the Corporal behind the desk.

"I think he's still out back in the corral." answered the Mountie. Henry raced around back to find Steele and another Mountie saddling up their horses.

"Hey Sam." he said as he came up to him.

"What can I do for ya Henry?" he answered.

"I was wondering if I could ask you a question before you leave?" he asked.

"You'll have to make it quick." said Steele, "Is it something about the trial?"

"No" answered Henry, "It's about a place. I was wondering if you might know where a place called Tombstone is?"

"I've only heard of Tombstone Mountain." answered Steele.

"Yes! That would be the place." said Henry, "Me and Elmer want to try some prospecting there, but we weren't sure where it was." Steele wasn't stupid and gave Henry a confused look. "It's kind of a tip we got." added Henry.

"Well, it's about fifty miles north of here." said Steele mounting his horse. "Your best bet is to go up the Klondike River until it splits. Then take the fork that goes north. There's a map in the office you can look at. It'll show ya pretty much everything I know."

"Thanks Sam." replied Henry as he began walking toward the office.

"Good luck." said Steele as he too began to leave.

Henry only looked at the map for a few seconds, before realizing that the best thing to do, was to copy down everything that could help them onto a piece of paper. After getting a paper and pencil from the Corporal, he was happy to see that the Tombstone Mountain on the Mounties map, was sharp on top and looked almost the same as the mountain on their map. It took a little while, but he finally finished copying everything he needed to, then thanked the Corporal and hurried back to tell Elmer in the restaurant.

While Henry was copying the map, the riverboat Leadtooth was on was already ten miles down the river, and the convict was complaining he was cold. They were going to move him inside anyway, so as the Captain held his pistol on him with one hand, he unlocked the cuff on the ring with the other. Standing behind the Captain was the First Mate with a rifle, partly because the Captain's revolver was almost as old as he was.

When Leadtooth began to stand up, he suddenly fell back down again. "My leg went to sleep." he said with a big smile.

It was a lie. As soon as the Captain reached for his arm to help pull him back up again, Leadtooth instantly grabbed for the gun, and tore it free from the old mans grip. Working all summer on the woodpile had changed him from being strong, to an extremely powerful man. Leaping to his feet and using the Captain for a shield, he shot the First Mate dead. Then he put the gun to the Captain's chest and pulled the trigger. But the cylinder was loose on the old weapon, and it never rotated far enough. The revolver just went 'click'.

Other members of the crew were yelling in the commotion now, so Leadtooth hit the Captain over the head with the gun, driving him to the deck in a daze. Then grabbing the handcuff key from him, he ran across the bow and took a huge leap into the river.

No one on the boat had even considered someone jumping into the water on purpose. First they'd probably be chopped up by the paddlewheel, but even if they weren't, with the temperature of the water they'd probably never make it to shore.

But Leadtooth had timed out his complaint of being cold, with the ship rounding a large bend in the river. It was on the outside of the turn where the water was the deepest, so the boat was actually not far from shore when he jumped. Not only that, but Leadtooth managed to escape the paddlewheel by just a few feet, and once he had, the wheel provided protection from anyone getting a clear shot at him. He had successfully escaped.

The riverboat would have to travel another thirty miles downstream before it could report what happened, so Leadtooth had at least a full day's headstart. Easily enough time to get back up to Dawson. Of course he wasn't heading for Dawson. He was heading for Elmer.

Back in Dawson City, Henry returned to the restaurant to find Elmer already gone. There was still a half bottle of whisky and an empty glass where he'd been sitting, as well as a plate with a steak bone and a couple of small potatoes left on it. "What happened to Elmer?" he asked Sid.

"Well he had more drinks waiting for his steak." answered Sid, "Then when he finished eating and you hadn't come back yet, he drank somemore. Then he staggered out the backdoor looking like he was gonna be sick. But that was about twenty minutes ago."

Henry followed out the back looking for him, and once outside saw an unnerving sight. Elmer had thrown up all over himself and passed out. Now he lay on his back, with about a dozen ravens standing all around, and on top of him. They'd moved in slowly until they were sure he was either dead or there was no danger. And now to anyone who didn't know better, it appeared as if Elmer was being pecked to death.

When Henry hurried over to him the ravens all scattered, and he woke Elmer up, in an extremely dishevelled condition. As Henry helped him back home to his bunk, they wobbled around so bad, that anyone who saw them would just assume they were both drunk. One thing was for sure. They wouldn't be going anywhere today.

Now came the best part for Henry, telling Rebecca about Tombstone. He found himself hurrying down to the Monte Carlo, not so much to begin their quest for gold as soon as possible, but rather to extract Becky from the dancehall as soon as possible. Before he even got there he was talking to himself sarcastically, "Take that Count Cheybee, or Echebee, or whatever yer name is! Now we'll see how important you are!"

When he entered the building, he waited to catch Becky's attention, then motioned her over to where no one could hear them talk. "What is it?" she asked, wondering if she should be concerned.

"I found Tombstone." answered Henry, "It's up north of here."

"Do you think we could find it okay?" she asked.

Henry had a sudden fear that maybe she'd changed her mind. "Yes I do." he assured her, "I copied a map directly from the Mountie's.

"Just a minute," she said, "I'll be right back." Then she turned and walked away. Henry wondered where she was going, and watched as she walked over to the bar, and then talked for about a minute. Then just like she said, she came right back.

"What did you do?" he asked.

"I quit my job." she said, "Let's go."

"This is great!" Henry thought to himself, "Advantage to Henry!"

As they left the Monte Carlo Henry suggested, "We better leave tomorrow. Me and Elmer already got pretty much everything we'll need, but we have to get some food and things."

"Do you think we'll have time to get everything we need tonight?" asked Becky.

"Of course" answered Henry smiling, "Dawson's always open." Then he added "If you don't mind, we should probably take all the supplies we buy to your place. If we take them to Belinda's where me and Elmer stay, people are going to ask a lot of questions. Questions we're not going to want to answer. Especially if they see us packing for a trip."

"Sure" answered Becky, "But when we get to my place, can I see the map you made? I'm pretty curious about it."

"You bet." replied Henry, "I'd show you right now except for other people being around." The more they talked, the more excited they both became.

Then she took his arm like he was so fond of, and asked "So how far is it to Tombstone?"

"He answered her right away, but was again thinking, 'Yes! Advantage to Henry!'

After they bought the food and additional supplies they were going to need, they took them to Becky's place down by the river. Once inside her tent, they sat down at her table and Henry showed her the map he'd made. They spent over an hour studying and pondering the paper, as well as guessing about any adversity or hardships they might encounter.

Then they took the halves they each had of Soapy's map, and taped them back together again. Trusting each other wasn't an issue anymore. They compared the two maps, and together they seemed to provide a clear path to exactly where they needed to go. "Let's hope when we get out there, it's as easy to follow as it looks." said Henry.

"I'm just hoping we find it." said Becky, "But getting there without any trouble would sure be nice."

"Well I better get back home and pack." said Henry as he stood up, "And I haven't even told Elmer about the map yet." Then he told her about their day in court, and what had happened to Elmer at the restaurant. "He'll have slept it off by now though." he said, and then added, "So if I go now we can probably leave in the morning."

"I'll pack too." answered Becky, as she too got to her feet, "I don't want to be holding us up tomorrow."

Henry didn't know what to do now. The way the last couple of weeks had unfolded, he wasn't sure what Becky expected either. "Well I guess I'll see you tomorrow." he finally said.

Becky walked straight over to him, and grabbing his face with both hands, gave him a big kiss. He quickly wrapped an arm around her waist, and then the other, as if trying to keep her from escaping. It seemed to work, causing her kiss to last much longer. "See you tomorrow." she said smiling.

Henry smiled back at her. He was much happier now, but more confused that ever. After taking a few steps towards the doorway, he stopped and turned around, and still holding his hat in his hands, he began fiddling with the lining. "I have to ask Becky. Who's this Count, or Lord Achebee I been hearing about?"

"Is that why you've been treating me like smallpox?" she answered. "I thought it was 'cause you didn't like me working in the Monte Carlo."

"I didn't." replied Henry, "But everybody's been telling me that you met someone new. Some guy with a title."

"I did." she admitted, "But he doesn't have a title, and he's not a Lord, or a Duke, and it's not Achebee."

"Well who is it?" he asked. "I gotta know."

"It's sir H.B." she explained,"...as in Henry Browning. It was you Henry! I told people that to keep men from bothering me."

Henry was relieved, glad, and flattered, all at once. "But why didn't you tell me?" he asked.

"I didn't think it'd be right to inform you that we're a couple. That you belong to me, as if you're being told." she said, "And I really didn't think they'd talk about it so much."

"So you mean I got these ulcers for nothing?" replied Henry.

"Yes." she answered, "Unless you don't want to be with me."

With that, Henry threw his hat on the table. Becky watched it land and said,"I thought you were going home to pack."

"We're gonna have to leave a little later tomorrow." he said, "I have two weeks of spooning to catch up on."

"But if you do it right," she smiled, "It could take a long time."

"Well I'm gonna do my best." promised Henry.

"You know Belle will be coming back before too long." said Becky, "So until then, I think you should pack them together and make 'em count."

"So do I." agreed Henry as he took her in his arms, "So do I."

By the time Henry got back home, Elmer was up again and drinking coffee. "Well that's it." he lamented, "From now on I don't drink for any reason. If I have to celebrate that bad, I'll jump up and down and clap my hands."

"I'm not sure," said Henry, "but I think you might still have to pay Sid for that steak."

"Yea" replied Elmer, "I guess I only rented that."

"Well," said Henry, "It didn't completely go to waste."

"What do ya mean?" asked Elmer.

"You don't wanna know." he answered.

Then Henry said "Anyway Elmer, have a look at this." and he gave him the map he'd drawn at the police compound.

Elmer took it, then immediately looked up and exclaimed "You found Tombstone!" "How'd you find it?"

"Right after we got to the restaurant, I thought that if there was one person in the Klondike that'd know where it is, It'd be Sam." said Henry, "So that's where I went."

"This is great!" remarked Elmer, "When do you think we should go?"

"I already told Becky," said Henry, "and we already bought the food and stuff we'll need to take. We figured we might as well leave tomorrow. All you have to do is come with me to quit your job, then pack."

"Do ya think Belinda will mind this time?" wondered Elmer.

"Naw" replied Henry, "She still knows why we're in the Klondike."

"Well, I'm wide awake now." said Elmer, "I might as well get started."

When they woke in the morning they were ready to go, and when they got to Rebecca's place, she was ready too and sitting out by her fire waiting for them. Belle was sitting with her, and another girl she'd become friends with while working at the Monte Carlo. "Henry, Elmer, this is Daisy." she said introducing them. "Daisy's gonna help look after my place while I'm gone."

Becky figured Daisy was more reliable than Belle, and could also be more discreet. In fact, she chose Daisy to tell people where they'd gone, if they didn't come back or ran into trouble.

So Henry and Elmer sat down to have a quick visit before they left, when Elmer said, "Look what I got last night." and showed them a spool of fishing line, along with some hooks and weights.

"That's a good idea." said Henry, "Fresh fish."

"It could be fun too." added Becky.

Before long, Belle and Daisy were wishing them good luck as they said good-bye, and they were off on their journey to find Tombstone.

Traveling up the Klondike River turned out to be a lot easier than they expected, as they found themselves walking along a well beaten path. By early afternoon they'd covered a full ten miles, and by late afternoon they'd reached the fork in the river, and began following North like the map said. There was still a path to follow, but it was less traveled now and a little tougher going. Then as they continued on, the land slowly began to rise up infront of them, until they were noticeably traveling uphill.

So far they'd been walking along under a cloudy sky, but now the sun began to shine through, lighting up the landscape and seeming to lighten their burdens. It was already into September and fully autumn in the Yukon. And as they moved through the poplar and aspen trees, the sun lit them up all yellow, orange, and gold, with many of the shorter plants shining back various shades of red.

Also as they traveled along, they continued to scare up grouse and ptarmigan, as well as a good many rabbits and the occasional porcupine. In fact the land looked to be full of birds and animals. Even all the little ponds they passed, no matter how small, seemed to have various breeds of ducks on it.

It was time consuming to cook meals while traveling, so they'd brought some food along they could eat straight from their packs. And when suppertime came, they did the same as they had for lunch and stopped to rest, while filling up on sandwiches and cookies.

They'd barely sat down when a few Whiskey Jack's began to gather, hanging around in the trees waiting for any crumbs or leftovers to eat.

When they finished eating, Elmer walked over to the side of the river. He knew there was no time for fishing, but was curious if he could see any fish in the water. The river was more like a large creek now, and peering into a big pool, he suddenly turned around with excitement. "There's lotsa fish in here!" he shouted, "And some of 'em are pretty big too! I think they're those arctic greyling."

Henry and Becky wanted to see for themselves, so went over and joined with Elmer a few minutes, staring into the water at the moving shapes. "I hope we see fish this good where we're going." said Becky, obviously wanting to try catching some herself.

"Yea, me too." added Elmer.

When they turned to leave, they were glad they'd wrapped up their food before walking away, as the Whiskey Jack's were cleaning up everything as fast as they could, with some even standing on their packs hoping to get at the source.

So now that they were both rested and fed again, they helped each other on with their packs, and continued on their way up the valley.

Meanwhile back in Dawson, Daisy was at Becky's place finishing supper herself, when a cousin of Henry and Elmer's appeared. He explained to her how he'd just arrived in the Klondike to prospect with them, but was having some trouble finding out where they were. "Some of the people in town said that you might be able to help me ma'am."

So Daisy described as best she could where they were heading, and the route they were traveling to get there.

"Thank you very kindly for your help Miss." he answered. Then with a big smile showing his lead colored tooth he added, "Boy are they gonna be surprised to see me."

With the changing of the season, it wasn't light out all night anymore, in fact it was now getting dark by ten o'clock. So after traveling a few more hours, Henry suggested they camp while there was still time to do a proper job of it.

When they woke the next morning the sun hadn't been up long yet, and the air was much crisper that they expected. So they quickly built a fire to warm themselves before getting started. Then as Henry sat looking at the map trying to figure out where they were, Becky sat tight against him, partly to look at the map, but mostly to get warm. But there really wasn't enough landmarks on the map to tell them anything, so after warming up and eating a little, they got back on their way again.

The valley continued to narrow as they made their way higher into the mountains. And so far, whenever they had to cross water, there had always been a small bridge in place. Usually just a couple of logs put together. But there was barely a path at all now, and whenever they had to cross a creek, they had to wade through excrutiatingly cold water. Anything taking longer than thirty seconds would become an incredible torture test. But they pressed on toward the mountain anyway, braving the frigid waters whenever it was necessary.

By late afternoon they'd crossed water a half a dozen times, and Henry began to worry. Becky had started to limp. She was doing her best to hide it, fearfull of becoming a burden to them.

But Henry didn't care about that at all. He just didn't want her to hurt.

When they stopped to rest awhile, he cut her a walking stick, telling her that it was to help keep her balance when they crossed creeks. It was believable, as most of the time when they crossed water, they were walking on various sized stones that were often quite slippery.

He also began feigning a sore back. "Nothing serious." he said, but began suggesting they stop and rest once in awhile.

A couple of hours later they had to cross the river yet again. They found a place where it was only about a foot and a half deep, and just as Henry was starting in, he heard a big splash in front of him. He looked up to see Becky face down in the middle of the river, with the current and the weight of her now wet pack holding her under! He quickly tore off his own pack, and went charging through the water to get to her!

Elmer had already crossed, and climbed the bank on the far side, but he too heard the splash, and throwing off his own pack went galloping towards her anyway!

Just before Henry got to her, Becky managed to pull her face from the water and get to her knees. Then he grabbed her by the arm to pull her to her feet, and he and Elmer helped her the rest of the way across.

When they all collapsed on the far bank, Becky had a look of guilt on her face, saying "I'm sorry guys. I tripped on a rock out there."

"Don't worry about it." replied Elmer, "I almost splashed in myself a couple a times."

Becky was already starting to shake from the wet cold, so they had to light a fire right away. "We might as well camp here anyway." said Henry, "It'll give us lot's of time, and we can use it to cook a hot meal." But mostly he was thinking how it would give Becky's foot a long rest.

Elmer too was glad they were going to camp early. "I'll get some firewood," he said as he stood up, "and then I'm gonna try out my fishin' gear." Then he hurried off towards the trees.

Henry looked over at Becky, "You have to be more careful." he said. Then shyly looking down at his own feet he added, "Gold wouldn't mean much to me now without you."

They were high in the mountains now, and the trees were a lot smaller. But even so, it didn't take them long to build a raging fire and gather a good supply of wood. Then all three of them stood by the blaze, vertically rotissing themselves to dry out.

Henry and Elmer weren't as soaked as Becky was, but after splashing through the water to get to her, they'd drenched themselves pretty good too. Anyway, they had lots of time, so supper could wait.

Elmer was first to get up from the fire. He wasn't completely dry yet, but couldn't wait any longer to try his luck fishing. So he took his big bowie knife into the trees, and before long was attaching some line to a long pole he'd cut. "Maybe we could have fish for supper." he said hopefully. Then he stepped up to the waters edge, and cast his line out as far as he could.

As it drifted downstream with the current, he watched closely, giving it small tugs with his rod as it went. He'd just begun thinking how nice it was here, with the sun out, and the mountains all around, when suddenly a fish slammed into his hook! His line stiffened straight and the end of his pole began jerking sporadically, and he quickly began working the fish towards him, while trying to make sure his line didn't break.

When he finally got the fish to shore, he quickly grabbed on to it, and holding it up for Henry and Becky to see, exclaimed "Look! I already got one!"

Then he set it on a rock and went right back to fishing. In less than a minute he caught another one. "Wow! Fishing in the Yukon is easy!" he yelled still excited.

"Bring it over here." said Henry, "Let's see what these greyling look like."

As they examined Elmer's prize he said, "At this rate I'll have enough for supper in no time."

While he was talking, Henry and Becky watched behind him as a large bald eagle came gliding down the valley, and without stopping or even slowing down, it suddenly dipped low to the ground and snatched up Elmer's other fish, then continue on it's way down the valley. Becky pointed behind Elmer and said, "Your other fish just flew away."

Elmer spun around with just enough time to watch both his fish and the eagle disappear. He looked back at Henry and Becky in disbelief. "Really!" he said, "Aren't there any birds in this country that don't steal from ya!"

It really didn't matter though, a short time later he'd already caught enough for supper. Even Becky enjoyed catching one. But before she had a chance to try again, she realized she wasn't quite dry enough yet, and quickly made her was back to the fire. They kept the fire high while eating the greyling, and by the time they were finished everyone was warm and dry again. They also agreed that arctic greyling was a very tasty fish.

When they woke in the morning, they again had a fire and ate before starting out. But this time Henry could tell where they were on the map, and figured they might see Tombstone before the end of the day.

They sat sipping their coffee and warming their legs, when Becky said, "Look, there's some other fires down the valley."

About three or four miles in the distance they could see a campfire, and a few miles past that another. "I wonder who they are?" said Elmer.

"The valleys wider down there, with more trees in it." said Henry, "Maybe we passed them without noticing."

"It could be smoke from some cabin's." suggested Elmer.

"I don't think it's cabin smoke," said Becky, "There would've been a better trail."

"Oh well," replied Henry, "as long as they don't have a map to the same place we do."

Henry took it on himself to finish packing up the rest of their things, and soon they were on their way again. As they traveled along, Henry continued to watch Becky's foot as closely as he could, and decided that though her foot was still hurting, it was still better than it had been, and the rest they'd taken must've helped her.

Then Becky noticed something. Elmer noticed it too. Henry was starting to struggle. Either he was short on energy, or his back was beginning to hurt like he said it had the day before.

It didn't seem to be slowing him down though, and they continued on until they came up over a rise, and there in front of them stood Tombstone. It had to be. The mountain looked almost exactly as it did on their maps. It seemed to stand alone, and soar incredibly high, with an extremely sharp point on top. "That's gotta be it." said Henry.

"It sure looks right." agreed Elmer, "Looks like we'll only be a few more hours getting there too.

"Sure hope so." replied Henry. He was still worried about Becky's foot.

From where they stood, the valley seemed to widen out into a high, giant, treeless plateau, with no apparent cover and very little to burn. "Does'nt look like there's many places to camp out there." said Henry.

"We should've brought horses." said Becky, "It would've made things a lot easier."

"Yea, but that can turn into a real nightmare when you don't know where your going." answered Henry. Then as they started towards the mountain again, they reluctantly told Becky about their experience buying horses in Skagway.

A few hours later the mountain appeared larger, but it still looked to be just as far away. Then a few more hours went by, and the weather began to change. The sky filled with dark boiling thunderheads, with huge shards of sunlight piercing through. It would've looked quite scenic if not so ominous.

They were getting tired now too, but with nowhere to camp and the foreboding sky, they kept on going. They had other problems as well. Henry was starting to really labour under his heavy pack, and Becky had begun to limp noticably. Even Elmer was beginning to tire, and speaking of Tombstone as a possible mirage.

Hour after hour they trudged forward, eventually willing to camp anywhere they could light a fire. The expansive plateau they'd been crossing had slowly begun to undulate. Until finally, when there was barely any time left to camp, they came over a slow rising mound, to see the land slope steeply down to a creek with a few acres of trees around it. "At last!" exclaimed Elmer, "I'm practically starving."

"And we didn't even get rained on." added Henry.

They quickly descended the small hill, and immediately began building their camp. Elmer started gathering wood while Henry got a fire going, and Becky began pulling things from their packs.

Suddenly Becky spun around and barked at Henry, "All right Henry!" she said, "I know what you been doing!"

Elmer dropped a load of wood by the fire, and thinking he missed something said, "What? What's he been doing?"

"He's been taking the heavy stuff out of my pack and putting it in his!" replied Becky, "That's why he's been struggling the last couple of days, because he's carrying twice as much. Not 'cause his back hurts!"

"Well it hurts a little bit now." answered Henry.

"Yea." protested Becky, "But in the meantime, I get to feel like I'm not doing my share."

"Look." said Henry, "I know your foot's been hurting. And back on the day when we first pulled Mace and the map out of the river, we made a deal. You said that if we found out where Tombstone was, you got to come with us, even if I had to carry you on my back. ...and truth be known, I relished the very idea. But now that we're out here, it seemed like it'd be better for both of us, if I tried carrying your stuff first. But I meant what I said. If it comes to it, I intend on carrying you wherever we need to go."

Becky thought for a bit then said, "It still feels like I'm not doing my part." then she asked "What do you think Elmer?"

Elmer didn't want any part of the conversation, and after rubbing his chin for a few seconds he answered, "Two things. First, if Henry's gonna carry you, I'm gonna carry your pack. Second. I think I'm gonna grow a beard." And with that he turned around and went for more firewood.

Henry and Becky looked at each other for a moment, then Becky walked straight over to Henry and hugged him tight. Henry quickly wrapped his arms around her, and hugged her back, trying his best not to squish her.

When Henry woke in the morning, he found that both Becky and Elmer had already been up for awhile. They must've figured he needed the extra sleep from the heavy pack he'd been carrying. Becky was sitting by herself at the fire, with coffee and breakfast already made.

"Where's Elmer?" asked Henry as he sat down.

"He already ate." said Becky, "Then he made another fishing pole and went up the creek. He just left a couple of minutes ago." Then she handed Henry a coffee.

He took a sip, then tried to look at their surroundings with sleep still in his eyes. "I wonder where we are?" he said. The mountain was looming larger that ever now, so they had to be very close. "I see you guys already ate." he noticed, "I didn't mean to be holding us up."

"Just Elmer ate." replied Becky, "I was waiting for you."

"Wow...what a girl." he answered.

They were sitting eating breakfast together, when Elmer suddenly came hurrying through the trees. "I know where we are!" he said throwing his fishing pole to the ground, "At least I think I do. And we're real close!"

He quickly dug Soapy's map from the pack and unfolded it. "Remember how two creeks joined into another one, at exactly the same place." he said, pointing his finger to it on the map, "That's gotta be pretty rare. Well I was looking for a fishin' hole when I found a place just like this. It's just a few hundred yards up the creek."

They were all getting excited now, and as Henry and Becky hurried to gobble up the rest of their breakfast, Elmer packed up everything around them.

When they got going again, rather than follow up the creek, they angled their way up the slope of the hill, so they could better see the land around them. When they reached the top, they compared the map to everything they could see, and it all fit. The creeks looked right, the distance to the mountain looked right, even the valleys in front of the mountain were all there. All they had to do was follow the creek on the left, and it should lead them right to where they were going. The spot marked on the map. The best part was, it looked to be only a couple of miles away. So they all headed off with a new spring in their step.

They followed the creek towards Tombstone, and before long started into one of the valleys separating the hills and ridges around the mountain. It appeared that at one time or another, the creek had travelled back and forth across the valley floor, leaving little behind but a sea of rocks and boulders, making it very difficult to walk over. But despite the tough going, the area was still scenic, and very pretty to look at.

About the time they thought they should be getting close, Elmer suddenly said "There it is!" and pointed across the valley to a fairly large cabin, nestled into a thick stand of trees. They had to cross the water to get to it, but the creek wasn't really big enough to present a problem any more.

As they walked over the rocks to get there, Henry had some things running through his mind that worried him. The cabin appeared to be vacant or abandoned, which could be a good thing. But few people would build a dwelling if they hadn't found any gold yet. And if they had, where were they? After all, the map they got from Soapy had the word gold written right on it.

But another thing bothering Henry, was that despite the sparce terrain he hadn't seen any claim posts yet. And who would discover gold, yet not stake a claim so they owned it?

Then there was Becky's foot. They hadn't had to walk nearly as far today, and her foot seemed somewhat better. But if they had to stumble over many more of these rocks, they could wreck her foot pretty fast.

When they arrived at the cabin, they all took their packs off setting them on the ground, eager to look around to see what they'd find. There was a fire pit in front of the cabin, and when they looked around the side, found a very large neatly stacked woodpile. Beside that was a big piece of canvas nailed to the wall of the cabin, and looking behind it they found shovels, gold pans, and many other tools. Then they noticed a small corral built in the trees. It was just big enough to hold a few horses, but by the looks of the ground, had never had any animals in it.

As they stood pondering the corral, Becky wandered around to the front again, and unlatched the door to the cabin. She then pushed it open and went in. Suddenly they heard her scream! Henry and Elmer both raced around front to find Becky outside again, stomping in a circle while wriggling her arms and shaking her hands, as if she'd been contaminated with something. "What's wrong?" exclaimed Henry not knowing what to do.

"There's a dead guy in there!" she answered grimacing.

While Henry made sure she was okay, Elmer went in to have a look. "Ahaaarg!" he gasped, as he stumbled backwards out the door. Then he looked at Becky and said,"I see what you mean."

The three of them then went in together, and Henry, despite being warned twice, still shuddered with a wave of goosebumps. A gruesome corpse sat in a chair fully dressed, yet seemed to be staring straight at the door, as if waiting for someone to walk in.

"I wonder what happened to him?" said Becky. They looked around the cabin but saw nothing else unusual. There didn't seem to be anything out of place.

In front of the dead man was the stove, with a large iron pot sitting on top of it. When Elmer peered into it he said, "There's nothing in here but a pair of leather gloves."

"I think the poor bugger starved to death." guessed Henry.

"Why wouldn't he just go to Dawson? wondered Becky, "It's only about three days away. I mean even if it's winter, he still could've made some kind of snowshoes."

Then noticing a strange lump on the corpse, but not wanting to touch it. Elmer took a large spoon off the counter, and slowly lifted up the dead man's pantleg, exposing a broken bone with a couple of pieces of wood tied to it. "Well, that'd be why he didn't go anywhere." he replied.

They all stood looking at him for a minute, thinking about the poor guys luck. "What should we do with him?" said Becky.

"Well for now let's wrap him up in that piece of canvas outside." replied Henry, "We're probably gonna have to bury him anyway."

So they took the canvas nailed to the outside of the cabin, and after securely wrapping the corpse, set him outside by the woodpile.

They were deciding what to do next, when Henry said "It doesn't look to me like anyone's dug for gold around here. So I think we should probably look further up the creek."

"I hope we find gold up there." said Elmer, "Otherwise the map was only to find the cabin, and the gold was just wishful thinking."

Then Becky said, "I saw a path in front of the cabin that seems to head that way, but mostly it goes down to the creekbed and disappears over the rocks."

They tried to consider their options, but there didn't seem to be any. "Well at least it's something to follow." said Henry, "Let's try it."

So they put their packs in the cabin, and as Elmer pulled out their shovel and a goldpan, Henry went to Becky and asked "How's your foot doing? Are you okay?"

"Its a little bit sore." she answered, "It's the uneven ground that bothers it, but without carrying a pack I should be fine." Then Elmer handed Henry the goldpan, and they started off across the rocks.

It was a few hundred yards to cross the rocky terrain, and as if it wasn't tough enough, when they got to about the middle, the rocks became bigger and it started to rain. Now they were slippery too. The good part was that when they finally finished crossing, they immediately found the trail again.

As they followed up the path, the valley continued to narrow in the bottom until it was no more than a hundred feet wide. Then the trail climbed up high on one side so they had to look down a steep bank to the creek. Which they could only see occasionally now, as both sides of the trail and much of the hillside was grown thick with high willows.

No sooner had the trail climbed up the bank when it began to descend again, and they saw a place where someone had worked with a shovel to widen it in places.

When they got down near the creek again, it'd been made much wider, and after walking just a few more feet, Elmer looked over to the water and said, "Look, there's a sluice box over there."

This seemed to be the place they were looking for. The path went down to the creek and ended, and various large holes had been dug on both sides of the water. They were old holes though, and the sluicebox, which had been dragged up the bank to keep from being lost in high water, had tall weeds growing all around it. Things looked promising though. No one would build a sluicebox without panning around first, to make sure there was a reason to build one.

They got excited now, and decided to look for gold first in the holes that were already there. Their hopes were high as they all started working. But as they tested each place, they'd only find enough gold to scratch out a living, and nothing that would make them anything close to wealthy. And by the time they finished testing all the holes, their moods began to sink again.

Things were starting to look bleak. So with the rain continuing to fall and further dampen their spirits, they started digging new holes. They tried on each side of the creek, then up and down the creek, then in the creek, always with the same results. Finally a very frustrated Henry said "There's nothing about this place that makes any sense to me." They didn't want to give up, but not knowing what to do next, they ended up just standing in the rain.

Then Elmer said to Henry, "Why don't you try digging a hole as deep as you can, and I'll go up the creek and see if this trail goes any further, and if there's anything up there we should know about."

Henry agreed, and before Elmer left told him, "Keep your eye open for any claim posts too, and if you find any, see if you can read the name on them."

After Elmer started up the creek, Henry looked at Becky and felt sorry for her. To him she appeared a near tragic looking creature standing there in the rain. He started digging, so he wouldn't have to look at her when he said "I'm sorry I drug you out here on some kinda misguided adventure. I thought thing's would go better than this."

She went straight over to him and stopped him from shoveling. "You didn't. I insisted, remember?" Then she said "Besides, it's not over, we haven't lost yet." Then she kissed him and picked up the gold pan, and holding it out with both hands said "Here, load me up."

So he filled up the pan while thinking out loud as he had before, "Wow, what a woman."

She continued trying panfulls as Henry dug the hole deeper, but it still didn't get any better. They kept on trying though, and about the time Henry hit the dreaded permafrost, Elmer returned from his search up the valley. "Well there's no more diggin's up the creek." he told them, "And the trail ends here. And I didn't see any claim posts either."

"It doesn't make any sense that there's no claim posts." said Henry.

"It does if they didn't find much gold." replied Elmer.

"Yea, but then the cabin and sluicebox don't make any sense." added Henry.

"Any better luck in the hole?" asked Elmer.

"No, just more of the same." answered Henry, "And then the permafrost."

"What should we do now?" asked Becky.

"Go back to the cabin and dry off while we think about it." suggested Elmer.

Becky and Elmer began heading for the trail, when Henry spoke up. "I'm gonna walk down the creek and see if there's anything we might a missed." he said. "I'll meet you guys down where the creek gets close to the trail again."

"I'll do it if you want." offered Elmer.

"Naw, you went up the creek." said Henry, "I'll do it."

So Becky and Elmer started up the trail, as Henry began plugging his way down the creek. As they made their way up the hillside, Elmer said to Becky "It could be tough for Henry walking down the creek. When we get back down to where we can meet him, we might have to wait awhile."

They hiked up the trail until they were high on the hill again, then walked carefully along so as not to slip on the rain soaked path. "You know, Henry's right about this place not making any sense." said Elmer, "It doesn't make any sense to me either."

"That's 'cause yer stupid." growled a deep voice behind them. They both spun around to see Leadtooth! They were shocked! He'd hidden in the willows until they passed by, and now he stood pointing a gun at them!

"I thought you were long gone." replied Elmer, "Off to start your life in hell." Elmer was doing his best not to look scared.

"I figured I'd finish off my business first." sneered Leadtooth, "But I had no idea you were gonna bring a girl for me." He looked at Becky with a taunting smile, "And such a pretty one too."

Becky looked at him like she was going to be sick, "You could make the flesh crawl on a squid." she answered.

"We'll see soon enough." he said still smiling, "And you'll have lots a time to get to know me." Like Elmer, Becky was doing her best not to appear afraid, but she was visibly starting to shake.

Then Elmer tried to get Leadtooth's attention away from Becky, saying "So how'd you get outta your handcuffs? Ya just rattle your tail and slither out?"

"That's funny." Leadtooth replied, "Now drop that big sticker a yours on the ground, and be careful doin' it."

Elmer had no choice, and slowly took out his bowie knife and dropped it to the ground. Then he tried to keep Leadtooth talking, "So how many people did ya have to kill to get away?"

"I don't know." he answered, "One or two. But who's counting? Now, where's that friend a yours?"

"He's back at the cabin." replied Elmer.

"Wrong answer." warned the thug, "Try again."

"He already struck it rich and went back to Dawson." lied Elmer again.

"Well if yer not gonna tell me," he said, "I don't need ya for anything." then he aimed the gun at Elmer and said, "This is gonna be great!" Then he pulled the trigger!

But the gun just went 'click'! Leadtooth instantly knew what happened, and he quickly put his other hand on the cylinder to help turn it! "Run Becky!" yelled Elmer, and he charged at Leadtooth! Before he could ready the gun to fire again, Elmer piled into him, sending them both crashing through the willows and down the bank! Becky didn't run! Instead she picked up Elmer's knife, and started down the hill to try and help.

When they tumbled to a stop, Elmer quickly jumped to his feet again, only to find Leadtooth about eight feet away still trying to fire the gun! Becky saw what was happening, and as fast as she could threw the knife at Leadtooth, hoping to hit him point first. But it was too late! This time the gun fired, and the loud explosion sent a bullet into the middle of Elmer's chest! Becky heard a loud groan out of both men, as Elmer careened over backwards and tumbled through the willows down the hill!

The instant after Leadtooth shot, Becky's lucky throw hit its mark. The big knife stabbed deep into his shoulder, causing him excrutiating pain! Now with Elmer gone, he suddenly glared up the bank at Becky, then seething with rage he pulled out the knife and started up the hill after her! She was terrified! She scrambled the few feet back up to the trail, and began running down the path as fast as she could go!

When Henry heard the gunshot he went into shock! He knew something horrible had happened to Becky and Elmer! He was going to yell out to them, but then thought it'd be better if whoever they encountered didn't know he was there, or at least didn't know where he was. The shot came from high on the hill ahead of him, and he wanted to rush straight towards the sound, but with the steep ground and thick wet willows, it would take far longer than just traveling down the stream then back up the trail. So he ran straight down the creek as fast as he could!

As he raced along, he kept looking up to the trail hoping to see something. Anything at all! Then when the path finally came down near the water again, he left the creekbed to scramble up the bank and back onto the trail. When he looked down the path he was instantly filled with horror! He saw Becky running for her life, with Leadtooth about thirty yards behind, chasing her with the big knife! He was even further behind Leadtooth, but charged off as fast as he could trying to catch up!

As all three of them raced down the valley, Leadtooth slowly gained on Becky, as Henry gained on Leadtooth. Then Becky reached the sea of rocks that stretched all the way across the valley to the cabin.

It was still a long way to go, and Leadtooth was closer than ever! Very quickly he too started crossing over the large stones, with Henry closing the gap behind him. The chase slowed to an agonizing crawl now, as all three of them slipped and stumbled their way over the rain soaked boulders towards the cabin. Becky was scared as she could be! Everytime she looked back, the big thug with the knife was closer!

As the chase went on, the space between them continued to narrow, until Henry realized he wasn't going to catch up in time. Now he prayed that Becky could reach the cabin in time to lock Leadtooth out. Then maybe he could get to the axe around the side of the cabin. He also prayed that her injured foot would get her there without breaking down. It had to be in terrible shape now.

Before long he could see Leadtooth was closing in on her, and she wasn't going to make it! All he could think to do now, was to try and get Leadtooth's attention on to him. So as he scrambled along, he started scooping up rocks and throwing them, trying to taunt the thug into turning around and dealing with him. "Poor scared Leadtooth!" he yelled, "The great woman fighter! You just afraid a me, or you afraid of all men!?" What Leadtooth was really afraid of, was that if Becky reached the cabin, there might be a gun inside.

Becky finished crossing the rocks with Leadtooth right behind her, and as she came up the bank to race the last few yards to the cabin, she could see that the door had been left slightly open! Then Leadtooth began to taunt her! He was so close now he didn't have to yell. "I'm gonna carve you up like a Christmas turkey!" He sneered. Then he raised up the knife to take a hack at her!

She looked back in horror as she saw the knife about to come down! Then she planted her ailing foot wrong and crashed to the ground exhausted!

"Don't worry," said Leadtooth, as he stopped and stood over her, "I'll put you outta your misery!" Then he drew back the knife to lunge down and stab her! Suddenly a rifle appeared in the cabin doorway, and fired a huge blast that ripped into Leadtooth's chest! He flew over backwards and landed on his back, stone dead!

Henry had just finished crossing the rocks, and not able to see who shot and what was going on, he dove down beside Becky! Becky didn't know what was happening either, and still panicked, she curled up in a ball covering her head with her hands! "Who's out there?" yelled a voice from the cabin, "Show yourselves!"

"Just friendly people now!" yelled back Henry, "We're not armed!" Then he stood up showing his open hands.

"Come over here to the door!" shouted the man, "And don't try no tricks!"

Henry helped Becky get back up, and then they started towards the cabin together.

Suddenly the door flung open all the way, and an old man stepped out. He had grey hair and a bushy beard, and the appearance of a lifelong goldminer. He seemed less afraid now, but with the gun still pointed at them, he stepped off to the side and said, "Go inside now."

Once they were all in the cabin he said, "So what are ya doing here?"

"We didn't have any luck prospecting around Dawson." said Henry, "So we came up here to try, and now it seems our luck's gotten a lot worse."

Then the old man pointed the gun at their packs. "Those yours?" he said.

Once he moved the rifle toward their packs, he never pointed it back at them again, appearing to start losing his fear of them. "Yea." said Henry, "We left 'em in here 'cause of the rain."

"There's three packs and only two a you." said the old man, "The other pack belong to that guy on the ground out there?"

"No." answered Henry, "It belongs to our friend. But that piece a crap out there ambushed us up the creek and shot my partner. I think he might be dead," said Henry sadly, "but I'd sure like to go check on him. He could be still alive."

Becky had seen what happened, and didn't want Henry to get his hopes up. "I think he shot Elmer square in the chest from just a few feet away." she reluctantly told him.

Then the old man said, "You better go check on him then. In fact, I better come with ya, in case you need to carry him."

So they left the cabin to hurry back up the valley and find Elmer.

As soon as they got outside, the old man said that they should go ahead, that he had to check his horses and would catch up to them. Then before they started off, Henry tried to talk Becky into staying behind, and not torturing her foot anymore. But she insisted, saying "I gotta show you where Elmer went down the bank, or you could be a long time finding him."

As they started to leave and were walking passed Leadtooth, she said "I wonder why his hand's all bloody?"

"He musta slipped on the rocks out there." answered Henry.

"But the rocks are all smooth." she said, "Besides, he's missing a finger."

Barely past him yet, Henry stopped and stepped back to have a better look. "Maybe it got cut off by the knife." added Becky.

"I don't think so." replied Henry," His hand's all mangled."

"It took him both hands to fire the gun." she said, "Maybe he shot his own finger off."

All of a sudden things didn't add up to Henry. "Why would he shoot Elmer," he said, "then leave the gun behind, and chase you all the way here with the knife?"

"Maybe the gun broke." suggested Becky, "The first time he tried to shoot it, it didn't work. It just went 'click'. That's when he used both hands."

"I think the gun blew up in his hands." realized Henry. Then he started to get excited, "If that's what happened, then there's a chance Elmer's still alive!" They immediately raced off to find out!

As soon as they got down to the rocks, they looked up ahead, and to their complete amazement, they saw Elmer staggering over the stones towards them clutching his chest! They hurried out to meet him, and before they could even ask, he said "It's alright, I'm okay. I'm only stumbling 'cause the rocks are slippery." But when they looked closer he didn't appear to be alright. His hand was on his lower chest, and both his hands and shirt were covered with blood.

"You don't look okay." said Henry, as he started helping him over the rough terrain.

"No really." he replied, "Look." and he lifted up his shirt to show a bullet lodged in beside his lowest rib. But there was enough of the bullet sticking out, that it could easily be pulled out by just using fingers. Then Elmer jokingly said, "See. It got stopped by my iron-like physique. I just left it in, so I wouldn't bleed so much on the way back." A little bit later he admitted, "I think the gun blew apart. When I was climbing back up the bank I found most of it. It's in my pocket."

Then he asked "What was that other shot I heard?"

So Henry told him "We got company. ...and it's a good thing too, that other shot you heard was him sending Leadtooth to meet god.

"Who is he?" asked Elmer.

"Don't know yet." answered Henry, but I'm guessing that's his cabin."

As he continued helping Elmer over the rocks, Henry began to realize that he could walk just about as well on his own, and really wasn't hurt that bad. When they finally reached the cabin, the old man had seen them coming, and was waiting with bandage strips and disinfectant to patch Elmer up.

After they all got inside, the old man looked at Henry and said "What's your name young fella?"

"Henry Browning." he answered. Then he introduced Becky and Elmer.

"My names Patrick" he said, "but everybody calls me Paddy." Then he added, "So Henry. While I'm patching up Elmer here, why don't you get that stove a cookin'. You're all soppin' wet, and the young lady there's starting to shake pretty good."

So while Henry got a fire going, Becky went into their packs to get what she needed to make coffee.

Then the old guy said "So I'm thinkin' it was you guys that wrapped up my brother in the canvas around back?"

"Yea, that was us." answered Henry apologetically, "We didn't know what else to do with him."

"Where was he when you found him?" asked Paddy.

Nobody said anything for a few seconds...they didn't want to tell him. Finally Henry spoke up and said, "He was sitting in the chair by the stove. He had a broken leg....It looked like he starved to death."

Paddy just stared at the floor with a sorrowful look for a bit, then finally said, "Well, that makes sense. I was supposed to be back last fall with supplies....He musta waited as long as he could, then had some kinda accident."

Then he said "I'm gonna go out back. I still have to unload the horses." He seemed to want to be alone, so they didn't offer to help.

After he'd gone Elmer said, "Since the old guy's here now, and there's not much for gold here anyway, maybe we should head back tomorrow."

Are you sure you're good enough to travel?" asked Henry.

"Sure." replied Elmer, "It might take us an extra day or two to get there though."

Then Henry looked at Becky, "How about you Becky? How's your foot?"

"Same as Elmer." she answered, "If we go slow and take an extra day or two, I should be okay." So they decided to start back for Dawson in the morning.

Then Elmer remembered the gun in his pocket, and pulled it out so everyone could have a good look at it. They all examined the revolver together, and with the cylinder blown off, they could easily see a huge gouge in the base of the barrel. And by the time the old man returned, they were matching up Elmer's flattened bullet with the heavily scarred barrel. Then Old Paddy had a look for himself and said, "Kid, yer the luckiest guy I ever saw."

When they finished studying the gun, they told Paddy about their plan to head back to Dawson in the morning. Then Elmer said, "Do you mind if I ask you a question Paddy?"

"Go ahead and shoot." replied the old prospector as he poured himself a coffee.

"Well we checked out the creek pretty good for gold." said Elmer, "In fact we tried everywhere....and well, we didn't find much. Are we missing something? I mean if there's not much here, why'd you build a cabin?"

Paddy answered "I been prospecting a long time. My brother too. And we figured there was enough gold in the creek to make the whole area worth checking out. There could be a lot better diggin's somewhere else around. Besides, at our age we prefer being away from the crowds....Well, I guess it's just me now.

It was starting to get dark now, and after Paddy opened the door to the cabin and stared outside for a moment, he said "I guess we better go bag up that snake before it gets too dark." "What'll we put him in?" said Henry. "I got a roll of canvas I brought from Dawson." said Paddy, "I'll cut a piece off that."

So Paddy and Henry went out to do the job, and when they'd finished wrapping Leadtooth up, Henry said "Should we put him around the woodpile beside your brother?"

"No!" replied Paddy, "Absolutely not! My brother shouldn't have to lay beside scum like this. We'll put him around the other side of the cabin." So they did.

When they woke in the morning, they were looking at blue sky and sunshine again. Paddy had a fire going in the pit in front of the cabin, so they sat around and talked for awhile, as they readied themselves to leave.

Eventually the conversation turned to the considerable distance it was back to Dawson, when Paddy asked "So what made you guys come this far north anyway? Not too many people come this far out to do their prospecting."

There was no reason to keep the map a secret anymore, so Henry told him, "We had a map we were following. We were kinda hoping it'd lead to the motherlode."

"Yea." added Elmer practically boasting, "Henry got it from Soapy Smith in a fight."

"A map!" repeated Paddy, "You followed a map! Do you mind if I have a look at it?" he asked.

"Naw, go ahead." answered Henry, and he dug it from his pocket and handed it to him.

When Paddy opened it up to have a look, he immediately exclaimed, "This is my map! I got it stole from me in Seattle!"

Soapy Smith stole it from you?" asked Elmer.

"No. It was some big bugger with a lead colored tooth." answered Paddy.

Then Henry said "You mean that big bugger with the leadtooth we got wrapped up around the corner?"

"What!" exclaimed Paddy. He immediately jumped up and hurried around the side of the cabin, with everyone else following behind. He quickly unwrapped Leadtooth to have a look, but when he tried to move the thugs top lip, he found it frozen in place.

Undaunted, he picked up a stick to use as a prybar, and after levering up the lip exclaimed "It's him! This is the leadtoothed bugger! It was dark when he stole the map from me, but I'd recognize that tooth anywhere! I knew it was one of Soapy's boys!"

He flopped the canvas back over Leadtooth's face, and as they walked back to the fire, Elmer asked "So how did Soapy find out about your map?"

"I'm sure it was either in Skagway or on the boat heading south." he told them as they all sat down again. "I still hadn't finished makin' the map yet, so I worked on it a couple a times. I thought I was being careful, but they must a spotted me and waited for their chance...a stupid mistake in hindsight."

"But it's one anybody could make." assured Henry, "Who'd guess that a whole town could be evil. We got skinned ourselves in Skagway."

"What I can't figure out." said Paddy "Was that if you guys had the map, how did Leadtooth find his way up here?"

"He was probably following us." said Elmer, "We've been dancin' with him since Seattle."

Then he told Paddy about their numerous confrontations, with Henry adding, "He's actually an escaped convict. He got sentenced twenty years in Dawson for trying to kill Elmer, and we watched him get put on a riverboat with our own eyes."

"Well, him being a convict doesn't surprise me." said Paddy, "My brother would still be alive if he hadn't a put me in the hospital for most a last winter."

"How'd that happen?" asked Elmer, as he started getting his pack ready for their trip.

"It was when he stole the map in Seattle." answered Paddy, "I was coming from buying my tickets back to Skagway, and a few blocks from the waterfront, he came out of an alley and started stabbin' me. He woulda killed me too, if not for a couple a guys scaring him off."

"Whaaat!" exclaimed Henry.

"Before he could say anything else, Elmer jumped up practically yelling "That was us! We're those guys!"

Old Paddy wasn't sure whether he should believe them or not, but "I don't believe it!" were the words that came out of his mouth.

"No!" said Elmer pointing a finger at him, "You had a grandson with you! In fact when they took you to the hospital, he gave us your tickets! We came to the Klondike on your tickets!"

Paddy thought for a few seconds, and knew they were telling the truth. "Well, I can't thank you guys enough for savin' me." he said.

Elmer started digging through his pack again and said to Paddy, "Your initials are P.D.R. right?"

"Yea" he answered, "Patrick David Ryan. How did you know?"

"It's right here on your cigar case." said Elmer, as he pulled it out and handed it to him.

"Wow." replied Paddy, "I never thought I'd see this again." Then he said "I guess this case has been on quite an adventure."

"You don't know the half of it" replied Elmer.

Then Henry said to him, "I'm curious Paddy, so I gotta ask. Why did you make the map?"

Paddy answered the question, but seemed distracted as he spoke, "I'd only made the trip out here a couple a times." he said, "And I know from experience that if you don't do something for awhile, it's easier to forget than you'd think. I just wanted to make sure I could find my way back."

They were ready to go now, but as they continued talking, Paddy's nature became increasingly distant. So finally they stood up to help each other on with their packs, and Paddy too stood up, seemingly to shake hands good-bye. But instead he began shuffling around, appearing extremely agitated. The shuffling quickly grew to pacing, then he suddenly came to a stop, and chopping his hand through the air like an axe he yelled "Alright!...Alright!...Alright." with his voice relaxing a little more each time he said it. "There's gold! Lots and lots a gold!"

They heard what Paddy said, but didn't quite know how to answer. "I know you guys are honest. "he said, "And I owe ya for saving me."

Then he looked at Becky and said, "And you young lady. There was only one person in the world I wanted to see dead, and you not only led him right to me, you gave me the perfect reason to send him to hell. So I figure I owe you too. .....So here's the deal. You guys help me mine 'till freeze up, and we'll split it four ways, an equal share for each of us. Then you guys go away and don't come back again. Agreed?"

Elmer shot forward before Paddy could change his mind, "Deal!" he said shaking his hand vigorously.

When Elmer let go, Henry and Becky stepped forward and also shook his hand, with Henry asking, "So where is the gold? We panned all over the place and we couldn't find anything."

"That's 'cause yer amateurs." grinned Paddy.

"Can we go have a look?" asked Elmer.

"There's no time for playin' around." answered Paddy, "Winter's gonna land on us soon, probably in four or five weeks. So we best get to mining right away."

As they took off their packs again, they quickly became excited about mining for gold. Paddy went around by the woodpile, and when he came back he was carrying four metal buckets and a couple of shovels. He looked at them all standing there holding gold pans, and said "Your not gonna need those. They'll just slow us down. But bring your picks and shovels, we can use them." Then they all started up the valley to go gold mining.

When they got up to where the sluicebox was again, they set down all their tools. Then Paddy and Henry packed the sluicebox from the bushes back down to the creek again. "You guys watch how to do this." he said, "In case you have to do it when I'm not around."

Then he proceeded to set up the sluicebox to catch gold. "If it's not steep enough," he told them, "nothin' will run through it. Not even the dirt. But if it's too steep, everything will run through it, even the gold. It's gotta be just right."

When they were finished setting it up, Elmer said, "So where do we get the gold from?"

"You still have'nt figured it out yet?" answered Paddy with a big smile on his face. Then he hurried across the creekbed and up onto the path. "You guys heard of the white channel?" he asked.

Suddenly Henry figured it out, and quietly said "The tricky ol' bugger's were mining the trail."

"This is just like the white channel." said Paddy, "The gold's in the bank. Didn't ya wonder why it's wide enough to drive a stagecoach up here?"

"Well how come you dug a big hole in the other bank, and all these holes in the creek?" asked Elmer.

"Fake diggin's and test holes." answered Paddy, as he came back down to the sluicebox. "All we have to do, is fill the buckets up there, pack 'em down here, and dump 'em in the box."

It was simple enough, and as they started working Paddy kept giving advice for everything to work smoothly. "It works best if we change jobs with each other every once in awhile." he said, "That way we don't strain muscles or get blisters. And when you dump the buckets into the sluicebox, it's better to just dump in half, and let the water wash it away before you put in the rest.

After about a half an hour, they couldn't resist any longer and had to stop to look in the box. When they gathered around, Paddy picked up a shovel and went to the bottom of the sluicebox, "We have to move the gravel from here every once in awhile." he said, "Otherwise it piles up and stops the box from workin' properly."

"I can't see any gold in here yet." said Elmer.

"Don't worry." answered Paddy, "It's in there. We just have to keep packin'." Then he took the axe and said, "You guys keep at it. I got some other work I gotta do. I shouldn't be too long." and he headed off up the creek.

When Paddy came back, instead of stopping to work with them, he continued on down the creek. Henry knew then that what he'd suspected was true. Paddy was staking the claim. As they filled the buckets with paydirt he mentioned it to Elmer. "Yea, I noticed that too." he answered, "I wonder why he didn't do it before?"

Then Becky yelled to them from the sluicebox, "Hey you guys! I can see gold in here now!"

They quickly picked up the filled buckets, and went down to see for themselves. When they got down to the creek, they peered into the box with Becky. "It's hard to see with the water rushing through," she said "but it's starting to look yellow here at the top."

They looked closer and she was right! The first riffle was yellow almost all the way across. "How much do you think is in there?" wondered Becky.

"It's pushed all the dirt out." said Henry, "So it's at least an inch deep."

They couldn't help just standing there and staring at it. "That's a lot a gold!" remarked Elmer. They wanted to reach in and grab some out with their hands, but not knowing a lot about sluiceboxes, they thought they'd best leave well enough alone.

When they went back to work, they found that even with their injuries the labor was easier now. Now that they knew there was gold in the box.

Before long Paddy returned and resumed working with them, to put even more gold in the box. And as the day wore on they watched the second riffle fill up, and awhile after that, the third. By the end of the day even the fourth riffle was showing signs of gold in it.

Finally Paddy said "We better clean up now."

The sun was still shining with lots of daylight left, but Paddy added "There's some things I wanna show you before dark. Besides, there's no sense in workin' ourselves into the ground the first day."

So they poured the last couple of buckets into the sluicebox, and after it washed through, Paddy grabbed the top of the box with both hands and said "When I lift it up, put a big rock underneath to keep it out of the water."

They did what he said, and when the water drained from the box, they saw a sight that dazzled their eyes! All the top riffles were packed with gold, and riddled through with large nuggets! "Wow!" exclaimed Becky, "I think I like gold mining."

"It might not be the richest claim in the Klondike," said Paddy, "but its rich enough, and it's probably the easiest one to work. No shafting, no tunneling, no overburden. And no permafrost, 'cause the sun keeps it melted. When you add in handy water and great scenery, I think it's the best mine in the whole Yukon."

They all looked at the big picture for a moment, with Henry finally saying "I believe you're right Paddy."

Very quickly their attention was drawn back to the sluicebox again, with Elmer asking "So how do we get the gold out a there?"

"That's one of the things I wanted to show you guys." said Paddy, "Every three or four days we'll have to clean out the whole box. And to do that, we have to lift the riffles out, then pan all the dirt that's in there. But on the other days we use these." he added, and he held up a large spoon and a square looking scoop that he'd fashioned from an apple juice tin. It looked perfect for getting between the riffles. "When we use these," he said, "Just do the riffles you see gold in. Otherwise we're just adding dirt to the gold, that we have to separate later."

Then he cleaned out a bucket with water and handed it to Henry, then handed the spoon and scoop to Becky and Elmer.

As they started scooping the gold from the riffles and putting it in the bucket, Becky said "It feels so heavy."

"Yea, it sure does." agreed Elmer, "But there's little bits a gravel mixed in with it."

"That's okay." answered Paddy, "I'll show you the best way to get it out when we get back to the cabin."

When they'd cleaned out the riffles as best they could, and were getting ready to leave, Paddy told them that, "When the weather's nice like this, it's best to leave the sluicebox just like it is. Then you just have to take the rock out from underneath, and set it back down to start mining again. But if the weather's bad, or looks like it's gonna be, we gotta set the box back up in the bush, so we don't lose it when the creek rises. Then he said "We can leave the other buckets and shovels here too. There's no sense in packin' them back and forth everyday."

Henry was carrying the loaded bucket as they started back, and said "There's a lot a gold in here! It must weigh twenty or twenty-five pounds!"

When they arrived back at the cabin, Paddy showed them how to pan out the small amount of gravel mixed in with the gold, and when he was finished, the gold was pure and lay in a heap.

Then he took the pan into the cabin and set it on the stove. Why'd you put it there?" asked Elmer.

"Well we're not trying to cook it." said Paddy, "But heating it up will help dry it out. You can't do nothin' with wet gold."

"What'll we keep it in?" asked Becky.

"I got some ore sacks just for that purpose." answered Paddy.

Then he said "There's a reason I was showing you all those things today too. Tomorrow morning I'm leaving for Dawson again."

"How come?" asked Elmer.

"A bunch a reasons." he answered, "This place is gonna get mined out one day, and when that happens, I don't want my brother buried in the middle a nowhere. So I'm gonna have him buried in the cemetary in Dawson."

"And then there's our lead toothed friend out there." he continued, "I thought about it, and I think the right thing to do is to take him to the Mounties and tell them what happened. Besides, I don't wanna bury him here and have him stinkin' up my claim."

Then Paddy added "There's another reason too. You mighta noticed me staking a claim today. Me and my brother found gold here almost a year ago, and I been itching to file a claim ever since.

"We did notice." said Henry, "And we saw there was no claimposts when we first got here, so I'm curious, why didn't you stake it back when you found the gold?"

"We couldn't." answered Paddy, "Because of that one claim per year law. When we got here we'd already staked a couple a bad claims on Goldbottom just outside of Dawson. So we had to wait a year before we could file anymore. That's when everything started to go bad. And that's why we tried to disguise our mining as part of the trail too.

"Well it worked." said Henry, "We couldn't find it." then he added, "But when you file your claim, aren't you worried people are gonna find out where you staked and show up out here?

"Not really." replied Paddy, "Lots a claims get staked. What gathers a crowd, is blabbin' like a bloody fool, or spraying money all over the place, and I won't be doing either."

"Well I hope it works out for you Paddy." answered Henry.

The next morning they helped Paddy load his brother and Leadtooth onto the horses, then watched as he mounted the third pony, and left for Dawson with the other horses in tow.

Once Paddy had gone, they traveled up the valley to go mining again, and it went pretty much as it did the day before. They watched the sluicebox riffles fill up one by one again, and by the end of the day, they carried about the same amount of gold back to the cabin.

They continued following Paddy's advice as they panned out the gravel, though it took them a lot longer than it had the old professional. And when they'd finished drying it out on the stove, and then played with it for awhile, they poured the gold into one of the ore sacks and placed it with their take from the day before.

There was still plenty of light when they finished their supper, so rather than sit around in the cabin, they decided to light a fire in the pit outside, both to keep warm and better enjoy their surroundings. Becky looked at the sun casting its long shadows over the scenery, and said "There sure is something different about the Yukon. I don't mean the gold." she added "I mean there's something special about this place."

"Your right." agreed Elmer as he looked around. "But in the winter it's just a trick. It's really tryin' to kill ya."

The sun slowly sank into the hills as they talked, and began that prolonged twilight only found in the north. They felt an instant chill with the loss of the sun, causing Elmer to throw more wood on the fire, and Becky to push even closer to Henry, though only partly to keep warm.

As they kept talking, their conversation was continually drawn back to the gold as if by a magnet. After all, they'd only been mining two days, and though they weren't rich yet, they could almost be considered 'well off' by southern standards.

When it started to get dark, they thought they'd be going back inside again, but instead they noticed the northern lights. Then they sat with their necks craned upwards for over an hour, as they watched the lights brightly shimmering green and blue, and dancing back and forth across the sky. "Wow! What a show!" declared Becky.

They mined for four more days before Paddy came back, each day adding more gold to their fast growing pile. They were surprised to see he brought all three horses back with him, but he brought some luxuries back too. So far the furniture in the cabin was comprised of a very rough-cut log table, and two even rougher made chairs, one of which Paddy's brother had died in. Now he'd brought back a large flat table top, and four comfortable chairs.

"How'd it go for you in town Paddy?" asked Henry, as he helped him unload their new comforts.

"Great!" answered Paddy, "I'm now the official owner of a very rich placer claim."

"That's good." replied henry, "You deserve some good luck."

"And I got out a Dawson without anybody following me too." he added. Then said, "Oh yea there's more. You should a seen how glad the Mounties were to see Leadtooth again. And they didn't mind seeing him draped over a horse either. But when you guys get back to Dawson, Steele wants to talk to you about what happened to him.

"I kinda expected that." answered Henry.

With Paddy's return from Dawson, their mining went better than ever. Not only did they mine more with an extra person, but since Paddy didn't have to hide the work anymore, he suggested they dig up the trail itself. "Lower is usually better." he said. So now when they traveled back to the cabin at night, they had to put the gold in two buckets, to even out the load for whoever carried it.

In the following days, they learned that Paddy had brought the table and chairs out for more than just making their meals more comfortable. He liked to play cards. He also seemed to enjoy that he could play more games with four people, than he could before with just his brother. They liked playing too, so the four of them often had games in the evening, sometimes playing much later than they should've.

Then one night Paddy wanted to use the table for a new game. He went and got four of the new ore bags, and as he wrote one of their names on each bag, he said "When I'm mining, there's something I like to do. I think the bigger nuggets are special. So when I take the gold to the bank, I like keeping them out for myself. They're good for making jewelry, or just saving, or I like giving 'em to people I know back home. Some of them never saw gold before, and they all seem most appreciative when you give 'em one."

So they took all the good sized nuggets from the bags they'd collected so far, and put them in the middle of the table. There was way over a hundred of them, ranging in size from beans, to some as big as strawberries.

Then Paddy put the deck of cards on the table and said "Whoever cuts the highest card goes first, and they get to take which ever nugget they want. Then the person to the left picks, and we keep going around clockwise until there's none left.

They all agreed and each cut a card, and Becky won. She looked the pile over, then picked out a giant nugget and put it in her bag. "I already like this game." she said.

In fact it was a game they all thoroughly enjoyed, and from then on as they dug up more gold, every fourth or fifth night they'd play the nugget game.

The next day when they'd finished mining, it was nice weather again, and knowing that winter was closing in on them, they took advantage to sit around the fire again. However when the sun went down and took the temperature with it, they moved back inside to play their usual game of cards, and that's when Paddy hatched a plan he didn't tell them about.

He waited until they'd played for awhile, and everybody sat relaxed in their chairs. Then as he shuffled the cards, he said "You know, I asked around about you guys in Dawson. To get a bead on what kinda characters I'm dealin' with out here." Then he suddenly dropped the cards and quickly leaned over the table into Elmer's face with an accusing look, "Scratchy the Claimjumper!" he snarled.

Elmer was shocked! "Now just hang on Paddy!" he protested, "That was an accident! Even if you talk to the guy that owned that claim, even he'll tell ya" Then Elmer quit talking, as Paddy was laughing so hard he wasn't really listening anyway. He'd cracked himself right up.

"Its okay." he finally said, "They told me you didn't do it on purpose. I just wanted to throw a stick a powder and see what happened."

As Paddy's laughter subsided, even Henry was chuckling. Then Elmer, as if trying to wriggle free from the attention, said "Didn't you hear anything about Henry?

"Naw, nothin' criminal." answered Paddy, "Just that in certain circumstances, he could be a dirty, slippery man."

Now Elmer cracked up and Becky sat giggling.

"Just deal." said Henry finally, "I feel I must punish you all with superior cardplay."

They woke the next morning to a thick layer of frost on everything, a sharp reminder of their limited time. It didn't take long to thaw out though, and they worked hard and steady the entire day with a new found urgency. Also throughout the day, they saw huge flocks of geese flying south in giant 'V' formations, another sign of winter's approach.

As the days turned into weeks, they continued getting shorter and colder, and their nights around the campfire became fewer and fewer. When they did sit outside, they'd often listen to wolves and coyotes howling in the distance, and watch spectacular northern lights.

On one special night, the lights appeared as huge shards of colored glass. They shone bright green on top, then turned to blue and then purple, with bright red tips on their bottoms. The sky was filled with thousands of them that not only shot all over the place, but seemed to beat straight down on top of them. "These lights would be scary if you didn't know what they were." said Henry.

As Becky stared up at them she said "This is probably once in a lifetime."

Then a day came when it didn't warm up much at all. It'd been cloudy all day, and when the sky began to clear about suppertime, Paddy suggested they clean out the whole sluicebox and put it back up on the bank. "I think that might be it." he said "Looks like it's gonna be real cold tomorrow, and if it is, the ground will be froze solid."

Then when they were ready to leave he said "We might as well take the buckets and shovels too. We can always bring 'em back if I'm wrong."

After they got back got to the cabin, Paddy started with panning the gravel from the gold again, as Becky and Henry took the buckets and shovels around the cabin to store with Paddy's other tools.

"You know Henry," said Becky, "I was trying my foot out on the way back today. Bending it every which way. I think after all these months it's finally healed. It feels like new again."

Henry could see she was happy, and he stepped up to her giving her a kiss and wrapping his arms around her.

He was still holding her tight when they heard Elmer yell "Hey Paddy! You probably wanna come and see this!"

They wondered what Elmer wanted him to see, so they too went to have a look. When they got to where he was standing, he pointed to the ground, and to their surprise they could see partially exposed bags of gold leading underneath the woodpile. "I was just gettin' wood for the stove," said Elmer "and there it was."

"I knew it!" exclaimed Paddy, "I knew my brother would have at least mined something last year. I just didn't know what he could've done with it."

"It looks like you're richer that you thought." said Elmer, "You want us to dig it out so you can see how much is there?"

"Na, just leave it there for now." answered Paddy, "I got some thinkin' to do first."

When they'd finished their work outside, they all went in and ate supper. Then after they finished clearing the table, but before they began their nightly game of cards, they played the nugget game for what would turn out to be the last time.

Paddy had been right about the weather. It was freezing cold when they woke the next morning. It had snowed a few inches, and the ground was solid as stone. There'd be warmer days ahead, but nothing that'd thaw the ground enough for them to mine again.

After they'd been outside awhile to better assess how cold it was, Paddy opened the door and saw them all standing there with frost on their breath. "What are you guys doin' out there?" he said.

"We're just tryin' to gauge the temperature." answered Henry.

"It's too cold to mine." replied Paddy, "That's all you need to know. Now come back inside and do your thinkin' in here." So they went back inside and headed straight for the stove to warm up.

"I guess we better pack up and get ready to leave." said Henry.

When he said it, he wasn't really sure how things were going to work, he knew they had more gold than they could possibly carry.

Then Paddy said, "When I came out here and found gold with my brother, we had a plan. But now that he's dead, I gotta change the plan."

Then he said "Have you guys noticed that the gold we've been mining is all rounded off and smooth?"

"Yes of course." answered Becky.

"Well that mean's it's traveled some distance to get where it is." he added, "Now I checked out that bank we been working in, all the way up and down the valley, and there's good gold for more that half a mile up the creek. Me and my brother figured we'd stake two claims a year and keep our mouths shut. And that way we'd get as much staked as we could before other people showed up. There's no way I can do that by myself, It'd just take too long."

"Don't you have any family that could help ya?" asked Elmer.

"Not much." answered Paddy, "And after I got stabbed in Seattle, what family I do have decided that Klondike gold mining is way too dangerous. They're city people anyway and not really cut out for this kinda living. If they did come, they'd only last about two days."

"Anyway," he continued, "without my brother, I'm gonna end up with neighbors out here whether I like it or not. And I could end up beside jerks or thieves, or anything at all. Now I already know you guys are honest." said Paddy. "You coulda staked claims anytime you wanted, but you stuck to our deal. And if I'm gonna end up with neighbors, I'd like to pick 'em myself."

Then Paddy offered, "So I'm suggesting you stake claims for youselves before you leave. But stake above where my claim is now. I'm gonna stay here 'till January when I'm allowed to stake another claim, and I wanna stake below where we been working. It looks as good as the ground above, but it's closer to my cabin."

"Aren't you coming to Dawson with us?" asked Becky, "I thought we'd all be leaving together. How are you gonna get out in January?"

"Snowshoes." replied Paddy.

"What about your gold and the horses?" she added.

"Well I brought the horses back for you guys to carry out your gold on." answered Paddy, "There's nothin' for 'em to eat up here in the winter. And when I go, I'll be carryin' more than enough gold to last me 'till spring. I'll hide the rest under my woodpile 'till I get back."

Henry shook Paddy's hand saying "Can't thank you enough Paddy. You're being more than generous." Then Becky and Elmer shook his hand too.

"Naw, you saved my life." said Paddy, and then he added "Tell ya what. When you guys start mining your own claims, you come by once a week and play cards with me, and we'll call it even."

"Deal." said Elmer.

So with Paddy changing their agreement, they went up the creek and staked their own claims. They'd hardly put up their posts, when they began getting excited about coming back next year. They couldn't wait to start mining their own claims, and building their own place, and to do it without worrying about money.

When they got back to the cabin, Paddy helped them load their gold onto the horses. "You know when you guys get back to Dawson." he said, "If you can keep it quiet where you got the gold from, and you get back here first thing in the spring, you should be able to stake three more claims. If people wanna know where you got the gold from, just tell 'em the truth. You got it from someone elses claim, and they wanna stay anonymous."

"That sounds like a pretty good plan." said Elmer.

Then Paddy added "But I was hopin' that if staking more claims in the spring works out, you could do me a favour."

"Sure" replied Elmer, "What is it?"

"I'd like you to sell me one." said Paddy.

"We'll sell ya which ever one you want for a dollar." offered Henry, "We at least owe you that much."

"Well Its all speculation right now." said Paddy, "Just come back in the spring."

It was only now that they began to realize, that old Paddy had gotten used to their company, and was actually going to miss them.

With the horses ready to go, they loaded on their packs as Paddy gave them one last piece of advice. "When you get to Dawson, just to be safe, you should probably deposit your gold in the bank before you go to the claims office. That way you won't be filing claims while there's hundreds of pounds of gold standin' behind you."

They agreed with Paddy, and after shaking hands goodbye, they began leading the horses away. "See you in the spring Paddy!" yelled back Elmer, and they were off on their way back to Dawson.

There was over six hundred pounds of gold loaded on the horses, and they were now very wealthy people. Of course they weren't Bonanza Creek rich, but once they filed their claims, there was a good chance they would be over the next year or two.

Traveling to Dawson turned out to be much easier than they expected. Thinking about the gold while carrying light packs, made their trip seem almost effortless, not to mention it was downhill the entire way.

Before they knew it a couple of days had passed, and they found themselves winding along the Klondike River not too far from Dawson. The horses seemed to know it too. Each time the trail crossed over a hump or small hill, the animals seemed to push them to walk faster. "I wonder what's wrong with these critters?" said Elmer. "It's like they got some kinda plan of their own."

"They probably know were not far from town," replied Henry, "and that they're gonna get fed when they get there."

Then Henry said "I wonder if we should make a plan? I mean, should we tell people we got money now? Or should we keep it a secret?

"Maybe they'll find out anyway." said Elmer.

"Well if they did," answered Henry "It'd be kinda like being redeemed for our past mistakes."

"That's something I noticed," said Becky "Whenever somebody gets rich, it doesn't seem to matter whether it was from hard work, or smart thinking, or good luck, or even stealing it. Everybody looks at them as if they've been chosen. Special people, no matter how they got it."

"One thing's for sure," said Henry "even if people find out we're loaded, we absolutely can't let on where we got it from."

They all knew it'd be better if no one even found out they had gold, but deep down they were all itching to tell at least their friends. Then Elmer said "As nice as being redeemed sounds, and not being 'Scratchy the Claim Jumper' anymore, we should probably try and keep it quiet."

"It might be out of our hands." said Becky, "If just one person we know sees us with these horses loaded down, it'll be all over town."

They led the horses over another small hill, then all three of them stopped and stood with their jaws dropped wide open. In front of them lay Dawson City. Burnt to the ground! The shining city of gold, the Paris of the north, was no more!

They never spoke much the rest of the way into town. They truly were in shock. From the edge of the city, they gazed out over a sea of charred rubble and ash, much of it still smoldering. Even the streets themselves were covered with debris, and spotted with numerous piles of singed articles rescued from the doomed establishments.

As the fire had raged through Paradise Alley, the whole city came out to fight it, and as it blazed towards Front Street, two thousand men with axes raced ahead, hacking buildings to the ground in a futile effort to stop its progress.

Then the flames began consuming Front Street. First the Tivoli Hotel went, then The Opera House, and the Bank of North America. Then The Worden Hotel, and Arkansas Jim's Greentree Hotel, The Northern Hotel, Silent Sam's Bank Saloon, and Bill McPhee's Pioneer Saloon. Building after building went up. Where the music had played, the women danced, and the gold had flowed.

In a final attempt to stop the inferno, they dynamited The Aurora Saloon and Dancehall, and then blew up Big Alex McDonald's Post Office Building. But to no avail. In the end 117 buildings burned. The opulent establishments, the lavish appointments, the fine art and furniture, all gone.

Though virtually all of Front Street lay in a smoldering heap, two buildings stood like bookends on opposite edges of a wasteland. It was Belinds's Fairview and the Monte Carlo. Both singed black, and caked with mud and ice, from buckets of dirty water being hurled at their smoking exteriors.

As they picked their way down Front Street with the horses in tow, many hundreds of very somber citizens dug through the rubble, or just stood staring at what used to be. Even though the heart of Dawson was destroyed, a few establishments on the fringe of the city had survived, as well as a good number of the smaller buildings in the back of the town. A couple of the banks had also come through unscathed, and as they made their way towards them to deposit their gold, they saw another surviving enterprise. It was Arizona Charlie's Palace Grand Theatre, and it remained completely untouched, as clean as the day it opened.

By the time they arrived at the bank, a number of people had seen them passing through town. People they knew. And the loaded horses were a dead give away. "Well I think it's safe to say our secrets out." said Henry as they began carrying their gold into the bank.

Inside they each got an account, and divided the money equally between them, except of course for their initialed bags of nuggets. They were weighed, and only left at the bank for safe keeping.

When they exited the building with their receipts and bankbooks, they went to see what things looked like at the claims office. It had escaped the fire, and when they saw no line up, as discreetly as they could they went in to stake their claims.

After registering the next three claims up the creek from Paddy on the map, they paid the fee and left, quickly putting as much distance as they could between themselves and the claims office. "I think we pulled it off." said Henry, as he looked around for familiar faces.

When they got even further away, Elmer said "Not only don't I see anybody we know, I don't think anyone's paying attention to us at all."

Then Becky, thinking about the gold said "You know, up until now I just felt like I always did. But now I actually feel like a rich woman."

"Me too." said Elmer without thinking."

"Yea." giggled Becky, "There's no chance you'll end up an old maid now."

Suddenly Henry said "Where are we going to anyway?" They all came to a stop and just stood there holding the horses.

They'd been so glad to get their claims filed and deposit their gold, that they hadn't thought any further.

So pondering their next move, they looked out over the devastation and Elmer said "It looks like our options are kinda limited." Then turning up his collar he said "And we can't take too long deciding, that's for sure, that winds gotta real bite to it."

The same stiff wind that had driven the fire through Dawson, had returned to sting at their hands and faces.

"What should we do with the horses?" asked Becky.

"I think we should give them to Belinda." suggested Elmer, "She could probably use them, and she helped us out a lot."

"That's a good idea." agreed Henry, then he added "I can't imagine the Fairview being anything but stuffed with people right now, but maybe we can at least get cleaned up there."

"You guys go ahead." said Becky, "I'm going home to my place. I'm curious how things are down there, especially since the fire." Then she told them "But if things don't work out for you at the Fairview, you can have a bath at my place. It's only a canvas tub, but I have a big cauldren for heating water." And with that, she turned and headed off down Front Street, towards her home by the river.

Henry immediately became distressed. She didn't kiss him good-bye or anything. Did she forget, or think it didn't matter. Or maybe it was because good girls didn't do that in public. That must be it he thought. But maybe she did it on purpose. After all, she didn't even agree to meet him somewhere later. "I don't know anything." he finally said out loud.

"Huh, what are you talkin' about?" asked Elmer.

"Oh nothing." he answered "Just thinking out loud."

"I been thinking too." said Elmer, "I was thinking about heading south for the winter. I haven't seen my mom and sisters for more that a year, and they had it pretty rough when I left home. I'd like to go back and fix things now that I can. Besides,

Dawson's not gonna have much to offer now,...at least not for awhile."

Henry hadn't thought about it, all his thoughts had been about Becky. But as they led the horses towards the Fairview, the more he thought about things, the more he knew Elmer was right. Finally he said "I think your right Elmer. Besides, we got no where to live now, and from everything I've heard, you don't know what cold is until you've spent a winter here."

"I think we should buy boat tickets before we do anything else." suggested Elmer, "There could be a real exodus with the fire and all."

So they turned down towards the river, and Henry went in to buy their tickets as Elmer held the horses. When he came back out, he said "I got good news and bad news."

"Tell me the good news first." replied Elmer.

"The good news is I got the tickets" answered Henry, "The bad news is, we only got about four hours before we go. It's all I could get."

"Well that's not so bad." said Elmer, "Remember, we got no place to live now."

Henry didn't tell him that he bought three tickets.

When they arrived at the Fairview, they found that Henry's prediction of it being stuffed with people was exactly right. A crowd was standing around outside, while on the inside the lobby floor was covered with sleeping people. Belinda was letting them sleep for a couple of hours in shifts, while the crowd outside waited for their turn. There was barely enough room for all the people in Dawson now, and just about every part of Belinda's establishment was packed.

When she saw Henry and Elmer, she came straight over to them and shook their hands. "Congratulations" she said, "I heard you guys finally struck it big."

They'd been right. Everyone in town already knew they'd found gold, and none of them had said a word to anybody yet.

"Yea." said Henry, "We had a lot a help, but we finally hit it."

"What's your plan now?" she asked.

"We need a couple a rooms." said Elmer.

She burst out laughing. "I'd need a shoehorn." she answered.

"Actually we're sailing south in a few hours." Henry told her, "We were wondering if there was any way we could get cleaned up here first?"

"Yea, I can arrange that." she said. Then she walked over and spoke to the man working at the front desk for a few seconds. When she came back she said "It's gonna take about fifteen minutes."

"Great" said Henry, "That'll give us time to give you our critters." And with that they went outside and gave Belinda their horses.

"Thanks you guys." she said, as she put them in her stable, "I can really use these animals."

Once back inside, Belinda led them to a room upstairs. "This is my room." she said, "There's some girls in here right now, but they've already been told they gotta move for a little while, so they're probably just sitting around visiting. They can visit downstairs until you guys get cleaned up." Then she added "They got burned out of their places like everybody else."

"How'd the fire start anyway?" asked Henry. Belinda was about to open the door, but instead she quickly turned around, and placing one hand firmly on her hip, growled "Belle Mitchell!"

"What?" replied Henry, "I thought she burned down Dawson last time?"

"She did!" answered Belinda, "And now she's done it again."

"How did she do that?" asked Elmer.

"She threw a lit lantern at another dancehall girl," replied Belinda, "and it smashed."

"That's unbelievable!" remarked Henry.

"Anyway you can get cleaned up in here." said Belinda, as she began opening the door again, "And I gotta couple a bathtubs waiting for you." Then as she walked through the doorway she added "You realize you're gonna be about the cleanest people in town right now."

"I have to be." said Henry following her through the door, "I'm gonna ask Becky to marry me." About a half a dozen girls had all stopped talking when the door opened, so all sat listening to what Henry said, and now looked at him with silly grins on their faces. Some with a romantic appearance, as if they'd just been asked themselves.

"That's great!" said Belinda shaking his hand, "Congratulations! She's smart and nice."

"Well I haven't asked her yet." replied Henry.

Then Belinda turned to the girls and said "Alright ladies. You have to visit downstairs for about an hour. I'll come and tell you when you can come back up again."

So they all filed out of the room, still grinning at Henry as they left. Then as Belinda followed them out of the room, she said back to Henry "I thought you should've asked her awhile ago."

After Belinda had closed the door, Henry said "So what do you think Elmer?"

"I think its great." he answered, "She's smart and nice, and really attractive, and I thought you should've asked her awhile ago."

"You're just repeating everything Belinda said." accused Henry.

"No I'm not." argued Elmer, "I said 'really attractive' too."

"Do you think those girls that were here will tell her what I said?" asked Henry.

"Naw. They might not even know her." Replied Elmer, "And even if they do, I doubt they'd walk all the way to her place in this weather."

When Becky arrived at her place, she was surprised to see that it too had a number of people milling about outside. And before she even got inside, they were congratulating her on striking it rich. The news really had rippled completely through town.

Inside she found a crowd of girls there too, most of them in their dancehall costumes. Daisy immediately came up and hugged her. "Congratulations" she said, "You deserve it."

Becky pretty much understood the situation her home was in, but asked Daisy anyway, "So what exactly's going on here Daisy?"

"I was letting most of the girls stay here." she answered, "every place in town that's still standing is full of people now. There's barely enough room for everybody. I kinda had to let them stay here."

Becky saw she was getting excited, so said "That's okay Daisy. You did the right thing. But I still want to get cleaned up. So I'll need you to move a few of the girls out of my bedroom for awhile, then help me heat some water for the tub."

"Of course." said Daisy. And she went and told some of the girls they had to move. Then as she helped Becky fill the tub, she told her about Belle starting the fire.

As Becky relished soaking in the hot water of her bath, she began pondering her future. She'd really enjoyed her time up at Tombstone, and actually looked forward to returning in the spring. But if she was going to live there for half of next year, she'd really prefer easier living conditions in the mean time, and almost anything seemed better than living through the Yukon winter in a tent. With the current conditions in Dawson, she could be in a pretty cramped situation as well. In fact the more she thought about it, the more traveling south seemed the most desirable option.

Daisy returned with more hot water for the tub, then came back a few minutes later with warm water to help wash her hair. "One thing's for sure," said Becky, "when I go mining next year, I'll be taking a bathtub with me."

After Daisy helped wash her hair, she left with the empty cauldren, and Becky's thoughts turned more to her immediate future. Like what she was going to do when she got out of the tub. She'd been weeks in the wilderness and really felt like doing something. But there wasn't much to do in her tent, nor was there room to do it. So she decided to go to the Monte Carlo. At least there she could listen to music, and it couldn't be any more crowded than her tent was.

After she got out of the tub and dried off, she wrapped a couple of towels around her, and went to her clothing trunk. When she opened the lid and looked inside, she was surprised to see that there was nothing in it but her dancehall outfit. "Hey Daisy." she said looking at her perplexed, "Where's my clothes?"

Daisy had a look of guilt on her face. "I gave them away." she confessed. Then she quickly added "Actually I only lent them. They're going to bring them back! Probably in a couple a days."

She continued to plead with Becky. "You don't understand." she said, "The fire went through town so fast, that a lot a people ended up with only what they were wearing. Some of the prostitutes ended up with nothing at all. It's why the girls here are wearing their dancehall costumes. It's all they have. ...I gave away my clothes too." she finally added.

Becky did understand, and knew she probably would've done the same thing, though she would've dressed in modest clothes first, as Daisy had.

Only Daisy and one other girl were dressed in regular attire, and they were both too small for Becky to trade clothes with.

"I'll just wear my mining clothes." she finally conceded, "It's not like anyone's wearing what they'd like to right now."

"You can't." said Daisy, looking guilty again.

"Why not?" asked Becky.

"Well I didn't know you wanted to go out." she answered, "So I'm washing them. They're soaking right now."

"Aw crap!" swore Becky.

"Just wear your dancehall clothes." suggested Daisy, "Like you said yourself, nobody's wearing what they'd like to right now."

So Becky finally relented.

At least she felt like a queen getting dressed. With the girls still left in her bedroom suffering from boredom, they jumped at the chance to help dress her. They fixed her hair, painting her nails, everything. And when they were done, she threw on her worn out mining coat and headed for the Monte Carlo.

Back at the Fairview, Henry and Elmer were finished getting cleaned up. It'd taken Henry a little longer than Elmer, as Elmer had decided not to shave his beard off.

"How long you gonna keep that thing?" teased Henry, "You're probably gonna scare away the girls."

"I'm not gonna keep it forever." replied Elmer, "But I wanna wear it 'till I get home, and see if people recognize me."

As Henry finished shaving, Elmer snuck downstairs and bought a bottle of champagne. He kept it hidden from Henry under his coat, figuring that if Becky said yes to his proposal, he'd surprise them with it, and if she said no, Henry could drown his sorrows.

They knew their time was already running short. So as soon as they were ready, they said good-bye to Belinda, and told her they'd see her again when they got back in the spring. Then with Henry already getting nervous, they hurried off to Becky's place by the river.

Even though the fire hadn't been out for a whole day yet, Dawson was already coming alive again. Debris was being cleaned up everywhere, and a large tent was already up where the Aurora Hotel had stood, with a new sign advertising the establishment. And though little snow covered the ground yet, there was more than enough to skid a sleigh on, and dogteams could be seen sprinting all over the place. It was as if both the owners and their dogs had been waiting all year to get running again.

They saw one of the Mounties magnificent teams go by, and suddenly Henry remembered, "Oh no! We still gotta talk to Steele about Leadtooth before we go. I forgot all about it." They all had. "Now we got even less time." he added.

Then to make it even worse Elmer reminded him. "And we still gotta go back to the bank and get a bunch of our money."

Becky was just arriving at the Monte Carlo, and as she entered the crowded building, it seemed as if almost everyone was staring at her.

In fact they were. The girls at her place had fixed her up to look beautiful, and with everyone else looking like they'd been through a fire, she almost shone in comparison. Not only that, but everyone knew she was rich, she didn't limp anymore, and she was wearing her dancehall clothes. So even though many of the onlookers were her friends, all the attention she was getting was still a little unnerving.

Then as the men smiled and tipped their hats, and the girls grinned and congratulated her, she made her way towards the bar where the girls she'd worked with were gathered.

Henry was surprised when they arrived down at Becky's place. He hadn't even considered there might be a crowd of people down there. He'd been imagining talking to Becky alone. He was even more surprised when Daisy told him that she wasn't even there. "Where'd she go to?" he asked, remembering that he was running out of time.

"She went to the Monte Carlo." said Daisy.

Then Henry threw his modesty aside and asked "Do you know if she was looking for me?"

"She didn't say anything." replied Daisy, "The girls helped get her fixed up to go out, and then she left."

As they started for the Monte Carlo, Elmer could tell that Henry was becoming concerned, if not outright worried. Despite having a stiff freezing wind blowing in their faces, Henry was walking faster now than he had on the way Becky's. "She probably just wanted to get away from that crowd a people in her tent." reasoned Henry, "I know I would."

Then hoping for assurance from Elmer, he asked "When I ask her to marry me, do you think she's gonna say yes?"

"I don't know." replied Elmer, "She seems to like you. What do you think?"

"I don't know either." he answered, "I was married before. And it turned out that what I knew, and what I thought I knew, was two different things."

"Well if she does marry you," said Elmer, "at least you'll know it's not for the money."

Henry thought to himself how it was true. Becky was rich. She didn't have to marry anybody if she didn't want to. "I'm gonna need some kinda plan." he decided, "It's bound to be crowded in there. I'm gonna have to get her alone somehow."

"You should get her to dance." suggested Elmer, "That's about as alone as your probably gonna be able to get. And you can't ask her to go outside, that's for sure. You'd lose her to frostbite." Then Elmer turned up his collar and pushed his hat down, to try and keep his ears from freezing.

"I need some kinda hook." said Henry, "I gotta be endearing to her in some way."

They both thought about it for awhile, then Henry said "Remember back when we first met her, and I dropped her in the mud?"

"Are you kidding?" said Elmer, "The whole town remembers."

"Well do you recall how she thought we were simple minded?"

"Yea I do." chuckled Elmer, remembering what they looked like that day.

"You see, you laughed." said Henry, "So I'm gonna ask her if she wants to dance with a simple man. ...I have to." he added, "...It's all I got."

"Well it should amuse her anyway." replied Elmer.

"Well that's my plan." said Henry.

When they got to the Monte Carlo there was lots of people outside. And when they went in, it was as crowded as they thought it'd be.

Before stepping down in from the doorway, they were looking around to see if they could see Becky anywhere, when they noticed all the eyes on them. "Half the place is staring at us." said Elmer, "It must be 'cause we're rich now."

"At least we know most of them." replied Henry.

Then he spied Becky's head through the crowd. "There she is," he said, "over there by the bar." She seemed to be the center of attention, with girls crowded all around her.

"How are you gonna talk to her?" asked Elmer, "It's like she's in a flock a chickens. And you know how hard it is to separate one from the flock. It's real easy to spook 'em all."

"Its okay." replied Henry, "I got the gift a gab. ...Remember?"

Neither one of them believed it.

"This is no time for crazy talk." said Elmer.

Then as Henry stiffened himself for his advance, he asked Elmer once more, "Got any advice?"

"Yea" he replied, "Don't make any big sudden arm movements."

There were still a lot of people looking at them as they moved towards Becky, and everyone seemed to step out of their way as they approached. It was unnerving Henry, just as it had Becky when she came in. He hadn't even gotten to her yet, but knowing what he had to do was starting to rattle him.

Even with all the time he'd spent with her, it was like he was starting all over again. Playing it by ear, or winging it, hadn't worked at all the first time they met. So, 'Just stick to the plan' he thought, 'ask her if she wants to dance with a simple man.'

As they got near to Becky, Elmer began to hang back a bit, and when the last couple of girls stepped out of the way, suddenly they could see not only how stunning she looked, but how she was dressed.

Henry was both shocked and dumbfounded, and as the rest of his confidence drained away, Elmer suddenly lost his grip on the champagne. He'd been heating it against his body since they left Belinda's, and when it hit the floor the cork blasted free, sizzling across the room and striking the champagne glass out of one girl's hand, before lodging into the piled high hair of another.

Seeing that some of the people were distracted by Elmer and the cork, Henry tried to seize the moment. But unable to think at all now, he quickly stepped up to Becky and with a sweeping arm motion towards the dancefloor blurted out "Da wincy watha sipple man?"

A couple of the girls quickly clamped their hands over their mouths trying to plug up a giggle, while others didn't even try. Becky seemed sympathetic, but shrugged her shoulders and said "I don't know what you said Henry."

"Well neither do I!" he answered back angry with himself.

He was going to ask her again, only this time using words, when he suddenly realized there was no music. When he looked over at the band, they were all just sitting there with the same stupid grins as everyone else.

Suddenly Henry realized what was going on. A few of the girls from Belinda's room had come to the Monte Carlo, and told Becky's friends about Henry's plan to ask her to marry him. Then they told the other girls, and the other girls told everyone else. Now practically everybody in the place knew. And without much good news in town lately, it was as if they all wanted to be part of it.

The whole place was listening now, so Henry loudly said to them "I know you all know!"

A ripple of giggling went through the crowd, so Henry added "And I don't have time to change my plans. So fine! Enjoy!"

Becky still didn't know what was happening, and looked at Henry to ask "What is it they all know?"

"Well first of all," he replied "I didn't expect to see you like this. I mean not wearing clothes and all. ...Damn, that didn't come out right."

Another wave of laughter swept through the crowd.

"Shut-up!" Henry yelled at them half kidding, "....Yer gonna blow it for me!"

Then a roar of laughter went up. But they quickly quieted themselves, not wanting to miss anything.

"Okay." started Henry again, "Well...I guess the cat's kinda out a the bag on how I feel about you."

"I thought the cat was outta the bag when you dropped me in the mud." replied Becky, as she began to realize what was going on.

Everyone laughed again, as they all knew the story. Then someone in the crowd yelled "Mudlover!" and someone else called out "What about poor Achebee?"

Then Henry asked her straight, "Will you marry me Becky?"

"Yes" she said, "Of course I will."

A huge cheering roar went up from the crowd, lasting for some time. Henry and Becky hugged each other, and then she gave him a really big kiss.

Suddenly they were being congratulated from all sides. Swiftwater Bill, Mizner, Rickard, Slavin and Boyle, Arizona Charlie, practically everyone Henry knew was patting him on the back and wanting to shake his hand.

It was the same for Becky. Kate and the Lamore sisters, and as many girls that could get close to her, were all hugging her and holding on to her hands and arms.

Suddenly Elmer plowed between them all, and grabbing some champagne glasses from the bar, thrust one into each of their hands and said "I wanna be the first to toast the newly betrothed." Then he poured them about half a glass each before draining the bottle. "That's all there is." he said looking down, "The rest we'd have to lick off the floor."

Then he raised his glass high with the rest of the Monte Carlo, and proudly proclaimed "To Henry and Becky! Two people with a slippery start, but a golden future!"

Everyone laughed, then cheered, then drank.

When Henry finished his glass, he turned and looked at the band, who was still just sitting and smiling. "Well play somethin'!" he said.

They immediately began churning out a slow waltz, and Henry reached into the crowd of girls to take Becky by the hand and said "Sorry ladies, but I wanna dance with my bride to be."

When they started dancing, Becky told him why she was dressed like she was, and what Daisy had done to her clothes. Then she said "And I gotta couple a questions for you Henry."

"Ask me anything you want." he replied.

"Well one thing I was curious about," she started, "was how did practically everyone in here know you were going to ask to marry me? And knew before you even got here."

So he told her what happened at the Fairview, and how the girls had overheard. And that when they were getting cleaned up, some of them had come down and told everyone.

"I was worried that they'd tell you." said Henry, "It never struck me that they'd tell everybody but you. But to be fair," he added, "they didn't know I was coming here."

"I was wondering about something else too." she said, "You told everyone you didn't have time to change your plans. What did you mean when you said that?"

"Glad you asked." said Henry, "I wanted to talk to you about that. I got us tickets south on the last boat out of here before freeze up, and we only got about two hours before it leaves."

"Goodie! Goodie! Goodie!" she squeeled hugging him. "I really didn't want to stay here this winter. Not the way it is."

"Fact is, we have to go right after this dance." said Henry, "We got some things we gotta do before we go."

"I just have to grab a few things from my tent, and give my place to Daisy." said Becky.

"But then we have to get our money and nuggets from the bank." added Henry, "And then we have to see Steele about Leadtooth."

"I forgot all about that." answered Becky. Then after the thought of missing the boat crossed her mind, she looked straight at Henry and said "We gotta go."

As soon as the dance ended, they said good-bye to everybody, as everyone wished them good luck. Then while Henry and Becky went to pick up Becky's things, Elmer left to gather their belongings from the Fairview.

When they met up again at the bank, Elmer had already borrowed the horses back from Belinda, to help carry their gold down to the boat. So after loading up the animals, they retrieved their heavy bags of nuggets, and headed off to their last stop at the police compound.

When they walked into Sam's office he was sitting at his desk. "I been waitin' for you guys to drop by." he said, "I thought I might have to go down and pull you off the boat."

"How'd you know we were leaving on the boat?" asked Elmer.

"Checked the passenger list." he answered. Then he stood up and said "Follow me." And with that, he led them into a room with a table and chairs, and a small kitchen. No one was in it, but it was obvious that the Mounties had coffee and meals there.

Then Henry said "I guess you want us to tell you all about how Leadtooth got killed."

"Make yourselves a coffee and sit down." he told them, "I'm gonna want to know about a lot more than that."

Steele's words made them very uneasy, and they were already anxious about how much time they had. "Sure." said Elmer, "But we gotta boat to catch."

"Let's hope so." replied Sam, "My advice to you," he suggested, "Is that if you wanna help your own cause, answer the questions truthfully, and don't leave anything out."

"Of course we will Sam." said Henry. They wanted to keep things as friendly as possible, so they poured themselves coffee's and sat down at the table.

Sam sat down too, but along with his coffee he set down a large notebook, and pulled a pencil from his pocket.

"Okay," he started, "I think we can all agree that Leadtooth was the scum of the earth, and Paddy already told me how he ended up shooting him. But I wanna hear from you guys how it happened." Then he added "Now, Paddy said he was chasing Becky here, so start with how he came upon you guys, and how things developed from there."

So they told Sam all about how he'd ambushed Becky and Elmer on the trail, and everything they could think of after that, including how the gun blew apart when he shot Elmer, and how it was Elmer's knife he'd chased Becky with.

"Thank god for old Paddy showing up when he did," said Becky, "or he would've killed me for sure."

Then Steele looked at Henry and said "Paddy told me all about how Leadtooth tried to kill him back in Seattle...for the silver case with the map in it. And how you guys saved him. Now, you asked me yourself where Tombstone was, and then copied our map here in the office. You also managed to find your own way up to Tombstone, and right onto Paddy's claim. So I'm guessin' by then you had Paddy's map."

"Now I know you weren't in cahoots with Leadtooth." continued Steele, "So I'm wondering how you got the map from him?"

"We didn't get it from him." answered Henry, "I got it from Soapy Smith. Remember when we got in that scuffle with him and his boys in Skagway? Well it fell out of his pocket when I was fighting with him in the mud. That's when I scooped it up."

Henry was embarrassed telling Sam that he actually stole it, and sheepishly added, "...Just tryin' to get even."

Then Elmer quickly added "But we were half way down Lake Bennet before we found out there was a map in it."

"Well Leadtooth was one of Soapy's boys." replied Steele, "There's no doubt about that. So it makes sense that he would of given the map to his boss. But here's my problem. A few months ago, one of my corporals' guarding the prisoners told me that Leadtooth threw a silver case at you guys. Hit Elmer in the head with it. He also said that you guys picked it up and took it with you. Now I don't believe the map was in it at the time. After all, Leadtooth mighta been mad enough to throw the case at you, but there's no way he's gonna throw you a treasure map."

Then Steele looked at Elmer and said "Okay, when we arrested him for attackin' you in the alley, we searched him, and he didn't have the case on him then. So what I don't know, and yet I think you guys do, is how did he end up with the case, while you ended up with the map?"

Henry and Elmer both thought for a bit without saying anything. Then Steele said "If you guys wanna catch that boat, I highly suggest you tell me everything, and in a clear way, so there's no confusion."

There was no way around it, they had to tell him about Mace.

"We're going to Sam." said Henry, "It's just that if we don't tell you everything just like it happened, we're gonna come off looking bad."

"Start at the beginning." he said.

Sam already knew about what happened in Skagway. And he knew about Elmer getting attacked on the trail too. That had come up in Leadtooth's trial. So they started by telling him about seeing Mace and Leadtooth on the island with some other thugs, just below Miles Canyon. And how they didn't know it at the time, but Mace had seen them too. Then they told him how Mace had subsequently snuck off with the boat, leaving Leadtooth and the others marooned on the island. At least until they could steal another boat. Then how Mace caught up to them on Lake Lebarge when the ice pushed them to shore.

"He came walking out of the bush with a gun on us while we were eating." said Henry, "Apparently he'd been following us, and the ice pushed him to shore too. He said that the ice had wrecked his boat, or pushed it way up on shore or something."

"Anyway," continued Henry, "when the ice cleared, he got in our boat and made us row out to the middle of the lake. Then he demanded the map and the silver case. It was obvious that the only reason we were way out in the lake, was 'cause he was hoping to drown us quietly, and not attract attention by shooting his gun."

"Then our bodies would sink out a sight too." added Elmer, "And not be left on shore for someone to find."

Then Henry said "And now for the part we were trying to forget." Then he and Elmer both went on to describe the gruesome battle to the death that ensued, including everything they could think of, right down to Mace shooting the boat full of holes.

Then looking a little puzzled Sam said, "So the silver case with the map in it, went down with Mace?"

"Yea." replied Henry, "For awhile."

"Well keep goin'." said Sam, "I gotta hear the rest of this."

"Well we were gonna tell you the whole story when we got to Dawson." said Henry, "But you were busy, and we were broke, and the town was crazy, and well, we just kept putting it off for awhile."

"And to be honest," added Elmer, "we were a little worried that you wouldn't believe us. Or something else would happen, and we would end up missing the gold rush."

Sam kept them nervous as they talked, continuously writing in his notebook. "So what happened next?" he asked.

"I guess it started with me takin' a shine to Becky here." admitted Henry, "I met her back when the streets were still muddy, and well....things didn't go so good for me."

"Heard all about it." said Sam cracking a smile, "But go on."

"Well about a week later I found out she lived down by the river." continued Henry, "So I went down one morning when I thought there wouldn't be a crowd of guys around, hopefully to apologize and get to meet her. When I got there, I saw her out on the end of the catwalk where the fishnets are. At first I thought she was just washing her hair, but then I realized something was wrong, and when I got to her, her hair was all tangled up with Maces corpse. Or what was left of his corpse. And the only way

I could get her head out of the water, was to pull the body out too. That's when I recognized it was Mace. Mainly by his coat."

Then Steele asked Becky "So how'd you get your hair tangled up with the body?"

"I was out checking the nets." she answered, "And at first I thought it was probably someone's lost cargo. But I couldn't see very good, and when I got down close for a better look, he came bobbing out of the water and his arm got tangled in my hair."

Then Sam looked back at Henry and said "So then what happened?"

"Well I could see the bulge in his coat from the silver case." replied Henry, "Then I thought a bunch a things. How he wouldn't be needing it anymore, and how he stole it from us in the first place. Then finding gold with the map crossed my mind. But mostly, I saw it as a way to tie myself to Becky for awhile."

"You bugger!" she said, piling her shoulder into his with a smile.

"Anyway," Henry went on, "when I took out the case, his coat kept the bulge it made. So I took the tube with the map in it out of the case, then put the case back in his coat. ....And well ...That's the whole story."

Steele kept writing for a minute, and then said "So how did Leadtooth get the case?"

"I don't know." replied Henry, "I mean I think I know, but I can't be positive."

"What do you mean?" asked Steele.

"When the Mounties came down to collect Mace," said Henry, "they brought some prisoners with them, and while one of the officers asked us some questions, the prisoners went out on the catwalk to bag up Mace. I never thought to look at them, but I'm guessin' one of them was Leadtooth, and that he recognized Mace's coat too. And that's when he got the case."

Steele finished writing. Then he stood up and said, "Just wait here, I'll be back in a few minutes." Then he left the room, closing the door behind him.

"Do you think we're in trouble Henry?" asked Elmer.

"I don't know." he answered, "I don't think we could be in too much trouble. But it probably wouldn't take much for us to miss the boat.

It wasn't long before Steele returned like he said, and sat down again at the table. "Well I checked the records," he said, "and Leadtooth was one of the prisoners we sent down to collect Mace. But even so, it appears by the evidence, that you should stay in town until we get all this sorted out. It's also apparent that we should confiscate any and all gold you collected from Tombstone."

They all went into shock! Their whole world just dropped out from under them. "Why?" exclaimed Elmer, "We didn't do anything! We're the good guys!"

"Well let's see." answered Steele, "First you robbed Soapy Smith, which ultimately led to the deaths of Mace and Leadtooth."

"But they were all despicable criminals!" protested Elmer.

"Doesn't matter." said Steele, "And then even if things happened the way you said they did with Mace, you still failed to report a crime, even if it was him that perpetrated it. You also failed to report a death."

They had no idea how to answer now, and their spirits sank even lower. Then Steele finished with, "And then when you pulled Mace out of the fishnets, you robbed a dead body, and in doing so, tampered with evidence of how he died."

Henry and Elmer both started feeling guilty now, and just stared down. "So what happens now?" asked Henry.

"Here's what's gonna happen." said Sam, "When you took the map and case from Soapy in Skagway, you were out of my jurisdiction, so that has nothin' to do with me. And the evidence, as well as common sense and Paddy's sworn statement, says that Leadtooth got himself killed. Now as far as robbing Mace's dead body goes, it was actually ol' Paddy's property, and seeing how you gave it back to him, and it was actually in your posession when you came into the country, we're gonna call it 'retrieving stolen property'. Besides, I saw Mace's remains, and he was only part of a dead body at best. Now, tampering with evidence. It's only tampering if an attempt is made to alter the situation in some way. By you guys volunteering the truth, no attempt was made.

Then Steele paused for a moment, before saying "Then there's Mace's death. Now knowing his character, and you not having any motive to rob or kill him, I find your story of how he died believable. But you still didn't report him trying to kill you, and you failed to report his death at the first opportunity." Then Steele said "So this is the only real stretch I'm gonna make. Now since I got to the Klondike, there's been nothin' normal about it. So I'm going to determine that this was your first opportunity to report it."

Suddenly Henry figured out what was going on, and said to Sam, "You been scarin' us to death on purpose."

"That's right." he replied, "It's your punishment for not coming to me about Mace as soon as you got to Dawson. Now I wrote down everything you told me," he said, "and if you all want to sign it, acknowledging that it's the truth as far as you know, I believe you have a boat to catch."

Suddenly it was like they could breathe again, they were free again, and they were rich again, and their moods began to soar. "Boy you sure made things look bleak for awhile there." admitted Elmer, "Thanks for being fair Sam." he added shaking his hand, "From now on if anything happens to us, we'll be tellin' you right away."

"You guys are coming back in the spring aren't ya?" asked Sam.

"That's for sure." replied Elmer, "We got good claims to work now."

"Well I look forward to seein' you again." he answered, "But next time, try not and bring me anymore work."

Then Henry and Becky thanked him for being fair about things like Elmer had, and they all left in a hurry to catch the last riverboat of the year.

They quickly made their way through Dawson, pulling the horses along at nearly a trot.

"Boy that Steele sure is a good cop." said Elmer.

"Yea." replied Henry, "Even though he was just scarin' us with most that stuff, I'm sure he could a made things real rough for us if he'd wanted to. Especially over Mace."

"Yea." said Elmer, "But I was thinkin' about how he put most of our story together with just bits of information. I mean, the guy's a busy man, he must a had a lot of other things to think about."

"Just be thankful he's not the type to get confused," said Henry, "and we still got time to catch this boat."

"I was wishing we had more time." said Becky, "I would've liked to have gotten married before we left."

"If you really want to, you can get married on the boat." said Elmer.

Henry was a little skeptical, "How's that?" he asked.

"A ships captain can marry people." answered Elmer.

"That's right!" remembered Becky and Henry together, both encouraged.

When they arrived down at the boat, they weren't the last people to board, but close to it. Some of the ships crew helped carry their gold into their staterooms, and when they were finished, they asked the captain if it was going to be safe there.

"Perfectly safe." he answered, "There's over forty tons of gold on board, and security abounds." He also assured them that he could marry people. So they locked up their rooms, and went out on deck to watch the ship pull away.

As they leaned over the railing looking over the charred remains of the city, Henry asked Elmer "So what are you going to do when we get to Seattle?"

"I'm goin' home." he answered, "My sisters make clothes for a living, but when I left home, they didn't have much to work with. So I'm gonna buy a wagon and team, then load it with some new sewing machines, and all the bolts of fabric and materials they need, right up to the finest. And oh yea, my ma always wanted a grandfather clock. And I'll probably get them some other presents too.

"Well that should use up a tiny bit a your money." said Henry, "But I mean what are your big plans?"

"I'm gonna build a big ranch house on my family's property." he answered, "To share with my mom and sisters. Then I think I'll start buyin' up some properties around us. I always wanted to be a cattle baron." He added smiling.

"I'm glad to hear that." said Henry, "Because I gotta favour to ask you."

"What is it?" asked Elmer.

"Well Becky and I are going for a holiday. So I wanna give you enough money to buy us a nice place near yours. Somethin' big with water on it. I always thought it was pretty where you guys live."

"That's a great idea!" agreed Elmer, "Then when we come back here to mine, my family can look after your place too." He really liked the idea of Henry and Becky living close to him, already envisioning them all as part of a great ranching empire. "So where you guys gonna go holiday?" he asked.

"Becky wants to go to a place she read about." said Henry, "It's suppose to have friendly people, and be warm all winter, plus we can still make it back here by spring. Some place called Hiwee."

"No Henry." corrected Becky, "Hawaii."

They watched as the last of the passengers came onboard, and the long gangplank get winched up into its sailing position. Then as the gears engaged the giant paddlewheel, it pushed a huge tide of water onto shore, freeing the ship to back out into the mighty Yukon River.

It was nearly sundown now, and a long stream of sunlight shone beneath the clouds, transforming even the burnt rubble of Dawson into a scenic sight. Becky wrapped her arm around Henry's and said "I'm glad you tied us together by taking the map."

"Smartest thing I ever did." he replied, and then kissed her on the forehead.

As the big riverboat gradually turned to point down river, they all kept watching shore, knowing that they'd been part of something special. "Well we sure had our big adventure." remarked Henry.

"Bigger and better that I ever dreamed." agreed Elmer.

Suddenly a girl stepped up to the rail beside them. It was Belle Mitchell. They were surprised to see her, and weren't quite sure what to say. Then Becky said "Hello Belle. I see you're going south too."

"Yea...." she replied, "They said they're making me leave for my own protection." Then she held up a cigarette and said "You gotta match?"

The End

Epilogue

Important:
Henry, Elmer, and Rebecca were fictitious characters, as were Mace, Leadtooth, and Old Paddy. Everyone else named in this story was a real person and portrayed accurate to history. Also historically accurate, are all events, dates, places, populations, distances, temperatures, gold weights, dollar amounts, and weather conditions. At no point was any embellishment employed, as none was needed. A few minor changes were made for continuity, all of which are listed in the following epilogue. Newspaper men of the old west had a saying, that "When the legend becomes fact, you print the legend." and a lot of that went on. However The Klondike Gold Rush took place in the latest and most recent period of the western era, providing a great wealth of photographs, meticulous records, and even some moving film.

Clarence Berry

Clarence Berry first climbed the Chilkoot Pass in 1894 in a party of forty people, where all but three turned back because of the hardships. Clarence continued on over the pass and down the Yukon River to a tiny settlement at the mouth of the Forty Mile River. There he found enough gold prospecting, that he traveled back to California and married Ethel, his childhood sweetheart. He had less luck prospecting after his return, and ended up taking a part time job in Bill McPhee's Saloon.

Then in the middle of August everything changed. George Carmack, one of the co-discoverers of Bonanza Creek, came into McPhee's saloon and dumped a shotgun shell full of nuggets onto the bar, and told everyone where he got it from. Within hours, Forty Mile looked like a ghost town, as the entire village paddled and pulled their way up river towards the discovery. Berry arrived early enough to stake #40 above on Bonanza, which he and Ethel worked until the following spring, when they headed south with over ten thousand ounces.

Two days before 'The Portland' sailed into Seattle and was met by more than five thousand people, another treasure ship 'The Excelsior' docked in San Francisco with Clarence and Ethel Berry onboard. There the same scene unfolded as many thousands watched the Klondike miners carry and drag their gold from the ship, including the Berry's, who had so much gold wrapped in Ethel's bedroll, they couldn't lift it. Then in the spring of 1898, returning to the Klondike to resume working their incredible mine, they climbed The Chilkoot Pass yet again, blending in with the thousands of stampeders, many of whom had been motivated by the Berry's own story.

The amount of gold mined from claims is usually measured in ounces. But from many of the claims in the Klondike it was actually measured in tons, and Clarence Berry had one of the best. By the time he sold it in 1912, he'd taken over four and a half tons from the ground.

He never forgot how Bill McPhee helped him with a job when he needed it in Forty Mile, and after the great fire when McPhee's Pioneer Saloon burnt in Dawson, Clarence gave him the money to rebuild again.

The Berry's eventually moved back home again, and bought both of California's professional baseball teams. Then Clarence started buying up oil leases near Bakersfield California, and created 'The Berry Petroleum Company', which still exists and pumps oil today, with it's stock traded on the New York Stock Exchange. Clarence Berry died from a burst appendix in 1930, with Ethel living on in Beverly Hills as a very wealthy woman, until her death in 1948.

'Silent' Sam Bonnifield

Bonnifield was dubbed "Silent' Sam, not only because he didn't speak much, but because when he gambled, his opponents found it nearly impossible to read his expressionless face. He was also refered to as 'Square Sam', for always running an honest game.

He built 'The Bank Saloon Dancehall and Gambling House' at the corner of Front Street and King Street, and actually gave Tex Rickard his start in the Klondike. He was known for very high stakes poker games where sometimes as many as half a dozen Mounties would be posted for security. In one such game he lost more than six thousand ounces of gold, plus his 'Bank Saloon', then over the next six hours won it all back and bankrupted his opponent.

His massive hand of poker (more than ten thousand ounces) with Goldie Golden, may still be the richest single hand of poker ever played.

After the gold rush Sam moved to Alaska, where with three million dollars in gold dust, he opened 'The First National Bank of the United States'. His bank failed during the great depression of the 1930s, after which he became homeless and destitute.

Sam Bonnifield died in Seattle, when in 1943 he was run over and killed by a car.

Joe Boyle

Boyle first came north in 1897 with his partner Frank Slavin, the previous heavyweight boxing champion of the British Empire. Boyle had been Slavin's sparring partner, and always maintained (along with Slavin) that he could have been world champion, had not John L. Sullivan and Jim Corbett, the title holders at the time, refused to fight him. A good number of boxing experts agreed, as the big Australian had disposed of many of the same top contenders that fought Sullivan and Corbett, but in a much quicker fashion.

When Boyle and Slavin arrived in Dawson, Boyle immediately landed a job as bouncer at the Monte Carlo, where Frank would give him a hand on particularly rough nights. Also as soon as they arrived, Frank became boxing champion of the Yukon, taking on all comers for the rest of the gold rush, with some contenders traveling half way around the world to get thumped by Slavin.

Near the end of the gold rush, Joe Boyle secured a huge land concession along the Klondike River, and built some of the largest wooden dredges in the world, taking out a staggering amount of gold. The wormlike tailings from these machines can still be seen along the Klondike River, and his giant dredge #4, is now a National Historic Site on Bonanza Creek.

In 1905 Joe formed 'The Dawson City Nuggets' hockey team, and Dawson became the smallest community to ever challenge for the Stanley Cup.

After the outbreak of World War, Boyle's exploits became almost too numerous to mention. He formed and financed 'The Yukon Machine Gun Brigade', which fought in many major battles including 'Vimy Ridge', and became the most decorated unit of the war, with more than sixty percent of the Yukoners winning medals of valour.

Boyle was then made an Honourary Lt. Colonel in England, and sent to Russia, where he was put in charge of (and fixed) the country's railroads and transportation systems. So successful was he, that he was decorated in the field by Russia's commander-in-chief.

He rescued the Romanian treasury and crown jewels, and later oversaw their return, and was then declared a 'Romanian National Hero', as well as 'The Uncrowned King of Romania'.

The Canadian Government never recognized Boyle for his accomplishments, however England awarded him 'The Distinguished Service Order', Russia gave him 'The Order of Saint Vladimir', France 'The Croix de Guerre', and Romania awarded him their top three medals including 'The Star of Romania'. Joe also won many other awards and honours, and after the war socialized with the Queen of Romania and Europe's other royal family's, as well as King George the Fifth and Herbert Hoover.

Joe Boyle died from a stroke in 1923 at the age of fifty six.

'Swiftwater' Bill Gates

'Swiftwater' Bill first came north from the mining region of Idaho, reportedly with his childhood friend Augustus Mack. He was working in Circle, Alaska when news of the strike first got out, and promptly quit his job as a dishwasher to make his way up river to the Klondike. After securing part of an extremely rich claim, (thirteen Eldorado, and not thirteen below on Bonanza as portrayed in the story) he proceeded to splurge and gamble his money away as fast as it came out of the ground.

Bill's sweetheart at the time was nineteen year old Gussie Lamore, who came up from Circle with him, with the famous 'egg incident' actually happening in 1897.

It was after this, with Bill owning half of the newly established Monte Carlo, that he went to San Francisco for 'upgrades', and Gussie renaged on her agreement to marry him.

Trying to win her back, he actually rented an entire passenger train to take her to New York City, but was ultimately jilted for good, when he learned that she was already married to one Emile Leglice.

It was then that Bill married Gussie's younger sister Grace. But after buying her a mansion, and lavishing her with expensive gifts, she dumped him after a mere three weeks. Undaunted, Bill began courting their youngest sister Nellie.

By the summer of 1898, all the Lamore sisters were in Dawson, with Gussie performing at the Monte Carlo, where she actually sang a song about being in love with Swiftwater Bill, sometimes directly to him.

At the same time at The Trivoli Theatre, one of Dawson's most popular plays was being staged. 'The Adventures of Stillwater Willie'. A thinly veiled parody mocking the life of Swiftwater Bill, with Nellie Lamore cast as the star performer. Often Bill himself would sit in the best box seat in the balcony, and cheer and applaud as loudly as anyone. So popular was it, that it was later performed at the Monte Carlo by public demand.

One change made to Bill's history, was that when he arrived in the freighter canoe with the dancehall girls and alcohol, and all the new appointments for his casino following on barges, he actually sold his half of the Monte Carlo that very day, rather than lose it gambling a few months later as portrayed in the story.

The only other change to Bill's history was that he didn't lose Chicago Charlie in San Francisco in 1897, with Charlie finding his way back in '98. While Charlie's story is completely accurate, Bill didn't lose him until the fall of '98, with Charlie finding his way back in 1899.

Bill was actually on his way to England with Joe Boyle at the time, to secure investment capital for Boyle's giant dredging operation. It was then on Lake Bennett, that Bill fell through the ice and Boyle was credited with saving his life, and right after that when he borrowed Charlie the packer from Augustus Mack.

After successfully securing investers in London, Bill and Boyle proceeded to travel Europe, hob-nobbing with royalty and the rich and famous alike, all eager to hear of adventures of the Klondike. For the entire trip, Bill was dapperly dressed as always, with a new fourteen karat diamond stick-pin, and publicly willing to bet anyone up to seven thousand dollars on the turn of a card.

When Bill returned to the Klondike he went broke again. Then he left the Yukon for good with his new wife, who he promptly dumped for another girl, whom he also married and then left. Then after a disgruntled mother in law caught up to him in a Seattle hotel room, he actually talked the woman into pawning her diamonds so he could travel north to Alaska to find another fortune in that gold rush, which he unbelievably did. (On Cleary Creek) Bill actually struck it rich and went broke twice in Alaska. (Again on Dexter Creek) His love life eventually became a convoluted history of marriages, elopements, mother in law chases, and bigamy.

Finally Bill ended up in Peru, where still possessing his silver tongue, he aquired for himself a gigantic twenty million acre silver mining concession. Then while living in a jungle hut and prospecting the concession, he was shot and killed in 1937 by two thieves, who mistakenly believed he still had some Klondike gold left.

It's thought that Hollywood's general image of 'the grizzled old prospector' was fashioned after Swiftwater Bill in his old age, with Walter Huston in the famous movie 'The Treasure of the Sierra Madre' even emulating Bill's speech patterns, talking quickly in short choppy sentences.

Sid Grauman

Sid was only nineteen years old when he arrived in The Klondike, and didn't become a waiter until after an unsuccessfull attempt at prospecting for gold.

It was during his time in Dawson, that from watching Klondike Kate and the other famous dancehall girls, as well as the fights promoted by Rickard and Mizner, that he realized how much money could be made in the entertainment industry.

So after leaving the north, he spent the rest of his life building and operating theatre's, culminating in 1926 when he built 'Grauman's Chinese Theatre' in Hollywood, California. After he had Hollywood's top movie stars of the time (Mary Pickford and Douglas Fairbanks) leave their footprints in wet concrete, Grauman's Chinese Theatre became the most famous theatre in the world, and still is. The practice of Hollywood's top stars leaving their footprints in the concrete continues to this day.

Sid Grauman died in 1950.

Eric Hegg

Hegg was working as a photographer in Bellingham, Washington when news of the Klondike first got out. And he quickly realized how big and unique it was going to be, so joined the rush immediately. Not on a quest for gold, but to document the entire event with a photographic record.

After photographing Skagway, a team of goats pulled his ton of food and hundreds of pounds of photographic supplies over the Chilkoot Pass, as he took pictures of everthing in temperatures down to -50 below.

He captured on film, the trail, the animals, the people, the struggle and the hardships. The great burdens, defeated men, the golden stairs, and the great avalanche that buried hundreds. The Mounties, the tent city at Bennett, the boat building, the incredible boat launch, and Miles Canyon and the rapids. Then after arriving in Dawson, he spent over a year photographing the city and its colorful inhabitants, as well as men mining on many of the claims.

By the time Hegg's photographs first went on public display in New York City in 1899, the whole outside world had been reading and dreaming about the Klondike for two years, and so great was the public's clamour to see them, that riot police had to be called to secure crowd control.

After the gold rush, Hegg returned to Washington and reopened his studio in Bellingham.

Eric Hegg died in 1955 at 88 years old. Today his gold rush photographs can be viewed at Washington State University.

Jack London

Jack London actually arrived in the Yukon fairly early in the rush, but after almost dying of scurvy in the winter of 1897-98, he spent a month in St. Marys Hospital in Dawson. In the following spring, not yet being physically strong enough to mine, he moved up river to earn a living piloting boats through Miles Canyon.

It's a credit to London, that during his time as a boat pilot, he only smashed up four vessels in the perilous section of river.

After moving back down river again to try his luck at prospecting, he had the misfortune of staking a claim on Henderson Creek, one of the poorer creeks around by Klondike standards. Then after building a cabin, and an unsuccessfull attempt at mining, London decided to return south again, partly in an effort to restore his health.

He built a boat on Dawson's waterfront with the aid of some friends, and then floated the twelve hundred miles down river to the Bering Sea and St. Michaels, Alaska. Then being flat broke, he earned passage on a south bound ship, by shovelling coal to the boat's boilers.

Though plagued by ill-health through the rest of his life, his memories of the Klondike provided him a career as one of the world's most famous authors. His fascination with Belinda Mulroney's giant dog 'Nero' inspired two of Jack London's most popular stories, 'White Fang' and 'Call of the Wild'.

Today Jack London's cabin has been moved from Henderson Creek to Dawson City, where it's visited by thousands of tourists every year.

Dick Lowe

While Bonanza and Eldorado Creeks were being staked, but before anyone had dug down to bedrock and revealed their true richness, the Mounties arrived with a survey crew to legally establish the exact length of each claim. When a small fraction became available just below where Bonanza and Eldorado converged, men were reluctant to stake it, as it disqualified them from staking a full size claim. The small pie-shaped piece of ground only measured eighty six feet on one side of the creek, and tapered down to nothing on the other.

Finally Dick Lowe took a chance and filed for it. But after digging a shaft down to bedrock, he didn't find a single speck. Depressed, he then tried to sell the tiny claim, but with no takers.

With men on other claims beginning to reach bedrock and discovering staggering amounts of gold, they convinced Lowe that before he abandoned his claim, he should at least try one more hole.

When Lowe hit the paystreak in his second shaft, the results were nothing less than spectacular. During the California gold rush not far from Sutter's Mill, a claim owner boasted that with fifty seven men, his ground had produced 250 pounds of gold in just two months. Dick Lowe dug up 256 pounds in his first eight hours, by himself.

After that, to say that he went on a drinking binge would be huge undersatement. He spent freely on booze, women, and gambling, and bought drinks for anyone and everyone he encountered. He frequently spent up to six hundred ounces of gold a day, and could often be seen riding around with 'guests' in an opulent carriage, being pulled by two matched Tennessee trotting horses.

With his fraction being mined by the invited and uninvited alike, it was impossible to determine how much gold actually came from the tiny piece of ground. Though it was known to have produced two and a half tons, the real amount could have easily been double that.

Less than seven years later, Dick Lowe was broke and carrying water in Fairbanks, Alaska for pennies a bucket. He died a pauper in San Francisco in 1907.

To this day, Dick Lowe's fraction remains the richest piece of placer ground ever found in the world.

'Big' Alex McDonald

Big Alex came over the Chilkoot Pass late in 1896, arriving early enough in the rush, that many of the men who staked on Bonanza and Eldorado still thought their claims were probably worthless. It was then that Big Alex bought #30 Eldorado for a sack of flour and a side of bacon, beginning his meteoric rise to become the richest man in the Yukon, and the bonifide 'King of the Klondike'.

He refrained from drinking or gambling, choosing rather to purchase more mining properties. And by the time he toured Europe in the winter of 1898-99, he owned all or part of more than fifty claims, and was being compared to the Count of Monte Cristo.

While in London, England a giant mining consortium offered McDonald ten million dollars for all his Klondike properties, a deal which depending on the source, he either turned down, or was thwarted by a greedy negotiator.

Then when in Rome, because of his generosity at donating a huge amount of money to build a hospital, and more than enough to build a new Catholic Church, he was granted an audience with the Pope, and made a 'Knight of the Order of Saint Gregory'.

After Big Alex returned to the Klondike in 1899, Dawson City had planned a farewell celebration for Sam Steele, who was being transfered from the Yukon. An elaborate speech had been prepared to honour Steele, and to thank him for his virtuous reign over the gold rush. And because Steele had made little more than a dollar a day like people in the outside world, the citizens had donated a large poke filled with nuggets, as a gift for the departing Mountie. And who better to give the speech and present the gift, than 'The King of the Klondike'. So after the farewell comittee rehearsed and prepared McDonald for days, when the appointed time came Big Alex stepped onto the platform and sauntered over to Steele, then cramming the poke into his hand, he edited the speech down to "Here Sam....here y'are. Poke for ya. Good-by."

Canada was still a British colony at the time of the gold rush, and the most powerful man in the country was The Governor General. So when he and his wife made an official visit to the Klondike in 1900, not having learned their lesson from a year earlier, they again chose Big Alex to deliver the speech and present the gift. The gift being a small golden bucket, heaped with oddly shaped nuggets. Again they repeatedly rehearsed a lengthy speech, bestowing the honour and respect their titles demanded. Until when the day came, and it was time in the ceremony for the speech and presentation, Big Alex simply walked across the podium, and thrusting the bucket out towards 'Lady Minto', said "Here. Take it. It's trash."

McDonald continually invested all his money back into Dawson and the surrounding creeks, so when the claims were mined, and the gold rush ended, Dawson went bust and so did Big Alex. By 1909 he was broke and living in a small cabin on Clear Creek outside of Dawson, where he died of a heart attack while chopping wood.

The huge bowl of gold he kept on his table throughout the Klondike's heyday, was weighed at one point, and contained over forty five pounds of nuggets.

Augustus Mack

It's believed that Mack first came north with his five brothers and 'Swiftwater' Bill Gates. Though Mack's history in the Klondike is vague, it's known that in October of 1898 he staked a claim on Mulberry Creek, and mined out between thirty and forty thousand ounces.

After the gold rush, he moved to Brooklyn, New York and bought a carriage company, and in 1909 moved it to Allentown, Pennsylvania, where it became the Mack Automobile Corporation, famous for its trucks.

Some sources have Mack using the 'bulldog' hood ornament, because troops in World War I said that when they took his trucks off road, they were like bulldogs. But other sources say that it was because when he was leaving the Klondike, his pet bulldog fell off the riverboat and drowned. Mack trucks with their familiar 'bulldog' hood ornament, are still being made and still seen on the road today.

'Arizona' Charlie Meadows

Arizona Charlie had a colorful past before he ever arrived in the Klondike. In 1879 when he was a teenager living in Arizona, his entire family was wiped out by Apache Indians. He fought hand to hand with Geronimo, and gained a famous reputation as a sharpshooter, with an ability to shoot the spots out of playing cards from thirty feet away.

With the taming of the west, his notoriety earned him a place in Buffalo Bill's Wild West Show, where he met another sharpshooter, and fellow stampeder to the Klondike, Calamity Jane.

Though he ended his Klondike experience a rich man, as told in the story it started out rough indeed. He lost everything and was nearly killed when the glacier crashed down on the Chilkoot Trail, then was nearly wiped out and killed again when his boat wrecked on Tagish Lake.

After the gold rush he moved to California with his wife, and bought up huge tracts of land in The Tiburon Islands, and became a cattle rancher. He also struck oil in the giant Kern County oil field, and had the second oil well in Tampico. He's also credited with starting the 'California Floral Carnival'.

The only change in the story made to Arizona Charlie's history, was that the Palace Grand Theatre didn't actually open until July 1st 1899, one year later than in the story.

Today The Palace Grand Theatre is still standing, and has been restored to its former glory as an historical site, and a heritage building of the Yukon. It's also a popular tourist attraction, where a period stage show can still be seen.

'Arizona' Charlie Meadows died in Yuma, Arizona in 1932.

Belle Mitchell

To be fair to Belle Mitchell, it was Dawson City's first fire in late November of 1897 (at -57 below), that she started by throwing a lit lantern at a rival. When she started the second fire in mid-October of 1898, it was after leaving for Lousetown and forgetting a burning candle on a block of wood in her room, which was more of an oversight than a stupid act. In the story the causes were reversed.

Though in the second fire much of Front Street went up again, it was limited to about forty buildings, and the great fire described in the story, didn't actually happen until April of the following spring, coincidently, also started by a dancehall girl.

By the time Dawson suffered its fourth major fire (Jan.1900) in a little over three years, when most of Front Street lay in rubble again, some of the population began to believe that God was allowing the city to burn repeatedly, because of its hedonistic lifestyle.

Dawson City burned again in 1904.

There's no evidence that Belle Mitchell smoked cigarettes, and it's also unknown if she was sent south 'for her own protection'.

The Mizner's

The only change in the story made to the Mizner's history, was that during the stampede over the Chilkoot Pass, Edgar Mizner was already in the Klondike working for the Alaska Commercial Company. That's when he wrote a letter to his brothers suggesting they come north.

By the 1920s, Addison Mizner had become the most popular designer and builder of mansions for the rich and super-rich, in the South Florida real estate boom. He was in such demand, that some avenues in South Beach were occupied almost exclusively with 'Mizner Mansion's', many of which have been preserved, some as historic sites that can be toured by the public today.

Wilson Mizner went on to become one of the most celebrated and successful playwrights on Broadway, and also became owner of Hollywood's famous 'Brown Derby Restaurant'.

Belinda Mulroney

Though Belinda came over the Chilkoot Pass as described in the story, shooting moose to earn money and feed other goldseekers, and having Nero pull her along in basket sleigh. It actually happened the previous winter, and her story is really two years compressed into one.

In the winter of 1897-98 during the great stampede, Belinda was already establishing her fortune in the Klondike, and using Nero (reportedly the largest dog in the north) to pull her sleigh back and forth between Dawson and Bonanza.

This was also when 'Gary' the mule developed his drinking problem, and it was probably Belinda's own fault. When the temperature that winter dropped to -60 and -70 below, Belinda began giving her animals rum, in an effort to keep them from freezing, with 'Gary' quickly gaining an affinity for the strong drink.

In addition to Belinda's businesses, she continued to buy and mine claims on Bonanza and Eldorado, ultimately owning six, with shares in a few others.

When the Canadian Government arrived in the Yukon, they changed the name of the little town that Belinda had started, from 'Bonanza' to 'Grand Forks', and by the end of the gold rush in August of '99, the population had swollen to ten thousand. But with new gold strikes in Nome, Alaska, in just months the population dwindled back down to only a few hundred, fast on it's way to becoming a ghost town.

By 1921, one of the giant dredges had worked its way up the valley, and with the town itself sitting on gold, practically the entire site was dredged up.

Today there's virtually no evidence that 'Bonanza' or Grand Forks ever existed.

The only other change in the story to Belinda's true history, was that when she found out that Joe Brooks and his packers had dumped her shipment of goods for the Fairview on the side of the trail, she was already in Skagway, and when she caught up to them with her new gang of hired 'packers', only Brooks foreman got beat up, and not the whole crew as portrayed in the story.

Throughout the gold rush, except to do business, Belinda didn't deposit any gold or money into the banks. Then just before leaving the Yukon for good, it was reported that she made a one time bank deposit of a staggering one and a half million ounces of gold, thus confirming her status as the richest woman in the Klondike.

In 1900, after being courted for months with a dozen roses everyday, Belinda married Charles Eugene Carbonneau, a French-Canadian champagne salesman. Then after leaving the Yukon, the newly named Belinda Carbonneau and her husband honeymooned in Paris, toured Europe, and being every bit as famous as the other Klondike celebrities, met with the Queen of England.

Returning to Washington State, they built a magnificent stone mansion on a large ranch outside of Yakima, and continued to travel to Europe each year to oversee their bank and shipping empire.

When World War I broke out, Belinda and her husband donated their entire fleet of ships for the allied cause, and Belinda's husband joined the military.

By the end of the war (depending on the source), Charles Carbonneau was either killed by a bomb while inspecting troops in the front-line trenches, or was psychologically damaged, and spent the rest of his life institutionalized.

Also by the end of the war, so many of Belinda's ships had been sunk, that she had to declare bankruptcy.

She continued to live in her mansion on her ranch in Yakima for as long as she could afford to, then lived out the rest of her life in virtual obscurity. When Belinda died in 1965, she was a little old lady living in a small house on the outskirts of Seattle, without even her friends or neighbors knowing of her incredible past.

About the same time 'Carbonneau Castle' was opened for tours by the public. Belinda was ninety five years old when she died.

Alexander Pantages

Before landing in the Klondike, Pantages had been a cabin boy, a prize fighter, and had worked on the Panama Canal, though none of his skills served him very well in Dawson. He eventually found work as a waiter, until in the eyes of many, he became the luckiest man in the Klondike, when Kate Rockwell fell in love with him. She lavished him with gifts and fashionable clothing, and used her influence in entertainment to secure him a part in a vaudville production at the Orpheum Theatre. Eventually Pantages became manager of the Orpheum, and thus began his remarkable career in the theatre industry.

When the gold rush ended they moved to Seattle together, where Kate lent Pantages $4,000 to build a theatre, to show the new 'moving pictures' that were beginning to flow from Hollywood.

Before long Pantages left Kate, and went on to build a huge theatre chain covering the continent. A great many were operated under the name 'Orpheum' or 'Savoy', but the most beautiful and opulent he called 'Pantages' Theatre's, a few of which have been restored, and are still in operation today.

Pantages lost almost everything in the stockmarket crash of 1929, and died of a heart attack in 1936.

George 'Tex' Rickard

Rickard was the full time Marshall and a part time gambler in Henrietta, Texas before he came north, and climbed the Chilkoot Pass early in 1896 with a friend of his. His friend turned back on the trail, but Tex pressed on to arrive in Circle, Alaska flat broke.

He quickly got a job dealing cards in Silent Sam Bonnifield's gambling establishment, and when news of the Bonanza strike reached Circle, Rickard raced up river towards the Klondike along with the rest of the community.

He arrived early enough to stake a good claim on Bonanza Creek, which he promptly sold for $60,000, and built 'The Northern Saloon' in Dawson. His good fortune didn't last though, and when his luck at the tables went bad, he lost everything he had including The Northern Saloon.

It was then that Swiftwater Bill gave him a job dealing cards at the Monte Carlo. And a fellow dealer and piano player Wilson Mizner, convinced him that they could make money by promoting and staging a fight between Hoffman and Frank Slavin, a fight which actually took place in the Monte Carlo.

Highly successful, Rickard staged more fights in Dawson. Then after leaving the Klondike in 1899, he continued promoting ever larger fights, until by 1916 he was staging matches in Madison Square Gardens in New York. Then after promoting a series of Jack Dempsey fights, he became a very rich man.

Tex then bought Madison Square Gardens, and while rebuilding it into 'the ultimate sports venue', a friend of his invited him to Montreal, where he witnessed a barn burner of a hockey game, between Montreal and 'The New York Americans' in front of 13,000 screaming fans. He immediately wired New York to stop work on the new Gardens, then reconfigured the new building to feature hockey games.

Rickard opened his new Madison Square Gardens in 1925 to great acclaim, and aquired a National Hockey League franchise. Dubbing his new team 'The New York Tex's Rangers', the game and the team were an instant hit. After Rickard's death, the name of the team was shortened to 'The New York Rangers'.

For Tex Rickard's entire life, he maintained that going over the Chilkoot Pass was the hardest thing he ever did.

'Klondike' Kate Rockwell

Kate or 'Kitty' Rockwell started her working life young, labouring in a sweatshop in New York City's garment district. She soon joined a travelling dance troupe, and while in Seattle, learned of the Klondike gold rush and decided to journey north.

She performed briefly in Skagway, before tackling the Chilkoot with three other girls, all of who turned back on the trail. Undaunted, Kate donned mens clothing and continued on alone.

It was said that Kate got so angry at being told she couldn't go through Miles Canyon because she was a woman, that she went through anyway, and then walked the five miles back up to the head of the gorge, and went through again.

There remains some controversy in Kate's history, and the confusion probably arises in that by the end of the gold rush, (and in the following years), there was no less than seventeen different women claiming to be 'the one and only Klondike Kate'.

But it is certain that Kate Rockwell was only eighteen years old when she arrived in Dawson, and it was her that sang and danced on the stages of the Orpheum, Monte Carlo, and Palace Grand, commanding huge sums of money. It was also her that possessed the violet eyes and the magnetic personality, and was hailed as, 'The Flower of the North', and 'The Golden Girl of Dawson'. And on Christmas Eve in 1900, she was officially crowned 'Queen of the Yukon' in a glittering ceremony at the Palace Grand.

Not long after, Kate left the Yukon with Pantages, and they lived in Seattle until 1905 when Pantages left her. Kate was apparently crushed by the break up, and began a spiral towards poverty.

Years later in the 1920s she was washing dishes for a living, when she learned that people were still fascinated with the Klondike, and still wanted to hear adventures and stories from the gold rush. She also realized that in the same vein as Samuel Clements, she could hold a crowds attention with just her personality and her tales and exploits of the Klondike. She then began a lucrative speaking career, which basically lasted the rest of her life.

Because during and after the gold rush, so many of the 'wanna be' Klondike Kate's publicized themselves with pictures, to this day a picture of Klondike Kate may or may not be a photograph of Kate Rockwell.

Kate died in 1957.

'Soapy' Smith

Captain Jefferson Randolph 'Soapy' Smith had earned the moniker 'Soapy', from being proficient at the 'Trip and Kyster' confidence game. A scam where paper money is wrapped around bars of soap.

Before coming to Alaska, Soapy had fought in the Civil War, and had also been a cowboy on the Chism Trail.

Then after becoming leader of the gang that terrorized Denver, Colorado, he increasingly found himself dancing with 'Bat Masterson'. So with the pickings getting slimmer anyway because of the depression, Soapy decided to move his gang north. He'd learned about the discovery of gold in the Klondike, and wisely determined that Skagway would become the big jumping off point, for a massive gold rush.

So he arrived in Alaska with a multitude of thieves, confidence men, thugs and scoundrels. They quickly seized control of the small town, and proceeded to fleece, rob, or mug, virtually everyone traveling to or from the Klondike. They did whatever it took to get a persons money, robbing and conning in too many ways to list.

Many were taken so completely, that a well respected and courteous citizen by the name of Captain Jefferson Smith would step forward, and 'generously' offer to buy them passage back south. A cheap fare, in that boats were practically empty sailing that direction. In this way, Soapy kept his town from filling up with penniless victims.

Mixed in with the goldseekers, was a steady stream of 'new' criminals arriving in Skagway, all to be either absorbed into Soapy's gang, or unceremoniously run out of town. Thus, Soapy's gang quickly grew into the hundreds.

Bigger and bolder, beatings and shootings became more and more common place, until Skagway became one of the few, if not only place in America, where when a gunfight broke out, people really would simply duck down, wait for it to end, then go back to what they were doing.

Sam Steele, who had a known prevalence for understatement, called Skagway 'Probably the roughest place on earth'. Other men of noteriety that passed through Skagway had similar characterizations, referring to it as 'Hell on earth' and 'Lawless beyond description'. In just one day, on February 15th 1898, eight seperate bodies were found on the American side of the Whitepass Trail. All dead from foul play.

Increasingly concerned with the situation in Skagway, the U.S. Government began posting troops six miles away in Dyea, and by the time Soapy marched his own armed militia of a few hundred men down Broadway Avenue, (Skagway's main street) they had over three hundred federal troops stationed there.

By July of 1898 the citizens of Skagway had had enough. Then as told in the story, when they tried to have a meeting on what to do about Soapy, and Smith tried to break it up, it resulted in a shoot-out between Soapy and Frank Reid, one of Skagway's leading citizens. Reid shot Soapy dead in the gun battle, but was mortally wounded himself, sending the already angry citizens of Skagway into a rage.

Many of Soapy's cohorts were standing behind him when he was killed, and immediately saw the writing on the wall. They fired a few shots at the onrushing mob, and quickly began making a run for it. Then as written in the story, Soapy's gang came to the horrible realization, that there was nowhere to run to. Hemmed in by steep mountains on both sides, the vigilantes on the waterfront, and the Canadian Mounties on the passes, they had to relegate themselves to hiding in willows and woodpiles, and underneath porches and the like.

After the gunfight, it took only minutes before men were being deputized to round up the gang, while at the same time, all around Skagway groups of vigilantes began arming themselves to join the hunt.

In just a few hours they caught dozens of Soapy's men, and forty eight hours after the shoot-out, they had the jail and townhall stuffed with Soapy's gang, with the overflow fast filling up the second floor of a hardware store.

By then an armed vigilante mob of a thousand people had gathered in the street, brandishing ropes and calling to hang certain gang members, while others in the crowd were yelling to 'Hang the whole damn gang!'

There was only twenty five temporary deputies to hold back the crowd, and they were fast losing ground when the Federal Troops arrived. Martial Law was declared, and the troops fixed their bayonets, and pushed their way through Skagway until they could seize control of the prisoners. It was one of very few times since the Civil War, that American troops had been used on American soil against American citizens.

Jefferson Randolph 'Soapy' Smith (The King of Skagway) was shot and killed on July 8th 1898.

Sam Steele

Samuel Benfield Steele (The Lion of the North), was held in high esteem for an exeptional career, before the gold rush ever began. At twenty two years old, he was just the third man in Canada to take the oath of the newly formed 'North West Mounted Police', and in 1874 was part of the Mounties 'Great March' west to Fort

Whoop-up, in an effort to establish Canadian sovereignty west of Manitoba.

In 1881, after the massacre of General Custer and his troops, The great Indian chief 'Sitting Bull' led thousands of warriors across the border into Canada, and when the Canadian Government decided to send a tiny contingent to negotiate their return, Sam Steele (known as a thinking man) was one of the six men chosen for the assignment. New York City newspapers marvelled at how a small handful of Mounties, could do what the U.S. Army could not.

Steele then kept peace on the railroad right-of-way as the Canadian National Railroad pushed its way west, and is pictured in the photograph of the 'Last Spike' driven in 1885.

When Steele was assigned to keep the law in the Kooteney's, such was his reputation for fairness with the Selkirk Indians, that 'Fort Steele' is one of few forts in North America, that was built without a protective wall. Fort Steele remains a popular tourist attraction today.

In fact, because of Steele's firm yet fair enforcement of law, and his extensive involvement in the development of the Canadian west, he's credited for being one of the main reasons that it was accomplished without 'The Indian Wars' and horrific bloodshed as in United States.

In the preceding story, only one small change was made to Steele's history. In the story he arrives in Skagway in September, and travels over the Chilkoot a few weeks later with a half a dozen men. He actually arrived in February, and proceeded over the pass with two dozen Mounties.

Everything else is true, including bullets ripping through the wall when he was trying to sleep in Skagway. And gunfights really were so common in Skagway, that neither Steele nor the other man trying to sleep in the room bothered to get up. The man almost killing him by nailing a soap dish to the wall with a twelve inch spike is also accurate.

After Steele made and enforced his own law concerning boats traveling through Miles Canyon, only eighteen more people drowned that summer. Some sources have as many as three hundred people drowning before Steele's arrival. (By July, one rock in the canyon had parts of nineteen different boats pushed on to it.) Later Steele was commended for his decision, and his quick thinking in a crisis situation, and that it no doubt had saved countless lives.

With Steele's vigorous and steadfast rule over the Klondike, there were no murders in 1898, and despite the huge volume of wealth spread throughout the population, violent crime and major thefts were almost non-existent. There were also no known cases of hi-grading or claim jumping, and only one laughable case of cross-filing.

Although Steele and his Mounties got free room and board in the police compound, their $1.25 a day wages would buy practically nothing in the Klondike. Yet even with incredible opportunities all around them to 'supplement' their incomes by 'bending' the law, to a man they remained squeaky clean throughout the goldrush.

When the rush was over, most of the gold seekers returned to their home countries, telling of the red uniformed Mounties of Canada, that were fair and honest, worked in any conditions, and always got their man. Thus began an international reputation that would make them the most famous police force in the world.

After the goldrush, Steele was asked what accomplishment he was most proud of. And it wasn't the stifling of crime, or even keeping Soapy and his gang out of the Yukon, it was that "A woman could walk anywhere she wanted, day or night, in complete safety."

Once Steele was transferred, he was promoted to be the top police officer for British Columbia and the Yukon.

Then when the Boer War wasn't going well for England, they asked him to form and lead a cavalry battalion, and so many wanted to join Sam Steele's 'Strathcona Horse Brigade' that thousands had to be turned down. His brigade fought with distinction during the war, and when the British later completed an inquiry, it was determined that Sam Steele had been their best commander in the entire war. The British then awarded him a Knighthood (an extremely rare honour for a foreigner), and by World War I he'd been made a General, and put in command of the 2nd Canadian Division.

On a personal note, Sam was an avid reader, a navigator, and a crack shot. He was also known for rarely getting cold, carrying 270 pound packs, and regularly dancing with his wife until dawn. By the time Steele died he was a bonifide Canadian hero, with his likeness found on everything from postcards to tea cups.

To this day, a troop of Sam Steele's scouts still ride every year in the world famous Calgary Stampede Parade.

Sam Steele died in 1919, and Canada named its 5th highest mountain after him.

———

One of the changes made in the story from true history, is that the 'Sour-toe Cocktail' that Elmer drank in the Monte Carlo, wasn't actually created until 1972 by Captain Dick Stevenson. The rule to get credit for drinking it is that the toe must touch the lips.

Another small change made in the story, was when Henry and Elmer were on the Chilkoot Pass, and came across the grave of a man who'd shot himself, and the words 'Bury me here where I failed' were carved on a nearby tree. While true, it actually happened on the Whitepass trail, where conditions were far worse for both men and animals.

There was one last small change made in the story to true history. When Sam Steele moved the prostitutes to Lousetown on the outskirts of Dawson, he didn't actually move them until a year later.

One of the side effects of Steele's 'deal' with the citizens, concerning the 'sins of the flesh', was that many of the stage acts in Dawson became increasingly salacious, until some were described as 'Lewd beyond belief'.

In the competition for customers and popularity, some of the girls, including the headliners, began dancing in the nude. Steele finally put a lid on how obscene they could be, when he stopped Little Egypt's 'Hoochie Coochie Dance'.

When the citizens of Dawson described how coarse and suggestive some acts were, they knew of which they spoke. Most had been through Skagway, where levels of indecency had been reached that probably went unmatched anywhere else in the world. Throughout the western era in virtually all the saloons and dancehalls, girls were hired to cavort with the customers, enticing them to drink more, gamble more, and to 'go upstairs'. In some of the establishments in Skagway, the girls even did that nude.

Only a few of the people and events of the Klondike are written into the previous story, when in reality the goldrush was saturated with incredible characters, unbelievable events, and eye rubbing spectacles. From girls who sold themselves to be 'a wife for a year' for their weight in gold, to A.J. Goddard and his wife, who packed an entire sternwheeler over the Chilkoot Pass, piece by piece.

Clarence Berry and others, who in early 1897 actually put boxes on the side of the trail beside their claims, containing a pile of nuggets and a bottle of whiskey, and with it a sign inviting anyone down on their luck to 'Help themselves'.

And Roddy Conners, who sold his claim on Bonanza for $50,000 so he could dance. Then slowly transfered almost all the money, to two sisters dubbed 'Vaseline' and 'Glycerine', at a dollar a dance.

It should be told that 'One-Eyed Riley', the man in the story who arrived at Bennett by dogsled, in an effort to escape the enticements of Dawson with his Faro winnings intact. Upon arriving in Skagway lost his entire fortune in three passes of the dice, in what was probably a rigged Craps game.

Three people not mentioned in the story by name, are the original discoverers of gold on Bonanza Creek. Skookum Jim, Tagish Charlie, and George Carmack. After their incredible find, they arrived in Seattle along with some of the other rich claim owners, and put themselves up at the most extravagant hotel in the city, 'The Butler Hotel'. It was they, that to amuse themselves, threw handfuls of nuggets from their hotel room window, to a near riotous crowd on the street below. The crowd Elmer was part of at the beginning of the story.

George Carmack had brought his wife Kate with him, a native woman who had never been outside the Yukon before. Kate found the many identical floors, doors, and hallways of the hotel extremely confusing. So after getting lost in the opulent structure, on her next trip down to the lobby she took her hatchet with her, and hacking Mahogany chunks out of the stairwells, door jambs and bannisters, she blazed a trail as she went, to help guide her on the return trip. A common practice in unfamiliar Yukon wilderness.

There really was a river of gold running beneath creeks and hills of the Klondike, producing rich claims all along the slopes of Cheechako Hill, French Hill, Gold Hill, Paradise Hill, and others. Down in the creeks it was ever better, not just Bonanza and Eldorado, but Bear Creek, Hunker, Sulpher, Clear, and Quartz Creeks, all generated prolific amounts of gold. Dominion

Creek alone flowed down from King Soloman's Dome, smearing gold for more that twenty miles.

Officially, less than half a million ounces were found in the Klondike in 1898. A number which is known to be highly inacurate. To give an idea of how inacurate, over two hundred riverboats landed in Dawson that summer, with many or most carrying gold back south. The last riverboat alone to leave that fall, (The one Henry and Elmer were on) was known to be carrying a million ounces.

One things for certain, gold flowed like water during the goldrush, and in 1897 before the stampeders arrived, it really was left in piles along Front Street. Even years later during the depression of the 1930s, men earned a living by panning spilled gold from underneath Dawson's boardwalks.

It's estimated that worldwide more than a million people started out for the Klondike. Though a great many barely made it out of the area they lived in, or at least fell far short of their goal. But between 100-150,000 made it all the way to Skagway, where another 30-50,000 were either robbed, or ran out of the money needed to continue. From there the rest pressed forward, with 40-60,000 more giving up in the formitable mountain passes, many when they first laid eyes on the Golden Stairs. Throughout the journey a good number of people died of sickness and accidents, as well as being frozen and drowned, but eventually 30-40,000 people succeeded in their quest, and made it all the way to the Klondike.

Ultimately, somewhere between three and four thousand people became wealthy to extremely rich, with a great many of them throwing away their fortunes in the cassinos and dancehalls as fast as they found it. Still others went broke in just a few years, from bad business decisions and lavish living. In the end, only about a hundred people benefitted throughout their lives from the fortunes they found in the Klondike.

The goldrush was such a huge physical as well as emotional test on people, that most who experienced it relished the memories the rest of their lives. It wasn't the richness of the Klondike, or the gaiety of Dawson that they were fond to remember, but the struggles and hardships they had to overcome. So in the following years when they gathered in reunions to reminisce about their experiences, it wasn't so much as gold seekers and citizens of the Klondike, but as veterans of the Golden Stairs.

Even today, the Klondike remains the most colorful goldrush in history. And every year tourists travel north to climb the Chilkoot Trail, paddle the Yukon River, and try their luck panning for gold. Camping in the Yukon wilderness now, is no different than it was during the goldrush, and sooner or later the Whiskey Jacks are still likely to show up and try and rob you. In Dawson City, you can still stroll the wooden boardwalks, see a show at the Palace Grand, and gamble at Diamond Tooth Gerties. And for those who think themselves able, can still order a Sour-toe Cocktail.

Resources

Arts and Entertainment Television Network: (Mansions, Monuments and Masterpieces

Burns, Ken: (American Stories, Episode - The Calender, Volume#1

Canadian Broadcasting Corporation: (Hockey- A Peoples History)

The Colorful Five Percent: (Jim Robb, Volume I, Number I 1984)

Dawson City Visitors Guide: (2000)

Dawson Daily News: (Sept. 1899)

Detroit Public Television: (Spectacular Views)

Gold Trails and Ghost Towns

Guide to the Goldfields: (Special Edition)

The History Channel: (The Canadians)

Klondike: Pierre Benton

The Klondike News: (April 1st 1898)

Knowledge Network Television Canada: (Sam Steele)

Law of the Yukon: Helene Dobrowolsky

One Man's Gold Rush: Murray Morgan

Tales of a Klondike Newsman: Stroller White

Weekend Magazine: (Volume 12, Number 27) 1962

The Whitehorse Star

The Yukon Archives

The Yukon News

The Yukon Public Library

The Yukon Reader

The Yukon Sun (May 22, 1900)

CPSIA information can be obtained at www.ICGtesting.com
Printed in the USA
LVOW12s0455240215

428028LV00002B/4/P